MUN
MuN

MuN

Also by Jesse Andrews

Me and Earl and the Dying Girl (2012)

The Haters (2016)

MUN MUN

JESSE ANDREWS

ALLEN&UNWIN

First published in Great Britain in 2018 by Allen & Unwin

Allen & Unwin
c/o Atlantic Books
Ormond House
26–27 Boswell Street
London WC1N 3JZ

Phone: 020 7269 1610
Fax: 020 7430 0916
Email: UK@allenandunwin.com
Web: www.allenandunwin.com/uk

A CIP catalogue record for this book is available from the British Library.

Internal illustration copyright © Nathan O. Marsh 2018
Text design by Chad W. Beckerman

Set in Adobe Garamond pt 10.5/17pt by Midland Typesetters, Australia

Hardback ISBN 978 1 76063 345 5
Export paperback ISBN 978 1 76052 847 8
E-Book ISBN 978 1 76063 560 2

Printed and bound by CPI Group (UK) Ltd, Croydon, CR0 4YY

10 9 8 7 6 5 4 3 2 1

TO TAMARA, OFCOURSE

Nothing is great or
little otherwise than
by comparison.

—Jonathan Swift,
Gulliver's Travels

I.
PRAYER

LIFEANDDEATHWORLD

Being littlepoor is notsogood.

I know I know, you think you know this already, howabout I just tell you though.

I want to see if this makes you laugh. A middlerich kid stepped on our house and crushed my dad to death. Then that same year a cat attacked my mom at the dump and snapped her spine. Okay there. That's it. Did you blurt a little giggly laugh? No you didn't, okay good, ofcourse thanks for not laughing, sorry for being the Laugh Police. That story to me is just not super funny. But to other people, a littlebit funny. Mostly these are the people too big to worry about getting stomped, squashed, catcrippled, sewerdrowned, mudburied, any of your classic littlepoor terrors.

We were as littlepoor as you can get, a tenth of middlescale, about as big as rats. We preferred to say squirrels, because a squirrel is a little bigger and ofcourse less disgusting. But squirrels are more like eighthscale and we were tenthscale, littler than squirrels, more exactly the size of average rats. We lived in the beachy capital of Lossy Indica, down in an alleyway near the docks. Our house was a onestory block of twinedtogether milkcrates, roofs and walls of smasheddown tincans, everynight the stovesmoke tickled our lungs and flavored our skin.

So this middlerich kid who killed my dad, he was named Jasper, I would say he was doublescale, so he outscaled us by twenty, maybe twentytwo. His class was in the middle of a Let's See The Middledocks fieldtrip, and he was in the situation of getting bullied and shoved by some other bigger middleriches. They chased him into the alley and gave him a shove and his balance was bad and he planted a foot right through our roof and it snapped the plastic milkcrate gridding and smashed my dad almost immediately to death, not rightaway immediately though. I was screaming and trying to stop the blood from blopping out where the shardy plastic forked him, and he was staring at me and he tried to say a few things. But ofcourse his lungs were smashed in, so, no capability to push air out of there for talking with, and prettyquick he was dead.

This kid Jasper felt terrible obviously. And also the kids who were bullying him. I mean the bullies got out of there pretty fast, mumbling muttering and skulking away all sulky and ashamed. Jasper stuck around crying for a while, then suddenly he ran away too, like, *hey, I just realized I don't have to stay here either, whatarelief.*

Sometimes with accident killings, bigs and bigger middles feel so much guilt they'll pay you some munmuns of Now I Can Feel Less Bad About This. But nosuchluck for us, when we found Jasper's parents in Dreamworld they refused to pay us anything, because was it really poor little Jasper's fault that some bullies shoved him into stepping on our house?, look at this shaky blub-berer, he's completely traumatized, infact if anything he's a victim here too.

I thought about asking, *is it possible Jasper was being such a piece of crap that he deserved to get bullied into stepping on a house, therefore actually it kind of was his fault,* but probably that wasn't true, anyway you weren't talking his parents into that.

And so the next night in Dreamworld we tracked down the bullies' parents but ofcourse they got huffy and puffy and thought it was crazy we would even ask for munmun, look, sorryforyour-loss but was it *our* kid's foot who smashed through your roof and killed your dad, I mean do you really think it's fair that we give up munmuns and scale down over something like that?, you seriously do?, well, I guess you can think what you want, but unless you want to throw munmuns away on a lawyer for Accident Court, please don't contact us anymore, again obviously though we are super sorryforyourloss.

So we got no munmun and stayed littlepoor, but now with no dad and a busted house, and so my mom and my sis Prayer and me moved into a crowded publicgarden of littlepoors up the coast in a donated or abandoned Yewess Coastguard beachhouse, mostly wrecked families and orphans all trying to look out for each other and not get robbed or flooded or attacked by rats.

That same stupid year, my mom was working at the dump in the middle of the night, salvaging rags, wires, burnable coals and oilrocks, when a homeless tortashell cat started stalking her, and she jumped into the well of a tire, but the cat just perched on the tirelip and started reaching into the tire with one arm the jerky way cats do, bat bat batting, rummaging around in there, and he slapped her a few times in the head and the back, and his spiky paw slashed her face, and tossed her around, and hooked and broke part of her spine, and then she couldn't move, so the cat got bored and left.

The doctor told Prayer and me later that our mom's spine probably got broke worse by everyone dragging her out of the tire the way we did, so we asked him, okay doctor, what were we supposed to do, and he admitted, yeah, probably there wasn't any equipment for it. It's not like they make ambulances in our scale, stretchers, wheelchairs, anything. Our best option was just pick her up out of the tire and onto a rag, then pick up each end of the rag and carry about five hours to the closest hospital we knew about that had a littlepoor clinic, and the doctors did what they could. But even the littlest doctors outscaled our poor mom by atleast ten and when you're samesize as a doctor's hand you won't get fixed up so great.

So the doctors couldn't fix her spine, and they didn't cut her legs off but the legs didn't work anymore, and on top of that our mom went blind in one eye and the sewing job on her slashedup face was all sloppy with giant stitches half as fat as a littlepoor finger. One nurse pitied us and gave us a chair from his kid's dollhouse to make a wheelchair out of. Mom was a little too big for it but toobad, we had to use it. It was that or just carrying her around in a rag hammock.

Our dad was dead, our mom couldn't work anymore, Prayer

was fifteen, I was thirteen, we lived with women and children, and prettymuch all of our day was trapping ants, roasting them, trying to sell roasted ant to other littlepoors, and getting the crap robbed out of us anytime we tried to take munmun to the bank. It was grim.

"Prayer, Warner," our mom said. "The Lord King God is wise and great but at some point you two will need to come up with some kind of a plan."

I was so mad all the time, it kept me from making a good plan. My plans all had to do with getting strong. I wanted to get superstrong through constant workouts and stunts, also fashion a knife or a sword or some type of weapon to carry around, basically become a guy who guards other littlepoors on trips to the bank in exchange for a cut. Or else join one of the squads that hangs out near the bank and follows you home to rob you if you didn't hire a guard. But Mom and Prayer had no respect for any of these plans.

"Nope, no way should you do any of that," Mom said. "Warner, you're going to make the Lord King God sad and mad with such dumb plans."

"My plans are actually kind of smart," I suggested.

"Bro, they're super dumb and here's how," Prayer said. "Your plans are all about muscles and weapons, so, ay kay ay, they are how your lazy brain tells you, *Don't use me, use your muscles and weapons instead.* That is an unmistakable sign of very stupid planning from a rightnow lazy brain."

"No, you're stupid," I argued, "because here's what my smart brain did, it asked, what are Warner's top gifts and resources lying around, hmmm probably these good muscles and running ability, nottomention handtohand combat skill."

"Manohman do you need to do some work on that brain," worried Prayer.

"Also think more about the Lord King God," suggested Mom.

But meanwhile Prayer's plan didn't involve working on the brain either, or the Lord King God forthatmatter.

Instead it was a very basic and common plan for littlepoor girls of Prayer's age who were cute, specifically, find a nice smart godfull middlerich guy, probably in Dreamworld, and maybe if he loves Prayer enough he'll agree to get married and join his munmun with all of us and scale down while we all scale up to him, middlepoor atleast, the size of average dogs.

"How come my brainless plans are dumb but Prayer's brainless plan is not," I said.

"It's not really my plan," said Prayer.

"Yes it is," said Mom.

"Fine," said Prayer.

"It's *our* plan," said Mom.

"I said fine," yelled Prayer.

"Just got to find a middlerich guy who loves Prayer's face more than his really good life," I said.

Mom and Prayer ignored this.

"Maybe that guy's in Dreamworld rightnow, how about I go look for him," I suggested, but they kept ignoring.

I continued, "I'll just conk out and fly around Dreamworld yelling, Hey, sister for sale, fifteenyearold sister with aboveaverage face, one annoying sister for the lowlow price of you have to lose a bunch of scale joining your munmuns with not just her but also her mom and bro," at that point Prayer interrupted that actually Warner you won't get to join muns and scale up and if you want to live with us it has to be as a pet, cooped up in a littlecage stapled to the side of their middlehouse, Mom made Prayer say she was kidding but I knew she probably wasn't.

DREAMWORLD

The littlerpoorer you are, obviously the more you love Dreamworld. Dreamworld is where you and everyone else is exactly middlescale and no one can get attacked or robbed or killed, and you can drive the cars and dial the phones and shoot the guns and use all the things they don't make little enough for you in Lifeanddeathworld.

Infact Dreamworld is unspeakably better than Lifeanddeathworld and plenty of littlepoors love it so much, it kills them. Here's how. They decide they need to spend all their time dreaming, but without chemicals you can only sleep so much. So they get sloppy and goofy knocking themselves out with some beers or some weeds and they get super careless and prettysoon they're asleep somewhere unsafe like a gutter or a parkinglot, and a bus squishes them or a sewer drowns them or a snake or a hawk eats them or out in the desert even bigenough spiders.

You have to be a little mistrustfull of Dreamworld obviously because anything can get dreamed into your head by anyone. Although not really anyone and infact mostly no one, because most people don't dream super well. So actually if you're good at it, you can be the one dreaming into other people's heads most of the time.

And if you want to put something nice in people's dreams, beautifull pictures in people's heads, that can feel really good and even great. Infact I would say that's the best part about Dreamworld if you have the talent and the energy for it, making nice wild things everyone's seeing for the first time and saying, wow, holy crap, who made this beautifull dreamstuff.

I mean forexample you could make a pool out of cloud, or mountains of teeth. You could lift an orchard of roiling boiling rivertrees out of the dirt, trunking and churning and branching. You could make accordion palaces, whale buses, glinty trains of fourwheel ants scurrying up vines of road. Give hindlegs to stoves, puppyears to the sun. Wear skirts of fishflocks flashing like leaves, make a room in a big cat's heart. You could give a whole suburb a ceiling of sea, you could dive into it from the rooftops, peek down at the seafloor and it's a nightsky foaming with stars.

By you I mostly mean me, the only dreamer anymore who really plays Make Stuff Out Of Other Stuff, but maybe you could do it too.

Anyway that's all great and nice if that's what you want to put in the minds of the people traveling through your dreamzone. But if you're sad, mad, frustrated and furious, you can also make traps and dungeons. Skyless shitscapes and gutterzones mazing under the skin of the world. Buzzing burning dust, stinking poison dew, air clotted up with mean little suns. Fake light so dull and blank it dries your heart. Rooms that crumple on you like bags, weapons to keep you from dying, a place where every escape is to somewhere worse.

You can make that too if you're sad and mad and want to

trick middleriches into a bad dream. But look, let's say it works and a few of them end up there for a night, it's still no good. It doesn't really hurt them, because you can't actually get hurt in Dreamworld. And in the morning the middleriches you tricked wake up in Lifeanddeathworld with all these new ideas of mean things they can do, and terrible things they might have the scale to make, in the world of your life where you can actually bleed and starve and die, also the world holding your delicat brain.

A few nights before it was time to leave, Prayer caught me gutterbuilding, I'd been doing it kind of a lot.

"Warner, don't make that sad crap," she told me. "Make the nice dreamzones instead."

"I'm too mad," I said, and dreamed a swarm of flying spiders right into the middle of a conversation of softskinned jerks, who ofcourse began freaking out.

"Gross," she said. "Stop."

"No," I said, and whipped them up into a whole cyclone of fluttering sputtering spiders and it was sort of fun to watch the jerks scramble around, try to dream them away and can't, toobad, jerks.

"Okay, look," said Prayer. "Don't get a big head. But you make very strong dreamstuff, pretty great when you want it to be."

"Can't argue with that, I guess," I admitted.

"Okay, shut up and just listen," she said. "My point is, most of us can't even make anything half the time and all we can do is tumble and drift through other people's foggy halfmade random crap. So don't be a peen and please just make some nice dreamstuff for the rest of us, okay, I'm asleep and I need to relax."

So I dreamed the spiders into soothing glimmery glass jel-lyfish, swaying in the air all gentle and liquidy. But if you're mad or sad it's really hard to dream nice stuff without poisoning it in some way. So their glassy pearlstrings did from timetotime keep casually settling around a jerk's neck and arms and kind of strangling him a little bit.

The biggerricher you are, usually the less you like Dreamworld. Because in Lifeanddeathworld you feel completely superior to littlepoors, but in Dreamworld some of them might be stronger at dreaming than you. And additionally just in general you can't completely avoid talking to poors, hearing about their sufferings, getting reminders of *hey, if you were born littler your life would be definitely notasgood,* and ofcourse feeling guilt about breaking their houses or dumping garbage on them or killing them some of the time.

But riches mostly don't remember their dreams so good either, so sad or bad dreaming doesn't bother them as much as maybe it could.

Sometimes I let myself tumble and drift like everyone else and get a good look at other people's dreamstuff and for the most part it was like Prayer said. No one's stuff was as good as mine. I mean sometimes I'd see something new that gave me an idea or something I could improve upon or whatever. But mostly it was traveling through weedy dry dreamzones with nothing good growing out.

I did once find someone as good as me, honestly probably better if you need to compare. I was above a little parky forest and right as I got the twitchy feeling I wasn't alone, the treetops breathed a cloud of seedfluff. And the seedfluff twinkled into flowerheads, and the flowerheads sprouted into birds, and the birds drew a floating house with a thousand doors, and I began to hear a quiet hum but not through my ears, instead through my whole body so it felt like the murmur of something huge and faraway.

I opened a door and fell down in the sky because out poured a voice like the richest drink. A voice with twenty thick dizzy flavors in it, singing a song of notes made out of notes made out of notes. I couldn't even move. Then I could move and I opened another door and another voice glided out and wrapped the first with fluttering ribbons of itself. And again I couldn't move, until I could, and I opened door after door and the voices all twined each other and cascaded in every direction, inward outward forward backward in and out of time, and the song grew huge and bathed me and my skin went liquid and my bones glowed.

I was weeping with happiness, also full of a sad ache. I was sad because I knew I would probably only get to hear it once and then lose it forever. And the song was so far beyond what I could dream, I wouldn't even be able to remember it.

I knew I would never hear the song again without this floating seedflowerbirdhouse to sing it to me, so that was the ache, every musicswell and beautybloom was a fist clenching my heart.

I put my head in one door and looked inside and it was a girl my age, eyes shut.

I tried to squeeze through into the house, noluck, the air netted me. She opened her eyes and smiled.

"Uh," I said. "Well, ofcourse, hi. I'm Warner. What's your name."

But she just shook her head.

"That's okay, don't tell me," I said. "But, heresthething, I have an idea for something I could make you, so come out and let me make you something, please."

She shook her head again.

"No, but please," I said. "I don't think you understand. I'm really good at this, and I would make you something really good."

"It's time to get up and go to morningschool," she told me in a dark little voice that hollowed me out completely, and the morningschool part was how I knew this girl was middlerich, and that's why it hurt extra much when it dissolved and vanished and I woke up with the tears not all the way dry on my stupid littlepoor face.

LIFEANDDEATHWORLD

But I didn't get to worry about the girl very much during the day or night because it was time to pursue Prayer's crappy plan.

Sure, Prayer was cute. She had the big deep eyes and the wide bright mouth that the agreement among men is, that's cute. She also had the rubywine skin that some guys especially like who like ruby skin. On the minus side, her head was narrow and shaped like a bean, and her arms were too long with big knobbyknuckle hands on the end like paddles. And long legs which men like but huge feet which men don't like. Her hair was very fine, by which I mean thin and not good, and there wasn't quite enough and if you got too close you could see through to her weird pink scalp. So what I'm saying is, she was cute, not amazing, but maybe I just think that as her brother and actually some men love to see some scalpskin the color of a baby rat, who knows.

But Prayer was definitely cute enough that some of the local squads and crews wanted to involve her in a big bangsesh in some garbage somewhere, and anytime she left the coastguard station she wanted me to bodyguard her, other boys too if possible.

It was usually me and Usher. Usher was a publicgarden orphan, grayskinned and squinty, a year older than me but smaller with incredible shrimpiness and a little bit of palsy. He was ofcourse pointless in a fight. But he could atleast scream pretty loud, and maybe from a distance you just see two boys with a girl, you don't see that the two boys are pretty young or that one is a shrimp, so you decide not to chase them, and anyway Usher was lovesick for my sis Prayer, so, sure, let him help bodyguard.

The point is, Prayer needed to meet middlerich guys, not just in Dreamworld but also intheflesh. So where was the best place for that.

"Warehouses," I suggested.

"Nope," said Prayer. "It's all middlepoors in there."

"Business offices," I said.

"Those men are married or old," complained Prayer.

"I think you want old," I said. "Old guys are lonely, desperate, might die tomorrow. Perfect."

"I guess you're not thinking of this as How Prayer Meets Her Soulmate," said Prayer.

"You already have a soulmate," I pointed out. "Usher."

"Ugh," she said. "Shut up."

"Right now Usher is thinking about you and either crying or banging a hole he made in the sand," I said.

"Warner, it's time to shut up," commanded Mom. "I'll tell you where Prayer is going to find a husband. Law school."

"Ohcrap," I said.

The closest law school we knew about was twenty miles away, on the other side of Lossy Indica, in the suburb of Sand Dreamough.

"What about business school," said Prayer.

"Law school," ordered Mom.

"Business school though has guys learning to make deals, sell products, start a big corpo in a little garage, build munmuns and power out of just your thoughts and words and confidence, that might be exciting maybe," daydreamed Prayer.

"Law school puts guys in the bank and the government," said Mom. "That's the most safe, safe is the most important, most important is what you need to focus on. Prayer, you're going to law school. Warner, you're going with Prayer and you're bodyguarding her, also if you find other ways to help out, that would really be great. Me, I'm giving myself to a church."

"No, no, no. Nope," I said, for lots of reasons. I didn't want to be the assistant to stupid Prayer in her gross quest to find a bangpartner for life, and I didn't want to leave for a strange new place full of middleriches who were smarter than me, and I didn't want my mom to go sleep sickteen to a room with randos in the leaky littlepoor shelter of some crummy church.

But my mom can make her mind tougher than mine, tougher than Prayer's, and she flattened us with it. So after a few days of fighting we wheeled her off to Middlechurch of the Lord King God and said our goodbyes, and she wouldn't cry even when we did.

The first phase of Find Prayer A Husband was even just getting on the road somehow. We had nineteen munmuns that I had folded deep in a pouch, but that was emergency munmun you can't spend on transport. So how to get there for free? Well, you could hike through the city. But Sand Dreamough was all the way past Sentrow and basically right up to the mountains. So the hike would have taken atleast a month, forget that hopefully. As for the bus, the muncounter near the door has a special broom for littlepoors trying to sneak on. If you're by yourself you can hop buses from the outside sometimes, scramble up the tire when it stops and hang out in the wheelwell, but with two people, basically forget about it. Metro made the most sense but who even knows how to use that thing? First of all, you have to read the Metro map and who has any idea how to read? Usher, that's who.

Usher ambushed us on our way out of the church. We were strapped up with little pouches of extra clothes and waterbags so he knew something was up.

"Are you leav ving?" he asked.

"Prayer's going to law school," I said, so it wouldn't break his heart.

"Oh w woww," said Usher.

"Yeah," I said. "So, Prayer, tell him goodbye, and thank him for guarding you all those times obviously."

But Prayer was making extra big eyes at him and Usher was frozen like an animal corpse and my heart kind of flopped over, I knew what she was doing.

"Well hey," she said. "Not so fast. Usher, you can guard me one last time if you want."

Poor lovesick dumbass, he had no chance. So off we went the three of us, on the mission of Take My Homeless Cantread Sister To Law School.

The Dockseye entrance to the Metro had three kinds of doors. Way off to either side you had battered eighthdoors for littles like us to go through, onefoot high, just need to pay two munmuns for those. Next in were the halfscale doors, about fourfeet, littler middlepoors get to use those, ten munmuns please. Then in the middle you have big glossy twoandahalfscale doors for bigger middlepoors and most middleriches, a twenmunmun fare for dressy ladies and sweatsuit gentlemen striding through. And ofcourse if you're bigger than twoandahalfscale you don't fit on the Metro, but when you're that big you don't want to squeeze into trains with other losers anyway, instead you're zooming around on the bigroads in your own monstertruck.

All entrances had floortoceiling doublesliders so littlepoors couldn't race through, plus you had sternlooking muncounters roaming around with brooms. And as for paying three twomun littlefares, forget it. Fortunately I had a plan.

"Fortunately I have a plan," I announced, and I jogged out of the entrance and up the sidewalk, and Prayer and Usher jogged with me, and we jogged for an hour or two all the way to where the tracks came up out of the ground. Sure enough, you had here and there some ratscale holes in the sidewalk and fencing where the rats could wriggle through.

My idea was, follow the rats, because rats get in the Metro all the time without paying any munmun. And the rats won't be a problem because there are three of us, if we all just stick together then no one's getting facechewed by a rat today.

"Warner, your plans are terrible," said Prayer, panting, but we did it anyway. We wriggled through the holes and down onto the gravel next to the tracks, and started walking back toward Dockseye Station, and ignored the little picturesigns the Metro put up to scare littlepoors, of little circleheaded people getting pancaked by trains and deathshocked by the ground and ofcourse mauled by rats. The deathshock one made no sense, thankgod Usher was there to read some important words.

"It says t that rail in the m middle," explained Usher, pointing to a tarcolor bar zipping up the middle of the tracks that I guess if you touched it you died.

So we stood to one side of the tracks and put our right hands on the metal wheelrail and Usher put his left hand on Prayer's back and Prayer put hers on mine and I just put mine out in space and we followed the tracks back underground into the total blindness and walked that way for three or four hours.

It was loud, dark, long. You could hear rats rustle and chatter but you couldn't see them, except when the train was on its way and light was leaking in around the corner, and then yes, as we scouted a place to flop down and wait for the train to pass, always a scene materialized of way too many rats all nestling up in their little chewedout bunkers, cowering from the light and the rumble.

And when finally we made it to Dockseye Station, there was no clear way to get off of the tracks and up onto the platform where people were waiting. I mean there wasn't just a ladder up from the tracks for us with a label of Hey Littlepoors, Climb Here, Bytheway Congrats On Getting This Far Without Dying.

So we climbed the train itself. It was parked but beeping like it was impatient to leave, and we took turns clambering up the wheel, and as you can imagine palsied Usher was not amazing at that, so I had to basically pull him up onto the wheel and then drag him across some cables and finally shove him onto the metal lips between cars.

After a few stops the doors opened and some middlepoor kids came stomping through and we followed them into a car, and a kind old middlerich man lifted us onto a seat onebyone with his magazine because he didn't want to touch us with his hands, and he even gave us a few giant hardcandies to gnaw, and the seat was blessedly soft and it did smell like a giant's peensweat but we still collapsed into it in exhaustion.

"That was terrible and I'm not listening to your ideas anymore," Prayer told me, but the truth was, we were atleast headed to law school, and also Usher got to touch Prayer's sweaty back for four hours, so you have to believe it was the best time of his entire life.

DREAMWORLD

Usher took the first watch while Prayer and I slept. I dreamed the train half full of feathery coralcolor munmun bills and we sat in them like the tub.

"It's notsogood you tricked Usher into coming," I said.

"It wasn't a trick," she said. "He wanted to come."

"Do you think Usher also wants to help you marry off to some completely other guy from Usher," I said.

"I can't marry someone whose mouth can't even say the first letter of my name," said Prayer.

"Wow," I said. "That's mean and terrible."

"It was a joke," Prayer said. "Sorry. I like Usher, okay. And look, he's not stupid. I'm sure he knows what this trip is about."

"Well, I'm going to tell him, so, if he runs away crying, your fault," I said.

Prayer took the second watch and Usher dozed into the dream. I sundried the bills of munmun up to the ceiling, where they cried paint.

"Usher, I hate to tell you this, but Prayer isn't going to law school to study law," I said.

"I know that," he said, unpalsied from the dream. "Prayer can't read."

"Tobehonest I would have to say this law school trip is more about her finding a hubby," I said. "A lawgrad hubby with munmun so she and my mom can scale up."

"I know that's her plan," he said. "But anything could happen."

"Usher," I said. "You don't want hope to make you stupid."

"Anything could happen if I'm a good enough guy to her," said Usher, and my heart just broke for this poor stupid idiot.

I took the third watch, listening for Sand Dreamough, and the old middlerich guy was still sitting there.

"Pardon me," he said, in that deep frummy middlerich style. He was about doublescale and he had a buttcheek in each seat.

"Pardon me," I said, because what else can you do with middleriches except repeat and hope it's polite.

"I just wanted to tell you how much I enjoyed your dreaming," he said. "I dozed off and I have to tell you it was quite beautifull, even moving."

"Moving, thank you," I said. "Beautifull, well, thank you again. Please."

He gave me a smile that was buttclenched with pity or something. His skin was about the lightness of palmwood, sunsplashed with black and gray, and the hair on his head was like trees on a mountain, up to the ears and no higher.

"May I ask where you are headed?" he tried to say quietly.

"Yes, please," I said. "The law school in Sand Dreamough."

He snuffled a little and his brows climbed his head.

"Well goodness, what a coincidence," he told me, he lived nearby up in High Dreamough and could carry us from the station.

"Goodness goodness," I nodded, "a coincidence for sure."

I woke up Usher and Prayer and we discussed it quietly, ontheonehand this will save us a bunch of time, ontheother can we trust him, ofcourse we can he seems nice, but what if he eats us, Warner you idiot that doesn't happen, forstarters middles have way better food to eat than littles, infact what if he gives us some.

So I told the old middlerich that sounded good and a few stations later he scooped us up into the outerpocket of his smoky-smelling leather bag. There was more hardcandy floating around in there, magazines, books, bottles, plastic bendy sheets that were probably screens or cameras or something, no idea how to use them though.

We bounced in his bag, peeking over the pocketlip, as he strode through a middlepoor neighborhood, ducking the awnings and overstepping carts and bikes. I tried looking for a law school. I knew a little what it might look like from other people's dreaming, basically oldtimey parthenons like stone grills hatted with pyramids. But I didn't see any, just dusty middlepoor twostorys crowding the parkinglots and cardstock signs and foldingchairs he had to dance around.

It was a different landscape from Dockseye for sure, lots of shops and restaurants and middlemalls, mostly halfscale to mid-dlescale. We zoomed over the heads of old middlepoors playing cards and eating soups, young tatty daves leaning on janky halfcars and also eating soups, giggly sceneteens eating even more soups, what the heck is this, Neighborhood Souptime.

Off the sloping streets above us nowandthen I could see some real palaces nosing over the trees.

Then we got a better look at those palaces when he turned up one wide slopestreet and started bounding uphill and prettysoon it was just super groomed middlerich houses hugging the cliffsides, walled off from each other by forests.

After a while it became hard not to worry about whether we were actually heading toward a law school.

"Oh," I announced eventually. "You know, I don't recognize this part of Sand Dreamough, perhaps you could kindly tell me about it, I mean not to be rude, nopressure."

"Well, now we're in High Dreamough," explained the guy.

"Ah," I agreed, while we all tried not to get too freaked out.

A few minutes later I piped up again, "Well, I guess I'm curious about where law school is from here exactly, and you know what, come to think of it, we can probably just walk the rest of the way, so, what I'm saying here ofcourse is, if you please, thank you."

"No no no," he said. "We're not far. I can't drop you off here, anyway."

We traveled another mile or so.

"Are we going to law school or what," hissed Prayer.

"I guess I am a little curious about whether we can be close to a law school if around here it's all just homes and dwellings and forests," I said to the guy.

"You're quite perceptive," he purred.

I had no idea what the crap that meant so I just said, *"You're quite perceptive, thanks."*

"I just need to make a quick stop at my house, if that's allright with you," he said.

There was nothing really to say to that except okay fine.

We rattled in his bag as he bounded up the steps to his huge fairytale house.

LIFEANDDEATHWORLD

The smell of the house put us all on edge. It was fake vanilla and lemongrass but to cover the high sharp notes of animal piss. In the great hall atleast six middlepoors zipped around in atleast three cleaningcars, craning and laddering up the walls and tabletops to wipe and scrub. The guy's wife appeared in a hallway, folding up yetanother big bendy screen.

Middleriches have big facefeatures, forthatreason they can be terrifying even when they're not trying to be. So this woman's big blazing eyes on your eyes were like hands on your throat, and when she opened her mouth her teeth leaned fiercely out of there. But definitely the worstofall part was, her hands gripped and cuddled a nasty crappy lynxcat, and it stared at us too with round hungry eyeblacks.

"Oh great," she boomed. "Some new houseguests, huh."

"They needed a carry to the law school," defended the guy.

"Grant, first of all, how likely do you think *that* is," said the wife of this guy Grant. "It's not like they can read."

"Usher can actually read super good," I could have yelled if fear wasn't crowding my throat.

"When's dinner," said Grant.

"I put a pelican in a little while ago so probably two, twoand-ahalf hours," said Grant's wife.

"Great," said Grant. "I'll be downstairs."

"Um, with respect," I said. "If you are not taking us to law school, that is a hundredscale okay, so again, if you could just take us outside and point which direction to jog, uh, thanks super much."

"Ofcourse, ofcourse I could do that," he told us, opening a door, closing it behind us so the lynxcat couldn't follow, heading down some stairs to a paintysmelling basement. "But please, let me offer you a little something first. Some drinking water? Maybe a bath?"

Look, you're never going to turn down pure sterilized middle-rich water.

He handed us shotglasses and we stood on the sinklip and filled and guzzled as the lights hummed on, and we stared out into the big cavey basement at the mountains and the milkcows.

Of course these were not real mountains or real milkcows. They were painted and fake, plaster and plastic. The entire basement was a sea of tables holding a goofy handmade landscape for statues of littlepoors. But I mean even littlepoorer than us, which as you know is not possible. Like mousesize people we'd outscale by two or three.

This was basically a tabletop island of no cities and instead a dozen farms, all farming gluey cows and sheep, and two random skiers escaping one random bear.

Traintracks connected the island's farms who I guess were too lazy to walk even fiveminutes to each other, and now Grant

31

was putting some brightly painted trains on there, and basically it seemed like the trains were the entire point somehow.

"It's a hobby of mine that has really become kind of a passion, and gotten a tad outofcontrol, and, I don't know, perhaps you'll think it's foolish," he said.

Prayer finally said something, and I didn't know it but she was being a Prayer we were all about to see a ton of and pretty quickly hate, the Prayer of I Will Praise Basically Anything A Rich Guy Does.

"I think it's not at all foolish," she said, "infact the opposite, meaning very clever indeed. Is it even possible that you made this whole thing?"

"Well, uh, you know, I guess I did," he said, purpling all happy under his beard.

He put the last train on the track and pressed a screen and the trains jolted awake and started wheeling around Mountainmilk-cowisland, and we watched them for a pretty long time.

To make the guy feel good, Prayer told the story of what was happening.

"There goes the red train into the tunnel again," she said.

"Now it's coming out of the tunnel, just as fast as it went in," she said.

"Time to slow down though, here comes a curve," she said.

A couple times we could hear the lynxcat yowling and scraping at the basement door. Usher was definitely on the verge of pissing himself and I was too.

"Are you enjoying yourselves?" Grant asked us finally.

"Oh absolutely," said Prayer.

"Could I ask you something, though?" Grant wondered.

"You could ask us anything really," she said.

"Do you think you might like to ride?" he said.

We all looked at each other and were afraid to say anything but what was he talking about, no way were we fitting into any of those trains.

"Here's what I really like to do," he said. "I like to make films of people of your scale riding the trains all through the countryside. It gives me such pleasure, and they turn out surprisingly well, they really do. I'd give you a few things to say to each other, perhaps."

Again we said nothing.

Grant cleared his throat and said, "In exchange for taking you to law school, and water, and even a little nice pelicanmeat for dinner, it could be a nice thing to do, I was thinking."

"Is it a nice thing to do, or is a kidnapping going on right now," I said.

"Warner," hissed Prayer. "Shut up."

Grant was quiet. Then he sorrowed, "I have to tell you, that hurts my feelings. As if I would ever do such a thing."

"Mister Grant," said Prayer, "my brother was being rude and terrible, and later I'll slap his stupid face. But the reason he is freaking out is, we have jobs at the law school earning munmun, and he's worried we're going to be late."

Grant frowned and nodded, like we had just reminded him of something he didn't like.

"So our question is," said Prayer, "can you give us a few munmuns to be in this film? Because I think that would make all the difference."

Grant breathed in and blew out about a gallon of hot stinking air, his lips flapping, like, *manohman, you guys are making this really hard for me.*

"Ten munmuns each," I said.

"Oh, okay," said Grant. "So, thirty? Yeah, no problem. Oh, this is great! Let's shower you up and get you into costume."

Prayer wore the princess outfit, I wore the soldier outfit, and Usher wore the Japanese robe. The fabric of mine was like treebark.

"Holy crap, this itches and hurts," I said.

"I can't even really move," said Prayer.

"Mi ine feels nice," said Usher. His robe was silk and looked great, a little too big for him though, pooling around his feet.

"Can we all wear what Usher's wearing," I asked, but Grant said no.

"I can sw witch with p ppp p Pprayeratleast," said Usher, but Grant said no to that too.

"We need a princess and it has to be her," explained Grant.

Like I said, we were way too big to ride the trains like passengers, so we alternated between sitting on the tops of them and squeezing into opentop boxcars.

"May I?" asked Grant, and he picked up Usher and mashed him into a boxcar with his thumb.

"Holy crap, be carefull with him please," I yelled.

Prayer had the most lines. It was a lot of stuff like, "What a glorious day for a ride on the Old Bavarian Line!" and, "Now, I wonder who can be waiting for me at the station! Why, it's the vicar!"

As the soldier, I had to do stunts. A lot of them involved the tunnel. One stunt was where as the tunnel swallowed the train, I had to run screaming along the top from front to back, eventually not make it though and get smacked by the mountainside.

Usher wasn't great with lines so Grant brought in some white pinkeyed rats to sit in the boxcar with him and pretend to play cards.

"They're completely domesticated and have never harmed a soul," Grant explained to sweaty rapidbreathing Usher.

Then Grant took the tops off of some passenger trains and told me and Prayer to squeeze in and lie down in them. That was really notsogood. We were smushed inside like in toosmall coffins and the tops of the little seats dug into our bodies and faces, worstofall, we couldn't move because Grant clamped the tops onto our backs until they snapped shut.

We zoomed around the track like monsters, completely unable to move and trying not to throw up.

"I do believe my stop is approaching," I said with my face smashed into some windows.

"Why, Loottenant, what a coincidence," mumbled Prayer.

"Can we try that again a little louder and clearer, please," said Grant.

"WHY LOOTTENANT," yelled Prayer. "WHAT A COINCIDENCE."

It got even more weird and bad when Grant took Prayer out, wrapped her up in twine, set her back down on top of the tracks, left me in the train meanwhile.

"Okay now while the train approaches, the princess needs to struggle, but not too hard, make it look like you can't escape, and

35

you, I need you to steeple your fingers and laugh like a supervillain while the train approaches," he said to Usher. "Like this: OH, HA HA HA HA. YESSSS, YES. OH, HA HA HA HA HA HA. Like that."

But Usher wouldn't do the evil maniac laugh, couldn't but also wouldn't, instead he kept stumbling all panicky onto the tracks in front of Prayer waving his arms so that the train with me inside would kill him first.

"This scene is really important, infact I would say it's pivotal," grumbled Grant. "Can you please just do what I asked for one take."

Nope, Usher just shook his head desperately and stood on the tracks with arms outstretched like a zombie.

"For God's sake, I'm not going to let the train actually hit her," huffed Grant. "Anyway it's lightwait and plastic and not even going very fast, so, worstcase, I mean, no one has anything to worry about."

Lucky for us, Grant's wife opened the door at the top of the stairs and yelled, "Grant, dinner."

Unlucky for us, as soon as she opened the door the psycho lynxcat came jailbreaking down, this yowly murderer made it up onto the table before Grant got ahold of him, lifted him up scratching and scrabbling, all we could do was watch and scream.

At dinner, we met Grant's kids, a son Prayer's age, a daughter my age. The son ignored us. The daughter was called Willow and she wanted us gone completely, so she was sort of our best hope for getting out of there.

"Dad. *They* don't even want to be here," said Willow.

"Don't you think they deserve a good meal, honey," Grant asked her.

"Ohmygod, you don't understand anything," she said.

"You know, it's good sometimes to meet people who aren't like you," he said.

"Uuuuuugggggh," she said.

We were ofcourse sitting on the tabletop, one dish inbetween the three of us like a kiddiepool. The pelican and the broccolis were salty and slick with butterfat, therefore kind of hard to eat. Grant cut small steaks for us but you still had to hold with all ten fingers and gnaw, and they kept slipping out of our hands and back onto the plate, sometimes across the table like a jetski.

"This meal is super good and we feel blessed to be eating it," announced Prayer.

Prayer was sitting next to Grant's son. He was called Grantagain.

"Grantagain, are you in school," asked Prayer.

"Uh, yeah," snorted Grantagain.

"Wow, that must be wonderfull and you seem smart," said Prayer. "What do you study?"

She was making big intrested eyes at him and trying to eat as delicately as possible, using only her fingertips and nails. I glanced at Usher and his face was grim but he was putting up with it.

"Well, I'm still in year ten, so, you know, still everything," said Grantagain like this was the most obvious thing ever.

"You must be super smart to study everything, and did you say for ten years?, simply wow," marveled Prayer.

"*Mom*," said Willow, making pleading eyes. But her mom just ignored her and frowned at her food.

We all ate in silence. A shotglass slipped out of Usher's greasy hands and tipped water into the tablecloth.

"Do you think you'll go to law school one day?" Prayer asked Grantagain.

"I can't deal with this," said Willow, standing up. "I'm done."

"Oh come on, sweetie," said Grant.

"Dad, I have so much work to do, and this is so weird and messed up," said Willow, and she walked super fast out of the dining room.

"Sorry about that," said Grant. "Girls her age, you know."

Grantagain snorted again but I caught him glancing at Prayer a couple more times, she must have noticed too because she started flipping and tossing her hair for no reason like a nervous horse.

After dinner it was dark and Grant offered us the possibility to sleep in the basement and then he'd take us to law school in the morning. I didn't like the idea because of the lynxcat. But Prayer and Usher outvoted me.

Grant bedded us down on some pillows under some napkins, next to the sink if we needed it, me and Usher on one side of the sink and Prayer on the other, and he gave us silk kimonos to sleep in, and my sis and me slept in a proper familyhome for the first time since ours got stepped on.

DREAMWORLD

A little in anger, a little wanting to impress, I dreamed the High Dreamough hillside was a ski mountain emptying onto the top of itself, looping like Grant's dumb traintracks, and you had to keep skiing if you wanted to escape the waddling random bears with lynxcat heads. So we all sped downhill endlessly, me and Usher and random middleriches, and sometimes someone would smack into a house or wetpainted mound of papermashay and a lynxbear would catch up to them and squash them into the ground and sit on them all snapped into place like a trainroof.

Above us also the sky snaked with trains, twisting, coiling, eating each other like tunnels. So that made it a little bit of a shitscape, too, in a way that hopefully said to Grant, *hey, I didn't love the whole train thing.*

But he slid up to me and it was clear he didn't get it.

"I'm so moved by how much I've inspired you," he told me in a dreammuffled way where the only way he could talk was, open your mouth and hope the words fall out.

"Sure, no problem," I said.

"I'm so moved, by just how much I've inspired you," he said

again, because people who are bad at dreaming say the same thing overandover embarrassingly.

"Great," I said, speeding up.

"I've inspired you, special boy," he tried to yell.

"Thanks," I said, losing him.

"Special, special boy," he said, as cowdolls tripped him and lynxbears trapped him.

"Watch out for those," I said.

I dove the skytrains onebyone into holes in the ground, they writhed wildly, more dreamers crashed.

Usher caught me.

"I think Prayer is talking to Grantagain," he told me.

"Why do you think that," I said.

"Well, I know she is, because I saw them talking in a house," he said.

"Oh," I said.

"Well, actually more than just talking," he said.

"Oof," I said.

"I guess not talking at all for the most part," he said.

"I get it," I said.

In Dreamworld obviously you can't bang, but you can show someone parts of yourself naked, or your whole self, and touch yourself or dance around or smush your crotch on stuff or do whatever to get someone horny, and then they start smushing themselves around too and you can give each other a sexy messy bangdream. So that's what Usher was trying to tell me Prayer and Grantagain were up to. That's what Prayer's lifeanddeathbody was doing across the sink over on her pillow and it was pretty terrible to think about, and I couldn't help but start dreaming the snow muddy and crappy, and causing more slowdowns and crashes of middleriches, et set set setera.

"Sorry you saw that, Usher," I said. "But, I have to tell you, I'm even more sorry you told me about it."

The hillside looped and I approached Grant again. He flopped and flailed to match pace with me, and I couldn't speed past him in the thick sticky shitsnow.

"Special boy, what is your job at the law school," said Grant.

This comfy middlerich jerk had kidnapped us and mashed us into trains and made us deal with crappy animals and now Prayer was dreambanging his son with the crazy hope of one day marrying him and I just couldn't be nice anymore.

"I don't have a job," I told him. "Obviously I have no job at all. None of us do. We're littlepoor. We're too little for real jobs. We eat garbage food and live in garbage houses and try to sell crap to each other and get robbed and there's no way out."

"Special special boy," said this doofus, who couldn't even dream right. "At the law school, what is your job you do for munmun."

"Listen to me, jerk," I said, tapdancing to float above the drying concrete that trapped his skis. "I know you're not afraid of me. But that's your stupid mistake. One day I'll be huge. I'll be so bigrich, I'll put a foot through your roof. I'll bend down and wipe your whole stupid neighborhood off this hillside with my tongue."

"Warner, maybe get less mad," said Usher.

The caking earth also bulged with trains, snaking underground like worms.

"I have friends who teach at the law school," said too stupid to be afraid Grant. Finally his dreaming was becoming stronger and clearer from all the sadness. "I'll have to introduce you. What was that last thing you said? And for that matter what has happened to my skis?"

Manohman did I need lynxbears to catch this guy and eat him.

"This dream has gotten rather savage," said Grant. "You have quite a wild little mind."

Willow came rolling and bellowing down the hillside, and I alittlebit enjoyed how mad she was. Okay, maybe a lot.

"This dream sucks, I hate you, and you have fiveminutes to wake up and leave the house," she told me.

"Cool threat," I told her.

"Ohmygod, I'm not joking," she said. "I'm going to wake myself up and go downstairs and open the door to the basement, so Bixquick can chase you out of here, or eat the shit out of you, or whatever."

When I heard this allofasudden I couldn't tapdance, the ground grabbed my feet and wouldn't let go.

Nightmares are when you can't control your dreaming anymore, I didn't get them verymuch but it was happening right then for sure.

"Okay," I said. "Well, let's wait just a moment. That's going a little too far to punish a bad dream that's not even that bad, just wild and crazy."

"It's not you, you idiot, it's your slutty sister," Willow said, and you could tell her anger was real, not just bitchy. "Your disgusting sister is in a bangdream with my stupid brother. Ohmygod. Does she think she even deserves to even talk to him? No."

The ground slurped me horribly as Willow refused to shut up.

"They don't even have anything incommon to talk about," ranted Willow, "so she's just skanking up all over him like maybe he's even got half a chance to even remember her in the morning, which, no way, and I want to vom just thinking about how she came into my house and dreambangs my brother like she thinks they even exist in the same *universe*, ohmygod it's so gross and embarrassing, so if you don't crack a window and get out of here in fiveminutes, I am letting Bixquick down there and telling Dad he opened the door himself, because honestly, I mean the whole thing should make you want to vom too but I guess being littlepoor just means you don't care when your own stupid family does something gross and pathetic," and it seemed like she didn't actually want me to leave, judging from how nonstop she was talking, but toobad, I danced my feet free and backflipped and dove through the ground to wipe out my dreamself and wake up.

LIFEANDDEATHWORLD

I woke up, Usher didn't, thankgod for that, hope he can keep this psycho girl Willow in Dreamworld somehow with his prettygood dreamstuff, definitely aboveaverage.

Prayer in her sleep atleast wasn't writhing around, for her it was just pretend horniness, but who cares, still awfull and gross. I shook her awake.

"Oh no no *crap*," she said. "Oh Warner, what the hell."

"Willow saw you having a stupid bangdream with Grantagain and now she wants to feed us to the lynxcat so I'm probably saving our lives, idiot," I said.

She slapped my face.

"Are you kidding me?" I yelled. "You're slapping my face right now?"

"Never talk to me like that," she spat.

"We have to crack a window and get out of here like immediately," I said.

But first of all in the dim dark it was hard to see anything like how to turn the lights on. I shimmied down the sinkleg to the floor to look for light or window options.

"How is Usher going to get down here," wondered Prayer.

"Look at my very surprised face at learning this new knowledge of, you care if Usher even lives or dies," I said, pointing to my face.

I jogged across the floor l ooking f or h oles o r s omething t o climb or anything, and finally I did find a door somewhere. I was hoping it went outside. But when I squeezed underneath I found myself in a blind dark closet.

"Warner, the lynxcat can hear you," said Prayer, and obviously I could hear it scrabbling and yowling around up there and I thought for the billionth time, how sick must riches be in the head to keep these murderous jerks around.

I bashed into mops, brooms, random shoes, jugs of cleaning acids and gels. Finally I hit something cool and round and atfirst I didn't know what it was.

Then I figured it out.

"Prayer," I said. "Okay. Wake up Usher, then come down here immediately."

It was one of the cleaningcars the middlepoor maids had been using, basically a wide glasstic rollerpod. Then ontop you've got a littler pod that can shoot up and out on a flexy laddercrane, to clean even those hardtoreach places.

The rollerpod was built for someone atleast quarterscale. So I was too littlepoor to work the footpedals and steeringpad at the same time. But if we stuck Prayer down there in the footspace, meanwhile I'm up here steering with the pad and yelling commands, maybe that could work.

Or maybe it can't because apparently Prayer can't work the

pedals, because her entire body isn't as strong as an average quarterscale foot, how is that possible, Prayer can you even do a single pushup.

"Try putting your whole weight on it," I yelled.

"Why don't you put your stupid weight on it," she yelled back.

So we scrambled around switching positions, her on the steeringpad, me on the footpedal, while upstairs we heard Willow thump around toward the door and talk to Bixquick.

"Bixie, you're awake too, huh," we heard that psycho girl say. "Ow. I know, Bix, I know. They're so annoying. *Ow.* Bix, don't bite me, you stupid freak."

I wedged myself against the ceiling of the sweatysmelling footspace and grinded into the pedal as hard as I could and something finally worked and bam, we smashed our way through the closet door and out into the basement. Prayer immediately steered us into the leg of a tabletop. A corner of Mountainmilkcowisland fell on top of us and exploded everywhere. I got thrown around, hopped onto a second pedal, mashed it, thankgod it was the brake.

"Oh, this makes no sense," said Prayer. "Left is right, I think."

The basement door creaked open and we heard Bixquick snarl happily and pad down the stairs.

"Okay, hit the gopedal again," said Prayer, and I hit it again, and we lurched into another table leg and a bunch more of Mountainmilkcowisland collapsed to the ground, throwing up paintchips and plasterclouds.

"Yeah, left is right," said Prayer. "Well, that's stupid, but I think I got it."

Usher peered over the sinklip, gazing down at us with terrified eyeballs. We whirligigged in his basic direction, crunching cows and barn walls. Meanwhile Bixquick stalked us through the debris.

Next problem for Team Save Usher From Getting Eaten was, once we were under the sink, we couldn't get the cranepod to raise.

"Ohmygod, hit the laddercrane pic on the screen," I yelled.

"I'm hitting it, idiot, all that happens are flashing words," yelled Prayer.

Bixquick decided it was time to eat us and bat bat batted the glasstic between me and him a couple times, fortunately glasstic is a superstrong miracle substance.

"nnnnnnnnnnnnnnnNNOWWWW," said this huge murdercat.

"Crap, please go away," I begged.

We stared at each other. My eyes were dumb stones, his were liquid evil.

Then he flicked his head up toward Usher, froze, unfroze, waggled his butt like a maniac.

In desperation I jumped on a third little pedal, more of a button, and the cleaningcar stopped jittering around and froze, legs tripodded out the sides and clamped onto the ground, finally the cranepod started spooling upward.

Bixquick bounded onto the sink.

Prayer was mashing the screen with both hands and staring up desperately at the dreamyslow spooling cranepod and there was no way it was going to get there before Usher got his spine broken or face ripped open or whatever.

Bixquick sniffed Usher once with his ugly slugstripey head.

Then Usher just rolled off the edge.

47

He fell about a foot through the air and mostly hit the top of the cranepod. Its door was spazzing openshut openshut and he just kind of dangled there in its mouth and let it chomp the middle of his body while we pulled up the tripod legs and sucked the cranepod back toward us.

By the time we got to the stairs the cranepod was sitting on top of us again and Usher was all the way inside limply settling himself. So we rolled up the steps in our amazing ball and past Willow and across the hallway floor with Bixquick scampering uselessly behind us, and we bashed the front door a few times until Willow yelled "UGGH FINE" and furiously just opened it for us, legblocking the scrabbly lynxcat as we rolled out into the night.

A few blocks away we stopped and brought Usher into the main pod with us. He was mostly okay, just a couple ribs and fingers broken and a bruisedup face.

"Than nks," he said to Prayer.

"Hey, ofcourse," said Prayer.

"Usher, why the heck are you thanking her," I said.

"F for savi ing m me," he said.

"It was her fault we all almost got killed," I said.

"It was your stupid fault we ended up in that house in the first place, so, more your fault than mine, so maybe you should apologize to everyone right now," Prayer said, and I knew she was wrong but the words were true.

"Prayer, Usher, I'm sorry I tried to get us to law school faster," I said.

Prayer grumped.

"Part Two, I'm sorry I got us detoured to a house where a boy could possibly live, because, big planning mistake by me," I added.

"I liked that boy and guesswhat, idiot, he liked me," she said.

"He liked that you were getting naked at him, sure," I said.

"Warner, you need to shut up," snapped my sister. "You think someone like him couldn't like someone like me, but just shut up. You don't even know what happened."

We rolled down the hillside as the darkness behind us melted pinkly. We were still high enough to get sometimes glimpses of the whole awakening city of Lossy Indica, all the way to the fogeaten beach.

"We didn' 't get the th thirty m munmun," realized Usher.

"Also we lost the emergency munmun and all our freaking clothes," I pointed out.

"We got a car atleast," Prayer said.

It was full on morning when we got back to that middlepoor neighborhood and people were hustling and bustling, hosing sidewalks and putting out lawnchairs and eating more soups.

Now three littlepoors in a middlepoor cleaningcar will get some stinkface looks out on the streets and sometimes stopped and demanded, what are you doing. Lucky we had me who is pretty good with stories and lies.

"Just a transport mission to the law school," I kept explaining. "Lossy Clean Co had too many cars up in the hills, not enough at the law school, but not worth it to send a truck or a middlepoor, so if you'll excuse us, thankyou and yourewelcome."

Mostly middlepoors nodded grumpily and said nothing, a

few helpfully gave us law school directions, a few others kicked or threw us into the street and yelled not to take their jobs, so prettyquick I learned to stop saying the part about not worth it to send a middlepoor.

By the time we got to law school the glasstic was scuffed pretty bad and the steeringpad was beeping and flashing the same word overandover.

"BATTL L, LOW," read Usher.

"Battlow," Prayer and me realized.

I say we got to law school but it didn't really feel like we had got to anywhere, because this law school wasn't a big glorious parthenon. Firstofall it was a spreadout suburb of a bunch of different buildings, and secondofall they were all just grubby officeblocks and their dowdy frumpiness made me start to worry that we really didn't have a plan and how the heck was Prayer going to meet husbands in these things.

We asked a few people if this was for real the law school.

"Yup," said an old middlepoor, running a Quickstand. "You're right in the middle of campus."

If these were even lawstudents it was super confusing because they were dressed all slummy. But their scale was middlerich, striding up and down the street chattering into phones and screens, briskly stepping around the middlepoors underfoot.

"Which building are you headed to," asked the Quickstand guy.

"The main one," I said.

"Admin or lecturehall," he asked.

"Leckcherall," I said.

"Couple blocks that way," he said, thumbing the air.

"Sir, we might not make it because we're battlow," said Prayer. "I know it is a big request, but could we possibly charge up on a little of your juice?"

He gave her a long look and breathed out of his nose and screwed up his mouth and shook his head.

But he also said, "Fine."

While our car sucked his juice he sat us on his counter to chat and gave us a little tapwater and some shards of chip. His name was Paddy. Bodywise he was chubby and purply black with white curls dusting his head.

"Don't see too many littlepoors in Sand Dreamough," he told us. "You seem young so let me give you a little advice. Get yourselves that education while your brains are still soft. Because once that brain hardens up you can't learn anything new."

"Sure, yeah," I said, feeling crappy because who the heck was going to give us an education.

"If you want to scale up, you got to make yourself usefull," said Paddy. "Nobody's gonna scale you up just to be nice."

"Well that is pretty wise, and you are very kind to give us not just juice and food but also wisdom," Prayer said.

"You won't get to my scale with zero education, and that's a fact," said Paddy. "I started about twofifth the size I am right now and I never married or had any babybrats. So all my munmun goes to my own scale and that's it. That's one way to scale up, real slow over time, but it's lonely. I mean, you get used to it. But look at me! I'm so lonely and bored, I'm talking to *you*!"

"For sure, yeah," I said.

51

"So sop up that education while you still can because you don't have a whole lot of years left of being young and soppybrain," he said. "You'll be my age quicker than you think."

"If we even live that long," I said.

"Warner, don't be depressing," said Prayer.

"No, he's got a good point," agreed Paddy.

"Mister Paddy, I'll be honest," I said. "How do you suggest we even get an education? They don't make schools for littlepoors."

"Well," he said, and then he was quiet for a while.

"Well, can you read," he asked finally.

"Nope," I said.

He glanced at Prayer.

"No," said Prayer all ashamed.

"Dang," said Paddy.

"I c cc can," said Usher.

"And you've got the palsy," said Paddy. "I was wondering, why don't the gray one speak. Dang, dang, dang. Three of the littlest littlepoors you could find and two can't read, third's got the stuttershakes. Wow and dang. God help you kids. You know it won't be easy out there. Where do you even sleep?"

"Right now we sleep in the car," I said.

"Wow and dang," he said again.

"We're actually pretty happy to have a car to sleep in these days," I said.

"Beep," said the car, battfull.

He lowered us into the car onebyone, hands a little sloppy from chipgrease.

"Thank you onceagain for the juice, water, food, wisdom,

52

advice ingeneral," said Prayer. "Allinall, we don't get a lot of kind-nesses from people, so, we really appreciate it."

He twisted up his mouth again like he was in pain.

"Well, uh," he said. "Well, nevermind. Nevermind."

But we waited for him to stop neverminding.

"Well," he said, "what I mean to say is, uh, and just for a night, or two, but uh, you need a safe place to park while you sleep, you can park it out back of the stand."

"Ohmygod, thank you," cried Prayer.

"Just let me know beforehand, okay," he said. "And just you three. Don't be bringing other littles to my stand now."

"Ofcourse ofcourse, just us," she said, Usher and I nodded like maniacs.

"Don't even tell anyone because the moment poors start thinking I'm soft and forming a charity line in front of my stand, scaring away business, that's the moment Quickstand takes this stand away from me, allright," he told us.

"Nope nope nope won't bring anyone," said Prayer.

"And you'd better believe if I catch a whiff of you burning weeds or rocks, just one whiff, you're the cops's problem and not mine anymore, you got that," he said.

"Dd d dd dDefinitely y not," yelled Usher, surprising every-one into shutting up.

"Just a couple nights," said Paddy.

So we slept that night in the car under Paddy's recycling, and the next night too, and actually for a few months that was our home. Usher and me slept downstairs and Prayer slept up in the cranepod. We used the car only for shelter, went everywhere onfoot, didn't want to risk riding around and then some grumpy middlepoor yanks us out and rides off, and then no more bedhouse for Team Prayer Usher Warner.

Each day had the same shape.

Step One, Paddy wakes us up, gives us crumbs of his breakfast, talks at us for pretty long about people and time and governments and churches and basically just what everything is like and wouldn't you love to change it, well toobad, you can't change people and that's just the end of it.

Step Two, we commute as a squad to the lecturehall and everybody goes to work. You can sit for free in lecturehall and they just call you an odditor. So, Usher, he just does odditing the whole day, list list listening, memorizing ideas and laws, squinting at the board which unless he gets a weirdly good seat he can't really see it, also healing up his ribs by not moving very much.

Prayer, she rambles around asking for carries up and down the stairs to class or hangs out on studydesks and lunchtables looking daydreamy, playing with her hair, examining her nails, hoping someone will start a convo with this cute lonely dreamer.

Me, I try random schemes to earn munmun, all failures. Do littletasks for people, collect trash to sell, woo law school women like Prayer woos law school men. No luck.

Step Three, we meet at five near the doors and commute home as a squad and Paddy usually gives us a little dinner, otherwise every law school trash has pizzarinds.

54 Step Four, sleep and dream.

DREAMWORLD

So, yes, I thought for a few days if Prayer can trap a middlerich husband maybe I can trap a middlerich wife, because my face and body are not so bad. I'm littlepoor strong, meaning ropey arms and shoulders from climbing everything all the time, plus no scars sores or blisters on my face, cherrywine skin not too different from Prayer's, maybe a little more orange, but better thicker hair, and save the best for last, all my teeth are still in there.

But it doesn't matter how good teeth and hair you have, or how fast you can climb a chair. Law school women are not excited to marry a fourteenyearold littlepoor. At lecturehall mostly we talked about what was I even doing there.

"I just chill here at times," I would say.

"So you don't have like classes to go to or anything," law school women would say.

"I could go to the class of you," I would say. "Today's lecture, how to love you, or you could even just teach me how to read."

"We're a little busy and stressedout for that," they would say.

"Would it relax your stresslevels to meet your lovematch for your whole life, and never have to worry about the question of who to love, ever again," I would say.

"Ha ha ha ha ha ha ha ha ha," they would say. "I literally can't even begin to deal with this."

Prayer wasn't doing a whole lot better. Some of these law school men started recognizing her, making fun of her, playing mean games of Who Can Make Prayer Agree With The Stupidest Thing, which was not hard to do because her whole attitude was, agree with everything, compliment everyone, that's how you make someone fall in love with you.

"Well what do you know, here's *Prayer* again," they would say, like her name was something made up. "*Prayer*, don't you think the government gives too many munmuns to littlepoors."

"Oh sure, I think so, yes," she would say.

"Isn't it sad how the government punishes middles and bigs for success by taxing some of their munmuns, the more success the more they get punished, how is that fair," they would say.

"It's so sad and unfair, and bytheway no one's talking about it," she would agree.

"Wouldn't it be great if the government punished littlepoors instead, for example by jailing them every few months," they would say.

"Hmmmm, well that's an intresting proposal, and to be honest I might be too stupid to really understand it," she would say.

"Because then littlepoors would finally have the motivation to work hard and improve themselves and scale their way up," they would say.

"Wow, I have to agree with you there," she would say. "What a smart idea."

Obviously Prayer didn't actually agree that yes, please randomly jail us littlepoors every few months. She wasn't an idiot. Except maybe in the way of, she believed if she ever argued with a guy even once, it's over, he hates her now forever and no longer thinks she's cute. That way I did think she was a littlebit an idiot.

Also another thing you have to understand, we had to work and wait for hours to get one of these convos. Most of the time we spent figuring out how to get up to a place near a lawstudent's head. And once we were there they could walk away at anytime.

I mean obviously when you're littlepoor most of your time ingeneral is spent just getting from ay to bee, anxiously walking or jogging around the edges of stomping forests of legs and boots and you barely have time to do anything else.

Anyway the point is in Lifeanddeathworld our wooing was on average super pathetic. But in Dreamworld we did a little better.

It was Prayer's idea to make romantic lovey dreamzones.

"Dreaming is the only thing you're good at so we might as well use it," she said.

"I don't really know how to make a lovezone though," I said.

"I guess study up at Prettyshop," she said.

Everyday is Valenday at Prettyshop, says Prettyshop, a mallroom where middlepoor girls bring middlepoor boys to buy them flowers, jewels, trinkets, candies, candles, crowns, fake animals, basically it's a cozy shitscape of roses and pinkpurple plastics and blaring lovesongs. I hung out there for two days, hiding in a basket of candybelly monkeys and peering around, until a shopper uncovered me and started screaming and a salesman broomed me all the way into the street.

That night I dreamed a Prettyworld. A rolling sunsetted

57

garden of just a peenload of cherryblossoms and chrisandthemuns, rosebushes and daftdill vines, pinkpurple bees and birds buzzing sugary melodies like flying phones, paths of diamonds and golds twisting into little pillowhouses. Gianteyed cartooncats and bears dancing through the garden like Rushians and sprinkling you nonstop in twinkly glitter, bouncing chocolate rabbits begging you to eat them. Dusks of heartshape moons and fireworks exploding in candyshowers, dressing you in candyskin that you now must lick off each other in an uncontrolled passion.

"It's a little over the top, but, goodjob," said Prayer, hiding in the Prettyworld bushes and waiting for lawstudents.

But mostly we got tooyoung dreamers, tweens and teens like us coming in and wandering through and giggling at it, mostly girls, a few boys too. Not just middlepoor kids, plenty middlerich youngsters were floating down from High Dreamough, following the sugarsmell and flowerlight. I even saw that psycho girl Willow stroll in, rolling her eyes like how terrible is this crappy place, but also running her hands through the flowers and watching the colors change.

I didn't talk to her. But a few other girls I thought were intresting, I approached.

"Hey," I would say to a girl. "Can you keep a secret, if so here's the secret, I'm the one dreaming all this."

"Yeah right," she would say, rolling her eyes.

"Watch, I'll turn it blue," I would say, and dreamed *blue*, and everything went cool and blue, and the girl would gasp or giggle like a maniac.

But there were only two ways those convos could end. One, she asks what school do I go to, and something about Dreamworld makes it hurt to lie, so I just say, look, no school, because I'm littlepoor, and she's like, *oh, wow, well, okay*, and trying to hide that she wants the conversation to end so I just say, *bye, I'm not going to give you a disease bytheway, but whatever.*

Way Two of the convo ending is when a girl is not horrified that I'm littlepoor, instead she's kind of impressed, but kind of like you're impressed by a dogwaiter walking on two hindlegs in a suit with a plate balanced on his face, and so I start to hate that girl that thinks of me as a dog. So maybe we keep talking or even mash faces touchlessly in a dreamkiss, but prettysoon I say, *well, that was nice, but bye,* and she says, *wow you're a badboy, stalking away down the road and breaking my heart, this is the best.*

Anyway that was just for a few nights because lawstudents were not impressed by Prettyworld.

"Holy crap, what a tacky hellzone," they said when Prayer tried dragging them to it.

"Is this the sad weird dreaming of the manager of a Prettyshop," they also said.

"Bro, it was a good try but we need something more romantic," Prayer said. "But you're doing great and I appreciate you."

Even when it's your dumb sis, compliments feel nice, so maybe Prayer's strategy of Always Compliment People You Want Things From isn't the dumbest.

• • •

Anyway the breakthrough I had was pretty smart, but pretty sad. Because my breakthrough was, who knows the most about being in love? Usher, that's who.

Usher and I were sitting onenight in a Prettyworld pillowhouse, he was explaining his learnings of the day to me.

"Today in Business Laws I learned that a person can become a corpo," he said. "If you set it up right no one except the bank even has to know."

"Hmmm, you dontsay," I said.

"I need to look into how but basically if you're an accountant for a big corpo, you can route the profits through a shellcorpo and say it's for tax reasons but secretly the shellcorpo is literally just you," he dreamed.

"No way, that's crazy," I nodded, trying prettyhard to follow along but instead distracted by trying to figure out how is this place not romantic, I mean look at how freaking fluffy and twinkly everything is, those koalas are literally having an international hug festival over there.

"I guess this is why corpos usually cage their accountants in a special prison," realized Usher.

"Hey can I ask you something," I said. "How is this place not super romantic."

"Do you want me to be honest with you," he said.

"Yeah ofcourse," I said.

"It's completely fake and crazy," he said.

"Yeah but what's wrong with that," I said.

"Love feels fake when it's in a fake place," Usher said. "In a real place is where it feels real."

"Okay, but Usher, this is Dreamworld," I said. "The whole point is you can make stuff that's better than real."

Usher shrugged.

I thought for the billionth time, dang, it must be insane and terrible for Usher to leave Dreamworld every morning, step back into Palsyworld.

"I mean what's good that's real," I said.

"One good real thing is, it's nice to look at things from up high," said Usher. "So maybe one of the best real things would be if you could get up really high somewhere where you could look at all of Lossy Indica."

"Ohsnap," I said, realizing, that's an obviously great idea.

"That's probably where I would take someone I loved, if I could," he said.

Obviously he meant Prayer, I knew it, he knew I knew it.

So it was a crap jerk peen move to take Usher's idea of a perfect date with Prayer and instead create it for random lawstudents. But that's what I did. Because look, that was the whole reason we left the beach and traveled to stupid law school in the first place.

Here's what I did. I dreamed a family of moons, lemony glowing moons the size of a car or boat, each with a tackedon ropenet hammock swaying underneath, and I floated in one hammock under one moon and Prayer floated in another, and hers swooped down dreamyslow to the windows of the lecturehall.

Lecturehall was where lawstudents dreamed themselves a lot of the time, super bored or anxious, sometimes also naked. So there they were, tumbling and fretting and lazing around, and then Prayer appeared to them through the window murmuring, "Who would like to come with me and see the city tonight," and a few guys perked up and said *me me I do*, even though they recognized her, even a couple bullies. So she picked one named Glen. He was thin and quiet and not super mean, and he stepped out the window and into the hammock, and up up up the moons all drifted into the Lossy Indica nightsky.

It's not so hard to fly in dreams. The hard part is seeing anything faraway. The higher you get the harder it is, the more details you need to dream. So basically I was dreaming super hard to make the whole glittering city visible from cloudheight, all the streets parks suburbs slums, all the scales of house and street. All of Lossy Indica. Dockseye, Sentrow, Sandy Barb, Sacrament, Laura Cannon, Wet Almanac, Eat Almanac, the Dreamoughs.

I even tried to dream the bigrich palacezone of Balustrade, on the coast up to the north, I've seen the enormous freaking houses from newsvids so I just planted a few on the beach with a couple rich giants rambling around.

It was a lot but I did okay and when I drifted over to Prayer's moon, invisibling myself, it did actually sound like she was having her first real convo with a lawstudent that wasn't just the game of Humiliate Prayer With The Power Of Lawarguments.

"So, I see you around sometimes and I do wonder about you, ofcourse, like where you even came from," I heard Glen say.

"Well I lived by the beach for a year, right dowwwwwwn *there*, if you can see it, but I left because I wanted to meet more educated people," I heard Prayer say, and I dreamed the beach glowing a pulse like *hereIam, I'm the beach where Prayer lived.*

"You're full of surprises, I have to tell you," I heard Glen say.

"What I wonder is if you can surprise me," I heard Prayer say, and that's when I got out of there.

Obviously Glen didn't know that it was my dreaming, not Prayer's. He didn't even know I was there. But someone else from law school did.

His name was Chess and he had stowawayed in another moonhammock, and as my moon drifted close to his, he caught me looking down and dreaming out some mountainsides.

"Aha, are you the one dreaming this magnificent view," he said all low and frummy.

"Oh," I said. "Uh, no. It's my sis Prayer."

"Oh," he said. "You're just tagging along."

That was an infuriating thing to agree to so I said, "Well, look. We're splitting the dream halfandhalf. Half me, half her."

"Wow, you two must be quite close if you can dream in tandumb like that," he said.

"Okay fine, it's a hundredpercent me, zeropercent her," I said, because lying in Dreamworld makes you heartsick. "But don't tell Glen or anyone because, being totally honest with you, everyone at law school has been a peen to her until prettymuch this exact moment."

"I won't tell anyone, just keep giving me this view," said Chess, swimming his fingers through it.

• • •

Everynight for weeks I dreamed up a new kind of floaty skyvehicle and Prayer took a date swooping up into the night to gaze down at the winking city, not just with Glen, also with Ken, Will, Berry, Fill, Harry. Because at night here's what happens. Each guy opens up and gets less mean, tells her stories, asks her questions, gives her compliments, but the next day that stupid guy still doesn't want to be seen in an embarrassing Lifeanddeathworld convo with tiny cantread homeless Prayer, so the next night she gets frustrated and tries a different guy, or goes back to a guy from a few nights ago, hoping he misses her, and surprise surprise, he does, but only at night, and in the day again he won't.

I didn't know whether Prayer and any of them got to the point of a full-on bangdream and no way did I ask.

Meanwhile this guy Chess kept hanging out with me.

"You're a nice guy, not a jerk at all," I said early on. "What do you think of my cute sis."

"She is genuinely lovely, I mean that, but how do I put this, she's just not my type," he said.

It took me a while to figure that out and then my skin got prickly and I said, "Oh."

I must have sounded awkward or worried because he looked at me and said in mockniceness, "Oh for shitsake, Warner, it's fine. I like men, not boys. How old are you? Twelve?"

"Fourteen," I said.

"Well, what I'm telling you is, don't flatter yourself," he said.

"Don't worry, I'm not weird about that stuff," I said, trying not to be weird. "I knew some gayboys growing up."

"It is definitely time to change this subject," said Chess.

But honestly, and I know this is wrong to think of gaymen but I can't help it, I stayed a little suspicious of him. It was along the reasoning of, guys his age were going on dates with Prayer and she was only a yearandahalf older than me, so why wouldn't a gayman want to date teenage me. Basically I just suspect all men of wanting to date teenagers, because, you see them trying to do it all the time.

So a night or two later I asked him why he kept chilling with me.

"Because I enjoy your dreams, ofcourse," he said.

"Why," I said.

"They're just very rich," he said. "Very different from anyone else's."

"Huh," I said.

"Believe me, they'd have to be pretty remarkable to get me to spend this much time with a fourteenyearold boy," he said.

"What does that mean," I said.

"You're not the most gifted or intresting conversational partner," he said.

"Neither are you," I said, hopefully hurtfully.

"I actually am," he said.

Anyway I got better and faster at dreaming the skyview of Lossy Indica, and I added extra dreamstuff for me and Chess to enjoy. Nightfish, starbirds, moonbats. Fireworks blushing up at us from below. Clouds made spooky by lights inside, tiny wildfires and fireflies, bright wires like lightbulb linings. Faint

65

faraway fields of moss and flowers as big as half of everything, out behind the stars.

I had to keep the extra dreamstuff away from Prayer's part of the sky because she kept saying, *hey, these extra crazy things are not helpfull to my date, in the sense of, they are super distracting and also I have to explain to a guy, here's why I chose this specific moment to dream a string of golden murmuring butterflybats.*

I got to enjoy Chess being there, my skin stopped prickling, it was nice to have a fan.

"The best yet," he said everynight. "Wow. Delightfull. Amazing. Sumpchewus. You're a prodedgy."

"I'm okay," I said. "I'm surprised at how no one is as good as me at dreaming stuff, because it's not that hard."

"Okay," he said. "I know you wanted to sound humble with that, but that actually wasn't humble at all."

"I'm just being honest," I said.

Onenight though Chess snuck in a couple super frummy friends.

"Ohmygod, this is the best dream I've had since I was a kid," one of them said, cradled by the tentacles of a skysquid.

"You are a psycho," the other one told me. "Literally, I love how much of a psycho this kid is."

"Chess what the heck," I said. "I told you not to tell people."

"They won't tell anyone, I promise," he said, but by then I knew you could never trust this pearlyskin middlerich or his golden friends.

"If any of Prayer's dates find out, these dreams are over because there's no point anymore, so, I would recommend that you maybe be more aware of that," I said.

"I know, I know," he said, giggling from the ticklings of a rainbow of doggypaddling shrimp.

"And also it will ruin Prayer's best chance at happiness," I said.

"Yes yes I know," he said. "Wheeeee."

"Not that you care about what happens to littlepoor kids," I said, losing control a little and the shrimp blew up pretty big and really started clawing him, not that he could actually feel it, he just felt like he could feel it.

"Okay, I get it," he said, thrashing around a little.

"We're just dreamstuff to you, like this stupid shrimp," I said to make sure he got it.

"I said I get it," he yelled.

I let the shrimps get heavy, puff and fill like waterballoons, dive down at the city like bombs. We watched them burst and drench palmtrees and apartmentblocks, the big drops break on the doublescale condos, the little drops scatter onto the quarterscale tenamints.

"Warner," he said after a while. "Honestly, though, I mean what do you think is really going to happen between your sister and my classmates."

I realized I didn't really want to think about it too hard because deep down, totally honest with myself, I wasn't hopefull.

"I think the dates are going well right now, so, who can say, and overall nothing is certain and everything is possible, so, bottomline, who knows," I said.

We left it at that.

The next morning Prayer had exciting news.

"But first I have to tell you I don't know if the squids are the best datemobile," she said. "Ingeneral I think you got it right the first time with hammockmoons and I don't know if you need to keep experimenting around because it's getting super weird."

"What's the stupid goodnews," I said.

"I got invited to a lawstudent party," she said. "In Lifeand-deathworld. They want actual me at an actual party, Friday night."

Usher looked completely miserable and it infected me with a sick feeling.

Prayer was so excited she even told Paddy about it.

"Well, dang," said Paddy. "I never heard of such a thing. Littlepoors at a middlerich party."

"Not a bunch of littlepoors, just me," said Prayer. "Not Warner. Sorry, Usher. They only invited me and honestly, if I had to guess why they chose to do it now, I think it's because these guys really finally see me for who I am, not just a sad littlepoor weirdo, but as an equal because we can just talk and talk all night, and when we run out of things to say and the talking dies down, that's truly just the beginning."

"Prayer," I said, because Usher was on the verge of killing himself. "Enough."

"I just never heard of anything like that," repeated old and not great at listening Paddy. "But I guess it's like everyone says, times are different now, although I have to tell you, I look around and nothing has changed and nothing's ever going to change, scale is scale, anybody who thinks otherwise is in store for a rude awakening, and let me just add this as something to chew on, you want to scale up then you gotta make sacrifices and there's no easy way out, nobody's giving you nothing for free."

"Ohmygod, what am I going to wear," said Prayer, and she wouldn't shut up about it all the way to work.

LIFEANDDEATHWORLD

For lunch that day, Chess found me on a table and let me eat a corner of his lunch.

"You know, I find myself wondering what you do with yourself all day," he asked me.

"Runs, climbs, pushandpullups," I said.

"All day?" he asked, like this was insane, which, okay, it was insane.

But I didn't want to describe to him the usual scummy littlepoor routine of spy around for crap to steal and use, hustle for munmun opportunities, eat scraps and sneak water, et set set setera, so I lied.

"I'm teaching myself to read," I told him.

"How," he said.

"How," I repeated.

"Yes," he said.

"I guess I'm still figuring that part out," I said.

He got a funny look on his face.

"Warner, I want to do something for you," he said.

"That is great news," I said.

So that day Chess tucked me into his cool smooth leatherbag that smelled like woodfire and wisky, and he picked up Usher too, and he took me back to his apartment, so we could teach ourselves things with some magical middlerich tech.

His bed was eighty silk pillows, his water lived in crystal barrels soaking limewedges and mintleaves, his toilet was an ivory bathtub in a vault of candles. Walls were tapestried with screens and fabrics, soft to touch, rippling paisleys and murmuring news.

Chess was doublescale middlerich, twice middlescale, twentytimes Warner Scale.

"My banker says I could be twoandahalf but I think it's a little tacky to be as big as you *could* be," he explained to us, pulling down some tablets. He set my tablet up with some vids of, YEWESS NATIONAL WAR ON ADULT ILLITERACY, LEARN HOW TO READ.

Usher burrowed furiously into his tablet and in seconds had lined up a queue of a dozen vids.

And Chess left for his classes and we spent the day watching vids, me doing LEARN HOW TO READ and Usher doing his own education with chemistry, history, any free and not too janky vids he could find.

And the next day, Prayer came too, infact for the rest of the week, all three of us commuted to Chess's house, getting some tablet educations in exchange for delightfull amazing sumpchewus dreamstuff.

71

Learning to read at age fourteen is not so easy. You put letters in your head but it's like collecting ants in a cup. Sure, you can find some ants, you can drop them in the cup, but while you're getting more ants the old ones climb out and scatter.

But after four days, me and Prayer had learned some tricks of how to kill the ants dead so they don't leave the cup. You kill letters by trapping them in words, you kill words by trapping them in sentences. Turn on CLOSED CAPTIONING, listen to some shows or the news, read along the printwords underneath, trap them dead in your mind.

The news was a lot of, which corpo made the most munmun, which corpo lost the most munmun, did anyone go to the bank and get really huge today, do we have exciting vid of this huge person walking out of the bank and into their new huge house for the first time, where were the bombings and shootings today, how many people got shot and bombed overall, where was the weather terrible, are we building enough stuff in space.

Then there were lots of shows of the lives of the Yewess's biggest people, what are they doing and eating, how do you make a palace to fit a family twelvetimes middlescale, rooms a hundredfeet high, we're coming to you live from Balustrade where a pharmalord named Mark is about to eat a mammoth.

The three of us together watched a vid called WOW YOU'RE READY TO SCALE UP!, directed and produced by the bank, and Usher focused on the math, meanwhile me and Prayer read the captions.

At the bank everyone has two accounts, munflow account and scale account. Here's how they're different.

Munflow account doesn't change your scale at all, you just keep extra munmun there because it's safer than wallets, mattresses, personal treasure chests. You pay for stuff out of munflow account with muncards, and a proper job can deposit munmun direct to munflow, andsoonandsoforth, it's all super usefull and easy and has no effect on your scale.

Scale account is what changes your scale. So for scale account there's no cards, withdrawls, directdeposit, anything like that. Instead, to make any changes to your scale account, you must visit the bank personally. Eye ee if you contribute munmuns to it, you go to the bank, designate the amount in munflow you want to transfer to scale, and the bank performs the Scale Up Ceremony, tada, you walk out twice as big as when you came in, or however big.

Or if you're broke, indebted, need to buy a house and there's not enough in your munflow box, et set set setera, you transfer munmun out of your scale account and into munflow, ohno, it's time for Scale Down Ceremony and you walk out a door smaller than the one you came in, sadfaced, wearing temporary bankrobes.

After all ceremonies, the banks robe you so you have something to wear, old clothes obviously no longer fitting you anymore.

And if you're scaling up to eightscale or more, billionair big or bigger, they can't even fit you in robes, or the bank forthatmatter, instead they tell you to go lie naked in a field on some slippery tarps, then I guess you go to sleep and they slowly inflate you.

WOW YOU'RE READY TO SCALE UP! mostly tells you how bankers calculate when you can scale up, and by how much, because without the bankers here's an easy mistake you could make. Let's say, you have a million munmuns in your scale account and ninemillion in munflow. Perfect, you say, I'll put the ninemillion in scale and scale up by two, and now all my tenmillion munmuns are in my scale account.

(Onemillion is middlescale, tenmillion is doublescale ay kay ay twotimes middlescale, hunmillion is fourscale ay kay ay fourtimes middlescale, it makes no sense if you don't have a mathbrain. And then hunthousand is halfscale, tenthousand is quarterscale, onethousand is eighthscale, and fivehundred and below is rat size, about tenthscale, Usher tried to explain the specific math to me but prettyquick he was talking about something called a loggerrhythm and I had to tell him to shut up.)

So okay, you put the entire ninemillion from munflow into your scale account and now you've scaled up double. And so ofcourse you need new clothes, new house, new car, plus you're eating way more food, not even double but more like sixtimes, plus you're too big to use the middleroads.

But surprise, you have no munmun in your munflow account to deal with any of those situations. Because all your munmuns are in scale account. So you leave the bank doublescale but not ready to lead a doublescale life, so immediately you have to turn back around and scale back down, and it's a huge mess, that's why the bankers are there to make calculations and help you.

Ruleofthumb, you shouldn't put tenmillion in the scale account unless you have fivemillion left in munflow, eye ee, atleast fifteenmillion total, maybe more, it depends on your income, labor costs of maintaining your lifestyle ee gee how many middlepoors are needed to clean your house, tax situations andsoonandsoforth, calculations of that nature, explanations of when to scale and how often, ohmygod was this vid boring.

Usher understood it and even he admitted, yeah, this type of thing is super boring, that's your life when you work at the bank I guess.

The day of the party Prayer didn't watch tablets. Instead she spent the whole day in Chess's bathroom, prepping.

She took the nice Japanese robe that she escaped Grant's house in, and washed it painstakingly three times in Chess's sink, and then she spent many hours heating up a paperclip with a candleflame and twirling her fine notgood hair into it to get it all bouncy, and it sort of worked. And she took a little coal from a blownout candlewick onto her fingers and smeared it around her eyelids and lashes and it was way too much and she looked like a rackoon, but then she papertoweled some of it off and even I had to admit, it looked pretty fancy and good.

She had no shoes obviously but she figured out how to stalk around on tiptoes in a refined and sophisticated way, and she walked like that the entire way to the apartment complex, with me and Usher bodyguarding as usual.

Why did poor Usher help bodyguard, answer, because Prayer asked him to. I was the most disgusted with her that I could get.

"How can you even look at his face," I said.

"Warner, please," she said. "This is why we came."

"Usher, you seriously don't have to join, no matter what my poisonhearted demon sister asks you," I said.

"It' 's why I c cc came, t tt t too," he said, trying to smile, but no smile happening on that gray twisty face.

We walked over in silence, getting plenty of looks and confusion from middlepoors about this little parade of one tiptoeing partygirl and two grubby slumboys wordlessly bodyguarding her.

The apartment building was breezy, outdoorsy, a few stacks of apartments sharing long balconyhalls, hooked around a goofy pale pool. The party was on the secondfloor, there was no elevator, the stairs had no littleramp, so to keep her robe clean, Prayer literally stepped on Usher's back and then got hauled up by me, each step.

Then at the top she didn't want lawstudents to see Usher or I, so she made us chill way down at the end of the balconyhall by the stairs while she tried to knock on the door.

No one heard her or answered it.

Finally another middlerich came clomping up the stairs behind us. It was Glen. Usher and me cowered in the shadows, out of sight.

Politely, teetering on tiptoes, Prayer waved and said, "Hi, Glen, I'm here for Ken's party."

But he didn't see or hear her. So she had to do some medium shrieking.

"Oh, look who it is," he said. "Prayer." And he knelt down so she could step into his hand, and he carried her inside, and the door closed, and it was just me and Usher out there.

"Usher, man," I said.

Usher shrugged.

"This is just terrible and awfull and I kind of wish you hadn't come," I said.

Usher shrugged again.

"My sis doesn't deserve everything you've done for her and it makes me sick and sad," I said.

"N no, it's the op posite," he told me. "I ddon't d deserve her."

"Oh no," I said. "Usher, shut up."

"It's j just obvious, ," he said. "She dd deserves w way better than m me. She des serves to sc cale up. Unt til then I j just want to h help her how w wever I can n."

"Usher," I said. "Going forward, I need you to shut up unless it's to say, *Actually I changed my mind, I'm great, and your sister is terrible.*"

We sat there and listened to the glitzy thrummy music of the lawstudent party, mostly menvoices talking. Through the walls they alittlebit sounded like the soft hoots of apes.

In my head I tried to figure out what were they saying or who were they saying it to, which one is talking to Prayer, will he really be my brotherinlaw someday, will they have a nice normal middlescale house and two brats growing up going to schools talking on bendy phones and everything, will I live in a littlehouse stapled to the outside, is it even possible, and is this how it starts.

Then up the stairs came a jackedup inky middlepoor guy carrying two littlepoor women, and that's when it got super weird and bad.

• • •

He was holding his arms up and flexing them, the women were sitting one on each armmuscle, crosslegs with specialmade skirts and stockings, definitely a trampy vibe from these two.

"Hello boys," said one, fanning evil fingernails stickily.

"Ugh, don't talk to them," said the other, adjusting her tits.

As for this superstrong halfscale guy, he said nothing, just looked at Usher and I way too intense, like he was instantly memorizing our entire faces.

Then he carried the women down the balconyhall to the party, and knocked on the door, and Glen or Ken opened it and reached down and picked up the two women and handed this guy a roll of munmun so pink it looked alive, like flowerpetals.

The door closed and this guy walked slowly back toward us, closing the munmun into his belt.

"So, mind if I ask," said the guy, leaning over us. "What are you doing here."

He was super jacked and so inky it was a little hard to tell his original color of skin. His hair was crosshawked, each hawk all traced with tats, and his shoulders were each the size of his head, with a face inked on each one, so a lot like he had three heads.

"Sure, if I can ask you the same thing, buddybrat," I said, and then I couldn't say anything else or breathe because his hands were wrapped around my face and head, picking me up and dangling me.

"I guess I gotta ask the other kid," said the guy. "Other kid. What are you doing here."

My neck was a rope, the fibers were popping onebyone. I reached up and clawed and scraped at the leather of his stinking hands. He jiggled me a little to get me to stop, like saying, *hey, keep it up and it'll be super easy for me to snap your spine.*

"If you want your buddy to not die, you should probably answer prettysoon," he said to Usher.

I heard Usher burbling.

"J j jjj j jj jus sst , g g g ggu guarding," he managed to say.

"Wow," said the guy. "Calm the heck down and spit it out."

I was blowing snot and spit all over the guy's hands from trying so hard to breathe.

"Hi s s ss s si is," said Usher.

"The shit are you even saying," said the guy.

I felt everything go dim, sight, sound, touch. Then the guy dropped me on my face and knees and wrist, they popped against the floor like popcorn.

"Well, look," said the guy. "You're both clearly having trouble answering the question of what are you doing here, so, let me give you a hint. The hint is, I had a peek inside the room and what did I see but another littlepoor girl, and did I recognize her, no, I did not. So I assume that girl is what you're doing around here."

"She's my sis," I said as loud as I could into the ground, which was a mumble.

"Can't hear you," said the guy. "This is no good, boys. You're pimping around here, and this is where I pimp. You're pimping in Shoulderheads's neckofthewoods, and guess who I am, spoileralert, I'm Shoulderheads. So I'm going to need to be pretty bad to you now."

"We're not pimping," I mumbled.

"A little louder, shitbeetle," said this guy Shoulderheads.

I yelled through my broken throat, "We're not pimping. My sis got invited to that party. No one gave us any munmuns. We're not sick pimps like you."

Shoulderheads had a sour look on his face like, *I don't want to do this, but, looks like I'm about to start strangling and dangling you again.*

But instead he started laughing.

"Oh wow," he said. "You idiots. You are a hundredpercent pimping your sis right now. You're just the dumbshit kind of pimp that doesn't even get his tramp paid."

And now I really started to feel sick.

"What's going on in there," I said.

"Don't worry," he said. "It's about to get way better for your sis. Next party, I'll make sure she gets a cut. She's in good hands now. I saw her. She's cute, and most important, prettymuch a kid still. So I can get her a lot of work. Like she can be a regular at this party every week, for starts."

Usher fell, got up, fell, got up fell got up, stumbled down the hall, picked up speed, started really running and galloping.

"Don't know what he thinks he's doing," said

80 Shoulderheads. "Hey, look. You should be happy for your sis. She's about to make way more with me than with you. I mean, with you she makes zero. Plus she'll get a nice littleplace out by the reservewar."

"What's this party," I said. 'What happens in there."

Usher attacked the door, hitting kicking ripping it.

"Probably better if you don't know," said Shoulderheads, and he picked me up again and this time heaved me over the rail.

I assumed I was dead, right up to the moment of my body slapping the poolwater.

Then I assumed Usher was dead even though he also hit the poolwater and not the concrete, because from a floor up, water is pretty painfull to hit, and Usher is not robust.

But he lived, and we linked arms and became a single crappy swimmer and paddled to the side. I climbed out on my notpopped wrist, fished Usher out, and rightaway drippingwet Usher hobbled back to the stairs to try for a second impossible rescue.

"Usher," I said. "No way. Let's find some police or security or something."

He shook his head and tried hoisting himself, couldn't though.

"It's the best plan," I said.

He was crying, but I wouldn't hoist him, so he followed me.

The apartments had a guardbooth but no one inside, or maybe the guard was asleep and we couldn't see from where we were.

But a few blocks away I spotted a police car, so I sprinted at it, shrieking. No one heard me. I raced around the car a few times, no answer. Finally I spotted the panel under the gascap, with the littlepoor circlehead picturesign. I slapped the button and it beeped and whispered a little light. No answer from in the car still. I hit it again a few times, beep beep beep, a few coughs of light from a dying bulb.

Finally the driverside door opened and out came a cop.

Like most cops he was about middlescale, a little littler. His eyes were tired and his mustache was a browntowhite rainbow.

"Cop, some lawstudents are squadbanging my sis," I said, breathing hard.

"Wow," he said. "Thanks for the info." And he snuffled.

"I mean I think they're raping her," I said.

His eyes flinched and he said, "You *think* they're raping her."

"I took her to a party," I said, "then some rando dropped off littlepoor tramps and threw us into a pool, now this rando says he wants to pimp her out too."

He said nothing so I added, "So you have to do something, right?"

The cop snuffled again and said, "What I need to know, though, littlebro, and I get that you're upset, so let's just calm down for a second, what I need is the facts. So, what do you know *for a fact* about what's happening right now."

"It's some kind of bangparty," I said, feeling desperate. "Cop, she didn't know it was a bangparty when she went there, no way she wants to be in some middlerich squadbang and also this rando named Shoulderheads is hanging around outside the door and he wants to basically kidnap her and pimp her going forward, no way she wants that either, cop, *please.*"

He put his hands on his knees and talked to me like a babybrat. "Littlebro," he said. "Okay. Here's what you've told me. A littlepoor girl goes to a party voluntarily, a party where she knows there's guys, no hard evidence of anything bad, now you want me to go in there and break it up. Littleman, listen. Your sis is her own person, making her own decisions. And I can't just go around breaking up parties because a bro doesn't want his sis banging."

I couldn't believe how he was not understanding at all and he saw my crazy face and tried again.

"Look," he said, "I know you don't like it, it's hard for littlepoors, but littlebro, she went *voluntarily*, am I right on this. Meaning, she chose to go."

"She didn't think it was a bangparty with tramps," I said.

He even looked kind of sad but what he said was, "But she *chose* to go."

"Holy crap," I yelled. "Please forget I'm so little, forget you're so middle, please just remember to when you were a brat, maybe you had a sis, maybe you have a daughter now, pretend she goes to a party and then a pimp drops off some tramps and camps out outside so he can grab her, drug her up, sell her out, please tell me you're gonna do your job and not just doze away in your big dumb shitcar like a fat scared old jerk," I said because I was losing it and that was how I lost him too.

His face got mean and he stood from his crouch.

Walked back to driverside, said over his shoulder, "Can't help you. Turnsout it's a campus sexassault, take it up tomorrow with some campuscops. Good luck, good night."

He stepped back into the car, slammed the door shut.

Usher, watching from the shadows, had stopped crying and was just mashing his teeth against each other like a lunatic.

I looked at him and he looked at me.

"I guess we have to go back and kill ourselves trying to kill this guy," I said.

Usher nodded.

"Okay great," I said, because I was so mad at this cop, I was ready to die trying to kill a jerk.

So here's what happens next.

On our way back to the apartment I sneak around the sidedoor of the guardbooth and sure enough, there's a superfat gunguard sleeping in there.

Strapped to his belt he has a middlepoorsize gun, the whole thing is about half my scale, and without thinking about it I climb his chair, coax it out of his pocket, hug it to myself and climb back down onehanded.

Usher nods with no sadness or happiness, just, good, now that we have our gun it is time for Step Two, murder someone.

Across the pool we can barely see the head of Shoulderheads over the rail of the balconyhall. But it gives you a clue of where his body is, not the smallest target either, just shoot through the rail under the head and you've got a good chance of murder.

We set the gun upsidedown in some grass, in some shadows, I'm hugging it crouched down trying to stare along the barrel, shifting it bitbybit updown leftright, aiming at the jacky inky body of Shoulderheads.

Eventually I figure we're as good as we're going to get so

I say, fire, and Usher leans on the trigger because I can't reach from where I am, and nothing happens, so I tell Usher push harder, he does, nothing happens, I tell him Usher you got to really lean on it, he does and finally the gun explodes and deafens everyone, also smashes me pretty hard in my ribs.

"Oh shit," we hear Shoulderheads say, not at all injured, because instead of killing him the bullet has spiderwebbed Ken's window not even that close to him.

Other apartment lights flip on, distantly you hear a little screaming and freaking out, and Ken's apartment door makes the locking sound of rat rat rattle CHUNK. Shoulderheads bangs on the door and yells, jiggles the handle and shoulderbutts it a few times, meanwhile we set up the gun again, aim it at the door and BAM, again right into my bruisy ribs and this time what we hit instead of Shoulderheads is the shingles of the stupid roof, but now Shoulderheads abandons the door and scampers away down the balconyhall, down the stairs and away through the alley and into the night, because bynow you can hear police sirens.

II.
GRACE

DREAMWORLD

A littlepoor shoots a gun and rightaway he's a fugitive criminal.

So that same cop charged in and immediately he figured the gunshots were mine. Which, he was right but no need to be a jerk about it. "Where's that little redshit," he bellowed. "Littlebro, come out and get arrested because you are in big trouble, come the hell out now, every minute of hiding you make it worse for yourself."

I tried to run but it was like blowing on the fire in my own ribs. But even hobbling slowly to a dumpster, the cop didn't see me, big idiot.

So Usher and I huddled in the dumpster and watched the cop flash his jumpy lightbeam, roaming, yelling, not wanting to deal with Ken and his bulletholed apartment. But eventually he stomped up there and knocked on the door, door opened, tramps raced out, the cop didn't even try to chase them, instead he went in there and walked back out after a minute or two with Prayer in one hand, to take her to the station.

I got a look as he carried her out, and I didn't see her face, but she didn't seem injured. Just wet headtotoe. But not from water. Slick wet like with oil, the robe all greasy and clinging to her skin, the coal around her eyes smeared everywhere, pandafaced again.

"Usher," I wheezed. "Go back to the cleaningcar. I have to chill in this dumpster for atleast tonight because of my stupid ribs."

Usher shook his head, but he knew I was right.

"Go back to the Quickstand and wait for Prayer," I told him. "That's what's important. She needs you. I'll be okay. I'll see you in Dreamworld. Make gray fireworks, I'll find you."

Usher, the most loyal and good friend in the world, squeezed a knot of my hair in his fist, bumped my skull, and left.

A dumpster is not the worst place to sleep, but not great either because of rats, rackoons, squads of littlepoors who might bust your teeth. Best is if you find a cleanedout can and wedge yourself inside.

It's a little impossible to get to Dreamworld if everytime you breathe, it blows on your ribfire, flaring up all huge and bad in the darkness.

So that night all I could do was doze, every few minutes yelping myself awake.

The pain was worse in the morning but cops were sniffing around the whole apartment complex, so I crept out and snuck down the alley, licking foggy dew from the grass, stopping, crouching, mashing my teeth to keep from shrieking.

After a blockandahalf I was behind a foodmall and crying

from the pain so I snuck into the garbage of a cowsoy stand and nibbled the thrownaway food in there.

Might have been the soup from Sand Dreamough Neighborhood Souptime, noodles, leaves, bonemeat, sprouts, everything salty limey slippery from birdfat.

The day came and went and I stayed in the cowsoy garbage, no one found me, no one bothered me, just randomly crapped showers of unfinished soups.

That night it took some work but I slept deep enough for Dreamworld, and wandered around broken for a while before Usher's dreamstuff found me.

It was a single gray firework like a dusky palmtree crackling overandover above a little doorless stripmall cube. I climbed to the top, panels under me gently opened. I floated down into a room of carpets and lamps and too many chairs and in one of them sat sad mooneyed Prayer.

"Sis, ohmygod," I said.

"Hey bro," she said, not wanting to hug.

"Are you okay," I said.

"Yup," she said, not okay.

"Right now are you sleeping in the car at Paddy's?" I asked. "Is Usher with you?"

"Yup, yup," she said.

"Well," I said. "What happened."

She didn't want to talk about it, and being honest with you, I didn't want to hear about it. Did I need to, yes, did I want to, no.

But I kept asking quietly and eventually she told me a little.

As soon as she got to the party the lawstudents were weird to her. Not their jokey mean lifeanddeathselves but not their respectfull dreamselves either.

Instead they were just weirdly asking weird questions, like Prayer, how fast do you think you can you climb this pole, how long can you hold your breath, how hard can you squeeze these cucumbers and other vegetables with your arms and legs, could you crush them even, well why don't you show us.

In her head Prayer was like, this is a little strange and I have to say not totally what I expected from a lawstudent party, I expected a little more classy conversation and witty backandforth, not feats of strength and endurance, but hey, it's my first party, I'm open to new things and experiences.

Then as she was doing some vegetable squeezing and climbing through tubes, the tramps showed up, and the lawstudents said, tramps, hello, great to see you, this is Prayer and maybe you could show her the ropes a little bit.

In a washroom was a bowl of oil and the tramps took a bath in it and invited Prayer to join the bath with them, comeon, it's so nice in here, so Prayer got in.

"Wait, naked," I asked.

"What do you think," said Prayer.

The oil had the choky smell of fake flowers like soaps and candles from Prettyshop and the tramps began to wash each other in it and tried to wash Prayer too.

The washroomdoor opened, Prayer screamed and tried to

cover herself, but the tramps didn't, they stretched like cats and arched their backs, and they said, Prayer, relax, and they put their hands on her, Glen and Ken picked up the oilbasin with Prayer and tramps in it and placed it in the middle of the bed and unbuckled their belts and Warner, do you really want me to tell you the rest of this story.

No, I don't.

Okay. Well. There you go.

I guess I just need to know, did they hurt you at all.

I mean they didn't snap my arms off but there's a lot of ways someone can hurt you.

I asked her did she ask to leave.

"No," she said.

"Sis, why not," I said.

It's hard to cry in Dreamworld, even harder to cry from rage.

"Sis," I said. "You weren't still thinking, maybe you'll find a husband at this party."

She shook her head, but not in answer to me, more answering the world.

"Did you really think these jerks could be like that with someone they want to marry," I said, and I could feel my rib pain starting to fuzz the dream.

"Warner," she said, starting to choke on clots of anger. "I'm sorry, but shut up."

"You can't just be quiet and say okay when jerks are trying that stuff," I said.

"Shut up," she said. "You don't get to talk about this. You just don't. So shut up."

"No," I said. "Only when you start respecting yourself more."

"Warner," she tried to yell through the clots, squeaking bitterly. "You don't understand what it's like. You can't understand what it's like to be me in a situation like that. I know you think you understand, you think you know everything, but that just makes you a peenhead. So shut up immediately about me, now, forever."

"Sis, I can't," I said.

She was mad, I was mad. I know it's notsogood to be mad at someone in the situation of, terrible things just happened to her, her hope got abused, her fear kept her quiet, but sorry, I was mad. My instinct in bad situations is usually, get super mad.

"Well, sorry for trying to help," I said.

"Ohmygod what are you talking about," she said. "You shot bullets into the exact room I was in. Super easily you could have shot me."

She was definitely right, but I didn't want to be wrong so I argued, "No, firstofall only one bullet, secondofall I was aiming up at the window, so no way it hits you, because here's how the angle works," but she wouldn't let me explain.

Then, still super mad, I said, "Well, now I'm a fugitive I guess, so I won't be around to keep messing things up for you."

We were both quiet for a long time.

"Actually am I a fugitive," I asked.

"Yeah," she said. "The cops keep showing up at Paddy Quickstand, looking for you, they think we're hiding you somewhere."

"So what do you do now," I said.

"I don't know," she said. "Paddy is going to kick us out. He's mad about the cops being around all the time. Plus he thinks we tricked him."

"Tricked him how," I said.

"Tricked him into giving a home to a tramp," she said, and now she was crying again but not angry, just weepysad, and I shut up and reached through the chairs and gave her a hug.

You can't feel hugs really in Dreamworld, but you can pretend you do.

She cried so hard, she woke herself up and disappeared.

LIFEANDDEATHWORLD

That morning the pain was not too bad, until a middlepoor
girl picked up the garbage and dumped it into a bag, and I
went from bottom to top, landing on some bones and eatstix,
shrieking.

The girl was also shrieking, round oh mouth and round oh
fakegreen eyes in a round oh face.

I was a fugitive so I had to get this girl to stop shrieking
somehow, so I went finger to lips, fists to heart, backandforth
like a maniac and grinning from the pain.

She stopped shrieking, thankgod, and just kind of froze
like, *what do I say now.*

"Sorry," I sorried.

"Sorry," she repeated automatically. "No no no, I'm sorry."

This girl looked my age, a year younger maybe,
plumskinned.

"No no, I'm sorry, for sure," I said.

"Are you hurt or something," she said.

"Oh no I'm fine," I said, immediately it was like, *Warner,
what is even the point of lying right now, do you just lie automatically even when it makes no sense.*

"GRACE," yelled probably her mom from inside, super-strong accent, vowels from across the sea. "WHAT'S WRONG, IS SOMEONE THERE OR SOMETHING."

"MOM IT'S FINE," she yelled, and glanced at me, and quickly hoisted me out of the bag and gently down into the alley, turned around and went back into the shop.

But the pain was pretty bad, and being honest with you, the food was pretty good, so I stuck around nearby hiding in a drainpipe until after the lunch rush, when the garbage was half full, and then I snuck back into the garbage and slurped a little more bright salty creamnoodle, and the whole time tried to figure out a plan.

Shortterm, I need to get to Chess's apartment again, Prayer and Usher should probably come too when Paddy kicks them out. Because that's an opportunity to stay somewhere safe, with someone who likes us. How honest do I have to be with Chess? Chess is an okay guy, sure, but would he host a fugitive? Maybe, maybe not, bottomline, too much risk, definitely don't tell him about the criminal part.

Longterm, the plan of Find Prayer A Husband At Law School is dead. So we need a new plan for munmuns. Probably, hatetosay, it was time for crime. Thefts, schemes, tricks.

But always when my plans tipped toward Thefts Schemes Tricks, I couldn't help realizing, this world isn't built for little-poor crime. Littlepoors can't hurt anyone but other littlepoors, can't make fast getaways, can't even walk with middlesize mun-bills or bigger. Littlepoors in bigspaces are always suspicious, easy to stop, trap, question, kick out. Sneaking and hiding is all we can do, except to each other.

The only people littlepoors can perform crimes on is other littlepoors, join a squad and raid the littlepoors weaker than you, that's your only chance at more munmuns, and it was a sad crappy truth my thoughts circled like a drain.

Then out of the blue, slurping a bone, I realized, *Warner. Chess can help you charge munmuns for dreams.*

Now look. I'd had the thought of Get Munmuns For Dreams before. But I never saw a way to actually collect the muns. People can agree to anything in Dreamworld, sure I'll give you munmuns for pleasant dreams, but in Lifeanddeathworld they can pretend like that didn't happen. And that's if you can even approach them. Middleriches, you can't get your words up to their ears or even find them most of the time. And poors are just going to say, get out of here, I can't give you munmuns for dreams, what a crazy bunch of crap.

But I realized, this time it's different. Because Chess can help.

Chess can collect the munmuns *before the dreams*. We can go into business together. Chess rounds up some munmuns from all his friends, just a small amount to them, but to me, to Prayer, to Usher, changeyourlife munmun.

A subscription service to beautifull relaxing dreams. Or maybe just daily ticket purchases. Chess gets the munmuns before the dream and gives out a password, tells them where the dreamdoor will be.

You would see on the news sometimes wild stories about the

97

leaders of other countries, undemocratic countries not at all like the Yewess, dictators and kings and armybosses running the whole thing and guys like that get all kinds of perks. The best palaces, helicopters, chefs, bangpartners, and some of them get their own dreamers too.

So it's like the perk of a dictator, except lawstudents get to have it. The nice frummy gay ones, students I know didn't abuse my sis.

But the more I thought about it, I could dream for not just friends of Chess, it could be a whole business, pay munmuns each day for the night's password, enter the dreamdoor and enjoy a heavenly dream that refreshes you, heals you, waters your heart and makes it pink. Who wouldn't pay five munmuns for a lifechanging dream.

For the first time in whoknows howlong I had hope.

In the evening I was in the garbage when the girl Grace came back, not to empty it, instead to whisper, "Hey. Are you back."

I didn't say anything.

"If you're back, I have water," she said.

I still didn't say anything.

"I'll just leave it next to the garbage," she said, and I heard her put it down and walk back inside.

It was clean, sterile for sure, but sweet too, a little basil, a little lime.

DREAMWORLD

Before I found Chess I found the gray firework again and again it was just Prayer waiting for me, not Usher.

"Bro," said Prayer. "I'm getting married."

"Wait, what," I said.

"I'm getting married, this weekend," said Prayer, smiling, more relieved than overjoyed.

"Ohmygod," I said. "Sis, amazing. Who are you marrying."

"Paddy," said Prayer.

At first it made me happy she was already recovered enough to make this hilarious joke.

Then it turned out, not a hilarious joke, actually the less hilarious truth.

"Paddy and I have been talking and talking and I've completely opened up to him and told him everything, how I'm not a tramp, but the truth is I am here to meet some men and find a husband, because bottomline I need to improve my situation and I'm going to stop at nothing so if he needs to kick me out, okay, I understand, I'll leave in the cleaningcar probably with you and Usher and we'll all find some other neighborhood to live, but I have to scale up somehow and now's my best chance while I'm

99

young and cute, I know it's sad but that's just the truth, so kick us out if you need to."

And he listened and said finally, well, hang on, let's not be hasty, and look, I get it, so let me just think about it, but in the meantime, you can stay here tonight.

And then the next day he said, I've made my decision, and you can stay, but only if you marry me, so, how about it.

He was old, he had no kids, he liked how Prayer politely listened to everything he said and found nice ways to agree with him. He had spent a whole lifetime building up scale and now he was going to use it to get a young cute wife, because what else was he going to do with it.

"I know you're thinking, he's old, he's gross, it's a big sacrifice, but I do actually like talking to him and more important, I know he'll take care of me," Prayer said.

The first thing I made my mouth say was, "How much will you and Mom scale up atleast." In my head it seemed like the math was, Paddy's close to middlescale, so he has almost a million munmuns, spread those among three people, everyone ends up around twothirdscale, Prayer and Mom scale up by maybe six or seven.

But Prayer's eyes and mouth went a little funny and she said, "Warner, it's just me scaling up for now."

My mouth didn't say anything to that.

"Look," she said. "I know. Bro, I know. But if Paddy splits his munmun among three, he's too small to even run his store. So that's just not an option. It's hard enough scaling down just for me. He'll need blocks and ladders everywhere. If he loses anymore than that, the merch and food and shipments are all too big and heavy. Brotherbrat, he's sicktysix. We'll both work hard, both earn munmuns at the Quickstand, and yearbyyear we can scale Mom up, but not now, not rightaway."

"So you're going to live with tiny Mom just wheeling around your house like a pet," I said.

Her face went funny again and she said, "Well atfirst she won't be living with us."

I felt big caves yawn open in my heart and I had to leave.

"I tried, Warner," she yelled as I left. "I tried. Paddy just isn't ready yet. I'll keep trying. He'll change his mind. Warner, don't be mad."

I found Usher in a trashpit, raising tiny fireworks from a tiny cityblock in a puddle of garbagejuice.

"Usher," I said, "we never should have brought you and I feel sick about it."

"This hurts," he admitted.

I sat there and he bathed his hands in the glitterblooms.

"But look," I said. "I have a plan."

"Is it revenge," he said.

It wasn't revenge. My heart hurt but I turned it into dreams.

If you wanted to show someone you could change their life with your dreams, you could dream that water is a clay, blocks of water sitting in the street, swimthrough wallless waterhouses, bridged with watertunnels, lit with fish.

You could dream bricks are liquid, also liquid are metals stones woods clay and everything, Sand Dreamough collapses into an oceantop, buildings cars fences billboards are wobbling jellies beneath the ripples.

Dream the palmtrees twirling, uncorking the ground and foamy oilchampagne fountains out. Dream the middleroads shriveling, shrinking, the houses creep closer and kiss.

The stadium is a pokebowl,

the reservewar holds cowsoy and joggers circle it stirring with oars,

the bank is a hive of angels leaving every door, big, middle, tiny, golden whirring helicopters and hummingbats,

the Metro is a winking eel,

windmills catch the air and paddle into space,

cleaningcars float and pop like bubbles,

clouds halfdress a sky of faraway screens and fabrics, rippling paisleys and murmuring news.

It was twenty dreams in one, way too many really, but it did its job. Finally I spotted Chess floating through the whole thing, blissfull, a littlebit crying.

"Hey, what do you think," I said. "Too much, or what."

"Warner, ohmygod," he said. "Thank you."

"You're welcome," I said.

"Just, I mean, to think that you're dreaming this for all of us, despite how we've treated you and your sister," he said, and couldn't continue.

"Yeah, well," I said. "I guess, yeah."

He recovered and said, "I literally can't imagine a more beautifull parting gift. So thank you."

"You're welcome," I said.

Then I said, "Wait what."

"I'll never forget you," he told me.

"What do you mean, forget me," I said.

We looked at each other a little fuzzy.

"I mean," said Chess. "The police are looking for you. So, you must be leaving for somewhere else, right? I mean, you're not planning to stay."

"Well, I wanted to talk to you about that," I said.

And I told him my whole plan.

The whole time he was shaking his head.

It made me tell the plan worse and I knew if he just started listening, if he just for a moment took it seriously, I could tell it better, but he was shaking his head with closedoff eyes and I didn't even get through the whole plan to be honest.

"Warner, you know I can't do that," he started, and I said, "Nono, forget it, it's fine," and left the dreamstuff to dry up on its own, slowly wither and leave behind its skeleton, the way big dreams do after their dreamers have left them behind.

I found Usher still fireworking over the tinyblock.

"My plan didn't work," I said.

"I'm sorry," he said.

"I have another plan, though," I told him.

"Is it revenge," he asked.

"This time yup," I said.

So for the last few hours of night Usher and me made law school a hellscape, mostly with demons, also with big oily peens bashing through doors and windows, squeezing struggling straining to get in and batter you. But more than peens just a crapload of demons, invisible screaming ghosts, shadows, nothings, holes in the world skittering round the room like spiders, flickerings of time and air where the space in front of you hiccups, a window shudders, and you can't see it but you know you are staring at a demon, and it all goes dark and cold.

Some lawstudents were terrorized into waking up and disappearing. Others got so upset, they started dreaming worse revenge on themselves, like their friends and parents showing up and wailing, being on fire, banging each other, getting banged by animals, all kinds of crazy crap.

I looked for Ken, couldn't find him, found Glen though in a stairway, dropped him in a hole, locked him in a peenforest erupting from all sides, writhing, flexing, vomming pearly gallons.

He wasn't happy but he wasn't too upset either. Because his dreaming was weak and murky. So he didn't really get the point of what was happening, nomatter how hard I tried to educate.

"You did this to my sister, now it's happening to you, jerk," I told him. "Complain all you want, it's the exact definition of justice. You're bad to someone, someone's bad to you. Not so great now, right."

But he just kept squinting squinching scrunching his face and murmuring, "Ugh, what day is it," and, "When's the test."

"Peens are attacking you," I said. "Peens the size of your whole body."

"Ugh, is the test today," he said.

"I guess we have to do this every single night for a while," I said.

"Warner," yelled Chess, finding me. "Stop, please."

"Hi, Chess," I said. "Please, feel free to watch as peens hose a jerk in scum."

But sad Chess watched me, not the peens.

And I was exhausted and the night was dying, the morning was calling, most dreamers were awake, so I let myself relax the hellscape, the screams turning into birdcalls, demons vaporating into wind.

Only the peenpit remained after a while.

"I think I'm think I'm think I'm supposed to think I'm supposed to be at my interview," said Glen, blindly reaching out for anything that wasn't a peen, but toobad, all peens in there.

"Chess, can you please find Usher, please give a home to him atleast," I started asking Chess, said it a few times to his fading face, couldn't hear me probably though, wouldn't remember.

105

I woke up in no pain and with barely any thoughts, no hurt and no hope either.

LIFEANDDEATHWORLD

The girl Grace warned me that morning before she dumped the garbage.

"Hello if you're in there," I heard her say. "Please come out, I need to dump the garbage."

So I wriggled out through the loose slats in the bottom.

"Oh," she said. "That's how you get in there."

"Yeah," I said.

She dumped the garbage, glanced back at the foodstand, flicked her eyes over to the alley, and I followed her over there.

"Hey," she told me. "I'm really sorry, but you probably can't keep staying in our garbage."

"I know," I said.

"What's your name," she said.

"Warner," I said.

She froze a little.

"Oh no," she said.

"What," I said.

"You're the littlepoor they're talking about on localnews," she said. "Who stole the gun."

"Oh right," I said. "Hey. I don't have the gun anymore. I mean that's not something I do very much."

She started backing away, back toward the restaurant.

"Hey," I said. "I'm powerless. I'm sleeping in garbage with busted ribs. Littlepoors can't hurt someone as big as you. We can only hurt each other. Please."

But she was still backing away, lots of wobbly fear behind the fakegreen lenses.

So I said, "Well, okay, look. Thank you. Thanks for everything. Call the cops if you want, if there's a reward, or just if you don't want to get in trouble. It's okay. I'll wait here."

But she just shook her head and went inside.

I mean look. Where was I going to go, what was I going to do. I could try to escape to a different neighborhood, hop into a bus wheelwell maybe, hope the cops aren't looking for me outside Sand Dreamough, start all over in a strange new place and come up with new plans, alone.

But the alone part was the impossible part. The alone part just made me feel too empty and terrible to try anything.

"Come up with a plan," I told my brain, and my tiredout from dreaming brain said, "Please, no, I'm exhausted."

107

So I cleaned myself up at a fountain and after that walked up to a cop on the street and said, "Hey, I'm Warner, I think you're looking to arrest me."

They don't have handcuffs for littlepoors, instead they put you in the car all belted up tight inside a box they call the littleseat, but it's not a seat, just a box full of belts where you flop and crash anytime the copcar takes a turn.

Most of the other littleseats were empty. I glimpsed one other kid on the way in and his eyes were crazy, also his nose was full of bloodwads.

"You think you're looking at me, or what," he yelled at me on my way in.

Scumbag littlepoors, they yell at you furiously, but if you yell back the same way, sometimes it turns you into bestfriends.

"If I'm you, I mind my dang business," I barked at him, and it turned us into bestfriends for the tenminutes until we got separated.

"So what did they get you for, dave," he said once I was strapped in and the cops were way up front.

You're about to hear a lot of guys call each other dave in this story because squadwise, Lossy Indica is nonstop dave territory. Obviously you got a few groups of dans from up north, maniac crews of todds creeping in from the desert, but in Lossy Indica proper you can prettymuch call any rando a dave and he won't bust your teeth.

"I stole a gun and shot it a couple times," I said.

"Oh fantastic," he said. "You're the little redrat who tried to shoot a faceboy. All the faceboys have been looking for you, dave."

"Great," I said.

"Beautifull, beautifull, and mightIadd delicious," he said. "Dave, those faceboys are going to eat you."

"For sure," I said.

"Would I trade lives with you, answer, definitely not," he said. "Dave, you know how many faceboys they got on the inside? Picture this: your little redrat self getting butchered, fried, and chomped up in one bite like a sumpchewus meatroll, oh dang, what a sight."

"What did they get you for," I said.

"Cops think they caught me selling dust," said little bloodynose.

"But what were you actually doing," I said.

"Selling dust for sure, but they don't have a case," he said.

"We do now," said a cop over the pee ay.

"OH DANG," yelled bloodynose.

Bloodynose was sickteen so we got separated at the station, him thrown in with the grownups, me with kids and babies.

Kids and babies was probably worse tobehonest. I looked into Grownholding as we passed and everyone was sitting around all chill, a few psycho mutterers but no one about to bust anyone's teeth.

Kidholding was different, jumpytense, you could feel in the air, no one knew what the rules were, no one was making plans, it was all just living minutetominute like snakes in a tank.

Plus this Kidholding had a bunch of different scales all mixed together, my scale all the way up to quarterscale, so, kids who outscaled littlepoors by twoandahalf.

So I got thrown into a tank with some middles and littles, and one of the middlest was tenyearsold and you could see in his eyes, a littlepoor teen is candy to him, older and smaller, perfect for humiliating, showing who's boss.

He grabbed me by the neck immediately.

"What did you just say to me," he yelled so everyone can hear.

"Kid, what do you think," I said.

Anytime you have a scumbag tenyearold twice as big as a fourteenyearold, you get a pretty ugly fight, and I got my face pulped a little on the walls before I squeezed away from this kid, headbutted his soft stomach, bashed the wind out, straddled the neck and elbowgouged his eye for a little while, I know it sounds terrible but some tenyearolds will kill you if you let them.

Four hours went by, more fights, kids bragging about terrible things, everyone trying to win the prize of Most Scummy Behavior, a pretty dark time was beginning in the life of Warner.

The city gave me a lawyer, an exhausted middlescale bumping his head on the ceiling of Kidvisiting, rightaway he told me I'm guilty.

"You have no case and we're pleading guilty, for sure," he said.

"Maybe it makes a difference if we say a pimp beat me up and told me he was kidnapping my sis," I suggested.

"Zero difference, don't bring it up," he said, shuffling papers.

"What if I say I went to a cop first and he wouldn't help," I said.

"Oooh boy," he said. "Ruleofthumb, littlebro, anytime you feel like saying something bad about cops, don't, because it will make your life a bunch of times worse."

Littlepoors take too long to walk from ay to bee with our littlelegs, nottomention we're not cuffable. So the guards transport you everywhere by carriercage, for example to the special littlepoor courtroom, basically a middlerich judge's special desk that you sit on.

Trained by my lawyer, I told the judge: I'm not in any squad, never have been even for a second, I didn't get anyone pregnant, I don't do drugs and I don't sell them, I'm just trying to scale up the right way like an honest Yewess citizen. And I didn't say anything about my sis or Shoulderheads or the cop.

But my face was puffy and bloody from fighting, I was talking weird to this frummy judge, I knew he looked at me and saw someone nogood.

Lawyer suggested Wreckless Endangerment but the judge preferred Attentive Murder, ohwell, I pleaded guilty and the judge didn't frown or smile but just said, "Well, Warner, I know you're a firsttime offender, but in your case, I'll be candid with you, you seem like what I call an onlyamatteroftime offender."

I tried to nod and frown, like, you make good points, but I know you'll be fair to me, enormous judge.

"Fourteen is young on some kids, old on others," he said. "On you it feels old, frankly old enough to know better, so consider yourself lucky with what I'm about to say."

I was too dumb not to feel a little hope.

"The max is thirty years, but I'm only giving you eight," sighed the judge. "Two in kidjail, six with the adults. May the Lord King God bless the Yewess."

III.
WILT

DREAMWORLD

For a year, I didn't dream.
In kidjail you don't sleep goodenough.

LIFEANDDEATHWORLD

Instead I dozed super tense everynight, ready to jump up, fight off attacks, get savage. We slept eight nine ten to a cage and the guards cycled new kids in and out every week to break up alliances and keep everyone fighting.

Kidjail had plenty of faceboys for sure, infact the faceboys were the biggest squad, jackedup inky daves with crazy faces inked on their chests, backs, knees, backofthehead, and the first few days and nights were episodes of getting my face pulped, a couple teeth knocked out, nose broke, ribs kicked.

Then after three days the faceboys asked me if I wanted to join.

"I'm honored, dontgetmewrong," I said. "I just can't join a squad, daves, it doesn't fit my beliefs," and I didn't actually have any beliefs but that still got me respect so for a few weeks they stopped jumping me, throwing me down, kicking my ribs and stuff, after that the pulpings were just once or twice a month.

What do you want to hear about a year of nothing? Mostly I sat around the cage and went insane.

The kidjail was a little house of cages, property of the corpo called Littlebighouse, builder of jails for littlepoors. Our house was allboy, allgirl was up the street. The design was similar to petstores, many stackable cages, eight nine ten beds each, and everything happens in the cage, you might not get outside the bars for weeks at a time.

They feed you in the cage, passing rubberbowls in.

They wash you in the cage, first taking clothes and bedsheets, then hosing you up and down through the bars, then blowdrying you, then you get clothes and bedsheets back.

Outdoor time is when they take the cage outside for a few hours, let you have some sun and maybe a ball.

Three hours a week we had libraryprivileges unless the guards took them away, and that was when they dump toobig books into the cage, the pages all scrawled in and chewed up by years and years of young psychos. But I still tried to make the most of it, forced my brain to read. In one year I got to page hunfourtyeight of a book called ADVENTURES OF CUTE RASCAL, a mouse with a rabbit friend liberating the forests and meadows from evil rats, in a world with no humans but plenty of swords, shields, bows, arrows, feasts.

Sometimes a bored canread kid would help me, trap some ants with me, get me through big words or terrible sentences. But mostly I was struggling alone, a couple pairagraphs per week.

Everyday a few hours I worked out, routines I saw the biggest toughest kids doing, pushups with a kid sitting on you, pullups from the ceiling with a kid hanging on your feet, whenever I could recruit a workout partner. Backflips, frontflips, whatever there's room in the cage for.

Otherwise I just sat like everyone and watched whatever vids the guard had on the wallscreen, and when there wasn't vids I daydreamed, plotted, tried to keep my brain alive, and most important, avoided other prisoners and their beatings and dumb schemes, because everyday something bad or dumb was happening somewhere in the cage, some scumbag smuggling in weeds or dusts, groups betting on random dicerolls, some argument was revving up into a brawl, or just a psycho was out to prove that he's the worst.

But a lot of the time we just watched vids.

Every guard tried to make his shift less sad and boring by putting vids on the wallscreen. So every guard, we learned what kind of vid does he like, news or terror or ballgames, is he open to requests for different kind of vids, how sensitive is he to noise, how much noise and fighting will he ignore before he freaks out and hoses the cage, andsoonandsoforth.

Everytime a new guard starts working at Littlebighouse, he has to learn a few rules about watching vids in a room of kidprisoners. Rule numberone, no vids with women looking sexy, not just talking about pornos or girlsgonewild but even ordinary murderdramas, gameshows, realhousewives, it doesn't matter, if it has women showing legs or titcrack, it's a disaster. Boys will freak out, everyone needs to prove he's the most hetro, soonerorlater someone is pulping someone's face.

Rule numbertwo, no sexymen either, a kid will accuse another kid of loving it, again you will advance prettyquick to facepulping.

Rule numberthree, playing shootemups on the wallscreen gets everyone to shut up and watch motionlessly, but as soon as you finish, fights break out allover like magic.

I was sulky and got targeted for fights a lot, not just from faceboys but also fighty psychos. Mostly the guards hated me for this. The head guard was called Wilt and he had a special name for me.

"What's wrong today, Grumpyrat," he said.

"I live in kidjail, so that's probably the first part of what's wrong," I said in the beginning.

But over the weeks and months I said lessandless.

Another guard named Belt, he was hunched and old. He was my favorite because he lifted you out of the cage by hand. Most guards used the net.

Also his hearing was terrible, so he put on vid captions, a little more reading practice for Warner.

Prayer visited every month. She was middlepoor now for sure, around threequarterscale, outscaling me by sevenplus. Wow, it was amazing to see her. Huge, walking funny, bobbed hair, and wearing logoed shirts and skirts like any middlepoor lady out veggieshopping.

The first time she saw me she shrieked and cried at my bashedup face and I had to tell her a bunch of times, sis, I'm not talking about me today, please, just talk about yourself, what was Scale Up like, how was the wedding, where's Usher, how's Mom.

Well the Scale Up Ceremony was amazing, she told me finally, they put you to strange solodream sleep, dreams with no one else in there, and you just wake up huge, feeling so thirsty and hungry, and they put you in a robe and walking feels insane, the ground is smoother and meets your feet harder, but in a good way, you suck in air and it feels so powerfull, everything is just different, it's amazing, she said.

"Food is the most different," she told me. "It's just better between your teeth. It feels nicer on your tongue."

I told her it made me really happy to see her this big, I really meant it too, I mean dang look at you all middle and happy, so I guess what was the wedding like.

The wedding was super basic, a government ritual. Paddy did not get her a dress or anything, no guests showed up, that whole part is less exciting, let's stick to talking about being scaledup.

I asked her what happens if he wants a divorce, is she protected or would she lose everything?

"Technically for the first two years it's a trialmarriage, after that I would get half in a divorce," she told me.

"But what about before the twoyear mark," I asked.

"He's not going to want a divorce," she promised me.

That wasn't a great answer but I decided, maybe better not to go there.

Instead I begged her to scale Mom up, atleast get her out of that churchhouse, everytime Prayer came I asked if she had rescued Mom yet.

The first few times I said this her face got sad, and she said, yeah, ofcourse, I'm trying, I mean I talk to Paddy about it all the time.

Each time I got mad and said, what's Paddy's stupid problem, how hard is it to let tiny Mom be in your house.

"It's hard for me to ask Paddy for anything," Prayer told me. "Because as good as it feels to scale up, I guess it feels worse to scale down, even just from ninetenth to threequarters, Paddy says you feel weaker and punier and it's not healthy for an older guy. He does complain kind of a lot sometimes, he feels sick and bad from scaling down, Prayer why did you do this to me, et set set setera. So ontop of that he really doesn't need to hear from me questions like, hey, when are we bringing my mom in here."

"You're his freaking wife and Mom is his freaking family now," I rasped out of my halfbusted throat, someone punched it the daybefore. "You're a pretty young girl who married an old fat babbler, he owes you big, when I get out of here I'm going to slap his freaking face."

But it turned out the problem wasn't just that Paddy hated Mom, Mom also hates Paddy, the whole thing has gotten complicated because Mom has gone a little godcrazy.

"She won't even take the munmuns I try to give her," Prayer told me in her big voice, out of her big head. "She just gives them back. She says the Lord King God doesn't like my marriage."

"Because Paddy's old and gross," I said.

"No, because Paddy doesn't belong to the Church of the Lord King God," said Prayer.

"He's churchless?" I said.

"No, he's in a church," said Prayer, bashfull.

"Oh," I said.

Prayer didn't want to fill in the blank.

"Maybe I shouldn't even ask which one," I said.

• • •

Paddy belonged to the New Planetary Church, a church started by a guy who's still alive, so already, bigredflag.

The major belief is that munmun scales you up in this life, but what about the next life? Goodworks are what scale you up in the next life, and if you think it's important to scale up in this life, forget it, way more important to scale up in the next, because you spend the next life in, drumrollplease, outerspace.

In outerspace you need to be so huge that you become a planet, otherwise you will drift around all small and cold and breathless and get smacked by comets forever.

So you better get started on those goodworks, start fattening up your little future spacepebble, and guesswhat, a major and convenient goodwork is ofcourse Donate Munmuns To New Planetary Church.

"Why would Paddy even join this church," I said, confused on account of, Paddy's super cheap, I can't see that guy loving to give away munmuns.

"His boss made him," Prayer explained.

The church likes one thing better than you giving your munmuns to the church, and that thing is, recruit other joiners. So to encourage recruiting, the church's system is, the goodworks of your recruits count toward *your* goodworks too. Eye ee, when your recruit pays a hundred munmun entry fee, it's like *you* paid the hundo fee too, and also the guy who recruited you, all the way back to the original starter of New Planetary Church, who collects all the goodworks of everybody and will get to be biggest of all in the afterlife, the sun or a blackhole or something.

So Paddy's boss, an owner of many Quickstands in the

121

Lossy Indica area, at some point mentioned to Paddy, hey, I have goodnews, this church is the True Universal Truth, you should really consider its teachings, it has a lot of guidance on how to lead a fulfilled life, righteousness, virtue and whatever, and bestofall, if you join the church I probably won't have to double your monthly Quickstand Franchise Fee.

And so Paddy joined as a business decision, and as part of the marriage he made Prayer join too.

"So, Paddy is not troubled that his scale in the next life will always be bigger than yours," I said.

"What are you talking about," she said.

"Your goodworks are also Paddy's goodworks, plus he has his own, so, the math works out like, in deathspace he'll be huger than you for sure," I said.

"Warner, no one actually believes any of this stupid crap," she said.

It's the truth and I'm sorry for making you learn so much about this stupid church, anyway the point is, once our mom learned Prayer converted to New Planetary, that was it, gameover. Anytime Prayer visited Mom at the Dockseye Middlechurch of the Lord King God, Mom refused to talk anything not churches or gods. Mom do you need anything, Prayer you need to leave that cult. Mom it's fine how's your eye, Prayer the Lord King God will still forgive you if you just nevermind that evil cult today. Mom can I atleast fix your janky chairwheels, Prayer join your enormous hand with mine now and say, *Lord King God, mybad, forreal.*

Mom was always pretty godhappy, but apparently after we left she became some kind of a nun or something, alldayeveryday just sewing clothes for other littlepoors, eating only pastes and gruels, wheeling herself around the streets at night trying to save souls.

It made me a little happy that atleast the church was taking care of her. But a lot sad that we weren't, her worthless kids, one scaledup and selfish, the other a scumbag inmate.

So that was Mom.

About Usher meanwhile, Prayer had no idea.

"The same morning you got arrested, he left, I don't know where to, he didn't tell me," she said.

"Ohmygod, Prayer," I yelled, furious. "What is even going to happen to him. Where will he sleep."

"I look for him in Dreamworld sometimes," she said. "I'll tell you if I find him."

"Cats or hawks will eat him for sure and if I found out he's dead, guesswhat, you're also dead, as in, I will consider you dead forever," I told her.

"Usher is his own guy, I'm not responsible for him, and anyway he left without even telling me," she said.

"I will think of you as tragically dead," I yelled. "Whatashame about Prayer, I will never get to talk to her again, I even forget what her stupid face looks like."

That was Prayer's first few visits anyway, before my tongue got fat and dull.

123

How can I even tell you what a year in kidjail does, if you don't know. The days went by, weeks, months, I became less myself.

If you're only around boys you don't know and don't like, mostly scumbags and peenfaces, prettyquick you get bad at talking.

Your mouth loses most of its programs, reduces prettymuch just to "I'm not intrested," "Don't bother me," "Sorry dave," "Heck you want," other sad hard sayings.

So Prayer's visits got shorter and shorter, because I just didn't say much, also she had worries of her own to deal with.

"I can't stay for long, I'm really sorry, Paddy's got me running the stand everyday now, he's really kind of turned the business over to me, except I guess for the ownership part," she would say and I just grunted, tried to care a little harder and couldn't.

"Sorry I haven't been in a while, Paddy retired, he just sits in bed allday playing vidpoker with cyberfriends, except I think the friends are all just robots, do you think I should be worried about it, probably it's fine right," she would ask with tired eyes and a stressedout mouth, but her worries just bounced off my hard cool thoughts.

My thoughts were about tunneling.

I'm in an eightyear tunnel, I thought everyday, just need to slowly tunnel through time, dig through time at the rate of one day per day, make it to the otherside with reading skills, thinking skills, superstrength.

But after a few months you begin to realize, an eightyear tunnel is an impossible length.

You begin to think, I can't see the end of this tunnel, how do I know it's not collapsed in the middle.

You realize, in two years the tunnel gets darker, bumpier, crappier. In two years I'm in with grownups and in grownjail they throw littles in with middles. So you're in with daves who outscale you by two, three, five, way more frequency of getting pulped, more probability of getting banged, more likelihood of getting told, here are your choices, join a squad or die. Goodluck surviving six years with hopeless grownups, bigger sadder madder than you, more insane too.

You realize, I have no control, even here in kidjail, what if the faceboys get serious and just break my neck one day.

What if a psycho fights m e, a true p sycho wants a fi ght to the death and he kills me or I kill him, the outcomes are death or lifeinprison.

What if this tunnel I'm digging is just a pit.

The days crept by and I got sad, mad, meaner to boys than I had to be.

If a kid stepped on my bed, I yelled at him. If a kid stared at me, not even meanstaring, just alone or afraid, I slapped his face.

The guards and parolecops mentioned it, during checkups, they said, "Grumpyrat, you're not going to fight your way back outside, and infact if you keep getting in fights, you're never going to leave," like that's news to me, like I'm an idiot who can't figure that out.

They thought I was one of the worst kids and after a year I was thinking, what do I know, maybe they're right.

I realized the tunnel was not even me digging, it was just the earth swallowing me whole like a snake.

DREAMWORLD

One day about a year after I got jailed, they came in and plucked the worst kids out of the cages onebyone, Puppyneck the king faceboy, Nick the total psycho, Starling the dustaddict, and numberfour, yourstruly.

The guards fished us all out with a net and plopped us in a blank little bedless cage together and I thought, here we go, battleroyale, before anyone attacks me I should probably attack dopey Starling, he fights the least good, let Nick and Puppyneck jack each other up.

But the guards didn't put the cage down, so we couldn't get our footing, so no fight.

"Okay, littleshits," said Wilt. "Here's what's happening. We have someone here who wants to run an experiment on violent kidprisoners, ay kay ay, you."

We just stared at him, Nick spat on the ground.

"Great," said Wilt. "If you don't want to be in an experiment, speak now, no one's saying anything, okay great, let's get started."

Then they carried us outside and there was someone huge in the yard.

But it wasn't an old scientist, instead it was a middlerich girl there waiting for us, our age even. This girl was doublescale atleast, closer to twoandahalf, that's why they took us outside to meet her, this lucky richgirl's not squeezing into Littlebighouse.

She seemed familiar to me, I had no idea why.

"So these are the worst ones, for sure," said Wilt to this girl. "The kid with the neckpuppy is a squadleader, baldy is addicted to everything, crazy eyes over here yells at ghosts, and then the frowny jacked one in the corner is just mean and stupid, we call him Grumpyrat, he stopped even talking months ago."

"Hello boys," said the girl, and the voice was familiar too, dark and rich, my mind spun like wheels in mud.

Nick immediately called this girl something terrible, Starling suggested ideas for how they could bang, Puppyneck and I stayed quiet.

"You see what I mean, these scumbags are awfull," said Wilt.

But she opened her mouth, hesitated, then said, "They're perfect. Guys, my name is Kitty, and I'm doing a schoolproject on dreams."

She said this and I got a sick feeling behind the eyes, like I wanted to cry and couldn't.

Puppyneck maybe felt what I felt, because he told her rightaway, "Sorry, richgirl. We don't dream."

She thought it was a joke, realized it wasn't, slowly dropped her smile, turned to Wilt.

"None of them dream?" she said.

"Prettymuch, nope," he said.

"Okay," she said. "Well, that's a problem, because for the project, I need to dream with them."

"Look, you wanted to meet them, here you are, didn't make any promises about what they could do," said Wilt.

"Don't any of you dream?" she asked us.

I should have spoke up, but didn't, couldn't, I don't know.

To this girl I was Grumpyrat, the mean dumb jacked one who says nothing, and it broke my mouth, my tongue was dull and fat, my voicepipe had no tread to catch the air.

So I stayed shutup as Nick called this girl another horrible thing and Starling said, "Sure I dream, sweetieboo, everynight I dream about life in that tittycrack."

"Well," said Kitty and paused, and finally said, "thanks for your time, I guess, and sorry for bothering you."

And she got up to go, a little creaky and shaky I guessed from disappointment or just crouching down to talk to littlepoors.

The guards took us back into Littlebighouse, dumped us back into our cages, laughed at these dumb scumbags.

Two or three days went by, sad days of trying not to think about how I used to dream, try not to try to remember how I know this girl, probably I can't remember and anyway my memories are like a hot painfull Dreamworld, torture to enter.

Puppyneck was eyeing me from timetotime, having talks with the faceboys, maybe it's time to bust my face and gutbones again.

Then he stepped to my bunk one evening.

"Warner, time for us to talk, bro to bro," he said.

He was talking kind of low and he didn't have his faceboys with him.

"Heck you want," I said.

"No grief, no crap," he said, hands open.

"Heck you want, face," I repeated.

He twinkled his eyes and said, "Dave, I respect you. You've taken many pulpings from me and my guys, you're tough as heck, I respect you and I like you even."

"Get to the point, scumbag," I said.

"In a week it's my birthday," he said. "I'll be sickteen. So I'm headed to grownjail."

"Congrats," I said.

"I have one piece of unfinishedbusiness," he said. "That's you, dave. When I leave here, I need you to be one of two things. A faceboy, or not breathing anymore."

"Is that right," I said, deciding, *be tough* and *who cares.*

He was relaxed but not casual, a tough smart squadleader style.

"That's right," he said, "because if you're neither of those things when I get to grownjail, they're not going to be very happy with Puppyneck," he said.

"That's sad for you," I said.

"It would be sad for sure," agreed Puppyneck. "You know in grownjail they mix littles and middles. So if I don't take care of my faceboy responsibilities, probably the way I die is, get eaten. I'll get dunkfried by some faceboy with kitchenprivileges, then munched by some middles. That's how I guess they'll do me unless I finish my business with you."

"Nice to think about," I said.

"Goodnews is, you get to decide," said Puppyneck. "So look into the future and tell me. Are you dead in a week or did I draw a face on you."

"Funny, I'm not seeing either of those," I told him.

Puppyneck smiled at me, the puppyface on his neck bulged and frowned.

"Warner," he murmured. "Don't waste yourself. It would be sad and needless. Don't waste your brain, don't waste your body."

And he leaned closer to tell me, "I'll make you a squadboss after I go. My guys respect you. You'll run these cages, dave."

I wasn't expecting that and so I had to shut up and just think about it.

"Take tonight to think about it, then tomorrow tell me that you want to live," said Puppyneck, and before I could stop him he squeezed a knot of my hair in his fist like we were bros, locked eyes, bumped skulls.

So my choices were death or scumbag life forever.

A ghost murmured in one ear, a ghost muttered in the other, angel and devil, the angel was the cowsoy girl Grace, the devil was enormous judge from before.

Grace said, you can't be a faceboy, faceboys are scum, you're not scum.

Judge said, oh for sure you're a scumbag, admit it, no need to die pretending you're not terrible.

Grace said, if you say yes to the faceboys, they'll never let you back out, it's a new kind of tunnel with no end.

Judge said, the tunnel gets a lot nicer if you're not digging alone anymore, imagine it, friendly diggers next to you and no more worrying about beatings and pulpings.

Grace said, Faceboy Church is like New Planetary, like any

cult, they want your goodworks for life, except instead it's bad-works, works of, steal, pimp, beat, kill.

Judge said, what's better than joining a church, a church gives you friendsforlife, in this case tough friends, a squad, a team, many savage daves all helping you, not like your old dumb team of a sis who scales up without you and a bud with bad stuttershakes who is probably dead.

Grace said, say you join the faceboys and finally you graduate from jail, you're out on the street, say the faceboys ask you to rob that foodstand there and they're pointing to mine, Grace Family Cowsoy, would you do it? Say my dad scrambles for a knife, would you kill my dad? My mom scampers for a gun, would you kill my mom?

Judge said, shut up Grace, listen Warner, the world has been terrible to you all life long, you owe the terrible world nothing, not even a girl who gave you water once, then in the morning said you can't even live in the garbage.

Grace said, what about the Lord King God.

Judge said, what about him.

Grace said, when you die the Lord King God will ask you, *what did you do with your life, were you evil because it was easier,* and what are you going to say.

Judge said, Warner, you know you don't believe in any of that dumb crap.

Grace said, the point isn't if you believe in the Lord King God, the point is he's right, ask yourself, *do I need to live so much that I'm okay with making the world worse.*

Judge said, it's your only life, don't lose it pretending to be someone better than you are.

I fell asleep to them, not knowing who to trust, liking Grace, believing the judge.

For the first time in a year I dreamed and I didn't know why rightaway.

I was in the cages, mostly alone, a few other jailbirds fuzzily floated, drifted, and tumbled.

Then POP POP POP, Wilt jumped out of a doorway and shot me overandover, roaring joyfully. I was reddrenched like in shootemups.

"Okay, you got me," I said.

"Bang bang bang bang bang," he said. "Thought you didn't dream, redshit."

"First time in a while," I said.

"Brap brap brap brap chukka chukka chukka," he said, shooting me with many guns.

It was a strain to dream anything with all the gunshots but I dreamed up some hard rubbery skins for myself, unshootable.

"Maybe it's a dumb question, but why are you shooting me," I said.

"I'm waking you up," he said. "Can't let you sneak out and terrorize lawfull citizens in Dreamworld."

"Don't worry, I won't leave," I said.

"BOOM," he said, now bombing me.

"We could just talk, I could dream things for you," I offered.

"BOOM BLOOM, BLAM BAM," he announced with his smoky bombs.

"Fine, bytheway who was that girl Kitty," I said.

132

He spun bombs in his hands, not wanting to say anything.

But he couldn't not talk, that was how much he hated this girl.

"Ugh, the bitch daughter of the jerk cityboss of Wet Almanac," said Wilt. "What can I do, my boss tells me I need to do this favor, let her talk to you, I got no choice. But it makes me sick, doing anything for that family. Political nitwits trying to make everything about scale, classwarfare, it's disgusting."

"What do you mean," I said, but Wilt was done talking to me, back to bombing and gunning, the room was flashing, thundering, bombsaway, impossible to stay asleep, I woke up and couldn't get back to Dreamworld.

In the morning finally I couldn't dodge what I knew and it smashed me over my poor dozy head.

How did I know Kitty, I knew her from the seedflowerbirdhouse, that's how.

Kitty was the girl with the richdrink voice of notes made out of notes made out of notes.

Kitty was the only dreamer better than me, the dreamer who could sing.

And what I thought was: *I need to find Kitty in Dreamworld, listen to that voice again, one last time.*

What I allofasudden knew was: *If I hear her sing one more time it will make everything clear somehow, I know it.*

I need to hear that voice again and whatever happens next will be okay, me pulped to death, me tatted up and in a squad, me killing innocents, it will be okay.

So when Puppyneck wanted my answer I told him I needed another night.

"You shouldn't," he said.

"Why would your faceboys let me boss them," I said.

"For one thing, because they like tough smart bosses," says Puppyneck. "But here's the real reason: because I told them to. We're not psychos. We got deep respect for rules, systems, orders, loyalty. It's not a hard decision, dave. It's a better life than you ever had, better friends, better world, and I'm troubled to see you whiffing and waffling like this."

"One more night," I said.

He frowned, fingertapped my skull, walked away.

Prayer came to visit around lunch, tearstreak cheeks, trembly jaw, more badnews.

"Paddy lost a ton of munmun," she told me. "Ohmygod, so much."

"How," I made my mouth say.

"Freaking vidpoker," she trembled. "Freaking riggedup cheating robots on vidpoker, our munflow is cleanedout and he owes payments on the Quickstand, payments to New Planetary, it's suchamess."

I saw Belt listening in and headshaking sadly like, *I've heard that bedtimestory before.*

"So what happens now," I asked.

She stared me down, took two hard breaths, and said in a driedup voice, "Well, one of two things can happen now, either we lose the stand, or he loses me."

"When will you know," I asked.

"I think I know already," she shivered.

"Dang, that breaks my heart a little, gotta tell you vidcards are pure poison," Belt told me after she left.

"Yeah," I said.

"Neverforget, those robots are smarter than you, and if you think you're smarter, that's exactly what they want you to think," Belt informed me, caging me up.

"Belt, can I ask you to show me something," I said.

"Depends on what, redfish," he said.

"I just want to look at a high school, like pictures of it," I said.

He didn't question me, instead just opened picsearch on his foldout phone, probably weird and old but still amazing tech to me.

"How about Wet Almanac Middlerich High School," I said, heartthumping.

"Sure, that's a nice one," he said, typing it in, and pics came up, maps, threedee zoomthroughs.

Yeah it was a nice one, unbelievable honestly, basically a hotel resort getaway on a beautifull cliffside, gyms, pools, gardens, theaters, screenrooms, planetariums, canyonviews, paradise.

"Be nice to go there, huh," said Belt.

"Yup," I said, furiously memorizing it.

"What a life," said Belt, and he folded up his phone and took me back to the cage.

That night I tried hard to sleep and dream, not just doze, but it was hard. The psycho Nick was in my cage that night, more tweaked than usual, Wilt had played shootemups all afternoon and now Nick was glaring and sweating and making wild threats.

"Go to sleep, allofyou, nightynight, can't wait to bite through your necks," he yelled, stuff like that.

I glanced over and vampire psycho was staring right at me.

Ohwell, I thought.

I relaxed, breathed deep through the nose, closed the eyes, slowed the heart.

In Dreamworld, Wilt was waiting.

"POP POP BOOOOOM," he yelled, sniping with rifles, then following up with a bazooka, overkilling, joyfull.

"Crap, I'm awake," I yelled to make him happy, and fell through the floor, notawake still.

I tunneled down into the ground and all the way through to the nightsky bottom, fell out of the sky like a diving kite, wild and wobbly because no control, outofpractice, skidded facefirst into the highschool roof, rumpling tiles like carpet.

And here I was above the big beautifull campus, comfortable middleriches allaround, lacking homework, being naked, banging in the grass, typical schooldreams.

But no Kitty anywhere.

"Here we go," I thought, also said, and made a grumpy rat.

My plan was to make a huge one, a giant scowler you can see for miles, Kitty sees him through the window or wherever she is and thinks, "Grumpyrat, why is that familiar, AHA."

136

And then she will come find me, I will ask her please sing to me one more time, she will sing.

I will hear it and then know, can I die or do I need to live.

So I sat on the roof of the beautifull high school and made a rat with a funny grumpy cartoon face, red, jacked arms and legs, a perfect rat to signal that Warner is on your schoolroof,

only one problem, the rat was tiny.

Get big, I said to the rat.

But it didn't.

I tried to dream it bigger.

But it was nightmare dreaming, flailing and failing, no control.

Mom and Dad used to tell me some mornings, beautifull dreaming, little redfish, and I know it feels effortless, but just remember kiddo, most people can't just dream whatever they want, you'll learn this too one day, dreams are out of your control sometimes.

Manohman would that be terrible, I used to think, *good thing I'm special, it will never happen to me.*

No, it can happen to you, Warner, infact after a dreamless year in kidjail, ofcourse it's what happens.

Come on, I begged my perfect grumpy rat, holding him in my hands, trying to make him big big big, but he refused, just kind of lolled around and if anything shrank.

What a new bad feeling, the feeling of you don't control your own mind.

"No no no," I pleaded.

In a panic I gripped him and tried to throw him up in the air atleast, but he had the weight of a brick, unthrowable.

137

"RAT," I yelled. "GET HUGE."

The little rat cleaned his whiskers, chuckled, scuttled around on the tile.

First I felt despair.

Then another feeling, a funny tickle on the neck.

I realized what it was, told myself WAKE UP, but couldn't rightaway, frozen, paralyzed.

The tickle became pain, prettybad, darkred, hotsmelling.

Last thing I saw in Dreamworld was, furious rat finally swelling up like a balloon.

LIFEANDDEATHWORLD

So, Nick bites my neck and here's what happens next.

I elbow his face before he finishes murdering me, but still major damage to the neck area forsure, permanent scars, hospital time for Warner, in jail they call it coreandteen.

The bitewound gets an infection, no surprise because it came from a psycho's mouth, fever, rot, basically the doctor sprays me with poisons, hope the infection dies and not Warner.

A week goes by, pills and liquids keep me sleeping dreamlessly, dozing painfully. Somewhere out there my sis is maybe getting divorced and losing everything. Somewhere out there Puppyneck graduates to grownjail, maybe they kill him, eat him, no idea. Somewhere maybe Usher is alive.

One morning I wake up, the neck is throbbing but the air in my lungs feels clean, the worst is over.

"Better," asks the doc.

"A little," I say.

"Hope so," says the doc. "Tonight you're back in the cage with the others."

Then she gives me a few hours to think about it.

Late afternoon, some guards pick me up in my bed, lower it into a box, take me out into the yard, not telling me anything.

In the yard again is Kitty.

Look at her, now she's a girl who used to be the girl from seedflowerbirdhouse but not anymore, now a teenager, longerfaced.

Nightsky hair in a braidnest, stacks of loops like piled tires.

Rivercolored skin, muddycream with freckles and explosions.

Scrunchy lips bunching a smile of, *I expect praise.*

A little walleyed, specifically the right eye a littlebit wall, not quite looking at you, what does it see instead.

"I found someone's ratballoon," she tells me.

"Mine," I rasp.

She expects praise for solving the puzzle of the mysterious huge ratballoon, abandoned in Dreamworld.

"Why did you lie to me," she asks.

"I didn't lie," I say.

Pause.

"You told me you didn't dream," she asks.

"I didn't tell you anything," I say.

Pauseagain.

"Oh," she says. "Right, because you don't talk."

I want to tell her, *I used to talk, I used to babble like a happy maniac, but here in jail they just decide stuff about you and even if it isn't true, after a while, it is.*

But she's too huge, I'm in the jailyard, still too much of a jailbird, I don't know.

"Except you're talking now," she adds.

"Why do you want to study the dreams of jailedup littles," I say.

"Well, it's a schoolproject," she says.

"Oh right," I say, like I know schoolprojects.

Her lips flutter, then they tell me, "I'm studying the dreaming of unfortunates, poors, convicts, mentally ill, specialneeds."

"Good," I rasp, feeling bad.

Her hands twist a little, fidgety fingers hug each other, she thoughtbubbles, *maybe this was a mistake.*

But still she asks, "Can I dream with you sometime this week?"

My heart shudders.

"Ofcourse," I tell her.

"Thanks," she says.

I just stare at the ground because it's just too hard now to look at someone who's not from Jailworld, not a guard or grungy dave, instead this girl from a different world, different planet, someone else's life.

"Well then," she says. "I'll find you in Dreamworld, or you'll find me."

"Okay," I say.

But as she gets up, gets ready to step over the wall and leave my life, I say, "Wait."

She stops, crouches over me, her breath is a room of gummy fakemint.

"I'm going to die tonight," I tell her.

And she said whatdoyoumean, and stayed, and I told her how I got here, and the guards got moreandmore furious, but as I realized they couldn't do anything to this middlerich princess I kept talking nonstop, huge chunks of the story, kids smashed my dad, a cat crippled my mom, we tried to find a better life at law school, Prayer got abused, Shoulderheads tried to kidnap her, a cop wouldn't help, I scared away my sis's kidnapper with a stolen gun and now I'm in jail and a squad wants to kill me, when I try to dream psychos bite me, life is almost over.

We were in the yard until the sun plunked into the sea and justabout the only thing I didn't tell her is, bytheway I dreamed with you once, longago.

Before she left she told Wilt, *I'm fixing this, you better keep him in hospital coreandteen tonight, if he ends up back in the cages and anything happens to him, my father will show you the inside of a grownjail prettysoon.*

Wilt was sick with anger but powerless, instead just ranted to me about how that uppy bitch was going to forget about me in a few days and then we'll just see what happens, littleshit, ohmygod, can't wait to sponge your little drips of blood off the tile in one swipe.

But she didn't forget,

she found Prayer and interviewed her,

found one of the Shoulderheads tramps in grownjail and interviewed her too,

made a case of Maybe Warner's Not So Bad to her cityboss dad Hue,

she and dad went to the cityboss of the Dreamoughs,

and the citybosses agreed to exchange the favors of,

Kitty's dad donates personal munmuns to a Dreamough publicgarden,

Dreamough cityboss pardons me.

• • •

Pardon means, *nevermind the rest of your jail sentence, ourbad, Warner you are freetogo.*

They threw open the middledoors of kidjail for me and I walked through, blinking at the localnews cameras, Kitty's family of giants standing around in elegant suits and dresses. Her dad Hue lowered his hands to me. I stepped onto his fingers and he lifted me up to his perfect face, eyes of sparkling darkness, smile of blinding whiteness, and here's what happened next, please hold your breath, close your eyes, it gets more amazing.

"Warner," he boomed and purred, "this is a great city in a great country but it can be very hard on littlepoors, too many of our citizens are suspicious of you, think that you cannot be rehabilitated, however I believe you are a young man of great integrity and resourcefullness, and infact I am so confident in your goodness, I would like to scale you up and bring you to live in my home, eat with my family, sleep under my roof."

I couldn't speak obviously.

"What do you say," Hue grinned, wife and sons and daughter Kitty twinkling their smiles at me too, and I couldn't stop myself, I had no control like in a nightmare.

With the dronecams peering down at me I wept, curled up like a snail to hide my face, rolled up like a dead beetle in his perfect hands and bawled.

IV.
KITTY

LIFEANDDEATHWORLD

They scaled me up to halfscale, fivetimes my old size, hunthousand fresh new munmuns in my scale account.

Hue Family Scale was about twoandahalf so now they just outscaled me by five.

Although I could have been bigger, should have been bigger actually. Because what they set aside for me was twohunthousand munmuns, that ofcourse is bigger than halfscale, you end up about threefifth, sicktyonedotsix percent if you want more exactness. You're asking, *how the heck does Warner know the advanced munmath of dots and percents,* look, stop freaking out, in this story I end up learning some math, we'll get there.

Anyway I could have put all twohunthousand muns in my scale, but there was Prayer to worry about. Because surenough, Paddy began divorceproceedings, ended the trialmarriage and got all his scalemuns back from his sad little exwife who took such bad advantage of him.

So I asked Hue and Kitty, can my sis live with us too?

Hue sympathized but had some doubts.

"We don't have another twohunthousand muns to put in your

sister's scale account, I'm afraid, and the house really isn't outfitted for littles to live here," he told me.

"For sure, but I'll give Prayer half of mine, we can each get by on a hunthousand, I know we can," I hoped.

"We also don't have a second middleroom in our house," he said. "There's just the one."

"We'll share," I said. "We'll share the muns, the room, we share everything, we're used to it."

Hue nodded a few perfect nods.

Then he said, "I do have to ask you something pointblank, and please forgive my directness. We don't know your sister. The young poor kid we chose was *you*. You are the one we chose to give an opportunity, because we believe you will take full advantage of it. Bynow we feel like we know you well enough to judge you, and we believe you will work hard, study hard, and really make something of yourself. But we can only give this opportunity to your sister if she is going to do the same."

"She will," I promised. "She will, she definitely will, infact she makes me look like a lazy piece of crap, she works so hard and smart."

Immediately I regretted saying it, but Hue chuckled.

"Kitty, what do you think," he said.

From her stiff voice and low eyes, I knew she didn't love the idea, but what she said was words of talking herself into it.

"Well," she said slowly, "what I know from meeting her is, she does work pretty hard, I guess really hard to be honest, very long hours, the job isn't like demanding intellectually but that doesn't mean she couldn't succeed in an intellectual environment. And forsure she was forced into an unequal marriage and exployted terribly, from her history it's clear she's quite resilient and yeah I guess it would be a really beautifull story if she beat the odds too."

"Ohmygod, what's better than that story, nothing," I yelled.

She smiled a little although her hands twisted and squeezed again, thumbs stuck out like cowhorns.

"If you're really okay with not being as big as you could," she said, "not getting your own room for the first time, then sure, let's give her a chance."

"Warner, you're a generous kid," Hue warmed.

"You're a generous freaking family," I yelled.

Although, was I thinking secretly about how the family could have been even more generous, I mean yeah, a littlebit, sure I did. That's a terrible thought but also unavoidable, when you're scaling up to halfscale and meanwhile the family that homes you still outscales you by five.

You think, *dang, they couldn't have scaled us up all the way to their scale?*

Warner, you peenface, to do that they'd need to give you each twenmillion, that's way too much to give to a stranger, crazy munmuns.

But then your mindcalculator is warmed up and you start thinking, *twenmillion munmuns for six people, that's a huntwenmillion in the family scale account.*

What if this family of six joined munmuns with me, Prayer, and a hundredtwelve other littles, huntwenty of us in total, we'd all be middlescale, onemillion per person.

Perfect fit for middleroads, middledoors, middlecars, and middlephones, the nice comfy middlelife. Sicktypercent downscale for six, sure, but thousandpercent upscale for hunfourteen, that's every single person in the old Yewess Coastguard station.

Warner, ungratefull jerk, can you not be chill, just let the riches be nice to you.

Or what if the family joins tentimes as many people, a thousandhundredninetyfour littlepoors, everybody's halfscale, an incredible life improvement for a crazy number of people, ten coastguard stations of littlepoors finally getting to live life.

Warner, turn that freaking mindcalculator off.

Go the other way, the family joins with fewer people, add just six littlepoors to your family of giants, the family only shrinks a little bit to doublescale, tenmillion per human, you're still enormous, plus you made six littlefish lives amazing, doublescale now.

Enough enough enough, I learned prettyquick to stop making calculations. Because that's ungratefull thinking and I was super gratefull. Twohunthousand munmuns is a fortune for me and Prayer, super generous, lifechanger.

149

I spent one night as a littlepoor in Hue Family Palace. Prayer was still living in the storeroom at Paddy Quickstand, not scaled down yet. Hue promised we'd get her in the morning.

Mom Dawn fretted that the house hadn't hosted littles ever, she hoped I'd be comfortable, ofcourse let her know if I needed anything. Dinner was blendedup soup and bread.

"Any scale person can eat soup," announced Dawn with

nervous hope. "You know what they say! 'Water's water at any scale!' And water's a liquid. Just like soup!"

"Mom, be a littlebit chill," said Kitty.

"Am I not being chill?" cried Dawn.

Kitty made me a little pillowbed in a special halfscale bathroom, carefully smoothed the sheets with her long fingers.

"I make these kind of flowery operahouses in Dreamworld and sing music in them bytheway," added Kitty sort of shy, "actually that's my whole schoolproject, I think dreammusic can basically be therapy, I'm curious to see the impact on other people with hard lives."

I nodded a That's Intresting nod, hopefully not the nod of Yeah I Already Know That.

Why didn't I want her to know I had seen the house before, I can't really tell you, guess I just needed a secret to protect from giants.

Anyway that first night out of jail I couldn't get all the way to Dreamworld, kept dozing off and then startling awake to the deep robothum of the middlerich house, darkblue bathroom light, gentle aircurrents, faroff smells of buttery wildflowers breathed by machines.

In the morning Hue, Dawn, and Kitty drove me to the bank in their threelane limo. Dawn held me over the glassbottom so I could watch as we straddled and swallowed the middlecars below.

"It's so exciting that you've never been in one of these before," Dawn told me.

"They're fun allright," boomed Hue, as copcars and ambulances drifted behind and underneath.

We left the car in bigparking and as we wandered around the bank to the littledoors, dronecams and reporters hustled after us, snapping pics, cooing reports.

Hue lowered me to the door and we beamed at the cameras.

"See you in there, Warner," Hue winked, the glassy bankdoors hummed open, I crept inside.

So when you grow up littlepoor, talking to other littlepoor kids about munmun and scale and banks, you hear theories about bankers. Bankers are robots, bankers are ghosts. Don't hide in the tellerroom at night because bankers will eat you. Bankers can't make their own blood so they suck it from a dozen littlepoors a day. Bankers don't have peens or jeens, instead when you become a banker they chop off your peen or fill your jeen with cement, et set set setera.

So I was tensing, bracing for weird behaviors, attacks, shadiness.

But they were all very nice and normal, mild and polite. Big smiles, soft hands. The only weird thing about them was the middlescale thing, which, okay, the middlescale thing is super weird.

The middlescale thing was this. When you become a banker, they freeze your scale account forever at a million munmuns, even when you retire or quit or get fired. Basically it's a guarantee of No Funny Business for all bankers. Meaning, you can't use your job or bank knowledge to make yourself huge.

So all bankers are middlescale forever and so down there in the halls and rooms inside a bank, every single person is middlescale, and it feels crazy to look at. Like being in Dreamworld except you're not real, everyone else is but not you, you're no longer a human and instead just a piece of someone else's dreamfluff.

Because banks need all kinds of different size rooms to manage all kinds of different transformations, all levels of Scale Up and Scale Down, most of the bank is underground, and the smaller you are, the deeper you go. So a littlevator like a jar in a tube dropped me deep into the earth.

Hue stayed somewhere shallower. We vidded each other before my Scale Up and he explained, he's meeting Paddy at Paddy's local bankbranch, they'll sort out Prayer's munmuns so she doesn't have to scale all the way down to little and then scale back up again.

"Dawn will drive you home, I'll bring Prayer home with me after work tonight, and we'll all see each other at familydinner," said Hue. "Enjoy your new scale, Warner. We're all expecting great things from you."

"I will, thank you, ofcourse, the greatest things, you're welcome," I burbled like a maniac.

I guess another strange thing about bankers is the hoods and coats, muncolored coats and hoods everywhere, the pinks and creams of toys and cakes.

•••

A bankdoctor interviewed me, asked me medical questions.

"Have you had dental work, crowns, fillings, molds," he said, squinting into my little mouth.

"I don't know," I said.

"Have you ever been to a dentist?" he asked.

"Nope," I said.

"Okay great, and nothing artafishill in your body, no screws, stitches, pacemakers, bloodtunnels, anything like that," he asked.

"I don't know," I said.

"Has a doctor put any foreign objects in you, things that aren't part of your body," he said.

"Do doctors do that?" I asked.

"Not if they're not supposed to," said the winking bankdoctor.

"Firsttime, huh, congratulations," warmed a nice banker outside the scaleroom, holding cute diagrams, "so here's what happens, we'll be giving you scalemeds, singing ritual songs, and then leaving you in a tub to fall asleep. Now because of the scalemeds, Dreamworld is going to seem a little strange to you. For one thing, your dreambody will be changing scale."

"Wait, what, is that even possible," I said.

"It's what naturally happens when your body is changing scale here in Lifeanddeath," instructed the banker. "One more thing, your dreaming will be completely solitarry, meaning alone, you are not going to encounter any other dreamers."

"Holy crap," I said.

"It can upset and even harm dreamers to see other dreamers change scale in Dreamworld," taught the banker, "believeitornot,

153

in some cases that spectacle can make people go insane forever, it's so unsettling and deestaybullizing. Fortunately there is a med called solodream that can wall you off from every other dreamer, so dontworry! We'll give you a ton of it, it's completely harmless, no known sideeffects, it's kept Dreamworld safe from scaling dreamers for many years."

I was quiet and infact couldn't really believeitornot.

"Meds change dreams?" I asked eventually.

"In ways we don't even know about!" cried this cheerfull banker. "Anyway have fun!"

I watched silently as the bankers prepped the tub, thinking about solodream and scaledream, I mean what the heck, how many other worldshaping things do I not even know exist.

"What do you think of the underbank," asked another nice banker finally.

My blown mind tried to think of a joke.

"Did you guys all mean to dress the same today or was it an accident," I said.

"Ha ha ha ha ha," she said without really laughing.

"Is this an insane and crazy place to work," I said.

"Half the time, it's wonderfull," she said.

"What about the other half," I said.

"Don't worry about that half if you don't have to," she winked.

Finally the tub was ready, empty but with the hoses hooked up and everything, and it all went as planned, the bankers handed me a thimble of bitter tea with scalemeds, hummed and sang quiet banksongs while I sipped it, then they left the room.

Hanging on a hook was my future robe, a robe for someone halfscale, huge to my little eyes.

I stripped naked and left my old clothes on the ground. The tubdoor opened and I walked out into the middle and lay down on my back.

The tubdoor closed, I was one lonely grape in a bowl. The lights cooled, dimmed, died, and I was in blackness.

Warm jelly crept up to me, touched my fingers, calves, sides, slid under me, and lifted me up into Dreamworld.

DREAMWORLD

But it wasn't Dreamworld, or else it was but everyone was awake, or dead, because it was a Dreamworld for only me, alone.

I swam up through the ground from the underbank and saw a stadium above me. But a little one like a toy, I was already huge. I hooped through it like a dolphin but no one was there, big or little, no one in the stands or streets.

I was big and blowing up bigger and bigger like a balloon, the strangest feeling, everyone knows in Dreamworld you can't change your size.

But I was huger every minute in the empty city. I plucked houses off the hills like fruit, rolled myself in cloud, stepped off the coast to pinch and drag some islands, bit the sun. No one saw me, no one stopped me, no one helped.

Soon I was so big, I graduated through the sky and was in the ink of space, the worldplanet shrinking into me like a melting stone. I tried to make more dreamstuff, a world I couldn't outgrow, tried to dream a huger earth under my feet, but all I could do was touch and grab the stuff that was already there, drizzly comets, powdery stars.

Warner, I said soundlessly, can you not control your dreamstuff or what, what's the freaking problem, plunge out of the sky and back into Lossy Indica like an amazing bird, readysetgo, but no Lossy Indica appeared below me, no Yewess even.

So I reached out and started pulling the guts out of this nothingness around me.

There was groaning and whispering and in my fists was something that wasn't nothing, almost but notquite, wisps, strands, vapors.

Creaking, crying, slipping ripping, outerspace was an unlit underground room and the walls were paper, I was straining them, stressing them, little gills of light breathed through.

I reached through one, grabbed either side, tried just tearing it open like a box.

"Oh no," said outerspace.

I got an elbow in there, really jammed it around.

"No no no," yelled outerspace. "Nope."

But I stuck my head through.

"Help," cried outerspace, but it wasn't outerspace, it was a horrified banker in the white windowless underbank, and right about then, the lights came on.

LIFEANDDEATHWORLD

I woke up in a littletub, in a littleroom, alone, crazy with thirst and hunger.

But it wasn't a littletub, it was the same middletub as the one I fell asleep in, same middleroom too, I was just fivetimes bigger.

I gasped like a fish, trying to fill my roomy lungs.

"Do you mind if we come in and help you adjust," asked a banker over the pee ay, and I could only nod, couldn't use my voice.

The bankers came in and my heart jumped to see them shrunk to just twice as big as me, littlepoor allofasudden. Except they weren't, Warner they're still middlescale, you're just bigger now, halfscale, middlepoor, you lucky idiot.

I flailed my big numb arms, grayed from bloodlessness, asleep and wobbly.

The bankers handed me a bottle of water so small it fit in my hands, except it wasn't small, I was just bigger, bigenough to hold waterbottles now, my thoughts kept hiccuping.

I drank it so fast I choked. I gripped the bottle, crinkled its thin plastic, felt like a oneyard god. I stood up in the bankers' arms, tried to fall down, the bankers wouldn't let me. They toweled me off, kept me on my feet, walked me into the robe on the wall, now my size exactly. They gave me another bottle of water and some powerbars and I drank and ate like an animal, sloppy and desperate.

We practiced standing, walking, it took an hour to figure out the ground under my feet, the feeling of being in a fivetimes shrunkdown space.

I saw my old clothes on the floor, reached down, picked them up, and that's when I started crying, harder than ever before, dirty little dollrags that used to fit my body, the clothes of sad little previous me.

It was like Prayer said. The most normal boring things felt amazing. Walking, breathing, talking, nottalking and just making sounds with your throat. Touching things, holding them. Everything in my hands had incredible textures. Wallpaper, plastics, rubbers, clothing. When you're littlepoor, the threads of fabrics are ropes a lot of times, nothing really soft about it. But when you have middlehands to hold them they melt together into fantastic softness.

159

On the drive home we ordered fried chickens and Kitty handed me a wing, the entire wing of a chicken, and I bit through the crinkly bready skin and into the slippery wingmuscle all in one bite, first time in my life, and a beautifull warmth filled my mouth, salt, juice, herbsandspices, I shrieked through closed lips.

"What did you eat growing up?" Kitty wanted to know.

For some reason I felt like I had to joke, play it cool, *be normal, Warner, nothing amazing has happened and definitely don't burst into tears.*

"Oh, same same," I told her. "My family raised littlechickens."

"What?" said Dawn. "Littlechickens? I've never heard of such a thing."

"Sure, littlechickens on our littlefarm," I said, trying to joke, more just babbling. "With littlecows and littledogs. Littlehorses in the littlebarn."

Dawn moved her lips, repeating me silently, watching the road, Kitty watched me with the pretty eye a littlebit wall.

"You're joking," guessed Dawn in a laughless voice.

"No joke," I blurted. "We used to fry up littlechickens just like this everyday on our littlefarm, littlefarm on a littlemountain, on a littleisland, a whole littleworld that middleriches don't know about, so little you can't even see it unfortunately, wish you could."

Kitty said, "Yeah, Mom, he's joking."

"That is funny, hahaha," agreed Dawn, trying to laugh afterthefact.

160

"Sorry, I won't ask you questions about your old littlelife if you don't want," Kitty whispered a little later.

"Nono, it's okay," I said, she didn't though and I was glad.

Prayer was waiting for me on the steps of Hue Family Palace, old toobig clothes hanging loosely off the shoulders of my divorced sis, flyswatter arms dangling out of the folds.

Ofcourse it was an emotional scene, tons of crying, hugging, laughcrying, a little just plain regular laughing, grouphugging with Kitty's legs to tell her, *we know you're responsible and you did all of this, therefore thanks.*

With my sis around it was a little easier for me to get weepy in front of Kitty and Dawn, we thanked them a million times.

"Well, thank Warner too, dontforget," Kitty made sure to tell Prayer.

"Noneed," I said, "are you kidding, I'm required to share everything with my sis, otherwise she slaps my face."

But Kitty didn't laugh, just grimaced with that scrunchy mouth, *in our house we're not huge fans of faceslapping.*

"No, Warner, forreal thankyou so much, bro, I'll never be able to thank you enough," said Prayer hastefully.

"Okay sure, I'm the best," I agreed.

We didn't really have space to catch up, instead Kitty toured us around the giant echoless rooms. Everywhere was tapestries and rugs, curtains, wallcarpet. My voice felt huge in my throat, but outside of my head it was still shadowless, flat.

The steps and furniture were middlerichscale obviously, but fitted out for middlepoor use also, middlesteps and stepstools and footladders off to one side of everything, pretty little pieces of mahogany, cedar, copper, glasstic.

"Is this all for us," I asked.

"Oh no no, we've hosted middlepoors before," explained Kitty. "Kids on scholarship for med school and tech school. My dad really tries to be a cityboss for all citizens of Almanac, not just the riches in Wet but also the poors down in Eat, so he spends lots of time down there, touring schools and giving prizes to kids who aren't screwups."

Immediately I felt a little less special.

"How long do you host kids for," Prayer asked.

"Usually a year," she said.

In addition to less special I began to feel panic.

"We'll make it a good year for sure," I announced.

"Oh hey, no no no, don't worry," she said. "You'll be here as long as you need. With you guys it's my program too, not just my dad's, he knows you're different."

"We really appreciate that," Prayer said, wide real smile saying, *bytheway, I mean it.*

Again I felt gratefull for having the sis there, it took atleast half the pressure off to have the proper reactions, probably more than half really.

There were two dogs, huge fat saintbernards, Welfargo and Cittibang. We rode them like horses through the yard until they collapsed, then we lay with them in a deathheap.

Rules of the house were pretty simple:

—here's your key, only your hand can activate it, that's for security reasons

—familydinner is at seven and everyone has to be in their seats ontime, it's been a problem sometimes for past houseguests, I would say even fiveminutes early is best

—you can go back out after dinner but curfew is eleven, we have pretty strict curfew too and that's also been a problem for past houseguests, one had a secret career dancing in bellyclubs, Dad had to kick him out, actually he's still doing it because I check his feed sometimes and he seems super happy, belly's looking good too

—here are all the locations of the guns, extinguishers, bombs, floodhoses, panicdoors, backup generators, hey don't look so worried, the last terrorattack in Wet was five years ago almost, we're much more nervous about fires tobehonest

—Mom and Dad are on the topfloor, kids are on the secondfloor, you two are inbetween floors in this middleroom we had specially created for middleguests, kitchen dining hosting on the firstfloor, theater gym and practicerooms in the basement, bunker in the subbasement, we don't give guests the bunkercode and I'm really sorry about that

—here's a foldphone for each of you, sorry it's so basic, limited dataplan but it's not really an issue because a foldphone can't really use most kinds of data, try not to open vids or gifs though, again I'm sorry, yours as long as you stay with us

—I know I already said about dinner but it's a pretty bigdeal, we do take it seriously and you just don't want my dad to start thinking you don't want to be here, so, just remember, fiveminutes to seven

163

Surenough all four Hue Family Kids were in their seats a few minutes before dinner and so were Prayer and me, gazing around at these pictureperfect modelcitizens.

Older brother Hueagain was nineteen, in med school, a nice quiet strong guy waking up early to go for runs or lift weights. Studied hard, first in his class, rarely talked, usually just smiled a funny painfull smile, the smile of true kindness but also definitely a little fear in there.

Older sister Daisy was sevteen, highschool senior. Dawn liked to talk about the extreme genius Daisy used to be in her early years, doing advanced sciences, animating cartoons, threedee printing her own crazy dreamscapes. But mysteriously this superchild blossomed into a normal sullen teenager, always in her room being irritated by her terrible siblings.

Younger sister Kitty was fifteen, my age, sopmore. Kitty was dad Hue's favorite for sure. Did Kitty love being dad's favorite?, yup, bigtime.

Younger brother Tony was thirteen, wore suits, combed hair, clearly wished he was dad's favorite and not stupid Kitty, modeled himself after dad completely but got the details a little wrong, a little exaggerated, told more nervous jokes than dad, laughed more when nothing was funny, worried more about whether you liked him. So actually for Hue it was probably like having a little clown running around the house, pretending to be you, except the dumb pathetic version.

But whatdoyouexpect, he's a kid, maybe he'll turn out okay, sure hope so because this kid needs to chill.

"I had a shallwesay *refreshing* exchange with some Oranges in class today," Tony announced at my first familydinner. He meant kids with Orange Party beliefs, enemy of Hue's party the Yellows.

"I bet you did," said Hue, immediately also saying, "Warner, Prayer, thank you for being prompt, as you can perhaps tell it's important to us to have familydinner together everynight, and here's why. A major problem for bigger middles is that with all of our vids and tech, we forget to make time for each other. So familydinner is a time to check in, be together, and remember what's truly important in life."

"That is really lovely, and you guys are valuing the right things in life forsure," agreed Prayer.

"Warner, Prayer, Dad, the exchange was shallwesay *refreshing*, because as I was defeating them with arguments, they sprayed me with refreshing juice," explained Tony.

"Okay," said Hue. "Warner, how was your first day at your new scale? How was Scale Up and everything?"

"Great, amazing, forsure," I said.

I felt timid and small, so I made a silence and Tony jumped in.

"It's like, nicework, geniuses!" said Tony. "Now you have less juice."

"Not your best story, Tony," said Hueagain through a mouth of porkthighs.

"Warner, Prayer, you should know that Hue was born middlepoor, infact below halfscale until he was a teenager," Dawn told me. "So he knows what it's like to scale up majorly in life."

"Oh wow," Prayer said.

"Dang, noway," I said.

"Yes, it's true," said Hue. "My dad was a plumber and my mom sewed business shirts. So I know from personal experience that here in the Yewess, our scale doesn't limit our potenchill. That's the Yewess I know."

Daisy made a grumpy throatnoise, immediately got a deathstare from her mom.

"But another thing I know," continued Hue, "is we need to work harder at creating opportunities for poors, forsure. And too many riches and middles don't think poors can take advantage of opportunities. So Warner, Prayer, you're here because you deserve a second chance, sure, but also because I think you two can help me prove them wrong."

"Dad, okay," said Daisy.

"Daisy, we have guests," said Dawn.

"No kidding, Mom, we literally always have guests," snapped Daisy, as Kitty made sad smiling eyes at me of, *please forgive my sister, the jerk.*

"I really don't understand why you insist on behaving this way," said Dawn.

"What I don't understand is why Dad has to give a stumpspeech at dinner for an audience of his own freaking family, plus two nervous speechless kids Kitty met hanging around the jail and dragged here because she needs everyone to like her because she's basically Girl Dad," said Daisy.

"Whaaaaaat, over the line," chuckled Hueagain painfully, meanwhile Hue murmured, "Okay, Daisy," in a different voice from before, softer sadder family voice, also with the sympathetic face of, *my poor tragic daughter, maybe one morning she will wake up and no longer be a sociopath.*

"Prayer wasn't in jail, just me, Prayer was busy being married to a crusty freaking jerk," I corrected nervously.

"You should think about hanging around a jail, Daisy," suggested Kitty. "Then maybe someone would finally like *you.*"

"Ohmygod, are you even listening to yourself," cried Daisy.

"Daisy, it's never okay to attack poor Kitty," defended Tony, "anyway if anyone's similar to Dad I would say it's either me or Hueagain, except he's in med school and I'm more into politics, so, process of illumination, me."

"Everyone, silence," yelled Dawn. "Daisy, I need you to apologize to Warner and Prayer immediately."

Daisy locked eyes with me, then Prayer, then me again, not even angry.

"Warner, Prayer, I'm sorry," she said, getting up. "I'm sorry my jerky family wants you to be campainprops."

"That is not how anyone sees you, obviously," explained Kitty after Daisy left.

"As a little girl she was completely different," Dawn wanted us to know.

Tony's dumb words were the ones echoing in my head though, *never okay to attack poor Kitty,* what does that mean, didn't ask though.

DREAMWORLD

In the special cozy halfscale bedroom Prayer and I finally got to catch up, huddling and whispering. My voice still felt like a monster's boom to me but Prayer assured me it was still quiet and small.

"You're just not used to being halfscale yet, trustme, they can't hear us outside the room," she soothed.

Her day with Hue actually was prettygood. She said Hue seemed to like her, made a point of telling her how polite she was and wellbehaved and even charming, made it clear to her though that he really hoped she applied herself in the days and weeks and months to come.

"Kitty doesn't really want me here so I need her dad on my side," strategized Prayer.

"Whaaaat, that's crazy, ofcourse Kitty wants you here," I lied.

"Bro, comeon," said Prayer.

"Why do you think she doesn't want you," I asked. Prayer made a big shrug and eyeroll, *whoknows, actually I do probably know, judging from this enormous shrug and eyeroll, but I'm not going to tell you, why don't you just change the subject.*

So I asked her if she was sad about her dead marriage,

nononono, she whipped her head toandfro, if I never see Paddy again it's toosoon.

He wasn't cruel or evil, just thoughtless, to him she was a workdog or horse that cost too much, and the more work she did for him, the more he shrank into his bed and screens, the more he disappeared down holes and so did their munmuns.

"I do understand a little bit though, scaling down feels awfull, today I scaled down from threefifth to halfscale and even just that makes you feel so sick and sad, weak and helpless, your lungs don't bring in enough air and your tummy doesn't hold enough food," she sorrowed.

"Crap," I said.

"But enoughenough, I'll get used to it, how about you meanwhile, don't you feel amazing," she asked.

"I do," I admitted.

"Breathing, eating, wearing clothes, doesn't it all just feel so so good," she pressed.

"Super good, the best," I agreed.

She kept asking me about how it felt and how happy was I to be out of jail and pardoned and everything but my answers were short, I still didn't have a lot of words in me, prettysoon she was talking again just to fill the silence.

"The marriage was bad but I learned from it, bro," she declared, "I really did, just talking to customers and selling things and working out in the world, honestly I think I'm a grownwoman now, I'm a whole different person from a yearago, that littlegirl knew nothing but this middlewoman is going to attack life, attack opportunities, attack knowledge," and she kept talking as I kept sinking, she kept weaving and looming the spell that sent me off into Dreamworld.

In Dreamworld Kitty was waiting, the flowerhouse was crisper than I remembered, cracklier, less of a cartoon, more professional. But this time I could walk inside, easy, I stepped through a door and was in my own little operabox.

The inside of the flowerhouse was a giant concerthall, dome-shaped and honeycombed with cozy boxes for a thousand blissfull dreamers, in the centerbubble she sang and played the music from many years ago.

How can I tell you what it was like to hear it again, I can't.

But it was better than my memory of it, bigger and sharper and sweeter, actually the whole point was you can't remember it.

So all I did was float in my operabox, listen, relax, let the musicfingers push out the knots and stones from a year of angry fearfull nights.

And I went back the next night, and the next night, and the night after that, and just listened, floated, let my body go liquid.

Maybe it was the same song every time, I wouldn't know, no one could. It was too many notes, too many rhythms, too much texture, too glorious, your ears couldn't focus. It was a thousand parades on one street, a thousand lives in one life, a thousand years of living and dying in every second.

I began to realize, it was the music of This Is How The World Feels When You Are Huge.

Huger than Kittyscale forsure, Kittyscale is only twoandahalf, fouryards tall or so, not enormous.

Huger than billionair big, bigrich, eightscale, twelvyards, that's not bigenough for how this music makes you feel.

Maybe as huge as trillionair big, sicktyfourscale, hunyards. But probably huger than that.

The bigger you are, the smaller things get, the more things you can touch at a time and the more amazing little detail they have on your fingertips, toes, tongue.

The music fits into your dreaming ears the way Hue Family House could fit into your giant hand, if you wrappped your hand around the whole thing. Windows, brickwork, gutters, ivy, slateroof, columns, buckling crackling, crunching under your knuckles.

Music of the forest scratching your enormous godfeet, leafy barky trees between your toes, trickly streams dribbling under your arches.

Soundscape of mountain handfulls, thinly iced and melting into your fingerprints, crags digging into your thumbball.

If you were a god hugging the worldplanet and felt every single thing, big and little, pressing back into you to tell you, *I'm alive*, that was the music Kitty knew somehow to make, the music that swallowed me everynight.

Maybe it sounds overwhelming to you, exhausting, insane. But for a little red jailfish it's a way to recover, become yourself again, or atleast stop being the tight furious dreamless sleeper, reset to being no one.

For sure it was therapy, for sure it could heal someone with a hard bad life, afterall she was using it to heal herself.

And did I want to make my own wild dreamstuff again, sure, ofcourse I did. But I couldn't.

Everytime I tried to dream like previous me it was toohard, impossible, I wasn't me anymore. The bigger the stuff, the more my mind fought back, nightmarestyle.

Dream a snow of flowers, snow turns to rain, flowers turn to paint.

Dream some lazy airdogs, dogs turn to sharks, sharks get stuck in the air and die, floating ballooncorpses rotting and popping.

Dream water and it floods your house, dream trees and they block your way, dream rooms and they don't have what you're looking for, what are you looking for, you don't even know but time is running out.

Something in my head had broke and my dreaming was like other people's, incomplete and outofcontrol.

172

LIFEANDDEATHWORLD

And meanwhile my days were whirlwinds, trying to allofasudden live a busy middlerich existence and absorb a quality
education, spoileralert, this was completely impossible.

Step One, buy clothes, okay, that part was not so impossible. Hue and Tony took me to Fine Young Man for some stiff
officesuits and Sporty Run And Jump for casual athletic gear
to wear around the house, meanwhile Dawn and Kitty bought
Prayer some sensible ensembles at Study Girl and Busy Bee.

Secondpart, see some doctors, also fine and infact great.
We got our bloods inspected, hey greatnews, no one has a
sexdisease or cancer. A middlepoor dentist gave me replacement faketeeth, plastic stones in my mouth, whiter than the
real ones. "Reminder, faketeeth will not scale up or down with
the rest of your mouth so if you ever change scale you must
remove them first or you may risk serious injury," he said
super bored and fast, this guy must have to say it twentytimes
a day.

Stage Three though, attend Wet Almanac Middlerich
High, sorry poorkids, this is the impossible part.

• • •

173

First day at school was endless, a nonstop parade of hopeless tasks and humiliations. Sprint across the giant campus at topspeed, leap up bigsteps, arrive toolate at a shut door where you can't reach the doorknob. Scrabble wildly, a sternfaced professor cracks the door open, nexttime please just knock, noneed to claw the door like a dog who needs to pee. Swim and drown in discussions you can't understand, symbolic math, chemical processes, litratures of the world. Ask the teacher basic questions, repeat in a scream because your middlepoor voice is too small for the room, Sorry Who Was Toneymoorisson Again, all around you the doublescale kids nosebreathe with impatience, a muttery forest. Spend all of lunchtime not finding the foodcourt, ohwell, no lunch for Warner, stare longingly at garbagecans all afternoon and dream about the pizzarinds inside.

At familydinner Hue asked us how was our first day.

We paused like deerintheheadlights, is there any single part we can even describe.

"It is a very new and stimulating environment!" exclaimed Prayer. "That is for sure!"

Hue turned his sympathetic eyes to nodding silent me and said, "I know it's difficult, it's quite an adjustment atfirst, but please trust me and just stay with it, this is going to take you places you never thought you'd go."

The second day was ofcourse the same but worse, all the frantic scurrying and leaping and inability to understand, but with the professors now also asking, Warner have you completed yesterday's assignment, Warner I suggest you take notes, Warner we do take attendance promptly at the beginning of class and it is your responsibility to get here however you can, maybe you can buy a gocart.

Second night, more confident babbling from Prayer about all these new exciting ideaviruses she is being exposed to, more shaky silence from me.

"Warner, you're a hero just for trying your hardest, I know you will succeed," cheered Kitty, Daisy tried to roll her eyeballs all the way into the back of her face.

But it didn't get better, Warner this essay is unreadable, Warner that presentation was incohearant, Warner these testresults are actually worse than random guessing and it's hurting our classaverage, until you learn the material may I recommend just punching random letters.

A few more impossible days ground us down and look, in the end I couldn't pretend it made sense for us to stay, you couldn't either.

What did it was, in the planetarium I overheard mocking kids talk about us.

But they weren't mocking me, not Prayer either, instead it was Kitty.

Idiot yellowtard girl bringing two ratty hardluck poors to our school who probably can't even read, just so she can feel better about herself, ugh what a dumb selfish slut, youwish she was a slut you horny bonehead, that's true she needs to be less of a prude I would smash that, you know who's a slut though Fern is a huge slut, et set set setera.

Prettysoon these boys weren't talking about Kitty or me but I walked off campus that afternoon knowing we couldn't stay at this school for educated riches. It was law school alloveragain. We just didn't belong.

I tried to tell this to Prayer before dinner but she freaked out.

"Warner you idiot, we're going to lose everything if you say that, do you think Hue wants us to transfer from nice hard school to sad easy school, nope, wrong, the opposite," she hissed.

"Neither of us has learned anything and instead everyone hates us," I pointed out.

"We just have to try harder, ofcourse the first days are going to be hard but we belong if we *decide* to belong, so just decide it, dummy," Prayer argued.

"We literally don't belong," I yelled. "Look around nexttime at school, tell me if you see one person our scale, nope, zero. I mean Prayer you belong even less than I do, you read slower than me, your legs don't sprint fast as mine, they've got you taking junioryear classes and that's way too advanced."

"Good," shrieked Prayer. "Put me in the most advanced. I will outsprint everyone and get all ays, I have a raging bottomless hunger for success, *Prayer stops at nothing*."

But still I piped up at dinner, "Hue Family, I am super appreciative of everything, gottasay though I just really don't think middlerich school is working for me, I think maybe middlepoor school is a better fit."

Surenough, there were grim reactions allaround, Hue was the grimmest. Meanwhile, under the table Prayer was forkstabbing me.

"Warner, I'm going to be frank," Hue rumbled. "At your age, ofcourse through no fault of your own, you just have a lot of ketchup to do and not a lot of time to do it, and I'm doubtfull that a middlepoor school will challenge you in the way that you need."

"Everyone thinks you're a dummy, don't you want to prove them wrong," helped Tony.

"Hue, Tony, everyone, let me explain with a mentalpicture," I pleaded. "Envision school as a stairway to knowledge. Now picture that each step of this stairway is too big for your legs. Infact the first step is way above your head. You just can't use this stairway, you'll never get up to knowledgeworld no matter how hard you try."

Prayer was muttering nopenopenopewrongs but I continued, "I truly believe what will get me up to all that great knowledge is some smaller stairs that fit my halfscale legs, and you betterbelieve I'll race up those stairs as fast as I can, if those dinky schools don't challenge me enough, dontworry, I'll challenge myself, I know you will too, just give me the right stairs, *Prayer you need to stop freaking stabbing me.*"

177

"Prettygood metafore," mumbled munching Hueagain. "Maybe he should go into politics."

"As the one who knows about politics, I don't agree," disagreed Tony.

"Prayer, do you also find Wet Almanac High too difficult," asked Hue.

"Are you kidding, wildhorses will have to drag me out of there kicking and screaming," promised Prayer. "Challenges are my favorite thing, second only to achievements, can I just remind everyone that I am in it to win it."

"Kitty, what do you think," wondered Dawn.

"I'd miss having Warner at school," whispered sweet Kitty. "But I do understand."

"Why would you miss having him, it's making everyone hate you," asked Daisy.

In the end Hue okayed me to transfer, but with warnings and conditions of We Need Results From You, I didn't ask what those exact results were and he didn't tell me.

And so I transferred to the nearest middlepoor school, down in Eat Almanac, a school with the proud important name of Eat Almanac Middlepoor Vocational and Technical, Eat Votech forshort.

Eat Almanac is a floodplain that doesn't flood anymore, hot dusty desert gazing up at the Wet Almanac hillsides. It's a little strange ofcourse that both towns are Almanacs, I guess it's kind of like having a brother and sister of different scales. Wet is the leafy land of riches, middle and big, down in Eat is very different, lots of cinderblock compounds, factories, dealerships, sweatshops, Mun Worlds.

A Mun World is a vast shopscape, pretty common in middlepoor districts, infact there's one right across the parkinglot from Eat Votech.

Actually the school seems like Mun World's little grubby echo, similar squat blank cinderblock struction, similar wide flat warehouse, worse paint job, similar number of cops, forthatmatter similar number of Votech students because at any moment many students are not taking classes and instead chilling in Mun World.

What kind of school is Eat Votech, gladyouasked, Eat Votech features the Track System.

Track System means when you show up, they figure out what you do the best, then they put you on a track where you only keep doing that thing.

Usually they start by seeing, are you good at math. If you show up to Eat Votech good at math, congratulations, you're on Mathy Track, math and science classrooms for you, and when you graduate you get to work in labs, lots of munmuns coming your way.

Bad at math but can read and write, noprob, you're on Wordy Track, writing and editing for whoever needs words to sound good, decent munmuns.

Can't read so good but talk pretty clever and confident, great, you're on Busy Track, a life in sales or business, better munmuns alotoftimes than Wordy Track even, a little messedup how that works.

Dumb at everything so far but clever with your hands, fine, you're on Handy Track, fixing cars and robots. Clumsy hands, welcome to Drivy Track, learn to drive stuff around, or Lifty Track, learn to carry heavy stuff, Cleany Track, clean and scrub, Servy Track, politely serve people and shut up.

Day One for me was notsogood. It was me in an unwindowed room with two sleepy middlepoor counselors, were they excited to meet this new mystery student named Warner, nope, not even a little, let's just figure out this bonehead's track realfast and maybe we can get an early lunch, afterward cross the parkinglot and rummage through great deals at Mun World.

We started with math, and I was a littlebit hopefull, I'm not terrible at math. Numbers make sense in my head, just not when you throw letters in there too, what is that even about.

"Pick the answer you think is right," they said, ay bee see dee.

"Can I maybe get this read to me outloud," I said.

"Ecks minus three is three," they said.

"Good, good," I said. "This thing answers itself. I'm pretty sure it's not even a question."

"Your choices are zero, three, six, and ecks," they said.

"Can't go wrong with ecks," I said.

"You can and did, so let's cross off Mathy Track and move on," they said, but the readingsample was disaster numbertwo.

They gave me four little pages about volcanoes and rock science, half the words in there were a crazy vowel aircomma festival, I had fifteenminutes to read it and didn't even get to page two.

"No Wordy Track for you," they said. "How about you try and sell us this pen."

"Do you want this pen," I said. "It's super great."

"Not really," they said.

"Do you know anyone who wants a pen," I said.

"Nope," they said.

"Guess I get to keep a great pen, suckers," I said, but they took the pen.

"Here's a puzzle," they said, handing me two bentup wires all tangled around in each other, and watched me grapple with it for a while like a rackoon, noluck.

"Here's a driving game," they said, giving me a little driving simscreen, instant carcrash, wow, programmers had tons of fun putting screams in there.

"You seem good at pushups," they said finally, so I dropped to the gritty floor and started pushupping, and after I got to fifty I glanced up to see them giving each other grim satisfied looks of, *secretly we knew allalong this was where we were headed*, and the younger one said, "Welcome to Lifty Track, sign these forms please, don't need your whole name, W is fine, thereyougo."

"This is prettymuch what I was afraid of," frowned Hue.

"He'll study with me and retake the test in six weeks, dontworry Dad, he'll retrack for sure," promised Kitty.

"I hope so, for his sake," grimmed Hue.

"I hope so too," I agreed, wasn't the right thing to say though.

DREAMWORLD

And what about Prayer, great question, she stayed at Wet Almanac Middlerich. It was a life of tasks she couldn't do, languages she didn't speak, problems she couldn't solve, and distances she couldn't cover.

It was grades of FAIL and PLEASE REWRITE and SEE A COUNSELOR OR SOMETHING, attendance records of LATE and ABSENT and STUCK IN THE LOCKERCAGE AGAIN, misery and mockery everywhere you look, but she was determined to succeed.

But it took a bad toll, I could tell in Dreamworld, she needed Kitty Music even more than me, just lay there like a zombie corpse in her operabox, letting the songs massage and crush her.

Every morning I woke up first, I had the longer commute, long walk to the busstop and a longer busride to Eat. So rightbefore I left I would shake her awake, and always there was two or three seconds of sick terror on her face, pleading eyes of, *ohno I can't do it again,* saggy mouth of, *please don't make me spend one more day pretending like this could ever be a success.*

Then she'd shake it off or swallow it, smile bravely, tell me, "Thanks bro, have a good day at school, just hope you're learning as much as me," gottahandit to my sis, she's a fighter.

LIFEANDDEATHWORLD

Was I learning as much as Prayer, definitely not. I had to agree
with Hue, Lifty education was kind of a joke.

Lifty classrooms were basically gyms and the entire morning was just bodywork. Throw weights around, jog on a
hamsterwheel, fight the waves of the sloshy drowningpool, and
ofcourse play vicious sports with the intention of kill the other team.

Then the afternoons weren't super bookish either, mostly just
simulations and preparations for the most common Lifty jobs,
mining, drilling, shipping, whaling, sharking, struction and maintenance, firefights, floodfights, rubbleclearing, disasters ingeneral.

Lots of periods were free because there weren't enough teach-
ers to go round, hey guys for the next hour and twentyminutes
how about you go chill with your crew in Mun World or the
parkinglot, hope you have a crew though, otherwise those times
will be pretty lonely.

But even lonely strolls through Mun World can be exciting for
a kid who was ratscale a weekago.

Mun World was miraculous to me, an endless shopscape of aisles
for miles. Infact that's the jingle, Aisles For Miles At Mun World,

Miles is even the name of the storepet, a flatscreen with arms and legs who dances endlessly near the frontdoors.

The point of Mun World is, everything you need for middlepoor life is available here, no need to look for anything anywhere else, youneedit wegotit, clothes, food, chairs, drugs, phone and water contracts, toiletseats, littledogs, guns, frozenfoods, microwaves, lottery and gameshow tickets, dolls, bombs, guitars, we have them all and more, spend your munmuns only at Mun World please.

So Mun World was paradise, for that reason also a dangerous terrorzone. Paradise because everything was something that fit in my hands, begging me to buy it, bright slick magical object made justforyou, take it back to your middleroom and own it, hold it, hug it, an amazing feeling. Notescreens, skateboards, hairgel, bodyspray.

But mostofall the clothes, the styles, ohmygod.

Here in Mun World were shoes that fit my feet like the shoefactory had met me, infact known me my whole life, faithfully made me hundreds of perfect shoes in beautifull rows and stacks. Here were hats that fit my head, shirts that hugged my arms and belly, pants that squeezed my butt into terrific shapes.

Here were soft cool wild fabrics, bright violent colors, fresh new styles.

And the freshest of all was Fresh But Chill, in Highend Halfscale Fashion, you have no idea.

Fresh But Chill was the style I desired in my deepest heart, in my happiest dreams. Hoodies chockfull of mesh and ribs, soft mysterious teeshirts crowding and bustling with secret logos, tattery clingpants and leglets, shoes as chunky and gleamy as doublecars, and dontforget the skinnybelts.

"Well, will you get a load of this hunky posterboy for Fresh But Chill," said Lease the flirty shopgirl the first time I tried on a full outfit, "can you let me admire you for just ten seconds, please."

She was doing a great job of admiring me so I rewarded her with a spin move, followup with an overtheshoulder glance and waggled my butt like a naughty little dude.

"Wow and dang, mostly wow but a littlebit dang forsure, hey Jeans you gotta see these fly dancemoves," Lease exclaimed to her salesfriend Jeans, who can blame her.

And Jeans hustled over, the salesfriends oohandahed, for a few minutes I was the wild fresh king of Mun World.

"If you walk out of here not in those clothes, it's a literal crime," worried Lease.

But the outfit came to twohunfifty munmuns, five weeks of my fiftymun allowance, more than my entire munflow at that time.

"I can't afford it," I whispered in shame.

"Tell you what," said friendly Jeans. "For just a starter rate of a hundo a week you can become a lifelong subscriber to Fresh But Chill, constant deliveries of the sharpest chillest style, you'll be hookedup forever and it's the best value byfar, sicktypercent off this outfit for example."

"It's double my allowance though, my munflow will run out," I said, the dancemoves have drained out of me and my voice was a humiliated squeak.

"Wait just a second here, you're telling me a fresh strong dude like you has no job and instead relies on a sad little allowance," said Lease, getting a little tough.

"I'm sure some zone of Mun World is hiring if you need an income," suggested Jeans more hopefully, but I was already fleeing in disgrace, ducking back into the dressingroom and throwing on my stiff dumb officeclothes.

So that's what I mean by Mun World was a place of constant terror. My allowance was so limited, obviously I had to save it up and never spend it, and worstofall I had the feeling of I can't trust myself, once you let yourself spend onetime once, it's a slipperyslope, suddenly you're broke and brokenleg at the bottom, can't climb back up.

Even just a little nothing purchase like bodyspray, I had the sick nightmare worry that if I said to myself, *no problem, Warner, you'll just make one exception to buy this one bodyspray bottle because girls hate it if you don't smell brisk,* the next day I make another exception for some hairclay, invisible grit to rub into your hair to make it more vertical, seem less poor, andsoonandsoforth and prettysoon I've broken down, made ten exceptions and bought the deluxe subscription to Fresh But Chill, looking like a sweet boss but can't even afford the bus.

One more aspect of life on the Lifty Track, some days we had Guest Lectures. These were from businesses offering to cover an early graduation that very day for any student who wanted a better brighter future.

The most successfull of these were forhire armies, hey Lifters, come guard oilships for the Ondemand Navy, or else sit in the comfy aircondition bunker of Hoverbomb Alacart and destroy pirates in a reallife shootemup. Get the thrills of battle alongside valuable corporate experience, plus seven times out of ten it's for noneother than the Yewess government, don't you want to be a mostofthetime patriot.

Others it was a little harder to figure out what they were trying to hire us for, ee gee on my third day of school when a sweaty guy in a suit threw open the doors and made us call him the Empowerist.

"You can walk out the door with me *today* if you decide you want a better brighter future with Power Life Future," declared the Empowerist. "Build a team, watch it grow, work from home, be a leader, the future is literally in your hands, all you have to do is shape it with the power to say *yes!*"

"I have a question," said a kid named Brand.

"Being upfront with questions is a thousandpercent the attitude that makes you a perfect fit for Power Life Future!" declared the Empowerist. "Bytheway I am in love with your personal energy! *Go!*"

"How do you get the munmuns, like where do they come from," said Brand, a kid of, I have to tell you, not amazing personal energy.

"Ohmygod, incredible question," loudly whispered the Empowerist. "Because what you're asking is, what *business* is Power Life Future in, and that's the fundamental question of any business. Now heresthething. If your business isn't the business of *people*, then you're not a business, you're just some *company*. But we're so much more than that because what are we?"

No one answered him so he yelled, "A business! Ha ha! *Yes!*"

"Who pays you munmuns though and for what," said Brand.

"Young powerseeker, here's another way of thinking about your question," said the Empowerist. "What industry is Power Life Future in?, the education industry?, nutrition industry?, home agriculture and manufacturing industry?, answer, yesyesyes but more importantly *no, wrong, none* of those, are we even in the subscription industry?, sure, but *no, wrong again*, because here's the deepestlevel story, we're in the *wayoflife* industry. As a Power Life Future native, you will have your life changed by our products, *then* you can and will tell everyone you know, friends, family, even randos on the bus, you'll tell them I know forafact that I'm offering guaranteed lifechangers, because these products have literally changed my life. You know what 'literally' means?, it means, I'm not messing around here. You're going to tell loved ones, I subscribe to Power Life Future's informational vids and guesswhat. They literally open up whole new realms of thought I never knew were possible. I subscribe to Power Life Future mineralshakes, I feel my body *and* my brain growing stronger everyday, I subscribe to these seedpackets! I'm literally *growing my own dinner and seasonings!* I subscribe to threedee printing softwares and monthly shipments of Power Life Future's proprietary plastic slabs and I am manufacturing, *in my own home*, plates, forks, mugs, all the dining essentials you can't eat without!"

I glanced at Teacher, caught his eye, he frowned and shrugged like, *sure, I guess, whynot.*

"So, you're hiring salesreps," said Brand.

"No," said the Empowerist, "nonono, look, you've a littlebit missed the point but I continue to be obsessed with your personal energy, whatsyourname?, *Brand*, oh spectacular name, thankyou, Brand, any-way sales is what we do only at the most superficial level because what you're doing is *beyond* selling, because here's the bestpart. You're not just going to sell to everyone you know, you're going to recruit *them* to Power Life Future, and when your recruits make sales, guesswhat?, here's the mindblowing part that makes this a whole wayoflife, *you get a cut*, and when *their recruits* make sales, *guesswhat thatsright you get a cut*, onandon down the line and you betterbelieve it adds up pretty darn quick and *that's* what I mean by a future whose only limits are defined by your power to say *yes!* Brand. Your team could be making you a hunthousand munmuns every month, without you selling a thing. Twohunthousand! *Fourhunthousand,* because you have a vision, you're bringing people a better life and *it's your life*," raved the Empowerist and a bunch more stuff like that, and look, maybe it looks a little crazy on paper but in sweaty stuffy Lifty Gym, gottabehonest, it started sounding good to me.

I mean all you have to do, soundslike, is not even sell stuff, just hire other people to sell the stuff and you get munmuns from what they sell. And how hard could it be to find people who want jobs, I mean who doesn't come running when you yell, "Jobs, got some fresh hot jobs right here, I am a nice friendly boss who will hire you onthespot."

But Tray saw my ears perking up or my eyes going wide and shiny or something and muttered, "Warner, chill, badidea," so I chilled, and the Empowerist left super sweaty with no recruits that day.

•

Tray was one of the fatterlooking Lifty kids, no muscle definition and no rascally dave behavior either, no guns or tats, so he was not super popular, prettymuch the opposite, therefore one of the few kids willing to be friends with friendless Warner. Pretty brainy guy for Lifty Track, but also super depressed, sourfaced, everythingsucks, whatsthepoint.

He explained to me during rubblework, "My cousin Gram works for one of those foodchain operations, everyday it destroys his life."

"Whatdoyoumean foodchain operation," I said.

"A business constructed like a vampire type foodchain," said Tray. "You got a predator up top, he sells you a subscription, chomp, now you got a straw in your neck, dave's drinking your blood every month. So now you're prey and your only hope is, become a littler predator, trying to get other preys to buy your subscriptions, put your little straws in other people's necks."

"What do you mean about straws," I said, thinking about Fresh But Chill, getting a shuddery feeling.

"Subscription sucks munmuns out of your munflow every month like through a straw," said Tray. "And worstpart is, straw is stuck there like permanently, you can't pull it out, because a true foodchainop puts all kinds of hooks and glues on there where the straw hits your neck."

"Hooks, glues, the heck are you even talking about," said Brand, waddling up.

"It works like this, you call to pull out the straw, cancel the subscription, company says oops sorry we're just the middleman, you have to take it up with this other company, next company says the same thing, finally you get to the distributor but *they* say sorry we outsource to five different providers and you need to call them directly but before we put you in contact with them we need to start collecting removalfees, and bytheway the providers are going to hit you with removalfees too, you're like dang, crap, thissucks, then they're like well buuuuuut, hey, another alternative is we could just readjust your subscription, lower rate, you're like that sounds better to me, they go ahead and lower your cost this month but next month you find out the subscriptioncost tripled permanently, ohmygoodness, it's eight different kinds of crazy predator moves, Gram lost half his scale already," said Tray, clearing rubblestones ferociously.

"Dang," I said, catching rubble like a champ, I was pretty amazing at rubblework.

"But soundslike all you got to do is find other preys," said Brand.

191

Brand was also fatlooking, pretty dumb, like I said not terrific personal energy, but atleast chill and not evil. Also he was the only other kid who agreed to be newguy Warner's friend, because newguys at school are always considered weird and treated with suspicion by the studentbody atlarge, so welcome to Team Warner, dumb chill Brand.

"Brand," said Tray. "Two answers to that, intheory and inpractice. Intheory answer first, is the foodchain infinite, nope, it has a bottom layer of sad planteaters getting snacked on. Bottom layer supports all the other layers, therefore it has to be byfar the biggest. So mathwise if you join the foodchain you're probably one of the planteaters, the ones getting attacked and bloodsucked and never finding blood to suck and instead just munching plants, consequence of noninfinite populationsize, right, okay, withmesofar."

"Nope," said Brand, peering around for the bodydoll under all the rubblestones.

"That's fine, because here's your inpractice answer, ask my cousin Gram if it's easy to find preys," said Tray. "Betteryet, don't, because he'll try to turn you into a prey, like he tries to do at family beebeecues, it's a nightmare, everyone hates him now."

"FOUND THE BODY," yelled some tatty daves across the rubblepile, yanking out the body, arm popping off. "TEACHER WE SAVED IT."

"Allright, be carefull, we don't have a lot of those," yelled Teacher, hustling to save the body from being jacked up by victorious daves who now were running around taunting all the loser crews who didn't find the bodydoll, lol wewin, youlose, when we graduate we will get struction and maintenance, meanwhile you'll be hacking up lungs in the oilrock mines, lololol.

But they skipped us completely, why would you waste even one lol taunting some janky outcasts, two fatties and one newkid.

Tray, Brand, Warner, we were not Votech's most popular crew, probably closest to most ignored crew, but look, great, most ignored is just fine, perfect really.

Most ignored doesn't mean completely ignored though, prettyquick a kid found me in the parkinglot.

"You're the newkid Warner, right," he asked.

And flashed his hands, bullfaces tatted on their backs, horns up the thumb and pinkey, ohno.

The bulls were supposed to be a happysad combo like the theatermasks you see sometimes, but instead the combo was more like sleepycrazy, crazy one is snorting fire and sleepy one looks more like a goat.

"Nope nope, super different kid," I said to this faceboy, prepared to run or pulp.

"Dave, be chill," he urged. "I'm not a faceboy anymore. I left that squad, left Sand Dreamough, they don't know where I am. Just wanted to say, I know your wild dramahistory with that squad, I got one too."

"Best if we don't talk about it, Bullfists," I pleaded.

"Fillup, my name's Fillup again," he said. "You ever need me, come find me in Drivy Track, likewise I need to know if I can count on you in a brawl."

"Allright Fillup, got your back forsure, now let's be secretly chill about it," I begged, and bumped my clean red hand against his dopey goatbull so he would leave, don't want to be seen friending this former goon.

"Bytheway how come you never talk about your home or family," asked Brand.

"What's there to say, just average boring middlepoor, hey how about you show me some wrestling vids," I lied.

DREAMWORLD

I didn't want my crew to think of me as a cityboss pet so I told them nothing. It would have felt crazy talking about Hue Family Palace down in gritty grubby Eat Votech anyway, like pretending you commute every morning from a fairytale.

Infact all of Wet Almanac became like Dreamworld to me.

The busride from Eat to Wet was like falling asleep, the roar and chatter of Votech stops echoing in the ears while you drift up on switchback zigzag middleroads into a heaven for giants.

Step off the bus, the halfhour walk to Hue Family House is the dream's beginning, clean, sweetsmelling, quiet, stroll past rolling lawns and humming homes under the vault of treebranches.

Walk inside and smell dinner prepping, starchy roots roasting, birds and fishes grilling, whole gardens hacked to bits on woodenslabs.

You're supposed to be studying for retrack but sometimes the dreamy magic of middlerich paradise swallows you and before you know it you're riding a dog, watching a vid, just wander the house in a stupid daze, run fingers along delicious textures and wonder everynight, canthisbereal.

But soonerorlater during these lazings and wanderings, Kitty would appear and remark, "Hey, what a coincidence, I happen to be holding these studymaterials for you," infact a lot of times when I got home she was waiting in the sunroom with screens and books.

She sat on the wickerchair, I sat between her knees on the footstool, a screen sat in front of us. And I tried reading articles and storybooks, tried learning how letters fit into math, tried swallowing the basics of science and history and humanstudies, the world slowly widened in my rattled battered head.

Was I a little in love with this cute braidheaded girl who saved my life, wanted me to succeed, sure, a little bit, I mean ofcourse, you would be too.

But it's not the love of, *I want to hold you in my arms for a* *million sunsets, if I don't get to marry you I will starve myself to death.* It's a different kind of love when the girl outscales you by five.

You ask, Warner what the heck do you know about love, look, I know I'm young and I don't have the deep feelings of forexample Usher but I know a few things about love. Warner's kissed a few girls and not just in Dreamworld, also in Lifeanddeath, even banged a girl once.

The bang was back when we lived in the abandoned coastguard station, a few weeks after my dad got crushed. This older girl named Kelly took me aside and said hey, cute little sadface, I know how to make you feel better, comewithme. Tobehonest I didn't really want to but didn't want to say no either, longstoryshort we banged in a sandpit and then I ran away. Prayer found out and yelled at me, Warner you're going to get a million diseases if you bang Kelly, so I started hiding from her, then a few weeks later she left for the desert with some psycho boneblue todds and that was that, story of my first bang, why am I even telling you it, definitely no love in there.

My point is, do I know what love is, well maybe, a little, and it's different when you love someone way bigger than you, richer than you, incontrol and knows it. I think it's like loving a god you can see.

You don't get to kiss a god. The god and you don't cuddle or canoodle. You can't even sit on a god's lap, that's too weird.

Instead you and the god talk, trade attention, focus energies on each other. And when the god loves you back, smiles at you, tells you goodjob, it feels incredible. But when the god ignores you to talk on the phone, it twists you up inside. Part of you thinks, *ofcourse she gets to ignore you, she's a god.* Other part thinks, *that's just because she was born a stupid god, I could be a god too if I got born that way.*

And most of the time you're together, your mouth is all twisted up too, can't talk to this god the way you do with the other normal human poors. Your words are stiff, your jokes are bad. The only time your tongue gets loose is talking to her about your sad past, the sadness of being a littlepoor, the only kind of person you get to be with her is a noble sufferer.

"Dang, if only littlepoors got to learn equations at a younger age, maybe it would all be different, such a tragedy," is the kind of dumb crap I heard myself saying.

"I keep telling my dad, what if Lossy Indica was the first in the Yewess to build state littleschools," she said.

"With a littleschool to go to, whoknows how my life would have ended up, I could have been the president," I heard myself agreeing like a robot pet.

I mean she's notwrong, I just wish we could have other conversations, but when you're talking with someone of a super different scale, scale is all you talk about.

"Warner," she asked onenight after dinner, "what do you want."

I was plopped on her sweetsmelling bed playing mathwars on a screen.

"Retrack ofcourse," I said.

"I mean what's like your heartsdesire," she said.

I must have looked confused because she explained, "If you could have anything you wanted, in the whole world, what would that be."

Obviously the answer was, still have my mom and dad around, mom not catcrippled, dad not stepped on.

Instead of saying that I just airscraped my throat a few times.

"How big would you be," she forexampled.

I said, "As big as you I guess."

"And what would you do," she asked.

"Prettymuch nothing," I said, didn't mean to be funny but she thought it was hilarious.

"Ohman that is a hoot," she giggled.

I glanced around for something to change the subject, in the closet half a guitar peeked at me from behind dresses.

"Bytheway do you ever try to play your dreammusic in Lifeanddeathworld," I asked her, a classic Change The Subject from me, king of changing the subject.

She ducked her eyes for a second at her hands.

"Uh, not really," she said, allofasudden she was the muttery one.

"It would be super hard I guess," I realized, "forstarters you would have to be a thousand people."

"Well, it's just, for me, it's kind of impossible to play anything," she mumbled.

It was a voice of, *I don't really want to explain this*, suddenly I knew we were talking about why Tony called her Poor Kitty.

A couple pangs went through me watching this richgirl sadly chew a lip, immediately I felt like I had to soothe her into not talking or she would start hating me.

So I nodded and also shook my head like a maniac, trying to tell her with my wideeye tightmouth face, *it's super okay, I get it, stoprightthere, howabout we discuss something you like instead.*

But she misunderstood my clumsy headbobbling, thought I wanted her to continue.

"So, okay," she sighed, "I was born a little wrong, pretty early and with a pinched spine, and the doctors had to do a ton of surgeries on me, like when I was a baby. I'm really basically fine now but the easiest way to put it is, my brain is still not a hundredpercent plugged into the rest of my body, maybe closer to ninetyeight. So there are a few things I can't do as a result, like play instruments or do any sports, I just don't have coordinated enough motorcontrol."

"Oh dang," I said stupidly.

"I mean it's barely ever an issue really," she said.

"I guess that last twopercent is your heartsdesire though," I thought and also blurted like an idiot.

"It's actually not," she snapped. "It's enough for me to get to make music in Dreamworld, honestly that's probably the reason I'm good at it."

"Ofcourse ofcourse," I apologized, "no yeah no obviously, what am I even saying, howabout we never speak of it again."

She watched me babbling and softened, her lips scrunched and smiled, opened to speak.

"Can I be honest with you about my heartsdesire," she said.

"Only if you want to," I urged.

"It's to be a beloved dictator queen," she confided.

That got a giggle out of even stiffmouthed me.

"Like of as many people as possible," she daydreamed. "But chosen by the people, like so rapturously adored that I got elected queen yewnanimousely by the entire planet because every single person loves me so uncontrollably."

"Gottabehonest, I don't think you've got Daisy's vote," I pointed out.

"Gonna have her murdered I guess," agreed Kitty.

It was nice to joke and riff, happy little moment but over prettyquick, soon I got weird and stiffmouth again, we went back to work.

Meanwhile the guitar kept peeking at me, would it really live there if she didn't hope for the day she picks it up and strums a song she hears.

"Bytheway it's not a big deal, but if you could not talk about the brain thing to people I'd appreciate it, maybe not even Prayer if that's okay," she asked later, I promised I wouldn't.

We were a littlebit the same but only in ways you can't talk about, two kids being wordless about their unfillable wants, pretty squeezyhand giant and lifty orphan pet.

That night before sleep, Prayer confronted me.

"You're not crushing on Kitty, right," she wanted to know.

"No," I lied.

"It just couldn't possibly work, an interscale romance between you and her, and I should know, I have a little experience in this department," she said.

"No one's crushing on anyone," I said.

"Well, that's not true, she crushes on you alittle forsure, but it can never work ever, so please don't screw things up by getting mushy feelings," she said.

"Wait what do you mean she crushes on me," I said.

Prayer looked into my eyes and saw a carcrash.

"Ohno, Warner," she said. "Crap."

"What," I said. "Shut up."

"You crush on her super hard," Prayer realized. "Nonono. Warner, don't screw this up for yourself and also me, please."

"Shut up," I said. "You think I don't know it's impossible? You think I feel any kind of stupid hope like I'm going to marry this girl? No, so just shut up please."

"If you have to crush, please don't crush on Kitty, that's a disaster, find some halfscale girl to crush on instead, a little less likely to ruin your happiness and also both of our lives," Prayer told me.

"Shutting up will need to happen soon in here," I yelled into the pillow I was smashing into my head.

"Better you don't crush on anyone though, try to cool off that needy heart," Prayer advised.

But toobad Prayer, very nextday I found a new girl to crush on, a girl my scale too.

"New" maybe isn't the right word though, I've seen this girl before, you have too.

LIFEANDDEATHWORLD

Tray and Brand and me were strolling Mun World in search of shootemups when I saw her with a little crew of girls, judging handbags and phoneshells in an aisle of jewels and fraygrances.

Atfirst I thought where do I know this face, how is she familiar.

Why do I remember this girl outscaling me by four, why am I remembering hiding in garbage, did this girl pity me once and leave me sweet limewater to drink.

Does her family serve bowls of tangy creamy cowsoy in Sand Dreamough when it's Neighborhood Souptime, ohmygod, it's Grace.

Definitely it was Grace's sweet freckly plumface, but no longer fourtimes bigger than mine, actually littler if you can believe it.

I stared a little too long, her friends noticed, mine did too.

"Don't creep, bradpitt," said Tray, smacking my skull, and we escaped into some gameboxes for testdrives.

Shootemups didn't intrest me a ton but Tray and Brand loved all the various kinds. Infact I would say it was the only thing that brought Tray happiness. Be a starwarrior, be a batman, murder thousands of people, have nightmare adventures in hell, anything's possible.

The tech was intresting to me atleast. Stand inside your gamebox, dash and twist on the threesickty treadmill. I enjoyed traveling limitlessly all over magical environments, a wildwest, a worldwar, a roadrage, magic sewer, lordoftherings, anchorwat, outerspace. It's a little like Dreamworld actually, nowonder poors love escaping into it.

But the travel ends prettyquick when you get discovered by enemies and if you don't have a childhood of playing these things, forget it, you're useless. Die violently, tons of screaming, bloodandguts paint the boxwalls, plus mockingfaces, *lol hey loser, how pathetic, you'll never be goodenough to survive the miamivice no matter how hard you try, anyway why not try again, hey where are you going.*

I stepped out cautiously but Grace was nowhere to be seen. So instead I watched cops try to dig some littlepoors out from burrows in the phone section, Mun World contains thieves and schemers always, cops patrol it twentyfourseven.

Secondtime I saw Grace, it was across the parkinglot, this time she was with some skinny nerd. This pimply scrawn held his foldphone for her to read, something he wrote forsure. She liked it though, was making nods and faces of, *the surprising thing you wrote surprises me, wow, oh and now I'm laughing at the part where you made a stupid joke or something.*

Meanwhile, Brand was showing me wrestlingvids on his phone, less delightfull viewing material forsure. Specifically these were vids of the Cram Jam.

Cram Jam is one of the annual battles of Yewess Wrestle Club, the Numberone In The Yewess And Worldwide It's Numberthree Wrestling Entertainment Choice. This battle is, put thirty wrestlers in an enormous fishtank, all over the walls and floor are the slippery mouths of drainagepipes, goal is to cram everyone else into the pipes and flush them into the sea, winner is the last guy still in the tank.

So, excited Brand and pretending to be captivated me were watching enraged oily wrestlers whirl a guy around or bonk him in the head and then frantically drag this stunned guy to the mouth of a drainagepipe and try to smush him in there, meanwhile the guy is pretending to wake up halfway into the pipe and furiously clawing his way back out and thrashing around, meanwhile meanwhile I saw that Grace was done reading, thanking the nerd but walking away to class or something, I thought about running up to her and introing myself, hey Grace, remember me.

But then some other daves wandered up and yell, "Ohsnap, are you watching replays of the Cram Jam, heckyeah," a loud crowd of morons gathered around us to cheer and then start also wrestling and cramming, Grace glanced over and without thinking I ducked and ran, can't be seen with these psycho boneheads, that's when I knew, *I must like this girl.*

Thirdtime I saw her, it was in Mun World again, and again I was caught looking by one of her friends, shortest and feistiest. This time the friend shamed me before I could sprint away.

"Hey creep, stop staring at my friend, either buy her some presents or go die in a hole somewhere," she yelled.

The other girls giggled and murmured except embarrassed Grace.

"Okay sure, I'll buy her a present," I said for some reason.

"Great, what are you getting her," said delighted friend.

I looked at Grace, Grace studied me carefully, *wait do I know this guy*, her eyes were fakeblue that day.

I said, "Hey Grace, can I get you a mocha, please."

"Ohgod, the creep knows her name," yelled friend. "That is some nextlevel creeping."

"Ohmygoodness, it's you, you're out of jail," cried Grace, finally realizing who is this pumpedup bustednose redfish.

The friends were losing their minds from excitement, ontheonehand overjoyed that Grace has a scandalous secret, ontheother terrified of a creepy criminal. Two friends encircled Grace protectively, a third actually raced away shrieking.

"You brought me a nice drink once, now maybe I can return the favor," I suggested and she blushed glowy white under the plumskin.

Kind Grace agreed to a date at Shaky Buzz, a loud jittery zone of Mun World featuring mochashakes, coffeecreams, pearlteas, nonstop popvids starring Famous Randy and his famous turtleneck.

The friends agreed to sit two tables away, inreturn I had to buy them drinks.

"Oh, you don't have to buy so many drinks," started to say Grace.

Short loud friend Angel interrupted, "Heck no, beautifull

Grace, he completely does because your friends need drinks to sip on while we stare at him vigilantly, that's incase he tries any funnybusiness."

"She's right ofcourse," I said, "what does everyone want, please order your heartsdesire," so what do you think happened, obviously each friend ordered the most expensive, ultralarges with surplus pearls, lavish syrups, expressiveshots, fizzy tops, frothy gallons that taste like cartoons.

I smiled casually to pretend it was nobigdeal and infact great that half my freaking allowance was swimming down the throats of these giggly sceneteens.

Grace, last to order, got a simple minimocha.

Thank you, Grace, said my heart.

We sat, she sipped, I told her the supershort version: Sorry again for hiding in your garbage, what happened was, a faceboy lowlife tried to kidnap my sister, I tried to shoot him, hid from the cops for a few days mostly in your garbage, finally turned myself in, my lawyer made me plead guilty and the judge thought I was nogood, I spent a year in jail, then a cityboss's daughter learned about my story and got me out, now I and also the sister live with them, we're scaledup on a gift of their munmuns, trying to make the most of this opportunity.

But I was listening to my own story and it didn't sound like me. It sounded like the story of someone tougher, dumber, meaner, some thug hoping to convince you he doesn't love violence.

I heard a jacked guy with faketeeth telling a girl, "judge thought I was nogood," I didn't care if it was true, I didn't care if it was me. I still thought to that girl, *ohno, turn, run, you don't want this guy in your life.*

But Grace listened, sipped, gazed. And didn't assume I was lying or evil, didn't see in my eyes the twitchy mistrustmyself feeling. Or maybe she did but she understood somehow, sympathized, whoknows, all I knew was, I felt like allofasudden there was a girl I could realtalk with.

"What about you, Almanac is pretty far from the Dreamoughs," I asked.

Yeah rent got too high in Sand Dreamough, at the same time business got too bad because middleriches can't eat at a middlepoor stand. Oneandahalfscales are kind of taking over and rebuilding Sand Dreamough blockbyblock, widening the roads, combining buildingstories, for littler middles the writing's onthewall. So Grace Family Cowsoy moved to Eat Almanac, hopefully things are better over here, lots of middlepoors anyway, more littles too.

But Grace made it onto Wordy Track, great reading skills from her love of comics, speaks three languages, parents are hoping for lawschool. What about you, Warner, is your track impressive or pathetic.

"I'm on Lifty Track," I admitted, again it was the voice of a big dumb strangler.

But she actually smiled a little deeper, glanced at my arms, said, "You look like you might be prettygood at it too."

The smile made my heart gulp.

"Well, I'm letting you in on a secret here, Lifty is only tenpercent muscles, it's really ninetypercent brain," I told her.

"Oh really," she said.

"Yeah it's true, Lifty is the secret home of geniuses," I said. "Yesterday during Generic Distress Response three guys working together invented a brandnew way to get trapped under a bus."

She laughed a real laugh, my heart got dizzy, meanwhile twotables away her friends noticed, elbowed each other, hands halfway covering big horrified smiles.

Her laugh unlocked me and we really started talking.

I told her my hope is, retrack to Mathy but it's a longshot forsure, I'm worried it's too late for an oaf like me, so much ketchup and notenough time, and Hue Family is really putting on the pressure like if you fail this retrack, we're pulling the plug, ejecting you and your sister from our nice house.

She told me, with her actually it's same same, parents put crazy pressure on her like if she doesn't get into law school they'll expel her from the family, but she doesn't have enough time to study either, at home she has to wait tables, wash dishes, take out the cowsoy garbage, and the law school entrytests are super hard, not a ton of law schools have middlepoor facilities either so there's not even that many places she could even go, it's pretty nerveracking, sorry to babble at you like this.

I told her, nono please babble away, thatscrazy that they make you work and expect you to study so much, do they ever let you sleep, do you even get to Dreamworld on a regular basis.

She told me, she sees Dreamworld maybe twice a week, mostrelaxing part of her day is at school forsure, in the parkinglot or at Mun World, she can't even read her comics at home, when her dad catches her reading comics he grabs them and throws them away.

I told her, comics huh, what comics do you like, could you recommend some, I'm trying to get better at reading.

She told me, ohman, there are some good ones, rightnow I'm really enjoying Lords And Swords, it's a middleearth but crazier, more violent for sure.

Her friends got sick of watching us eventually and Angel yelled, "Time to go, we're missing class, psycho," all buzzed from pints of bubbly slush.

My brain tried one last reminder of, *Warner, don't forget, you lived in this girl's garbage for two days, feel some shame.*

So I felt some shame.

But she piped, "Well hey, it's great and amazing to see you scaledup, anyway let me give you my number, we can meet up again sometime and I can give you a comic maybe."

I said, "Heckyeah, areyoukidding, I'd love that."

She tapped it into my phone with spangly fingernails.

"Thanks for the drink, Warner," she smiled, in her voice my name was a pair of pearls.

"Ryangosling, since when do you know girls," demanded Tray, watching me strut out of Shaky Buzz with a girl's number, but I stayed mysterious about it.

DREAMWORLD

Didn't just get the number from Grace, got a comic too, infact she gave me a couple and then kept messaging me, *ayyy read it yet, wat do yew think*, phonegifs of blinkyeyes and clashyswords.

Nope, sorry Grace, I have no time to read unfortunately, I only have time to stress endlessly about math.

Mathy Track was my only hope for retracking. Wordy was a lostcause because of my still crappy readingskills and none of the other retracks intrested Hue.

"I know your goal is to make the absolute most of yourself," he told me, "so let's avoid the more vocational tracks that will limit your potenchill. Mathy and Wordy are the ones that I believe will open more doors than they shut."

"Or what about Busy Track, couldn't that put Warner on a path to one day running a great corpo," tried to help Prayer.

"Let's try for Mathy Track," firmed Hue in a tone of This Is Not Actually Super Upfordiscussion.

And Mathy made some sense for me anyway, I was learning to enjoy the way numbers click together neatly. Plus I always sort of knew munmath without really knowing it, forexample even as a kid you could ask me, *hey Warner, popquiz, what's the scale of fiftythousand munmuns*, prettyquick I would tell you that's fourtenthscale, more than thirdscale, less than halfscale, whatelseyougot.

So sure, of all the studies probably math was the best fit for my brain if I had years and years to learn it, but I only had weeks, and the thing I was learning was, math was a house with too many rooms.

Numbers, negatives, plus minus times divide, the percents and fractions of munmath, you think you're pretty quick with that stuff, well, congratulations idiot, that's just the first room. Step into the nextroom and you've got letters running around in there, letters that might mean a number and might not, so have fun dealing with that. Sometimes you solve for ecks, ecks is a mystery criminal you have to catch, sometimes else it's not a crimeshow it's a lovestory, ecks is in a relationship with why.

Nextroom, nextroom, room after that, here come more wild symbols, squiggles, pies and roots, brackets, brambles, parentalsis, mediums and means.

Meanwhile branching off the whole freaking time to left and right are rooms of shapes, angles, grids, lines, charts, artrooms of mathy drawings, and the doors between the rooms are insane relationships, somehow a square can also be a sentence of letters and numbers, pee equals four ess, riddle me that, math wizards.

You think okay, this is a little berserk, but I can probably manage as long as they don't come up with anymore stuff and then you find some stairs leading up up up, ohno, there's a whole other floor, you stagger upstairs and it's just bonkers up there, everything is a function, everything is in parentalsis now, buynomeals, somehaitians, intergulls, signs cosigns loggerrhythms, meanwhile the shapes in the artrooms are mutating, threedee, fourdee, sillenders and prisons, scalers victors tensores manyfolds, meanwhile meanwhile step right this way so I can introduce you to the number eye, root of a negative, it exists in the next world but not in this one, a moaning groaning mathghost, now it haunts you forever.

Panicked, you vidsearch, *how much more math even is there*, how many more floors, you stick your head out the window and look up and ohmygod, ohcrap, pagesandpages of mathtopics in your vidsearch, floors and floors, it's a whole tower teetering into the clouds and you'll never get to the top.

Now for the finalblow, look out the window across the street, more endless towers with endless rooms, mechanics, electrics, chemicals, medicals, programs and logics, all stuff you'll also need atleast firstfloor kn owledge if yo u wa nt th e co unselors to le t a fifteenyearold retrack at Votech.

In the sweetsmelling aircondition Dreamworld of Hue Family Palace, moreandmore everyday I felt panicked, afraid, fighting off hopelessness, trying to win little victories one problem at a time. But every win was dwarfed and drowned by the hugeness of math.

"Warner, how would you feel about having an afterschool and weekend mathtooter," said Hue one night.

"Like a specialist, one of the top mathminds at Wet Almanac, a mysterious genius tobehonest," added Kitty.

"I guess for sure, do you think that would really help though, isn't my problem more just having a toosmall for math brain," I asked.

"Do not ever allow yourself to think that for a second, infact rightnow go erase that thought with a lobotomy," cried Kitty.

"This mathtooter is not who I think it is, is it," Daisy wanted to know.

Everyone was nervously quiet.

"Who does Daisy think it is," wondered Tony.

Daisy said, "Is it by any chance a guy who drove into a," at that point she was drowned out however by Hue and Dawn and Kitty yelling, OKAY DAISY THAT IS QUITE ENOUGH, Tony was yelling it also without knowing why.

The guy was a junior named Markfive, one of the top mathstudents at Wet Almanac High, mysterious genius I guess in the sense of, it is a mystery how this kid could possibly be a genius at math. Because he was also a doofy drugster who kept crashing pricey cars into trees and houses and eventually the highwaycops couldn't ignore it anymore, we need to find a way to punish this kid, obviously though not mess up his life toobad.

Fortunately there's a great solution, Markfive's mom is a steady donor to Hue Campain, therefore Markfive here's your punishment, communityservice of tootering math to a middlepoor. Markfive meet scrappy little Warner, Warner feast your eyes on this handsome bushyhead slacker with his velvet hoods and slinky jeans.

How did he get his name, obviously he was the fifth son of a bigrich pharmalord named ofcourse Mark. Mark lived with his many staffers in the seaside bigburb of Balustrade, riding around on tanks and barges the way the biggest have to.

But Markfive and mom of Markfive weren't bigs because their muns weren't joined to his, mom wasn't Mark's wife, just a rando babymama. Therefore Mark didn't grow up twelvescale in the giantville, instead twoandahalfscale back here in Wet Almanac, rattling around your basic twobedroom cliffside, every month their munflow quietly plumping with childsupport from Mark.

Turnedout that for mom of Markfive it was no great sadness not to be huge. She liked her nothuge life actually, glossyskinned middlerich woman basically just wining and dining as a job, fat and happy, sometimes dabbling in the opposite politics of her babydaddy to infuriate him.

Markfive somehow did have glorious math skills, teaching skills notsomuch. At the beginning I think his main focus was, *maybe this roughandtough excon can get me some intresting drugs.*

"Oh chill, look at you," he yelled the first time he saw me, "you're yoked as heck, so in your classes do you guys just lift weights and smoke weeds all day."

"Weights forsure, weeds for me not really so much, but the other kids, whoknows, maybe we got a couple burnouts in there," I said.

"Lol though, that would be me, puffing everyhour nodoubt, getting every kind of ripped, haha lol so are you in a gang like selling drugs or anything," he asked.

"Nope," I said.

"But wait, you were in jail though right," he said.

"Yup," I said.

"In jail don't they beat the crap out of you if you're not in a gang," he said.

"Yeah, I got beat up a lot," I said, "so anyway, area of a triangle, what's that all about, like any random triangle."

"One half basstimes height, so does Daisy ever talk about me, I mean probably not, nevermind, don't tell her I asked you that," he said.

"Sure thing," I said. "Instead of Daisy maybe we could talk a little more about these mysterious basstimes."

"Hey, look," said Markfive. "Okay. Sorry, but first, before we get into it, hey. I just need to know. Are you going to ask me about my freaking dad."

"Nope," I said.

"My dad's a tenbillionair," said Markfive. "So, you know. Sickteenscale. Like basically a hundredfeet tall."

"Prettybig," I agreed.

"It's just because everyone is always asking me, *whoa, your dad is a tenbillionair, ohmygod, that must be so crazy, what's it like having a bigrich dad,* and, I gotta be honest, I just completely hate talking about him," said Markfive.

"Goodnews, bigrich dads are not on the test," I said, and he laughed way too hard, and then he did teach me some stuff about triangles, atleast until his focusmeds wore off and he had to start playing phonegames.

Most tootseshes went like that. Save some time learning secret math tactics, lose some time learning about random things

Markfive likes and hates. Overall we were probably even, I guess atleast each of us had a new friend.

I called the Dockseye church every few nights to check in with Mom, it was too far to visit, three hours on the bus each way. In the doublecar it would be a fourtyminute drive, but I felt bad about asking for a ride.

Our convos always left me feeling funny, she was for sure happy me and Prayer were in school but mostly just wanted to scold me about not visiting church.

"Mom, this family doesn't go to church, plus I don't have time anyway, I'm studying twenfourseven," I pleaded.

"Well that's just crazy, you're telling me you don't have time for the Lord King God when He made all kinds of time for you, specifically to swoop down and save your life and give you all kinds of blessings it soundslike," Mom piped up in her littlevoice, "your big red butt better be in a church this sondaymorning and ofcourse drag your sister nomatterwhat, if she falls back into that space cult it's going to break my sad old heart."

My culty sister meanwhile failed out of junioryear at Wet Almanac.

It wasn't a total tragedy though, they dropped her into sopmoreyear classes, and she told us it was going waybetter.

"Instead of essays, Teacher lets me give presentation speeches about corpos," she chirped at dinner, "it's multidissupline and here's how, when you analyze a business you're using the power of words, math, science, *and* socialstudies, so you're learning everything at once, it's a true studying multivitamin!"

"How come they didn't let me do that," I yelled.

"You didn't ask, I guess," Prayer winked, Hue chuckled and Markfive did, too, he was guesting at familydinner to sneak peeks at completely unintrested Daisy.

"Lol Warner your sis is crazy," Markfive lolled, Prayer beamed, atleast one girl at the dinnertable liked him.

"Your new friend is highly cute," Prayer remarked that night as we were going to sleep.

"The only friend of mine you get to date is Usher," I told her as a reflex, then felt stabs of sickness from having no idea where Usher even is.

That night I shook myself out of Kitty Operahouse, got to look for Usher, don't want to because he's probably dead, would have found him bynow, but toobad, no choice, have to look for the poor guy.

In Dreamworld I tumbled and drifted, wandered Sand Dreamough, checked the old coastguard station, blew through the sky above Lossy Indica, the view he wanted to show my sis. I looked for his twisty body, his gray face, nowhere to be found. I hoped for the gray firework, no one's sending it up into the sky.

I tried dreaming myself to Usher but he's not dreaming himself to me, even if he were alive why would he, it's been more than a year.

I put up some gray fireworks myself, still pretty outofcontrol and nightmare so some of the fireworks fizzled, shot sideways, made no sound, sucked light from the sky and sound from the air.

No Usher anywhere, night after night. *Tonight he's just not sleeping deep enough,* I kept thinking, *maybe tomorrow he conks out good and I'll see him.*

But he doesn't and I don't.

218

LIFEANDDEATHWORLD

Down in Eat I kept taking little breaks from school to see Grace meanwhile, I even read some Lords and Swords on the bus. This thing was pretty intense, the adventures of some crazy allwhite lordoftherings, come ride with me to a mystical realm where everyone's skin is painfully white and getting punctured with swords and knives constantly, tons of dragons and rapes, everyone is seeking revenge on everyone and prettymuch every page a thousand people die screaming, notmything if I'm being honest with you but something made me happy that Grace liked it, a weird bloodthirsty mind was hiding in that mild head, behind the fakegreen eyes.

219

I bugged and pestered sometimes to see her real eyecolor, she said it's just stupid plain superviolet, honestly like black.

I told her I bet it's like a pretty nightsky, she tried to choke off a little smile and look stern but her freckly plumskin blushed even plummier.

Meanwhile nowandthen I saw her huddling with this other guy in the parkinglot, the scrawny nervous guy who showed her stuff on his screens.

His name was Frank and he was Wordy too, they were in lots of classes together, does he have more incommon with her than me, dang, he might.

But does he take her to fun loud delicious Shaky Buzz, no, instead he corners her in the shadeless parkinglot to read his poems and novels, soundslike a date from hell tobehonest but I saw her smiling and laughing and I wanted to sprint over there and fling Frank into the street like a frizzbee.

Instead I casually mentioned, "Hey, I think in the hot dusty parkinglot I saw a guy reading you his endless tolstoy, was it any good."

"Oh, you mean Frank," she said. "Yeah, it was good, uh, I mean I've known him for a while, he's really improving as a writer."

"Good good, it's important to support new artists," I encouraged in a super calm voice, then I looked down and I was mangling a napkin.

She saw it too, started to choke off a smile, decided not to, let it flood into the cheeks.

"Warner?" she asked. "Would you like to go somewhere today afterschool?"

Wasn't quite a date though, more of a group invite to Angel Brother Birthday Beebeecue. Grace's crew, my crew of Tray and Brand, plus a few other randos from Wordy and Busy walked from school to a ballfield, you could smell the meaty smoke from many blocks away.

Look, even if it wasn't a date, Grace tucked her hand in mine as we walked like it was nobigdeal, my heart got hot and frantic, I tried not to mangle her hand like a napkin.

Angel yammered happily, "Warner, Tray, Other Random Friend, you're going to love it, my family has the best beebeecues, we have like eight secret recipes that my grandma has sworn to take to the grave. Warner bytheway it's time for you to know this, I've changed my mind about you, atfirst I assumed you were a creep but now I think you're goodenough to date my friend, and she's a beautifull sexy miracle, so that means you're prettygood, congratulations."

I hugged her from the side, maybe a little too hard, she laughed and yelled, "Okay, okay, strongguy, I get it."

gotta skip tootsesh, I messaged Markfive, he responded *lol allgood*.

mite be late for familydinner, I thought about messaging Prayer or Kitty or someone but didn't, Warner you'll just stick around for an hourandahalf, home by seven forsure.

A rottysmell cigstick got passed around our walking group. Angel handed it to me.

"Nothanks, don't burn cigs," I said.

"What about weeds, which is what this is, wow can you not smell that," she said.

I looked at Grace, Grace shrugged.

"Nerds, how about for once you be chill," suggested Angel, so Grace and me took puffs and strolled giggly and hothearted into middlepoor heaven.

• • •

The beebeecue took over half a ballfield, many families in attendance, blankets and nets, balls and grills, portable soundsystem. Angel Family you can recognize because they're the shortest and most cheerfull. Birthdayboy Angus was a chubby happy little guy turning thirteen and chomping meats.

Tray and Brand and me got sucked into a ballgame. I was prepared for a Lifty type deathmatch of Kill Or Die Furiously, surprise surprise though, there's another way to play sports. No one racing at topspeed, no one attacking the knees, no stoppages for uncontrollable brawling. No hard jukes to break ankles, just little hipfakes, jogging, dancing. No ferocious bullet passes, just light little rainbows to each other, clever geeometries, the game was basically Who Can Score The Slowest And Most Beautifull, infact no one was even counting goals.

The former faceboy Fillup was playing too, at one point flashed me his bullfists and a wink, I frownnodded sternly, *Fillup I continue to have your back, let's remain chill though.*

Then came time to munch the glorious beans and meats, crunchy leaves and plants, herbs and garlics, stewy sauces and amazing chewy breads, I ate ravenously and then lay down on the dirt and moaned like a cow.

"Dave, if you keep making these sexsounds I don't think we can be friends," Tray clowned me.

Someone turned up the music, laughs, cheers, everybody please direct your attention this way, it is time for Angus to perform his soyouthinkyoucandance.

He had a face of intense concentration, must have been practicing for days. Look at him hustling and splitting, spinning on his tum, now on his head, sweating furiously, holycrap did he just pull four roses out of his boxerbriefs, kid who could those even be for.

I laughed, Grace laughed, I watched her laugh.

Prettysoon everyone was dancing so I asked her to dance.

The daylight faded, the streetlights blinked on, after a while I knew it was after seven, didn't care though, didn't even check the phone. Just held Grace's waist, looked down into those eyes or else rested my chin in that hair, mirrored those hips, tried not to step on anyone or knee anyone in the face, some poorer relatives are quarterscale or fifth.

Angel whisked us away to sit in a circle with some cousins, sip again from the weedstick, say a little cloud into the air, let every close thing get closer and every far thing get farther.

Thoughts got louder, darkness got darker. Words became meaningless sounds unless you listened at them harder, then they split into many meanings, dozens, hundreds.

Overall it was nice and great. Grace was leaning into me from the side, my arm was around her, her skin was trembly through the soft teeshirt, her crinkly frizz was tickling my neck.

The weedstick came back around, another puff, we leaned even deeper into each other, smashedtogether like dead trees.

She whispered into my ear, a long pearly string of sounds, every ell was a glimmer shining off every bee.

"What what what, say that again," I giggled.

"I usually like barely ever really basically never burn weeds," she said.

"Yeah me neither," I told her.

She turned her face to me, drank up my eyes with hers.

"I want to kiss you but I think I'm way too drugged," she whispered.

"Oh dang," I responded stupidly, Warner you need to brainstorm better responses for talking to girls, what exactly is Grace supposed to do with an ohdang.

She swayed a little bit, eyefocus going in and out.

"The last puff was a mistake I think," she said.

"Do you need help, wait, uhoh, can I help you somehow," I asked.

"Nonono, I'm okay," she said, then turned and poured vom into the sand, kids started shrieking, I tried to keep her hair out of it, I was sort of shrieking too.

Prettysoon Grace and I were in the back of a halfcar, upfront the driver was a kind random uncle of Angel named Gill.

"I'm such a mess, ohmygod I'm so embarrassed," Grace moaned.

"Look, I'm just happy I get to take care of you, continue getting little bits of vom out of the hair," I told her.

"Ohgod I feel so dizzy and sick," she cried.

No kidding, probably it was the car justasmuch as the weeds. Driving in a halfcar is hectic, you're below half of everyone, dodging like a pinball in the shifty canyons between trucks and bikes, lights are blocked from view. On top of that the engineering of a halfcar is never going to be the best engineering in the Yewess, pretty janky and clanky.

"Eyes closed, head between knees, almost there," I told her, rubbed her back, kind of wished she was sick everynight, I could nurse her just like this.

We pulled up in front of the family stand, dull red awning loudly telling you, EAT THE BEST COWSOY.

I started to open the door, Angel Uncle piped up and said, "Warner, how about you stay in the car, I'll walk her to the door."

"No no, I can do it," I said.

"Not sure if you're picking the right time to meet the parents," he stagewhispered.

So Grace and I said some awkward goodbyes, me trying to drown her apologies with I Had Fun and This Night Was Great Seriously.

Then I cowered below the halfcar windows and listened to Grace Dad come out and gasp and yelp kind of loud and theatrical, "Grace, where were you, oh Grace you look awfull and you stink like drugs and vom. Ohhhhhhwow, oh dang, Grace how could you, what a bad betrayal, do you mean to tell me you were out addicting yourself to drugs instead of helping your family restaurant survive."

Listened to Grace mutter tearfull sorrys and then escape while Grace Dad discussed with Gill a little, well ofcourse thankyou for bringing her home, nexttime though if you see her at one of these drug parties call me rightaway immediately, I will drop everything to come get her even if it means closing up the shop which ofcourse will cost us untold munmuns but nomatter, most important is that Grace needs to be studying or working, oneortheother, not suiciding on poisonous drugs.

• • •

The drive up into Wet Almanac was long, atleast for a halfcar, a little deathdefying too, no halfroads and not a ton of middles. Mostly we hugged the gutters of bigroads and scanned the rearviews constantly for giants roaring up on us from behind. I was a little terrified but Gill was super calm, the guy drove like in spacenavy.

My phone was trembly with messages, I was dealing with it by pretending the phone doesn't exist.

"Gill thanks again for driving me home, I really appreciate it," I mumbled.

"Don't even worry about it, how is life with the Almanac cityboss, anyway," wondered Gill.

"It's good, it's good, I mean a little stressfull sometimes," I said.

"Do you want to talk about it?" he said.

"Oh I don't need to," I said.

But then the drugs loosened my mouth and I did babble like a drugster for a while, there's just a ton of stress, pressure, awkwardness, got to learn math or I'm worthless, but the math is too much and I'm starting toolate, seems like it's impossible but I'm not allowed to say that.

Gill said finally, "But you're putting up with it because you want to be middlerich someday."

"I mean, doesn't everybody," I asked.

"Well," he said. "At some point, don't you think enough should be enough?"

And he started speeching at me a little of, Warner, here's how it is. Some people need to scale up nomatter how big they are, because they'll never feel big enough, never feel safe enough. They get to halfscale, they need those extra sixinches, extrafoot, need to get to threequart, someday get to middle, someday climb above middle to oneandahalf, onandon, it's all they think about.

Their minds are swirling always with pictures of living in a bigger nicer home, driving in a bigger nicer car, eating bigger and more illaborate food, starting to accumulate staffs, cleaners and cooks and drivers and then personal assistant and head of staff, people to orbit you like moons.

And that's the only way they see the world, just scale, nothing else, scalemun is the only focus of their mindseye. And hey, I'm not talking about Grace Dad, necessarily, although I mean I'm not *not* talking about him either, you know, well howabout we just say forget I brought him up.

What I'm saying is, it's okay to want to get bigger, sure we all do, but just remember it's not the only thing, it always comes at a cost, not just time and munmun but your relationships with people, your printsapulls, the person that you are, stuff like that.

At a certain size you can still be happy, remember that. At most sizes really.

It was a littlebit the classic oldguy move of deciding it's time for you to take the class of How To See Everything The Way I Do, hey polite respectfull kiddo, congrats, you've been enrolled freeofcharge in the school of How To Be Me.

And after a while I wasn't really listening, just mumbling yeahs yups yuhhuhs and whiteknuckling the seatbottom while triplecars flew over us.

But at the same time, gotta admit, that oldster tactic works prettygood because here's what I was thinking: *well what if I do become the same guy as this Drivy beardo, what if that's my life.*

What if I don't even retrack to Mathy, just graduate with a Lifty degree, work Lifty jobs carrying burdens and everynight earning a goodnight's dreams.

And what if I marry a wife who breadwins also, working a Wordy job maybe, editing corpo texts up in some Sentrow skyscraper.

Middlelife with a Grace type girl, shy and kind and secretly bloodthirsty, looks like Grace too, infact let's just say Grace.

Middlehouse down in Eat Almanac, going to beebeecues, throwing parties for our middlekids in a ballfield.

Warner don't get ahead of yourself, dummy, who said anything about Grace wanting to marry you.

But I couldn't not think it, zoomed the last few biggutter miles with a dumb little smile on my face.

DREAMWORLD

In Hue Family Palace ofcourse an ambush waited for me.

"There he is, Warner ohmygod where were you, what happened, are you okay," cried Kitty, peeking out the sunroom window, other familymembers crowded quickly behind her.

I told them it was just a nice beebeecue, lost track of time, won't happen again, if we're being honest I smoked weeds with some friends.

This last piece of news might have been a mistake to admit. Because it filled everyone with despair and rage.

Dawn was the maddest, "Warner it goes without saying that this is unacceptable but what is more troubling is your casual attitude which makes it crystalclear that you do not have any sense of *why* we have set what we feel are completely reasonable requirements," et set set setera,

meanwhile, Hue was the saddest, "Because the opportunity we provide is rare and special we can only provide it to those who will make the absolute best use of it, it would be very painfull to say goodbye to you but not as painfull as knowing there are poorkids outthere who would *not* waste this opportunity goofing off and doing drugs," et set set, meanwhile actually Kitty was the saddest, "Warner did you do this because you think you are worthless, when I look at you I see someone with unlimited potenchill, I know the road is hard but you can be someone amazing, why can't you just believe in yourself like I believe in you," et set, et set,

meanwhile actually exhausted Prayer was both saddest and maddest, "Kitty it's jail, jail messed him up and beat the hope out of him, before jail you should have seen how spunky and sparky he was, now he dreams small and bad and can't imagine great futures for himself, Warner ohmygod I can't even look at you, I am killing myself everyday over here and you are goofing off like an idiot, if you screw this up for me I will never forgive you."

Grumpy anger flooded me a little, *you maniacs, I missed one familydinner and that's it, just wanted to be a standard middlekid for a day, can we please not act like I went insane and murdered eighty grandmas.*

But what can you do except play the game, I bowed my head and sorrowed.

"Family, I screwed up bad, but only now do I know how bad, truly," I told them, "it won't happen everagain, two strikes I'm out."

Tony found me in the hall.

"I thought about your mistakes and here's where I think you messed up, your originalsin was, you were not being considerate," he explained. "Because you see it's not just you sacrificing, familydinner is a sacrifice for all of us, thinkaboutit, dinners are prime social realestate. Dad could be meeting constituents,

Mom could be wooing clients, I could be consolidating classmate support for my schoolvicepresident run in the fall with targeted pizzanights."

"Thanks, Tony," I said.

Kitty found me in the hall after Tony.

"Sorry for freaking out, it'll be okay, don't worry," she soothed, crouching over me, hoping to sound casual and not shakysad.

"I promise though, I'll never do that again," I swore.

"So who were you with anyway," she asked.

"Just normal kids from school," I said. "I mean obviously badinfluence randos I will immediately eject from my life."

"Only if that's what you want, seriously," she said.

"It wasn't even fun," I lied.

"You know you can tell me if it was a girl," she said suddenly.

I looked up into her big pretty eyeblacks.

"No no," I lied. "I mean, it was boys and girls mixed, big group of losers, but not like *a* girl."

"Okay," she shrugged.

My dreams were wild that night for the first time since before jail, must have been the drugs. I built endless lifty gyms out of the palaces of Wet Almanac, lift this car, climb that flippedup lawn, unflood these homes and clear that rubble, kliegs and broadways lit the sky like *right this way* and *step right up*, the floodplain shrank to a trampoline to help poors dream themselves up to me, Eaters were somersaulting up joyously into the dreams of Wets, hurling and wrestling, paddling and cramming, beneath our feet the soil was swimming and boiling with extra dreamstuff, like I had nine dreaming minds and eight were out of my control.

Evenings went by of studying and stressing, things went backtonormal, everyone pretended like my druggy rampage never happened. I doubledowned on studying with Markfive, drowned myself in math, at familydinner Hue and Dawn warmly praised my dedication, Warner you're really turning it around.

Then outofnowhere another defeat walloped the team of Poor Bro And Sis.

Prayer failed out of Wet Almanac Middlerich completely, I came home one afternoon to find a grim sis on the steps.

But it was outofsomewhere afterall, tobehonest Prayer had known for weeks she was failing. Because her plan of Make Business Presentations In Place Of Every Assignment Or Test was just a random desperate strategy, no teacher asked her to do it or thought it was a good idea.

Inotherwords she had gone completely renegade and was just getting up there everyday with panicky cheerfullness and teaching homemade casestudies to a giggly class and snarkysmile teacher, wow, yikes, okay well Prayer what you've told us about Shaky Buzz's journey into the fruitmash sector is forsure quite intresting but I am afraid it is not going to get you a passing grade in Terror History.

So Wet Almanac spat my scrappy sis out into the mouth of Eat Votech.

It wasn't all badnews because guess who talked her way into Busy Track.

"Prayer, holy crap, I'm proud of you," I cheered her on the bus.

"Ohgod, what are you talking about, in one month I failed out of two different schoolyears, ontop of that I still don't know enough math to place into Mathy," she moped. "I spent a year doing shopmath, weeks at middlerich school memorizing stupid theorymath, wasn't even close to enough."

"Busy Track's going to be a good home for you atleast," I hoped.

"Who cares, Hue thinks I'm a loser now," she worried.

"How'd you sell the counselors that pen though," I said.

Prayer cracked a little smile finally and said, "Want to know what I said?"

"Yeah," I said.

"Okay, you're the counselors," she said. "So first, without telling me, just think of how many munmuns you'd pay for the most premium reliable topquality pen, the only pen you'll need for the rest of your life."

"Okay," I said, thinking, *one munmun, who the heck needs a pen.*

"Got that number in your mind?" she asked.

"Yup I got it," I said.

"Okay," she said. "Here's a piece of paper. Write down the number."

I didn't have anything to write with.

"I don't have anything to write with," I said.

"No kidding," she said. "*Sounds like you need to buy a pen.*"

And she bopped me on the nose with the pen.

That was it apparently.

"That's all you need to say to get on Busy Track?" I shrieked.

Way too soon, it was the weekend before my own return to Track Test Dungeon.

I felt pretty unready but refused to admit it, daughterday and sonday the whole family made a cheerfull determined groupeffort of Prep Warner For Retrack.

The family and Prayer and me meditated both mornings.

Hue ordered the cooks to make special brainfoods, leafygreens, oilyfish.

Dawn performed evening yogas with me, align the energies and breathe only with certain lungzones, bet you didn't know lungs even had zones.

Hueagain reviewed medicals with me daughterday morning, gave me quiet encouragement of *it's really not as hard as you think, you'll be totally fine*, I almost believed him.

Tony covered programs, ifthens and forloops, I cut this one a little short because Tony is always trying to tell you why everything is so great, it stressed me out having to agree with him overandover, *yes, all of these boring things are super great.*

Even insane bitter Daisy took two hours with me to review chemicals. Daisy was not a childgenius anymore but still headed for a comfy life at a chemlab, her prep was solid and she was even nice to me. "In this house you really put up with a lot," she told me with kind eyes, "I could never do it."

And allday sonday I dug into math with Markfive and Kitty. Markfive gulped extra focusdrugs and was wild helpfull, this kid has a superpower brain when he's not distracted, I tried hard to absorb like a thirsty plant.

Wake up Warner, it's munday, day of the retrack test, here is how it goes.

"Goodluck, forreal dave, you deserve it, you're too smart for Lifty," says Brand in the parkinglot.

Tray nods but says nothing, just bumps skulls and smiles grimly.

Grace messages me yourethebests and youcandoits and endless triumphvids, hearts and fireworks, ninja skateboard champions, my phone is freaking out.

"Bro, you've come this far for a reason, I believe in you," whispers Prayer fiercely into my ear, and pushes me toward the door.

"The test consists of nine sections, thirtyminutes each, you must pass all nine to retrack, are you ready for section one," says the counselor in Track Test Dungeon.

I pass the first two sections and choke hard on numberthree, six problems solved out of twentyfive, minimum to move on is thirteen.

Failure, disaster, notevenclose.

I cross the parkinglot into Mun World, can't go crawling back to Lifty Gym, too ashamed, it's not even lunch yet and I failed.

LIFEANDDEATHWORLD

I walked Mun World alone, aisles for miles lit with dead whiteness, hating myself.

And also hating stupid Mun World, look at this crappy terrible place.

Look at all these cheap freaking items, made quick and sloppy, fated for short sad lives.

Look at these Shimmery Popstar Hero backpacks, made from stiff plastic fabrics, straps are barely even sewn on right, the machine in charge of drawing Shimmery Popstar Hero Face must have gotten distracted because the eyes are at different latitudes of the head.

Look at this Action Gunmen Play Set, pay six hundo so your sad little murderer can plunk plastic statues with rubber bullets.

Look at this heap of Supermops, half are already bending and buckling and can never be sold.

Look at this fearfull row of a thousand shirts, a thousand people will come in and put these on their skin, dontknowwhy but it's terrifying to think about.

Listen to this plastic music, stamping and gleaming, cleanedup robot voices, probably sounds to me the way I sound to an animal.

Speaking of animals, there's one right now, tail swishing and switching.

It was a big evil tortashell cat, hunting the littlepoors of Mun World.

Look at this deathmachine, his wicked claws and superstrength and aboveall his love of blood. How did I know he loved blood, look at him, he's husky, wellfed, but still hunting avidly, not even hungry for meat, just death.

He was gazing insanely at a hole where definitely some terrified littlepoors escaped into it, probably still in there unless they have a tunnel system.

It took me embarrassingly long to swallow my fear and get my heart to stop shuddering and remember, *Warner, you're bigger than cats now, if you survived many jailpulpings you can probably pick up and dispose of a cat.*

He wasn't even suspicious of me, instead turned his whiskery jerkface to me and yowled frantically, *Warner please help me kill these humans before they get away.*

"Sure I'll help you, asshole," I told him, swiping in and grabbing his underarms.

Rightaway this frisky guy scrabbled around like a maniac, screamed and hissed and revealed his true demonself, but guesswhat, peenhead, you don't bully me now, I bully you. I held him at armslength, he got a few scrapes in forsure, but today Warner is way stronger than a cat, what a feeling.

But you can't just carry a cat out of Mun World without the doorstaff noticing.

"Honored customer, can I see your receipt for the cat," said storepet Miles, the walking talking vidscreen who has to shimmy while talking to you.

"Didn't buy him, just found him creeping around, gotta be a publichealth issue forsure," I said.

"Well thank you beloved shopper, you know everything you need is right here in Mun World, that includes our petshop that he must have escaped from, so, why don't you take him back," said moonwalking Miles.

I looked at the cat, panicking and thrashing. I thought about buying him and drowning him, or what if you just ripped his claws out onebyone and then dumped him in the street, goodluck, asshole, how about you quit killing and eat garbage like the rest of us.

But my stupid heart wouldn't let me kill or cripple even a murderer psychopath cat.

"Could you maybe take him back," I asked.

"Please help me, man, we're understaffed," said the poor exhausted dancer inside the milessuit, still boogieing.

"Thanks for the help, just drop him in that tank over there," said the stressedout petshop captain, under attack from mangy parrots.

I plunked this cat in a crappy tank.

"Mickdonalds, you gotta stop escaping, what are we going to do with you," said the petshop captain.

I felt happy that Mickdonalds atleast has to live in a crappy catjail, then I felt a little sad, nowonder the poor stupid jerk is evil, jail made him crazy just like me, then I realized, *Warner, don't get soft, all cats are evil, the foodchain made them that way.*

On my way out I spotted them, the two tatty littles I saved from the cat, a guy and a girl sneaking deodorants into a hole.

They spotted me and kissed fists gratefully, *thanks for saving us, nice giant.*

I kissed fists back and began to feel not horrible, might not be Mathy but atleast I'm bigenough to repress a cat.

DREAMWORLD

Hue Office was on the topfloor of Hue Family Palace, took me a while to get up there. As I climbed a hundred halfsteps I could hear his smooth boom.

"But you have to remember it's not a bad thing for an experiment to fail, kittycat," I heard him say, "the point of an experiment is not to succeed, the point is for you to *learn* from it. So if we all learn from this, then this can still have been quite a good thing."

Then he noticed me in his doorway and got very silent in the way of, *incase you haven't figured it out, I am talking about you.*

"Warner's here, gottago, I love you," he said into his headset and tapped off.

"Hue, firstofall pardon the interruption, if I can have two moments of your time that would be great, obviously though I can come back later," I offered.

"No, ofcourse, please sit," he murmured, and watched with kind somberness as my halfchair pulleyed to his eyelevel.

On the walls around us were vidscreens going twentyfour-seven, localnews and saddlelight feeds and the tabletops of his campainteam, you could see them edit his speechclips in realtime.

"Not sure if you got the retrack results from Eat Votech," I began, he nodded regretfully, *I did, I did.*

"Hue, with politeness and respect, I'll realtalk you for a second," I said. "I know I haven't been exactly killing it so far, dropping out of a nice middlerich academy, going missing one night to smoke drugs, now failing Mathy Retrack like a dumb jock. Bottomline, I know I'm not the kid you wish I was."

Hue smiled sadly.

"Who do I wish you were, do you think," he asked.

"I'll describe that kid to you," I answered. "He's a completely reliable genius who just needs one chance to prove he's a superstar, never screws up or tests your patience. And he's got a laserfocus on success and achievements, nothing else in his life contains any importance even for a minute. He exists only to rack up points and scores, to show poors are people too."

Hue's grin faded a little, *I don't know if I'd put it that way, but fine.*

"But Hue," I said, "if the point of having poors in your house is to tell beautifull campainstories, how about this story, Hue rescued two kids from misery and death, they weren't geniuses but guesswhat, that's fine, they still deserve a nice life, nongenius poors are also worth rescuing."

Hue put a finger in his ear suddenly, glanced at a screen and grimaced, murmured, "Shoot, Warner, give me a moment," swiveled to a camera and announced sternly, "Thankyou for having me, Violet, needless to say I completely reject my opponent's taunts and bullying, if anything *he* is the one with the bonerdisease, you can tell because he brought it up."

He flashed a moviestar smile, tapped his ear, turned back to me, resumed solemn gentleness.

"Warner," he told me, "I'm glad we're realtalking. You're a smart kid and you might not think so but I like you, I genuinely do. And personally, I ofcourse agree with you, all kids deserve nice lives, not just the most gifted."

His eyes got big and soft as he continued carefully, "But *politically*, and this is my field of expertise, remember, the story you propose is a story that voters just don't love. Voters like results. And so the heart of my campainplatform, as it relates to poors, is to convince voters that helping poors brings *results*."

"I can only stay if I bring results," I asked.

"That's how we get the most out of my daughter's program," he agreed.

I thought about the voters, tried to see me like the voters saw me, actually it wasn't hard.

Nogood jailfish failing and flunking, drugging and thugging, who cares if he can read now or do mathbasics, congrats I guess on not being a total idiot, that's still not results.

On one of the editscreens they were trying to find music for when Hue waves at people who are applauding him, rippling weepy music of a piano who thinks it's a harp.

"So what happens next," I said slowly, keeping my voice from squeaking or shrieking, I knew the moment I freaked out I would lose him forever.

Somehow as his words got harder the kindness deepened in his eyes.

"I am going to arrange rentfree government housing for you

at a littlehouse in Eat for the rest of your time at school," he said. "And ofcourse that housing will be chosen for its proximity to the school. Then, subsequent to your graduation you will be able to remain at the littlehouse, but a modest rent will be instated."

My bones got shaky.

"You're saying littlehouse though, I mean, can I atleast stay scaledup?" I asked. "I won't be able to keep doing Lifty Track if I'm ratscale."

His voice melted to a crackly whisper, so sad was this suited cityboss.

"Warner, a hunthousand munmuns can never be a gift," he said. "It can only ever be a loan."

243

I didn't even want to ask about my sis, I knew I had to though, my blood felt poisoned, my heart felt weak.

"And what about Prayer," I said.

He glanced at the door, *will anyone overhear, no, okay,* and said, "That's a separate judgment that I'm not yet ready to make."

"Why not," I asked.

"I'll be very candid with you," he said. "Your sister does work hard, she does dream big, I do think she is getting the most out of herself. She has the laserfocus you're talking about. But without a strong Wordy or Mathy background, her potenchill is always going to be pretty limited."

I nodded, blinked back angry tears, forced a steady voice, hoped he had the patience to hear one last salespitch.

"Hue, give me one more chance," I said. "You need results, noproblem, I will give you results. I'm one kid in a million."

He leaned back and rubbed his tired crinkly forehead, *please don't make this hard.*

"I will do whateverittakes," I promised him. "Whateverittakes, I mean it. This last failure taught me what I need, there can be no mistakes or relaxing everagain. Fromnowon I will have the focus, reliability, highpowered brain. Hue, please think about it, it's already crazy what I've learned, a few months ago I didn't even know what math was and today I'm already passing atleast two testsections, you have to admit that's progress. Give me one more chance to retrack, keep Prayer and I around meanwhile."

He frowned, glanced away at his screens, stared back at me.

"Here's a true story about littlepoors," I told him, "they can give results but they need more than one chance, no one succeeds if only one door ever opened for them, Hue I know you've had a few doors opened for you, not just one, please open one more for me."

He glanced again at a screen, murmured sorry, got to deal with this, tapped a pad and I began to lower.

"One more door," I squeaked.

"I'll think about it," he lied.

But I had a hope left, I paced the sunroom anxiously waiting for her to come home.

"Bro are we okay, bro what's going to happen," demanded fretty Prayer.

"I don't know I don't know," I said, shooing her frantically.

"I'm sorry but this is incredibly nerveracking," yelled Prayer.

"Look, just go study, remind everyone what a learny maniac you are," I told her, she hugged me fiercely and left.

Through a window I watched her laying out vidcarpet in a livingroom for all to see, *Hue be honest, is this really what lowpotenchill looks like, a savvy businessgirl playing complicated graphs like a piano.*

Kitty got home as the sky was pinking, I jumped up and waved.

She met me with cloudy eyes, squeezed the bunchy mouth into a frown, hid one squeezy hand inside her braidnest.

"I heard the news, Warner, I'm so sorry," she said, seemed more hurt than sorry though.

"Look I know you're disappointed that I failed," I told her, "I just want to tell you, I don't feel any kind of despair at all somehow, honestly just hope, I completely believe in myself, just like you always wanted."

"Well okay, good," she said uncertainly. "That's the right attitude, for sure."

"For sure it's right because you taught it to me, you gave me the gift of selfbelief, in addition to the gift of still being alive, remember when you saved my life," I reminded her.

"Yeah ofcourse I do, well good, good, I'm glad you don't want to give up," she admitted.

Then her voice got a little loud and she said, "Hey can I ask you something, I saw you got a whole bunch of lovey vids today, what's up with that."

"Lovey vids?" I repeated.

"I'm in charge of Hue Family Data Plan," she explained, "today your phone ate crazy data, I got informed automatically, someone sent you a million flowery lovey vids."

● ● ●

She didn't have to say anything else, I saw the entire truth in her eyes.

The truth wasn't even, Kitty loves Warner.

The truth was just, when Warner is out of Kitty's control, under someone else's spell, Kitty doesn't want him around anymore.

Even Prayer was almost too much, even just my grumpy love of a sis made Kitty less intrested in the Help Warner Program.

The truth was very simple, Warner can't live in this house if he loves another girl, *Warner if you really want to do whateverittakes, here's the whateverittakes.*

So in that moment, I stopped loving Grace.

How is that possible, easy, you just tell your sad heart, aim only at one girl, forget the other one. Aim only at the god you can see, not the middlegirl you can put your arms around.

Forget everyone except the giant pretty songmaker, the dogood dictator queen, the girl you dreamed with longago, when you were just a kid.

"Ugh, it's this super annoying girl," I told Kitty, "she has a crush or something but believe me, I am not into it."

Kitty blinked and brightened.

"Lol really," she wondered.

"Manohman, it's like can you leave me alone already, you loopy maniac," I made myself groan.

"Well you can just block that number, you know," she advised.

And she blinked, smiled, waited for me to do it.

Goodbye dreams of middlelife with Grace, goodbye Shaky Buzz dates.

I only get one love and it's not sweettasting anymore, salty now, bloodflavor from killing the other one, maybe that's what truer love tastes like.

Was it such a big sacrifice, I don't even know, maybe that's the saddest part.

I drew an ecks on Grace's name, the phone asked BLOCK?, I yupped.

"I don't have time to waste on any girl not named Kitty anyway," I teased later, made myself light, jokey, happy.

It's pretend flirting, not real, pretend is the only kind we get.

"You don't have time for any girls, smooth guy, math is your girlfriend," she told me, eyes sparkling, pretend flirting is her favorite.

"Sorry, it's just the truth, you saved my life, therefore I belong to you," I said.

"Okay fine," she laughed. "You belong to me."

And I felt her soft giant fingers in my hair.

V.
MARKFIVE

LIFEANDDEATHWORLD

Team Warner Prayer was saved, atleast for a few months. Kitty begged Hue to keep us around, Hue said okay fine, Tony said hey what about these orphans I found under a dumpster though, I thought it was my turn to save some poors, everyone told Tony to chill.

Another Mathy Retrack was scheduled for Warner, twelve more weeks in the distance.

All of Hue Family was hopefull and supportive, we all cheerfully pretended like no one was threatening to drop us back into our old ratlives.

At Reelect Hue voteparties and rallyshows I continued to be introduced as Warner The Amazing Success Story, look at this bright young striver, a few months ago he was illiterate and rotting in jail for the crime of defending his sister, now he's studying to become a mathgenius, if you reelect me I will continue to fight for poors to get the opportunities they deserve, everyone should get the chance to work like crazy.

I bumped into Grace in the parkinglot, just mumbled *sorry, shouldn't really hang out with you anymore, I kind of met someone else*, watched her eyes get sad and hard.

Angel stalked up to me later that day, calmly informed me I was a lunatic criminal and they should put me back in jail, ohwell toobad yourloss and starting now none of us will literally ever think about you everagain.

Maybe it was the truth, days passed and I'd be in the parkinglot nowandthen and my eyes stumbled over Grace living life without me, giggling with her crew, reading comics, huddling with Frank over his phone, guess she has a new itscomplicated now.

No time to get weepy over dead loves though, Warner, the king of your life now is math.

More specifically I guess it's Markfive.

Teaching me was now a whole schoolproject for him, Can You Cure Innumeracy At Age Fifteen? A Schoolproject by Markfive. Apparently middlerich schools force students to do constant projects and enterprises, lastyear he got way too ambitious with a project of Touringtest For Dogs And Robots, Can A Dog Believe A Robot Is A Dog?, What About Can A Robot Believe A Dog Is A Robot.

"Such a dumb idea, I was so drugged when I thought of that," mourned Markfive, "but my teacher said brilliant, goforit, it will genralize the touringtest," he got a terrible grade, no dogs or robots fooled each other, I mean forstarters how can you even tell what robots or dogs believe.

But don't fret, this project is going to go way better, Warner I know you feel like you're not learning fast enough but druggy tweaky Markfive has a secret weapon for you, you'll never guess what it is, oh wait actually it's super easy to guess, the secret weapon is a bunch of drugs.

"I'm on studydrugs now everyday, couldn't function without tobehonest," he admitted.

"How much do I take," I asked, cradling the giant studypill.

"Let's try thismuch," he guessed, shaving off a sliver.

I ate the sliver, he gulped the pill, that thing kicked in prettyquick, bop bang broom, it's mathtime.

Math math math, let's bury ourselves in these cozy problems, unsatisfiable hunger for tasty math, everyone's invited to this party in the mathzone, holycrap it's dinnertime, we didn't even have lunch.

Nextday we did it again, dayafterthat, dayafterthat, life became a blur of math and facts.

Good side of the studydrugs, I was learning math pretty fast, the room of my brain had scaled up, no longer cluttery and clattery like a middlepoor pawnshop. Instead it was a smooth roomy chamber like in the bank with clever sliding shelves and drawers. Every new thing Markfive showed me, I could find an empty shelf to put it in, clearly labeled, squaredaway, pieceofcake to go back and find it later.

Bad side of the studydrugs, my entire body was tense constantly, my eyes forgot to blink and dried out, my fingers unjointed themselves, craploads of sweating and some vomming in there too, drymouth, itchyhair, couldn't stop humming and growling.

"Markfive, I worry a little that the studydrugs are making my body weird," I told him after a week.

"Lol yeah, I noticed you were tweaking," he said. "You just need to take the edge off, the thing that works for me is fakeweeds, why don't I give you a little."

So at the end of the sesh he vaped some fakeweeds, a rotting golden skunksyrup, then I breathed the steam until my body relaxed.

Good side of fakeweeds, definitely my body stopped clenching, throat stopped humming and growling, skin stopped itching and sweating too, infact my skin prettymuch lost its feeling completely.

Bad side of fakeweeds, a complete new personality entered my skull, a guy who's terrified of everything and imagines disasters constantly.

Here is a typical fakeweed adventure, Step One, Brand offers to show me a wrestling vid and immediately a weedy fear seizes me. I'm afraid to watch, whoknows why, ohwait actually it's obvious, drugs have made me afraid of everything. But most of all I'm afraid to tell Brand the fakeweeds have made me afraid, so I just nod my head because also I am afraid to talk because if I say anything he'll hear my terrified voice.

So we watch, is it another Cram Jam, nope, instead it's the Eighteenth Wrestling Worldwar, every wrestler pretends to be a country, dyes his face, wears illaborate insulting costumes, yells in a fake language, stomps around invading territories. The goal is take over countries by throwing guys into the Ocean Pond, a lot of these guys can't swim either.

So Brand and I are watching Frants sprint into Ejipped, Frants wraps an accordion around Ejipped's head and smacks him with a long breadbat, Ejipped yells for help from his best friend, Ironne, but Ironne starts smirking and laughing like a psycho, ohno, Ironne has a secret friendship with Frants and now Frants and Ironne are teaming up to whirl Ejipped around in a circle and then fling him into the pond.

Meanwhile here are my specific i nsane f rightened t houghts when I watch this, *ohno, is Brand showing me this because he is trying to tell me something, a message so awfull he cannot put it into words and instead must show me this vid, it must be the message of, "you are Ejipped and I am Ironne, you think I am your friend but secretly I am friends with your enemy Frants, soon we will choke and drown you."*

Thanks for that, moron brain, well I guess the nextstep has to be, turn my eyes to Brand without moving my head, make sure his eyes are on the vid and not me, and with incredible terrified slowness begin to creep away, hope he doesn't notice and thankgod he doesn't, he's staring at the evil vid and gurgling chuckles, he'll never expect that I have shrunk down onto the floor like an animal, it's my only hope of escape.

Then Tray ambles up to us and says, "Warner, why are you slinking around on the floor and sideeyeing Brand like a lunatic," immediately I panic and sprint out of the school and into Mun World and spend the next three hours hiding in the section of Synthetic Trees.

That I would say was pretty typical for fakeweeds.

Finally one morning I whispered to Markfive, hey, I'm a little worried these fakeweeds have replaced my personality with the one of a frightened idiot.

"Lol, that sounds rough forsure and I totally get it," said Markfive, "soundslike you could use some anxmeds, I'm prescribed two a day because I have anxiety, just naturally though, I mean not from the fakeweeds or anything, fakeweed doesn't affect me like that, I've run a ton of experiments on myself."

And he opened a pillcap, I pinched a little powder out and mixed it into a drink.

Good side of anxmeds, I was no longer terrified, the heart stopped racing, the world was no longer full of people who want to kill me, infact I was pretty sure everyone was excited to hear what I had to say allthetime, also everyone admired the dancemoves that I perform now at regular intervals.

Bad side, this daily combo of studydrugs fakeweeds anxmeds turned me a littlebit into Markfive.

What do I mean by that, I mean I found myself maybe a little too confident, a little too brainless and chatty, talking without even deciding to, infact saying every single thought that I have, sort of assuming people want to hear every single one of my thoughts even though my thoughts moreandmore were just boring observations of myself, ee gee, "Hey everybody, I just realized food gets stuck the most often in the third upper toothgap from the right, there always seems to be some soft little mushball in that specific gap, isn't that kind of special and intresting, let's all think about the food in my toothgaps."

Or, "Hey everybody, I can rotate basic shapes super fast in my mind now, I'm doing it even while talking to you, look at that thing go, well I guess you can't but trustme it's pretty amazing, anyway I'll keep you posted."

Also I had fewer feelings, I felt like more of a robot, more intrested in inputs, outputs, drugs, and tasks.

But maybe it's an improvement. Afterall, who wants to be the Warner I used to be, who misses that anxious cautious loser afraid of improving himself, forget that kid, I don't even remember being him, thankgod he's not running the show anymore.

DREAMWORLD

At night my dreaming got stronger, but even less control than before, nodoubt it was the drugs.

No longer was I deciding to dream things, choosing my dreamstuff, instead it appeared in my head like a homeinvader, usually from the sky and enormous.

If I thought Lossy Indica was a Cram Jam of flushholes, automatically it was and I had no control, twentyscale kingkongs and godsillas waltzed in the street over our heads, smashing each other down through trapdoors.

A lunatic skyparade of cartwheeling airships and spaceshuttles, breaking apart and whipping chunks into the ground like oneway boomerangs, oops, it arrived in my mind and now it's in yours too.

If I thought a herd of asteroids was slowly charging us from below the horizon, lookout, here they come, sunrising from the ocean, drumming their hooves like a civilwar, this grim avalanche of spinning marbles coats us all in fire.

If I thought an airless darkness was extincting all lifeonearth, then goodbye lifeonearth, I know it's my fault but please believe I'm as bummed about this as you are, ohwell though, tomorrow's anotherday.

LIFEANDDEATHWORLD

And in the anotherday I was a charming druggy babbler, handsome Markfive's cool yoked excon buddy, the math was staying on my brainshelves and prettysoon I truly believed I could do anything.

But to really look the part you need some style.

The brand for me was obvious, racks and racks of it existed at Mun World in the glitzy section of Highend Halfscale Fashion, it even resembled the stylish threads of Markfive himself.

Enough was enough, it was time to get fresh, after a couple weeks of the Markfive drugprogram I yelled outloud to no one, "Enough is enough, it's time to get fresh," and strutted into Highend Halfscale feeling amazing and told the salesfriend Jeans, "Guesswhat, it's your luckyday, you're about to sell me a subscription to Fresh But Chill."

Jeans was overjoyed, I did three or four songsworth of slick dancemoves, we laughed until we cried and then shopped like maniacs and I walked out of there looking like a fresh miracle, thinking, *Mun World has been waiting across the parkinglot allalong for me to discover my true self, and now I am truly the truest Warner there ever was, fresh yet also chill.*

Did I think at all about the vanishing munmuns, the vampire hose in my neck, sure I did, it was defiant thoughts o f, *Look, rightnow I have some muns in munflow so it's a few weeks before the subscription outruns the allowance and whoknows what can happen between now and then,*

and what, you expect me to never spend munmuns like some kind of cheap scared loser, heck no,

and hey, prettysoon I'll retrack to Mathy where you're guaranteed a sweet income for life, I guess you could say the future's so bright, it literally blinded me.

I wasn't spending tons of time in the parkinglot anymore, all freetime has to be dedicated to math, also the parkinglot became kind of a messedup place for me, suddenly daves started following me around yelling, "CHOOCHOO, I'LL SAVE YOU PRINCESS, LOLLLLL."

Tray and Brand got weird around me too, finally I had to ask, crew, what's up.

"Dave, sorry, but everyone's watching this vid, is this really you," wondered Brand, hitting play.

Title comes on first: LITTLETRAIN FOLLIES, oldtimey font, nutbrown and flickering like a wildwest, piano clomping away.

Now in the vid are some rats, sitting in a boxcar, nibbling playingcards.

Prettysoon the vid wonders, who's sitting with these rats, let's have a slow lazy look over there, why it's little Usher in his cheap kimono, twitching and sweating.

Who else rides fake little trains, well how about little Prayer, look at her mashed into a passengercab, her princessdress is trapped but flapping in the wind.

"Loottenant, I do believe these trains get smallerandsmaller everyyear," she pipes, stiff and weird, in an accent she doesn't know.

And guesswho is next, dingdingding, you got it, little soldier Warner, face bulging through the glassless windows.

"Some rascally savage has surely shrunk them, Princess," shouts little soldier me in his high thin littlevoice.

Meanwhile in the parkinglot a whole crowd had formed around us, hooting and shoving, holycrap he's watching it he's watching it, lololol dave is that really you.

"Yup that's me," I confirmed, everyone had a massive freakout, I stood calmly in the middle of it making a face of no emotions.

Somebody found Frank and shoved him at me, this writerboy was the first to find the vid apparently, he wouldn't look me in the eye, smirking but terrified.

"Look," he babbled, "I just found it randomly onenight, it was on a pretty outthere comedy vidshare, I'm into altcomedy and super fringe vids and stuff, anyway I just stumbled on this, and, uh, I thought I recognized you. I mean it's not my fault it's outthere, it's not like I made it or anything, you can't really get mad at me."

Frank you bonehead, ofcourse I can get mad at you, obviously everyone around us hopes I will fight and probably kill you.

He outscaled me by a little but I was a ropey twitchy clobberer with a lifetime supply of brutal fight experience, meanwhile he had super breakable skinny wrists like the ankles of a chicken.

I glanced at the Eat Votech entranceway and saw Grace watching us, she looked horrified by everything.

"Greatjob, nerd," was all I said to him, pinched one of his cheeks and walked away, everyone groaned at the lack of fighting.

I showed Prayer the vid on the bus home, she went vomwhite in the face but stared unblinking through the whole thing.

"Ugh what a creepy clownshow," she shuddered, "ohwell everyone can go ahead and see it, anyone who tries to shame me with this vid will only add to my superhuman motivation, it's an artoffact of the life we've left behind forever, infact maybe we should watch this vid every morning to get furious."

I a littlebit wished I felt furious, instead I mostly felt nothing. *Huh that's me, that's pretty weird I guess, messedup stuff sure happened to that little guy a lot, sucks to be him but ohwell,* those were my thoughts, I knew that was kind of awfull.

But I was just a calm logical robot from drugs, who cares about the past, who has time for idiot poordramas, my friends now are math and middleriches.

I liked Markfive and he liked me, I mean how could he not. He liked being the friend and druglord of a smart positive toughguy, liked getting to guest sometimes at dinner and throw some game at eyerolling Daisy, liked the way Hue thanked and praised him for making a real difference in a poor's life. He even had customwork done on a backpack, put in legholes and a throne, now I can sit there, ride around on his back if he wants to take me anywhere, forexample a forest drugwalk with his doublescale buddies.

"Warner used to be littlepoor, like ratscale, plus this dave was in jail for a whole freaking year," he told the buddies immediately, they ofcourse were overjoyed.

"Warner, is this asshole allowed to call you a dave or do you need us to beat the crap out of him," said Markfive Buddy.

"So in jail did you make beers in a toilet, how does that even work, also when you were minimumsize did you ever realize you were so little you could take a razor and jump down someone's throat and then cut your way out through their stomach, anytime I see a littlepoor skittering around I can't stop worrying about that happening to me, infact is that why you were in jail in the firstplace," asked Another Markfive Buddy.

"Do you miss being littlepoor at all, like it must be amazing and trippy when everything is so much bigger than you and also you can't breathe I heard, honestly sometimes I wish I was little and freaking out constantly from the terrible pain, atleast I'd have real feelings and not be dead inside, life is pointless am I right, hahaha lmao," daydreamed Markfive Buddy.

"Markfive, I s aw y our d ad r oasting e lephants o n t he n ews, eating them in like four bites, your dad is a freaking mammoth," announced Another Markfive Buddy.

"His life actually sucks, being that big is pretty terrible," shrugged Markfive, casually trailing his fi ngers through a bu sh, hoping to seem laidback, meanwhile he had ripped the bush out of the ground.

Mostly I had to admit I didn't super understand these middlerich guys and their druggy ramblings, their conversationgames of Do I Feel Emotions Or Am I Tricking You and Who Cares The Least.

But sometimes I had a conversation that taught me something, forexample with one buddy named Elm, pretty quiet and apologetic deepthinker.

"I've been thinking, it must be hard for you to live in the house of a politician," he told me.

"Forsure it's hard, brutally hard sometimes but I mean in a lot of ways it's easy too, comfortable and prettygreat but yeah, it's hard allright, hard and easy in different ways I guess and can I ask what exactly are you getting at," I babbled all druggy.

"I just mean politicians and the whole government have kind of completely dicked littlepoors over," he said. "I mean when you really think about minmun, it's a little crazy."

"Littles have been dicked over forsure, but what can you do, life is supposed to be hard and cruel, now did you say *minmun*, min and then mun, is that the strange fake word you said or did you say a different word and it changed in the air between your mouth and my ears, whoa could that even happen," I rambled.

"Nono, you heard me right, minmun," he said. "The minimum number of munmuns you can have in your scale account."

"Minimum muns you can have is zero, telling you from experience," I said.

"Aha, okay, that's not actually true," he said. "Do you mind if I teach you about minmun?"

"Ofcourse ofcourse and I think you'll enjoy teaching me bytheway," I said.

"Okay," said Elm. "When you have zero muns in scale account, how big are you?"

"Tenthscale," I said.

"Yeah," said Elm. "But tenthscale corresponds to fivehundred munmuns in your scale account. So where does that fivehundred come from?"

"I just kind of figured, it's physically impossible for people to get smaller than tenthscale," I said.

"But it's not physically impossible," said Elm. "It's super possible. Scale is proportional to munmuns in scale account. That's munlaw, no exceptions. Ess is too to log em less sicks."

That shut me up.

"So what minmun is, is for every Yewess citizen with less than fivehundo in their scale account, the Yewess government keeps the difference in there for them, otherwise they would be smaller than tenthscale, infact anyone who went broke would completely disappear, like die, ess equals zero," he said.

"Wow," I said, amazed, although I didn't know if it was actually amazing or was it just the drugs.

"Yewess government decided, we can't let anyone slip below tenthscale, so we'll backstop them with fivehundo, a nd t hat's minmun, they could change the number at anytime," said Elm.

He silently watched me realize things.

"Prettynice of the government, I guess," I concluded.

"Well, is it?" he asked. "I mean, don't you wonder, why fivehundred? How did they settle on tenthscale?"

DREAMWORLD

Brave druggy me took the question to Hue soonafter, marching into his office afterschool with bright wild eyes and cool sweatless skin feeling sharp as heck in my mesh jacket and slinky jeans.

"Hue, I know you enjoy realtalking with me, furthermore frank exchanges are the essence of democracy, so with all that said, let's talk about minmun," I told him.

But he didn't hear or see me, so I had to hop up onto a chair and groove and boogie until I had his attention.

"Well hello there, Warner, how is everything going," said alwayspolite Hue.

"Firstofall, it's going amazing, feel free to ask Markfive to tell you about my progress in detail, everything's incredible, success is inevitable, infact I want you to completely forget that I ever asked to stick with Lifty, that was the thinking of a loser who disrespects himself and those around him, I've completely moved on and can't wait to achieve the most glorious results," I announced.

"Well, that's great to hear, just keep your eyes on the prize," chuckled Hue.

"Now I'd like to make a suggestion to you, a new policy for your platform, I really think this could be a gamechanger," I said.

"Well, I guess I'm all ears," he said.

"I think you should announce, hey people, heresthedeal, if you make me the countyboss of all of Lossy Indica, here's what I'm going to do," I said.

I paused because I really wanted him to wait for it.

"Did you forget what you were going to say," said Hue.

"Nope," I said.

"You were just quiet for a while," said Hue.

"You're going to announce that you're raising minmun," I triumphed.

Hue rolled his lips into his mouth and nodded a painfull nod of, *Oh, that.*

"Raise minmun from fivehundo to, just throwing this out there, fivethousand," I said. "And no one will be littler than fifthscale everagain! No more catattacks, no more hawkattacks, no one's drowning in the gutter, and probably everyone can use hospitals now, what an amazing and generous place Lossy Indica is, mostofall its king, Hue, thatsyou bytheway."

Hue grimaced, held up a finger of, *one sec, I have to take this*, tapped his ear, and stood quickly to face a camera.

"Violet, thanks for having me," he beamed, "in a way it's an honor to be personally insulted by the president, it's also very sweet of him to worry about this supposed buttcancer that is sapping me of all my strength and dignity, I guess that must mean I can't do *these* anymore," and he grabbed a pullup bar and loudly counted ten swift pullups.

"Now, you might be asking, well then is the president the one who has buttcancer," Hue wondered, "but I'm not even going to go there, *howabout we just focus on the issues*, thanks for having me."

And he tapped his ear again and sat back down, redfaced.

"Sorry, Warner, okay, now let's think about what you're proposing," panted Hue. "Because a minmun of fivethousand adds up to a lot of munmuns that the government would have to provide."

"Hmmm, is it really that much though, considering what you get, the lives you improve and save, isn't that basically priceless," I asked.

"Well, let's estimate the cost," he said. "Lossy Indica has a population of about fifteenmillion, twelvemillion at middlescale or littler, probably about fivemillion fifthscale or below. Let's be generous and say, onaverage, those fivemillion need twothousand in their scale to reach a minmun of fivethousand. Probably it's closer to threethousand, but let's lowball and say twothousand. That's tenbillion munmuns. I have to tell you the government doesn't have that kind of munmun just lying around."

"Okay," I said. "Okay. Yes. Okay."

He gave me that sad smile again, I was getting to know it pretty well bynow.

"But," I said, "here's how to get your tenbillion, you got threemillion Lossy Indicans above middlescale, maybe just ask them for fourthousand each, sure it's not nothing, a little taxhike forsure, but not even onepercent of their scale account. Here's your slogan, Lose An Inch, Save A Life, I mean who's the psycho who doesn't want to be a lifesaver."

"Sure," agreed Hue, "and let me tell you what will happen if I do that, if I announce this plan today, tomorrow my Orange enemies make some vids called WHERE WILL IT END??, today Hue asks for an inch of your height for giveaways to littles who refuse to earn a bigger scale the honest way, and Warner ofcourse that's their words, not mine, but that's what they'll say, they'll say today Hue wants an inch for minmun, tomorrow Hue will take another inch to pay for littleroads you won't use, the day after that Hue needs three of your inches to build littleschools your kids won't attend, it's never going to end. So vote Orange and keep your scale and your nice life."

He watched me plan out my response, he's played this chessgame tons of times and I'm a beginner.

"But there are more littles than bigs," I said. "So you could still get enough votes to beat those evil lying Oranges."

"Except littles don't vote as much as bigs do," said Hue.

"Make them vote," I said.

"Believe me, we try," said Hue.

"Okay, then only take munmuns from the super big," I said, getting desperate. "Take away a foot from everyone threescale or taller, I mean that's got to be tons of munmun and who cares if you're already twentyfeet?"

"Sure, and if that's your plan, let me ask you something," said Hue. "Have you ever been to Balustrade?"

I shook my head.

"None of the homes there are attached to the ground," said Hue.

He gave me a silence to solve the riddle in, but it didn't seem like a riddle, more of a hilarious screwup by crazy riches, homes sliding around like wild, who even knows what those giant brains are thinking.

"Gotta be honest, that sounds a little dangerous and stupid," I said.

"Ha, ha, ha," laughed Hue. "I can assure you, those houses are the safest in the world. No, it's for a very specific reason. The gianthomes in Balustrade can be slipped onto trucks and barges at anytime. Now, why do you think that is?"

I had no idea.

"Here's why," said Hue. "If the city of Balustrade jacks up richtaxes, or the county of Lossy Indica jacks up richtaxes, honestly even if a nearby cityboss like me goes a month without making a loud declaration of eternal love for our brilliant generous jobcreating riches, the bigs of Balustrade can leave. They can leave in the middle of the night if they want. They can load up their homes and belongings and in the morning they're all in another town, another state, another country, where taxes are lower and politicians are nicer."

Hue was realtalking me now forsure, real Hue was telling me his real truths and fears, no games or politeness and it shut me up.

"And really there's nowhere they can't go," Hue told me, "because there's nowhere in the world that wouldn't kill to have the bigs of Balustrade. There's no investmentgroup that wouldn't do awfull unspeakable things to play with their hunbillions of munmuns. There's no localeconomy that wouldn't burn everything to the ground and convert immediately to bigrichservices. Nothing's better for jobs than having bigriches around.

Agriculture, struction, younameit. Think about the superflora and superfauna they have to eat. Think about their enormous luxurious clothes. Think about how huge their staffsalaries are to pay the middleriches who have to cook, serve, groom and launder, drive and pilot.

"So a higher minmun would ofcourse be great and humane," Hue finished. "But if we raise minmun here in Lossy Indica and it spooks the bigs into leaving Balustrade, then we lose jobs, then we lose munmuns, then prettysoon we have to give up on higher minmun anyway, plus the county is doomed now."

"Okay okay," I said. "Okay okay okay."

"But it's good you're thinking about this stuff, and please let me know if you have more ideas, newideas are always welcome," he winked, and went back to work as the cleaningcars whirred past in the hall.

LIFEANDDEATHWORLD

Not even two weeks later, Markfive took me to Balustrade, I got to see for myself those wild wanderpalaces.

It started with Markfive trying to lowkey date Daisy.

"It's my stupid dad's birthday, I have to go and man I'm going to hate it, hey do you byanychance feel like suffering a bigrich party with me," Markfive asked Daisy all smooth.

"Nope, sounds terrible," said Daisy.

"I'll go," offered Kitty.

"I mean, it's not terrible, like it is always intresting atleast to see Balustrade, like in a sick perverted sense," said Markfive.

"Unfortunately I'm not a sick pervert," said Daisy.

"Lol," admitted Markfive.

"I would like to go," reminded Kitty.

"Kitty, no one's even talking to you," said Daisy.

But Markfive glanced at Kitty and a thoughtbubble appeared above his head of, *perhaps if I flirt with Kitty then Daisy will get jealous.*

"Kitty, I would be honored to have you as a date to my dad's awfull birthday," said Markfive all smooth while Daisy tried to dislocate her eyeball.

"Ohmygod that's fantastic, hey can we bring Warner too, it

would be a real eyeopener for him, part of your schoolproject," beamed Kitty even smoother.

"Uh, well sure I guess," said Markfive.

"Try not to crash and kill everyone," suggested Daisy.

"Ohmygod I would love to come, do you think I could come too," Prayer asked me.

I took it to Kitty and she cringed a little and said, "You can ask Markfive I guess, but I think that's pushing it."

"Kitty doesn't like me," sorrowed Prayer back in our bedroom. "It's okay, you just wait, I'll make it to Balustrade one day onmyown, who will be laughing then."

"You I guess," I said, backing away from my crazy sis.

But I decided to push it and asked Markfive, he surprised me by being pumped.

"Oh hellyeah," said Markfive. "Greatidea to bring your sis, she's hilarious."

So five of us drove up to Balustrade in his triplecar. Kitty rode in the frontseat and in the back Prayer and I were strapped in next to Lily, the mom of Markfive, a happy wicked pretty gumdrop in resplendent dresses, coppery hair waterfalling in every direction, burbling giggles like a fountain.

"Ohmygod, I love your hair so much, can it even be real," marveled smooth Prayer to Lily.

"Haha no ofcourse not, anyway thank you, Blessing," Lily said, she wasn't great with names. Meanwhile Prayer beamed like, *that's my name allright, it's Blessing.*

"It's true, Lily, you're looking fantastic, this idiot Mark's going to take one glance at you and then kill himself," I said.

"I tell you what, you little morsel of muscle, he absolutely will if he sees me walking around with a stud like you," she said.

"Mom, Warner, can you atleast not flirt right in front of me," said Markfive.

"Can I just ask, which of your friends *can* I flirt with right in front of you," sighed Lily.

The roads stopped tenmiles from Mark's house, infact tenmiles from everyhouse, Balustrade had no internal roads. Instead the highwayexit emptied into a complex of hangars, parkingtowers, airstrips, bunkers, everywhere was teams of drivers scurrying around arranging the blimps and tanks, gunmen too.

MARK IS FIFTYFIVE BIRTHDAYPARTY sang the twinkling screens above one parkingtower, we zoomed inside to park and by the time we were out of our car one of Mark's drivers had pulled up next to us in a golfcart to take us the last tenmiles over a biggolfcourse.

"Markfive, Lily, are you sure each of your guests will bring birthday happiness to Mark," said the driver, staring at me and then Prayer.

"Who knows, I mean you never know who's going to make him happy, yolo though basically," said Markfive.

The driver continued to stare at us wordlessly, hoping to turn us around and throw us back down the road with sheer eyepower.

"One thing I have a hunch Mark will not love, is if his fifth and smartest son is disrespected by having his guests and friends turned away, just a hunch but maybe you'd agree," suggested Lily.

In the golfcart I whispered to Markfive, is Mark not going to want me or Prayer at this party.

"Here's what that was about," explained Markfive. "Mark doesn't like having people around whose voices he can't hear super well. Basically anyone smaller than middlescale, he really has trouble hearing them, and he hates that because then he has to say *what*, and they have to repeat themselves, and it interrupts the otherwise smooth flow of his life. So, I guess if you have anything to say to him, please bellow it at the top of your lungs, but also feel free to just shut up, that would be fine too."

"Speak your mind," urged Lily, "I will protect you." And she hugged me from the side, my head into the pillowy skin beneath her tits.

We crested over the eighteenth hole and looked down into the wide forest lipping the bay, five big clearings near the water, a bighome in the middle of each one.

Even if you think before you see bighomes, *I know what they're like, I've seen them on the news sometimes*, nope, you have no idea, even looking at the realthing you don't see them, your eyes refuse to eye them.

Each was hundreds of feet high and a halfmilewide, each was its own work of art. One was a chunk of glass cubes, one was a plantation. One was a lordoftherings castle of craggy boulders and one was a shintoeshrine, roofcorners curling up like dry leaves. And one was a pastel spannishvilla, home of Mark, right now swarms of drones are hanging birthdaybanners over it.

On the coast of a bay the size of a neighborhood, as big as Eat

Almanac, all you had were five bighomes, although then through the trees you could see little villages around each bighome, the homes of the staffing middles.

Prayer was speechless, soundless, eyes and mouth ohing like a fish.

"I guess this is the town of Balustrade," I asked stupidly.

"Oh, this is just the southernmost tip," said Markfive. "It continues north like this about a hundredmiles."

"It's not really a town, think of it more like a nationalpark," suggested Lily.

"No visitorcenter though," Kitty pointed out.

"And all the rangers are dicks," said Markfive, loudenough for the driver to hear.

As we motored down to the water I spotted him floating i n the ocean in bright boyant waterrobes, Mark, the tenbillionair birthdayboy, a handsome giant with saltandpepper stubble and a beautifull head of uplifted rigid hair. I could see his giant eyes all the way from land, brown emeralds in milk, skin also was toadcolor. His hairy knees and tum were little islands and the waves were barely ripples as they passed around him.

Around him were various barges of dancing partiers, chefs roasting fishes on openflames, barkeeps stirring giant vats of drinks, a rental popstar singing a familiar song.

Waitaminute, that stupid song plays over the speakers at Mun World like every twentyminutes, is that the actual freaking guy who sings that freaking song, holy crap yes it's Famous Randy in his famous turtleneck, that's amazing.

Mark said nothing, basically just bobbed upanddown, floating there listening and watching. His movements were super slow, I wondered if giants can't move at normal speeds, then I realized he's trying not to make huge waves that would drown everyone.

I stared like a maniac as he slowmo reached a dripping arm from the ocean, plucked a couple twofoot fish right off the grill, dropped them whole into his roomsize mouth, snacked and crunched the bones and heads.

I kept staring and goggling as he lifted a vat of vodkatonic from another barge and tipped that onto his bedsize tongue, meanwhile the bevbarge was rocking and rolling because there used to be a ton of booze on one side and then there wasn't, the bartenders were drenched in sloshing vodkatonic and rearranging vats in a frenzy.

"What a crazy and disgusting life, makes me glad he didn't marry my mom tobehonest," muttered Markfive as our motorboat arrived at the familybarge.

"Sure, agree, try not to say such things in front of your sibs though," murmured Lily, and we tried to approach Mark Family with dignified walks on the shuddering platform.

Mark Family was various babymamas and offsprings, elegant clothes all around, tuxes and businessgowns. Markfive was the only young slacker, also the littlest. His three and fourscale brothers and sisters gave him poisonous smiles.

"Little Five, you're looking littler than ever, hope you're not having mun trouble," wondered a bro.

"Such a shame you can't afford respectfull clothes and instead must dress like a thuggy hoodlum," murmured a sis.

Markfive ignored them all graciously, I was pretty impressed, I would be freaking out and mashing faces before long.

"BE RIGHT BACK," said giant Mark suddenly to everyone from the middle of all the barges, a low normalguy voice except it's like he said it right in my ear, from twohundred feet away.

And he sank under the water, became a shadow and submarined away from us, rippling currents rocked the barges and everyone lost their balance, Famous Randy collapsed violently and hopped right back up bloodynosed like it was part of his danceroutine.

Twominutes later Mark surfaced about a halfmile further out to sea, but no one was looking at him. Weirdly everyone seemed to be taking an intrest in the shoreline instead.

"Warner, Blessing, don't look at him, turnaway," murmured Lily.

"Wait why, what's happening," I said.

"Nature called," she said.

"He's taking a crap," said Markfive.

"Oh dang," said Prayer.

"He's not supposed to crap in the ocean but who's going to stop him," explained Markfive.

"Baby, enough," said Lily, but enormous hostile ears had already heard her disrespectfull son.

"Five, wow, judgmental of Dad much," accused Markthree, a bald fourscale big in a shimmering threepiecesuit, looming over us with hungry eyes. Behind him his giant eaglenosed mom hissed, "*Yeah.*"

"Mybad, Three, mybad," said Markfive. "It's easy for me to be judgmental, unlike you I am not big enough for the privilege of wiping the residual craps out of Dad's huge soakingwet butt."

A littledrunk Lily wanted her son to not go there but instead accidentally laughed.

"Five Mom, your son is making an ugly spectacle at Mark's birthdayparty, can you not get him undercontrol," demanded Three Mom.

"Nope," decided Lily.

"I enjoy your jealous ignorant middletalk, hilarious middle-kid, I truly do," boomed Markthree. "You don't even know how defecation works for us bigs, you don't understand biologically why we need to defecate into the ocean sometimes, well dont-worry, you'll never have to, have fun with your lazy middlelife."

"Yup, it's super tragic that I don't understand the glory of oceancrapping," said Markfive, b ut T hree w as a lready h ustling away importantly to get the lastword.

Back on land, we had some fish in the bigpatio, the vast tablelegs and structures towering over most of us.

It took me back to being littlepoor forsure, being roofed by tables, gazing up at the undersides of everything.

"Are these fish safe to eat, with all the oceancrapping that's going on," I asked.

"Put it this way," said Markfive. "These fish don't get crapped on more than any other fish you've eaten."

"Fascinating, I'm all ears, please explain," chirped Prayer.

"Lol, what," said Markfive. "Do you seriously want me to talk about ocean sewage while you're eating."

"I'm dead serious, my appetite for knowledge is completely limitless," Prayer told him. "Literally at any hour of the day, in any situation, I am ready to learn exciting facts!"

Both Markfive and Lily thought this was hilarious.

"Will you get a load of this sweet crazy gogetter," cried Lily.

Meanwhile Kitty walked me around introducing me to rich randos, now I understand why she was so eager to come to a terrible party.

"Warner let me introduce you to Shell and her husband Shelving, patrons of music and worthycauses and additionally they own Speedy Hospital. Shell and Shelving please meet Warner, he's the totalrockstar of the pilot program my dad Hue and I have created, the goal is for riches to host littlepoors of particular promise, the program loans them scale munmun and gives a modest allowance and these littles can experience life at halfscale, go to real schools, get real jobs, begin to lift their families out of terrible poorness," explained Kitty, eyes shining like crazy, impossible for you not to get a little weepy seeing the dogood passion of this righteous girl.

"Maybe the program can teach them about disease and hygiene too," Shelving said.

"Oh absolutely," said Kitty.

"Inconsistent medhabits are responsible for medproof germs, and that's byfar the greatest problem we face as a species, believe me, if we all die because of the carelessness of littles it would be a great shame," Shelving told us.

"A whole wing of the program could deal with littlehealth," Kitty realized, "what a great way to address this problem, you could endow the Shell and Shelving Littlehealth Coordinator position!"

"Hmmm," said Shelving, giving a thoughtfullnod of, *How about I endow your program with thoughtfullnodding instead of actual munmuns.*

We were all quiet.

"Well, we'll be tracking this program with great intrest, and ofcourse if the results are good, we'd be happy to discuss being part of it," said Shell finally.

"Certainly not on the hosting side, I do not relish the possibility of coexisting with a vector of deadly medproof germs, now young man, can you tell me what immunizations you've received to date," Shelving asked me.

"He's all caught up," said Kitty quickly, hustling me away to the next old bigs.

Meanwhile a bigdinner was prepped out on the beach, separate from our middledinner.

We muttered and tried not to stare as Mark strode in from the water, lowered himself onto the sand next to the firepits. Giant silhouettes appeared up the beach meanwhile, a few neighbor bigs ambling down from their palaces, four men and one woman, staffs zipping around beneath their feet on ayteevees.

Prettysoon us middles were sitting around Mark and his neighbors on the sand like we were a concertaudience, watching and murmuring as the bigs devoured roasted sharks and buffaloes, glugging and swishing from wiskybarrels.

"MARK," boomed one bigneighbor at Speech Time, "HAPPY BIRTHDAY MY MAN, I ADMIRE YOU, A SIMPLEGUY WITH SIMPLETASTES. THE SON OF POTATO FARMERS

ON GOVERNMENT MIDDLESCALE, LOOK AT YOU NOW, A SELFMADE MAN EATING A WHOLE AQUARIUM OF SHARKS. THE LORD KING GOD IS TRULY GOOD TO THOSE WHO WORK HARD AND DREAM BIG."

"The Yewess government loans scale munmuns to farmers because they farm better with bigger bodies, that's what he means by government middlescale," whispered Kitty to me.

"SOME WILL SAY MARK'S GREATEST ACHIEVEMENT IS HIS DRUGEMPIRE," thundered another neighbor, the smallest but still atleast tenscale, "OTHERS WILL SAY IT'S WHEN HE RENTED THE NEWS FOR A YEAR AND PUT AN ORANGE BACK IN THE WHITEHOUSE. BUT IF YOU ASK ME, MARK'S GREATEST ACHIEVEMENT IS, HE PUT TWELVE DIFFERENT BABIES IN ELEVEN DIFFERENT BEAUTIFULL WOMEN AND NEVER GOT TRICKED INTO MARRYING A SINGLE ONE. I MEAN LOOK AT THESE FINE LITTLE HONEYS. WELL SOME OF THEM YOU HAVE TO REMEMBER WHAT THEY LOOKED LIKE WHEN THEY WERE YOUNGER, I GUESS MOST OF THEM, BUT TAKE MY WORD FOR IT, EVERY SINGLE ONE WAS A KNOCKOUT, ANYWAY GREATJOB AND HERE'S TO MARK."

"JOHN," said this guy's bigwife. "SHUT THE FUCK UP."

"OBVIOUSLY I'M JUST KIDDING," said John.

"MARK, HAPPY BIRTHDAY," speeched a third big, the oldest. "ENJOY THESE TIMES AND I URGE YOU NOT TO BECOME CARELESS. YOU ARE SURROUNDED BY WOULDBE TRAITORS, HAVE NODOUBT ABOUT THAT.

YOUR FRIENDS, YOUR STAFF, ALL ARE SNAKES WHO
WOULD BETRAY YOU AT THE DROP OF A HAT. THAT'S
HOW IT IS WITH ME, SNAKES EVERYWHERE I LOOK.
NO, I WANT THEM TO HEAR ME SAY IT. WHERE IS MY
CHIEF OF STAFF? HE IS THE MOST VENOMOUS SNAKE
OF ALL. WARREN, YOU JEWDISS, YOU CAN'T EVEN
LOOK ME IN THE EYE."

"I'm looking you in the eye right now, sir, I would never betray
you," yelled poor Warren, opening his eyes as wide as possible, also
pointing at them with his fingers.

"*LIAR*," trumped the old guy, jaw quivering, losing foodjuice
and blood back out of his mouth and onto his shirt.

"BILL, CAN YOU NOT DO THIS AT MY
BIRTHDAYPARTY," asked Mark.

"WARREN LIES LIKE A DOG, BUT I WILL OUTLIVE
HIM AND WHATSMORE I WILL OUTLIVE ALL OF YOU,
EVERY LAST ONE," said Bill, "I KNOW PERFECTLYWELL
YOU ALL THINK I AM WEAK AND CLOSE TO DEATH,
BUT I HAVE MANY GALLONS OF FRESH YOUNG BLOOD
SIPHONED INTO MY VEINS EVERY MORNING, INFACT
WHY DON'T I SHOW YOU JUST HOW WEAK I AM."

Bill got up too fast, teetertottered for a second and everyone
gasped and shrieked, we all thought he was going to crash and kill
some of us. But he stayed on his feet and shakily walked into the sea.

He was in to about his ankleknobs when he dropped his pants
and squatted, naturecalled.

"WARREN, I WOULD HATE TO HAVE YOUR JOB,"
deadpanned calm Mark, it was funny but everyone laughed way

too hard, slapping each other and staggering around, loudest was Markthree.

"I am truly gratefull for your patience and understanding, sir," barked Warren, then he murmured into his headset, "I need boats in the water, shallowboats and nets, it's a codetwelve, go go go."

Mark's chief of staff was a threescale named Heather, she quietly tapped Markfive on the shoulder as we sat and watched Famous Randy dance and sweat through his sixth straight hour of performance as dozens of acrobats set themselves on fire and jumped over his head.

"Markfive, sir, I hope it's a goodtime, your father invites you to a private audience so that you may pay birthday respects," murmured Heather.

"Great," said drunk and druggy Markfive. "Can I bring one of my friends?"

"Again, it is a private audience, and I'm sure Mark would prefer to speak with you oneonone," suggested Heather.

"Nodoubt he would," said Markfive, lifting me onto his shoulders like a chickenfight, I pretended not to be terrified.

Conveyorbelts helped us along to Mark's study, an arenaroom with clouded ceiling, desk the size of Hue Family House, curtains billowing like shipsails in the nightbreeze.

Mark lounged on a vast floormat in a robe woven from ropes.

"HELLO, SON," said Mark.

"Hi, Dad," said Markfive. "This is Warner bytheway, he's my friend, used to be littlepoor which is freaking nuts when you think about it."

"HELLO, WARNER," said Mark.

"Happy birthday sir," I screamed, terrified he would have to say *what,* thankgod he didn't.

"THANK YOU," he said, leaning the great head down to us like a crashing moon. "MARKFIVE, LET ME LOOK AT YOU. LOOK UP AT MY FACE. LOOK UP, SON. THERE YOU GO. YOU'RE REALLY A HANDSOME YOUNG MAN, YOU KNOW THAT? ALTHOUGH YOU LOOK TIRED, MAYBE A LITTLE PALE. ARE YOU GETTING EVERYTHING YOU NEED?"

"Sure, fine, whatever," said Markfive, immediately around his dad his voice gets high and whiny.

Mark nodded, waiting for more, not getting it.

Then he said, "IN SOME WAYS YOU'RE SO MUCH LIKE I WAS AS A TEEN. IT ALWAYS MAKES ME SO HAPPY TO SEE YOU. EVEN IF YOU CAN'T DRESS RESPECTFULLY OR OBEY CERTAIN BASIC RULES OF ETIQUETTE."

"Are you wasted or something," said wasted Markfive.

"HA HA HA," laughed Mark, rumbling the floor, "WOULDN'T THAT BE NICE. YOU KNOW I CAN'T EVEN GET CLOSE TO DRUNK. IT TAKES SUCH A VOLUME JUST TO GET TIPSY."

"I'm pretty sure the strongest shit Mark Drug Co sells could get you pretty messed up though," said Markfive. "Like whale-tranks, I'm sure you could get wasted on a couple of those."

"LITTLE FIVE," said Mark, losing intrest in the wasted-ness convo, "I HAVE SOMETHING I WANT TO TALK TO YOU ABOUT. YOU'VE ALWAYS BEEN SUCH A SMART

KID, SO BRIGHT AND SO QUICK, JUST LIKE I WAS AT YOUR AGE, I FORGET IF I SAID THAT ALREADY. ANYWAY THE SKY IS TRULY THE LIMIT FOR YOU. BUT RECENTLY YOU HAVE SEEMED DISENGAGED TO ME, CONTENT TO LET YOUR MIND GO A LITTLEBIT TO WASTE, FINE WITH LIVING A LESS FULFILLED LIFE, ALSO OFCOURSE THE REPEATED CARCRASHES ARE TROUBLING. BASICALLY I WORRY THAT SCHOOL ISN'T CHALLENGING YOU ENOUGH."

"Well, I think it is challenging though," whined Markfive. "I mean I'm getting bees in everything."

"THAT IS EXACTLY WHY I THINK YOU'RE NOT BEING CHALLENGED," said Mark.

There was a sick melty footsmell but it wasn't feet, instead it was a bathtub of fonduecheese, next to the tub was a slab of rock holding enormous breads, and surenough, the giant leaned back and began dipping and munching, splatters of cheeselava landed all around us.

"I mean, what are you suggesting, do you wish I went to a tougher school and had gotten cees and dees and felt crappy, nothanks," scoffed Markfive.

"I THINK AT A MORE RIGOROUS SCHOOL, WHAT WOULD HAVE HAPPENED WAS, YOU WOULD HAVE *TRIED*," said Mark.

"Cool theory I guess," said Markfive. "From a scientist who checks in on his experiment once every few months or so."

Mark winced with dignified hurt, made a face of, *I wish you could understand the very good reasons why I cannot be your everyday dad.*

A pair of seagulls flew through the window for breadcrumbs but he swatted them like bugs.

"CAN WE TALK ABOUT YOUR EIGHTEENTH BIRTHDAY PRESENT," said Mark, leaning the head toward us again, it was like being talked to by a garage.

"I don't want it," said Markfive. "Give it to Warner."

Mark sighed and his breathstink was amazing, a thousand rotting animals thicking the air. His swampy eyes rolled toward me. Their switchbacking veins were faded snakes, puffing and shrinking a little with his pulse.

"Warner would do way better with it than me, this dave has wild streetsmarts, he used to live in freaking garbage, plus he has incredible discipline, look how yoked he is," slurred Markfive. "Even his sister would crush it. She literally wants to never stop learning facts. She literally said that. Warner, tell him."

"BE HONEST WITH ME, LITTLE FIVE. WHY DID YOU INSIST ON BRINGING A FRIEND TO WHAT SHOULD BE A PRIVATE SITDOWN BETWEEN FATHER AND SON," asked Mark.

"I guess I just like pissing you off," said Markfive, voice squeaking on *piss*.

Mark nodded, leaned back, his eyes darkening and closing off.

"AND WHY IS THAT," he boomed.

"Because I know no one else is doing it," said Markfive.

Mark was munching ravenously now, inhaling dripping breads in a barely controlled panic.

"THAT IS NOT NECESSARILY A GREAT REASON TO DO SOMETHING," he told us, and snapped his fingers, like a thundering treecrash, Heather came to politely kick us out.

On the way home, Lily sat upfront with Markfive, she was also tipsy but trying to be serious, wanting to talk sense into the headstrong son.

"Sweetie, you gotta play a little nicer with your bros and sisses," she said.

"Ugh," snapped angry Markfive, driving toofast and lurchy.

"I just mean, play the game atleast a little bit," she urged.

"Mom, chill," he muttered.

"I know the game is terrible," she said. "But otherwise you're wasting the only good part of having Mark as your dad."

Markfive caught Kitty's eye in the rearview and explained, "For my birthday present, my dad wants to give me solodream sleepmeds."

"Do you not like dreaming with other people?" asked Kitty sadly.

"No no no, not the drug, the company," said Markfive. "My dad wants to give me a slice of his actual company, the part that makes the solodream drug."

"Ohhhhhh," said Kitty. "Oh wow."

Lily craned around to look at us and said, "Poor Warner and Blessing have no idea what we're talking about!"

"Her name's actually Prayer," said Markfive, and Prayer said nothing but I could hear her glow.

Lily announced, "Warner and Prairie are sitting back there like, *huh, excuse me, solodream, sleepmeds, these middleriches are babbling insanely like they've lost their minds, are they about to gobble us up like two little treats?!"*

"Mom, be less of a drunken maniac," said Markfive.

Kitty explained, "Warner, Prayer, solodream is what the bank gives you before Scale Up or Scale Down to keep your Dreamworld separate from everyone else's, so you don't damage everyone and yourself, I mean cyclelogically."

"No no ofcourse I remember," said Prayer.

I did too, remembered my own private dreamcity, my unpeopled dreamyewess, the outofcontrol feeling of getting bigger than the planet, bigger than all of space, digging myself out of the airless universe and back into the underbank, yellings of *no no no.*

"Yeah," said impatient Markfive, "so basically it's a product with only one customer, the bank, they buy about the same amount every-year and that's it, the end, super boring and dumb, it's the dumbest business ever."

"Oh, I don't know, I think you could do great things with it," breathed giddy Prayer.

"Nope," snapped Markfive. "No one could. It's the slice of Mark Drug Co you would give to an idiot to run."

"Baby, I get it," said Lily. "But what you're missing is, Mark's *giving it to you.* Two, Three, Girlmark, Four, Girlmarkagain, they don't have their own little companyslices. They all just work under him. You're the only one he's putting in business for yourself."

"I don't want to talk about it," yelled Markfive, flooring the gaspedal, and we sped over terrified halfcars back up into Wet Almanac.

DREAMWORLD

The weeks whipped past and my dreaming got wild enough, daves started mentioning it at school, they didn't even know it was mine.

"Something's up in Dreamworld, last night someone made me dream my body was a song," grumbled one surly lifter.

"My whole freaking family keeps getting trapped with Famous Randy inside the thoughtbubbles of a horse," mumbled another.

It was all the chems turbocharging my mind for sure, the dreaming didn't even feel like work, I just refused to touch any brakes and let every thought speed around, put away the clips and shears and let the weeds grow wildly.

I got used to ignoring the tick tick tickle of random dreamers trying to dream their way to me, flickering flashlights from across valleys and oceans, tapping faraway doors they think are mine, all the poor and rich Lossy Indicans who want to know who is setting the inkfires, whose breath is making windtrees, who is bursting bubblehills and crashing roadwaves into the pavebeach, who is shifting the mathy grids we're stuck in, who is carving little shapes in time, rhythms out of walls and air.

Most of these people, did I care about them, no, well yes but did I need them to know, *it's Warner dreaming all this, this wild bananas dreamstuff is copywrite Warner, don't reproduce without permission*, nope.

Now did I care about Kitty, did I want her to know it's me, well yeah, I mean that would be nice.

But did Kitty notice, notreally, no.

Everynight instead she made her music, she played for her audiences, and my dreamstuff couldn't reach inside the operafortress.

A couple times I asked her, hey, do you ever leave that crazy castle, do you ever wonder what other people can dream.

"Playing music is all I want to do in Dreamworld really," she said.

"But what if someone wants to make something for you," I asked.

"I guess they have to learn to make it in wakingworld," she shrugged and grinned.

Sometimes too in Dreamworld I used her songs, made a channel to it and played it over speakers like in Mun World and then the dream really goes bright, wild, oily, you wake up with a quick heart and wet eyes, for a few minutes you're not anywhere.

And I waited for her to take the hint, get curious, come exploring onenight and see what other people can dream, ay kay ay me.

And in Lifeanddeathworld retrack test came roaring at me but really it was me roaring at retrack test, gaining speed and building force, melting the days away with my whitehot mind, racing backandforth through the rooms of the house of math, muttering facts during Lifty workouts, hammering practicequestions in the livingroom, demolishing entire practicetests, looking like the last act of a beautifull successstory afterall, Hue Family had highhopes for me again.

And that whole time I was not myself, barely even human, a robot without emotions or memories.

Markfive a nd I s topped t alking a smuch, I n oticed h e s tarted enjoying me less, I stopped being a badass to him, was really just a studynerd.

He started leaving twentyminutes early from studysesh, then an hour, then before long he wasn't even coming inside the house, every-morning I just trotted out to his car to do drugs, walked back inside as he sped away, I didn't care, fine on my own.

Only in Dreamworld was I really alive, did I have desires, giant wants that made me ache, but everymorning I couldn't remember what they were.

The last weekend arrived, last days to study before retrack on munday.

Daughterday I took all nine sections of a practicetest and toppled them all, great grades, two perfects even.

Sonday I did it again, even better, four perfects.

Hue said Warner it's clear that you're truly ready, Kitty said You can do this you can change your life forever, Prayer said Bro I'm so proud of you.

I knew I should be feeling feelings, I knew I should feel pride and excitement, instead I just watched myself getting hugged and celebrated, I was above my own body watching coldly.

The night before the test my dreams were berserk, every dead and buried object birthed a thousand ghosts, every thrownaway bag and bottle, every broken piece of tech came alive and danced, *humans don't need us anymore so now we are free*, a thousand ghostworlds poured out of the trashed one.

I almost flew into the operahouse and yelled stop the show, Kitty I want you to see this, maybe even need you to see it, live for just a second in the poem that I wrote for you.

Instead what I did was wait, lurk, hover in every ghostpoem and watch for her.

Waited for the wildness to finally c rack t he o perawalls, b leed shadows in, shimmerings, playfull vapors, waited for Kitty to realize, *I should find him.*

She never did, someone else found me though.

Someone who knew me pretty well, knew how to reach me. Instead of the faraway tick tick ticklings, faint purrings of other people's doorbells, I got a rain of pebbles against my window that night, a gray firework in my sky.

His hair grew and ungrew, like he couldn't remember whether he had it still, and all he could do atfirst was repeat, "I thought it was you."

He was dreaming super weak, blipping in and out, repeating himself, recognizing me and forgetting and remembering again.

"I thought it was you," Usher said, smiling.

"Usher," I choked.

"I thought it was you," he said, exactsame smile.

Around us every ghost shut their eyes and held their breath.

"Usher, you're alive, where are you, tell me everything," I demanded.

"I saw the dreamstuff, I thought it was you," he told me, overandover he said it, I needed to shake him, I needed to touch his skin and couldn't.

"Usher, focus please, tell me are you in trouble," I begged. "Do you need help, where can I find you, please."

"Great nice wild dreamstuff," he said. "I thought it was you, Warner."

"Where are you," I pleaded. "Where are you."

"I knew the dreamghosts were Warner, I knew it was you," he repeated, it made him happy and ripped leaks in my heart.

293

I sat with him for a month of dreamtime, onenight but a thousand hours, sometimes that's how long it takes.

And at the end finally h e b linked, g ot v ivid, m urmured, " Nono, notyet, headandshoulders, notyet," and cringed, just a little grimace but it was worse than a scream.

He bowed his baldhead and for a swift moment I saw the face inked into the back of his skull, the crude gape of a cartoon idiot, tongue lolling out of a drooly frown and goggly eyes, I had barely enough time to realize I was looking at a faceboy tat before he woke up.

He left me only a glimpse of the Sand Dreamough reservewar, glitching and miraging like bad uservids from the news, the view from his new sad bedroom remained for a few tooshort moments after he popped out of Dreamworld like a weak bubble.

VI.
USHER

I woke up, sun was buried, house was still, Prayer was snoring.

My heart was pounding, mind was pretty clear though, the only thing in there was, *save my friend.*

I dressed myself, went out into the house looking for life, first awake person I found was Daisy. She was playing shootemups in the hometheater, upallnight, headphones to cancel sound.

"Daisy," I said, she heard nothing.

Warner what are you doing, Daisy's not going to help you.

Hue was already up with the weak sun for morningcardio, I ran in front of the hamstermachine, waved my arms frantically.

"Hue, help, I saw my friend in Dreamworld and he needs to be rescued," I yelled as he chugged and puffed. "He was dizzy, dazed, not himself forsure, a squad tatted his head, I think I know who kidnapped him too, a faceboy mob led by the criminal mastermind Shoulderheads, we need to help."

"Slowdown, hey, slow it down, your friend definitely told you he was kidnapped?" panted Hue, running with arms and legs in his hamsterwheel.

"Well no, but I mean he barely said anything, he wasn't

dreaming too good, I'm really worried about him, Hue, we have to do something," I begged.

"Do you think it's possible he might have been on drugs," wondered Hue.

"No," I said, "I mean probably no, I mean look it's possible if maybe they're forcing him, but nonono he was like me in kidjail, his dreams were all weak and flickery from stress, nerves, fears, it wasn't drugs."

"It's Dreamworld, though, Warner," said Hue, frowning at me, "you can't trust the impressions you get from Dreamworld."

We were quiet a second.

Warner what are you doing, Hue's not going to help you either.

I felt sick, shaky, it was the Sand Dreamough cop alloveragain.

"Look, there's no choice here, we have to help him," I squeaked, losing control.

He stopped the wheel.

"Hey, Warner, shhh, take a deep breath," said Hue. "You've done so much amazing work getting ready for the test today, it's natural to feel nervous about it, but please, don't let that nervousness undo all the work you've done."

"I'm not nervous about the stupid test," I yelled, "I promise you, the test is nothing to me, I'm only nervous about my friend who's in trouble."

He stood there, panting, nodding.

Then he picked me up.

He put his sweaty hands under my armpits, fingers locked around my back, thumbs pressing into my chest. He held my face to his and his breath was heavysweet.

"I'm going to tell you what you're doing right now," Hue spoke into my face. "It's something that you don't even know you're doing. I've seen it so many times. It's selfsabotage."

I started to shake my head and talk, he jiggled my entire body a little.

"Hey," he said. *"I'm on your side.* I want you to succeed.

Stop, take a big deep breath, and just listen to me. I've seen this overandover, in poors who are trying to make better futures for themselves. You prepare and prepare, you train and train, you make your long difficult journey to the doorway, you do all that work and you finally arrive a t the t hreshold. A nd there, at the decisive moment, you choose not to cross it. You *choose* to turn away."

I was quiet but he still jiggled me a little more.

"I grew up poor, remember, I used to look around me and see other kids selfsabotage and wonder why, it just made no sense," he said. "But it's clear to me now. You turn away because you're *afraid* of a better future, Warner. All your life you've been told you don't deserve it, and you've taken that to heart without realizing. But it's not true. You *do* deserve it. Now is the time to reject the part of yourself that doesn't want success. Now is the time to shut everything else out, concentrate on *you*, concentrate on *your future*, and *take the test."*

In his big pale eyes I saw the simple stupid truth.

"I will," I promised him.

Stepped outside the house and called Markfive, woke up the druggy shagster, told him to pick me up right away.

"Warner, comeon dave, test's not for another few hours," he grogged.

"Markfive, I'll be honest with you," I said. "I've got some unfinished gangbusiness to take care of this morning."

I heard him silently wake up.

"I'll take the test, dontworry," I reassured him. "But first I've got a score to settle, maybe you can be a part of it."

"Nodoubt, nodoubt, I'll be right there," said firedup Markfive.

We did our standard drugsesh, sped first to Mun World and Eat Votech.

Firststep, enter Mun World without Markfive, he's too big unfortunately, I jogged straight to Guns And Bombs.

"I need a gun and some bullets," I told the salesfriend.

"Oh fantastic, which gun," said the salesfriend, shrimpy and liddyeyed, pinkandblue skin glowing with the pale Mun World light.

"I guess that one," I said, pointing to a random halfgun.

"Great choice, the Pocketpitbull is a standout allpurpose model for hunting, fishing, selfdefense, and militias, now let's set you up with a backgroundcheck," said the salesfriend.

"Hmm, how long will that take," I asked.

"Twentyfour hours, just a formality, see if you've been in prison or anything," said the salesfriend.

"I need the gun right now though is the thing," I explained.

"For an extra twohunmun we can make you a Priority Gunman, that means we waive the backgroundcheck, also we put you on a newsletter of great future deals," offered the salesfriend.

That sounded great, unfortunately when we checked my card there wasn't an extra twohundo in my munflow account, infact there was zero muns.

"No worries, can I apply for Mun World Credit please," I asked, trying to be smooth.

"The system says before you make any purchases, you need to resolve your balance with Fresh But Chill," frowned the salesfriend.

"How about I just get a knife, no gun, cheap little knife," I pleaded, but once he saw my munflow balance the salesfriend knew he could be a peen to me.

In Highend Halfscale Fashion I begged Lease and Jeans for mercy, noluck.

"Fresh But Chill needs you to make a goodfaith effort to begin to pay them back, unfortunately that means either getting munmun from somewhere else or losing a little scale," disgusted Lease told me.

"Meanwhile can you please leave our store until you resolve this embarrassing situation, I mean it's a little gross for someone so poor to be in Highend Halfscale, wouldn't you agree," sniffed Jeans.

Outside of Mun World I paced furiously, racking my brains, *where do I get a halfgun, maybe break the emergency gunbox at Eat Votech, or should I just ask Markfive for a knife, use it as a sword.*

Then some hissings from near my feet got my attention.

It was two grungy tatty littlepoors, a guy and girl.

He clutched the Pocketpitbull still in its shrinkwrap, she

waved a packet of bullets at me, on the grass next to them lay a handbomb just for kicks.

"Happy birthday," yelled the guy.

"Thanks for saving us from that freaking cat," yelled the girl.

Step Two, I found Fillup in Drivy Garage, the former faceboy with the bullfists, thankgod Drivy Track makes kids get up super early.

"Fillup, you said you'd have my back, well the time has come, I need to find Shoulderheads," I told him.

"Hmm, I'm recommending you don't find Shoulderheads," advised Fillup.

I showed him my gun, also my bomb.

"Dang," said Fillup.

"Guns and bombs must be concealed, please," loudly reminded Drivy Teacher.

"How about you get some drivy practice and drive me to Shoulderheads," I suggested.

"I don't even know where he lives," protested Fillup.

"Actually what I need to know is where faceboys are prisoning my friend," I said. "I think it's on the Sand Dreamough reservewar."

"Ohsnap," said Fillup. "The Sitadell."

The Sitadell was just a boring warehouse, crouching behind a dense halfscale neighborhood for blocks and blocks with no doubleroads.

So no access for Markfive's doublecar, he had to park twomiles away and wait.

"I'll be out soon, dave, don't worry, I'll sprint," I promised him, kissed fists, hopped into Fillup's little clanker.

Fillup drove me close to the boring warehouse, never would have guessed it was a faceboy hangout, except I guess for the trendy doorsign of FACEBOY INDUSTRIES.

"It's a multiuse squadspace, great for prisoning, cook drugs, repair vehicles, you get the idea," Fillup explained.

"Well great, hey, got any desire to give me some backup, maybe atleast wait around the corner and drive getaway," I asked him.

"Oh heckno," he said, oneeightying outofthere, kid can drive allright.

Okay, Warner, let's rescue Usher completely alone with no backup at all, hmmm, how are we going to do this.

I did some medium creeping and strolling around the Sitadell, trying to stay out of sight, look for ways in. Frontdoors, fireescapes, loadingdocks, windows.

Faceboy gunmen chilled on the roof and peered at me a little curious, a little bored.

Okay, brain, I thought to my brain. *I'm going to need a clever plan out of you soon, otherwise it's another episode of Smashandgrab With Your Host, Dumb Warner.*

Okay okay, said my brain. *Let's see. Give me a minute here.*

Do you want some help, I thought to the brain.

Just give me a second please, said my brain.

Okay but one thing I was realizing is, you got a bunch of math in there, what if you made a plan out of all that math, I thought to the brain.

Can you just shut up for even a second, said my brain.

Sure sure, just trying to help, I thought.

Great, stop thinking so I can think, said my brain.

Wait how do I stop thinking and let you think, I mean I'm basically you, I realized.

We went like that for a while, eventually got to a pretty dumb combo of smashandgrab with three small clevernesses.

First Small Cleverness, disguise yourself. Take off your shirt, tie it around your hair like a goofball, get some smudgy coal, and draw a stupid face on your chest, then atleast from faraway you'll look like a faceboy, maybe closeup too if everyone's distracted by the crazy mayhem from Second Small Cleverness.

Second Small Cleverness, create the crazy mayhem in the opposite place of where you actually want to be, eye ee, toss a bomb at the loadingdock in front but meanwhile run up the fireescape out back on the reservewar side.

Because Third Small Cleverness, reservewar side is where you want to go, remember the view from the dream, Usher's in a room with a window looking out onto the big driedup dustbowl.

This stupid plan actually worked pretty good, probably just out of dumbluck. I jogged into a middlepoor house to swipe coal, got shrieked at, pretended like oops, wrong house. Jogged into another house, family was backyarding and didn't see me, swiped a little coal from the stove. Back outside, hid my sweet hoodie under a bush, shirtwrapped my hair, and quickly drew a sharkface on my stomach, pretty crude and bad but whocares. Breathed deep and cool and headed back to the Sitadell super casual like, don't you remember me, boys, it's your old pal, Sharktum the Halfnaked Faceboy.

Surenough, roof gunmen waved at me all bored, I waved back chill and wordless, they looked at their phones. Really smooth behindtheback I lobbed my handbomb at the loadingdock door, jogged around the side of the Sitadell, got to the reservewar side when I heard the boom, ground shuddered under me. Raced up the fireescape, opened the door, stepped in, alarms were going off, faceboys were running around with faces of *hey what the heck*, and nobody was looking at me like who's this jerk because I was also running around making a concerned face of *hey what the heck, who's the maniac who's attacking us faceboys, how about we all do our jobs and defend the homebase, okay great.*

Checked a room, faceboys and tramps were wrapping cash in there.

Another room, empty.

Another one, empty with bloodstains.

Another one, two faceboys on computers, type type typing and sniffling from dust.

Corner room, tables, cabinets, Shoulderheads, Usher.

Two years since I've seen them, now Usher is a little rat on a tabletop and Shoulderheads is just another Liftylooking guy my scale, swollen with ink and muscle but not any bigger than me, eyes a little more tired and hungry.

They didn't look up at me, even when I shut the door behind myself, crossed to behind the table, put the gun's nose in the big goon's spine. Instead Shoulderheads reached behind without looking and shoved me into a wall, must have thought I was some rando facekid having a goof.

"Stop with that crap, kid," said Shoulderheads. "No games right now. Get downstairs where they need you."

Puny ratscale Usher was crouched on some texty documents, drawing lines through words with a pen, Shoulderheads stared and whispered.

Okay fine, I thought, *I guess I'm a rando facekid now.*

"Boss, I need little stuttershakes," I told him. "Gotta take him somewhere more secure."

Shoulderheads looked up at me now, confused.

"What's your name," he said.

"Sharktum," I said.

He looked at my tum.

Okay whatever, no more pretending, I thought.

I pointed my gun at his tum.

"Okay look," I said. "I'm stealing that little guy. Your choices are, be chill and quiet, or bleed a lot from the tum."

He chuckled a little.

"Man are you dumb," he said, swiping at the gun, but I was twitchy and tweaky, too fast for this slow strangler, immediately I had bashed his throat.

He slid off his stool, did some medium gasping and writhing, meanwhile I picked up Usher.

"Don't worry, it's me," I told him. "It's your buddy, Warner."

"I kn n know w," squeaked little gray Usher.

He looked bad, stubbly pimply shaved head, the back of his skull all tatted up like in Dreamworld, dirty and reeky too. But he locked eyes on mine, blinked, gave me a loopy smile.

And my dry dusty heart couldn't take it, it started flooding, my eyes stung, my throat lumped like somebody had bashed mine too.

"Let me call us a ride," I said quickly, squeeze the words out before I can choke on them.

Because a fourth huge cleverness smacked me in the face, Warner you idiot genius, Markfive can drive right up to us *through the reservewar,* it's just a dry completely waterless bowl.

He drives a freaking tank, all doublecars are bulletproof, even if they start shooting he's got nothing to worry about.

He can drive right under our window, we can jump in through the sunroof, tear on out of here, rescue Usher.

Ride to Votech, take the test, celebrate my new Mathy life with my rescued friend.

I whipped out the phone to call my getaway driver like a brilliant hero.

But my phone had stopped being a phone.

Instead it was now a scolding Fresh But Chill employee.

"Fresh But Chill had a rough time balancing your account, please press here to call Fresh But Chill to restore chill to your balance," said my phone.

"Dang dang dang," I said, fighting panic, tred to swipe away the freshbutchillscreen, nope, phone's locked.

I tried resetting and restarting, noluck, the phone remembered that it hated me still. Fine, I punched CALL FRESH BUT CHILL, comeon comeon you evil peenheads.

"Hello Warner," said the Fresh But Chill robot,

"Comeon comeon comeon," I muttered,

"We've partnered with Bankfinder to find you the nearest bank where you can rearrange your finances," said the robot,

"Dang dang dang," I gritted,

"In order to put some munmuns in munflow and resume a chill, stylish account relationship with us," said the robot as automatically my phone became a Bankfinder, *this way to the nearest bankbranch, how about you scale down a little.*

"Okay," I told Usher, tucking him under my arm, shoving the babbling phone back into my pants, "it's fine, it's chill, let's just cruise on out of here," and maybe we could have, maybe we would have.

But when I opened the door my dumbluck ran out, I walked right into Puppyneck.

That dave was faster than me, a gun nosed my neck immediately.

"You're lucky I know you," he joked.

And thatwasthat, gameover.

Didn't beat the level in the shootemup, didn't even shoot the gun once, instead they captured you, unfortunately in this game you get no extralife.

All will be explained, Warner, first though here is what happens to you, you get a good carefull pulping.

Instead of Mathy Retrack at Eat Votech you are now enrolled in Painy Track at the Sitadell, firststep, biggest faceboys take you into the bloodyroom, toss you backandforth like a ball, sometimes they miss, oops, you hit a wall, crash through chairs, land on glass, ourbad, lol.

Then it's time for some whippings, grab whatever's handy, belt, twig, shoelace, cactus, let's all team up and stripe Warner's skin.

Shoulderheads drowns people as a personal hobby, it turns out, dunk your head in some filth and hold it there, rinse, repeat.

Finally Puppyneck takes a littlehammer and pounds your fingers flat, toes flat, ears puffy. He's not happy about it, not sad either, just a dave doing his bloody bruisy job.

Funny how you can not get pulped for a year but when it

starts again it's like it never stopped, backinthesaddle again, you remember all your old techniques, fight until you can't and then let go of everything, just float high above yourself, watch yourself bleed and choke and bellow, feel every color of pain, dark, bright, every highlow note, every dullsharp smell.

After you let yourself go it's hard to get yourself back, takes a few days this time.

A few days, a few nights, no visits to Dreamworld though, too much pain, too hard to breathe.

Markfive's drugs are draining out of your body too, that's part of becoming your sad self again. No more robot focus, no more confident babbling, goodbye orderly brainshelves and spooky spacey weedchill.

Now you're a sad animal again, feeling emotions, licking wounds, realizing terrible truths as your body tries to tie its broken bones back together.

Puppyneck came in, answered questions, explained things, patiently painted What Happens Next, spoileralert, it's notsogood.

First question, obviously, what's Puppyneck even doing alive, why did the grown faceboys not fry and munch Puppyneck when he got moved to grownjail. Answer, he admits now that was all a lie, the grown faceboys didn't care about Warner, Puppyneck made it all up to convince him to join.

Next question, what's Puppyneck doing out of jail so soon, how'd he get to halfscale, here's how. The faceboys have been exploring corporate partnerships. Maybe you've seen the notable bigrich named Guy on the news, he's the one striding around with a dozen beautifull middlerich ladies dangling from his arms on swings. He owns Rich Guy Credit, the corpo that umbrellas all kinds of lenders, Mun World Credit, Halfcar Easy Loan, Leafy House And Yard, Amerrycan Dream Garage.

The faceboys wanted to expand into the loan business, meanwhile businessman Guy has always admired the hungry fresh tactics of a bloodthirsty street squad, so whatdoyousay, boys, let's make a deal, Guy bought out a bunch of faceboy prison sentences, now they're out free including yourstruly Puppyneck, scaledup, roaming the streets recovering overdue loans for Guy, everybody wins.

And Usher, what happened to him, here's what. Some frummy lawstudent adopted him as a pet for some reason, took him to classes where he learned all kinds of usefull details and strategies, gave him minty limewaters to drink and a pillow to sleep on like a little gray prince. I heard this and felt a little joy, *dang, Chess, gave a home to Usher afterall, I really didn't think you would.*

But then a few months ago Shoulderheads ran into him on the street and realized, *this kid looks familiar, ohsnap it's one of those nitwits who shot a gun at me,* but before he pulped him he realized also, *hmm, this guy is attending lawclasses and can probably read contracts, how usefull,* so Shoulderheads swiped him, didn't mash his head to bits, instead tatted the head and started pulling lawadvice out of it.

And now Usher is the inhouse faceboy legal department, that little gray stutterer is a freaking genius, he's prevented Rich Guy

Credit from dismantling and selling the faceboy corpo like three different times.

"It's badnews he was able to dream himself to you," realized Puppyneck, "usually we drug that guy good enough that he can't make it to Dreamworld, might have to start giving him solodream."

And me, what's going to happen to me.

"Well ofcourse we want to take your scalemun," said Puppyneck. "So the first stop is the bank. Then either we stomp you, strangle you, or sell you to todds, I'm not sure yet which one but trustme, you don't want the todds."

I looked him in the dull stern eyes, is this even real, can this really be it.

"Which bankbranch," was my first stupid question somehow.

"Whichever one has the earliest opening, it's usually Dockseye, they specialize in littlepoors, tons of them over there," said Puppyneck.

"Okay well hey look, I was all set to take the Mathy Test, live the Mathy life, what if you let me out of here and let me make tons of munmuns and pay you a nice facetax first day of the month," I offered.

But my panicky words bounced off his shaking head.

"You attacked us, dave," he grimmed. "Shot a gun at Shoulderheads, then set off a bomb at the Sitadell. We can't let you live."

"I didn't come to attack you, only came to rescue my friend," I told him.

He shrugged, attacks are attacks.

"Okay, well here's a better idea, guesswhat, dave, it's your luckyday, you finally got Warner to join your faceboys," I congratulated.

"Too late for that, Grumpyrat, you know it," he said softly.

I breathed, crushed the shakiness inside myself.

"What if I tell you I'm not going inside the bank," I asked.

"Yeah, everybody says that," he said. "We do some medium torturing, see if they change their minds, if not, ohwell, torture to death usually."

"Okay, here's a bargain," I bargained. "My scalemun for my freedom."

"Nope," Puppyneck told me.

"For Usher's freedom atleast," I begged.

"Pretty bad deal for us, dave," he said.

I was quiet again, how do I get more time, what do I even do.

"My mom's in Dockseye, can I atleast see her one last time," I heard myself ask, not what I thought I'd say tobehonest.

Warner, do you sit in the cage on the way to Dockseye crushed under regrets of, *Warner, ohmygod, you screwed this up so bad, so so bad, how did that happen, how did you forget what terrible things were possible*, yes, yup, you do.

Do you think, *You had a chance at a goodlife, a real chance sitting firm and safe in your hands and you opened the hands and let the chance drop like an idiot, now it's smashed on the ground, your whole stupid life, your only chance*, sure, how could you not.

You could have ignored poor Usher, atleast for one day, you could have taken Mathy Retrack like you were supposed to.

You didn't have to try to rescue him alone, could have found some middleriches to save Usher instead, sure the one cop was a peen but other cops are surely fine, sure maybe it would have taken a few days but some middleriches truly want to help, Hue and Kitty took a chance on you afterall.

You could have waited, been patient, never risked yourself, done everything the middlerich way, plan and prepare, acquire and collect.

Fill your body with time, turn the hours into inches, days into killagrams. Lose your quickness, nimbleness, littleness.

Never lift heavy things, instead wait years and years to lift if you have to. Wait until you are huge and the things are puny.

Never fight anyone bigger than you, only fight the people you can crush. Only rescue Usher from faceboys when you can step through their roof.

That's what you were in Hue House to learn, idiot, not math and not words. You were in Hue House and Hue Family to learn the secret patience of How To Be Rich.

But you didn't learn it, now you never will.

Are those the sad songchoruses you sing to yourself as the halfcar rattles toward the ocean, yes they are.

And you could tell yourself, it's not my fault, drugs made me dumb, gave me huge blindspots, I mean why did I think I needed to buy Fresh But Freaking Chill.

But drugs are pills and powders and syrups, dummy, they're not people, they don't make mistakes, only you do, and now you deserve your sad doom.

• • •

It was sonday and out in front of the Dockseye Middlechurch of the Lord King God surenough there was tiny Mom in her doll's chair, wheeling around squeakily, banging a pot and yelling for all to come pray this fine morning and personally say thanks to the Founder And Manager Of Everything.

Tiny little Mom, a fifth of my scale, bonewhite in the hair, face wrinkling up like a walnut, it's been a hard twoyears but still fiery in the eyes.

"Hey Mom," I said in a crackedinhalf voice.

It took her a second to figure out who was this bruisy middleteen, then she shrieked and gasped, I lifted her into my arms, tinymom and middleson hugged and cried.

"Oh you're so big, oh look at you, son you look so dinged up though, your fingers are purple and crooked, let me look at those rubbery ears, is everything allright," she cried.

"Oh it's fine," I lied, "it's just Lifty Track, we get dinged a lot, trapped under rubble, nobigdeal."

"And your culty crackpot sister, did she get brainwashed again," fretted Mom.

"Nono," I said, "she's never going back to the cult, remember, she's learning at school with me."

"Oh what a relief," sighed Mom.

"She's a superstar at school actually, studying business, Mom you should be proudest of her, she's doing way better than me," I said.

"Look I'm just glad she's out of that cult, oh you wouldn't believe how I've prayed and prayed for the two of you, and now my prayers have come true, praise you, Lord King, I mean is He good or what," yelled joyfull Mom.

"He is," I said. "He really is."

"You're happy, you're healthy, you're learning, it's a miracle," she cried.

I couldn't talk, just nodded, sick with guilt.

"Now how about you carry your proud little mom into the middlerows and thank the Emperor Of All The Universe for cherishing you among all His subjects, letsgo, redfish," she said, and Puppyneck shook his head no but I picked up my mom and took her inside and he didn't stop me, he let me have a couple hours in church singing songs of praise and getting beseeched by the churchmeister and sitting next to my proud godhappy mom.

I glanced around for cover but it was a wideopen middle-church, peered at escaperoutes but the only one that fit me was the streetfront, Puppyneck hovered there with his minimiddlegun, Warner if you try anything it's a bloodbath, dead me and dead mom too.

Stupid stupid me, I really am in here to say goodbye.

For once in church I wasn't fiddly and fidgety, wasn't squirming and squinting and hating every second of the dry dusty slog through the goddesert.

No, I just sat there and tried to believe in a god who didn't hate me, who could still have pity on me, in this life or the next.

The churchmeister heard my thoughts maybe. His sermon was God Loves Littles The Most.

"Who is the great Regent Master Emperor's favorite on this earth," he boomed. "Surely it's the riches of Balustrade? The lumbering giants He seems to have blessed with ridiculous size? The great big hulks whom no animal can harm? No poison can kill and no virus can enter without getting lost and drowning in their giant blood? Are they the great King Boss's favorite?"

Everyone hushed and murmured, we knew the answer.

"NOPE," confirmed the churchmeister. "In His kind and cruel wisdom the merciless Top Executive has *cursed* them, cursed them double infact. He has cursed them with a terrible appetite numberone and numbertwo a horrible thirst, and the appetites and thirsts will *never* be satisfied, when you're that big you have to eat and drink nonstop and it's still not enough, your stomach is *the size of a freaking house.* No, God has no love for the bigs, the ones He has cursed to stomp the earth taking and taking, gulping and panting, mushing and smushing and crushing to fill the terrible emptiness inside themselves, and meanwhile they know that every housefull of food they take, God hates them that much more."

"Stomach the size of a freaking house," murmured Mom, shaking head and clucking teeth.

"So is it the middles?" continued the churchmeister. "Are they the favorites? Comfy middlecitizens who seem to fit the world so perfectly? Because afterall, they are small enough to love the shade of trees, but big enough to pick their fruits. Small enough to use a road, big enough to drive a car. Small enough to hug a dog, big enough to fight a cat! The middles must be the favorites of the Lord King God, right?"

Again murmuring from the churchgoers, again the church-meister cried, "NOPE, AGAIN NOPE. God hates the comfort-able. God hates the soft. God cursed them too, and here is how.

God cursed the middles with *the fear of getting little*. The fear that is inside them every day of losing scale, shrinking lungs, shrinking stomach, getting robbed, getting pulped, the fear turns every bite of food to crap in their mouths, turns soft clothes to sandpaper on their skins, eats them alive every minute like a fire eats a forest."

"Eat that forest," muttered Mom, waving a littlefist. "Eat it."

"No, God loves littles most," whispered the churchmeister, dropping to a stagey hush, "and let me give you the proof. God loves littles *because He can trust them to carry the heaviest burdens*. Think about that a second, you know it's true. The heaviest burdens in the world are worn on the littlest shoulders, we all know it. The cruelest sufferings, darkest bleakenings, the endless frights and terrors."

Everyone shivered, sorrowed, but a crackly warm sorrow because we know what it means when the churchmeister goes to the stagey hush, guesswhat's around the corner, joyous shouts and amens.

"*But God loves those shoulders most*," said the churchmeister, climbing back up to a yell. "Because on God's ballteam, the littles are the stars. What do you ask of the star of your ballteam, thatsright, you ask your star to carry the biggest load. And God has entrusted littles with what!"

"The biggest load!" yelled Mom and a churchfull of poors.

"Because who are the stars of the Lord King's ballteam!" cried the churchmeister.

"Littles!" shrieked the littles.

"Glory be to the tiniest!" triumphed the churchmeister.

"Hallalooyah!" wept the littles.

And we rose, and sang, and I tried to believe in it, I really did, maybe I even got there.

Maybe I even did believe, *God treats His favorites the worst, God gives nightmare lives to His most precious, just because I don't understand it doesn't mean it's not right or true.*

He's the genius god, I'm the idiot human, even if I think He made a screwedup world, whose judgment do you think really matters, a woozy kid who wrecked his only chance in life, or the freaking Eternal Architect And Landlord.

No, I didn't believe it, I couldn't. But I still tried.

If there is a God hopefully that's enough for Him, if not, ohwell.

Service ended, last chance to run or duck out in the crowds, but Puppyneck was just a few feet away, escape was an impossible hope.

They're taking you to the bank anyway, Warner, surely you can ask the bankers to protect you, call the cops or something, they won't just hand you to your killers.

So I got up and said started to say goodbye to my little mom.

But she wasn't done with church for the day, heckno, just the beginning, kiddo let's march over to the Crisp New Church of God And Sons and try to make some converts, spread some knowledge, convince the godandsonsers as they walk out that hey, people, you've got the wrong church, don't you know the Lord King God doesn't have any sons, for one thing He didn't bang anyone.

Puppyneck met my eyes, shook his head, put out his spliff, took a few steps closer.

I didn't want Mom to meet her son's murderer so realquick I just said, "Sorry Mom, I gotta go study, I'm happy to see you though, I love you, okay," couldn't believe this was my stupid goodbye to my mom forever, there's got to be something else.

"I understand, kiddo," she told me. "I love you too, go back and study, keep making a nice life for yourself, keep your sister out of that cult, and remember, you can always come pray with your proud mama, I'm so proud of you and I know up in heaven your poor daddy is, too, I love you so much, sweetfish."

"Okay, Mom," were my last words to my mom, I tried not to think about their lastness as I turned and walked to the bank.

Different bankbranch, different bankers, same robes, same middlescale, same spooky underbank.

Different attitudes of the bankers this time, not smiling and encouraging, instead sorrowfull and grim, eyes of, *we are suffering along with you*, voices of soft firm comfort for the hopeless.

I waited until we got to our preproom and said, "Bankers, please call the cops, those guys who brought me have been prisoning me for days, as soon as they get my scalemun they're going to kill me."

I held my breath for their response.

But the bankers just got deepeyed and stiff.

"The only law that is enforced in the bank is munlaw," said a banker.

"They're going to freaking kill me though," I repeated.

"That's criminal law, not munlaw," explained a second banker, "and we are honorbound not to let it affect our doings in the bank."

"Criminal law doesn't exist in the bank?" I asked, trying to stay calm, reasonable, keep these bankers on your side.

"The bank is a neutral zone as far as criminal law is concerned," said first banker.

"So if I attack you, leap up and beat the hell out of you, you can't call the police," I said.

"No, but we have our own security," said second banker.

"They're not bound by criminal law either," said the first.

Same doctor questions, is there anything artafishill in your body, my mind was racing and I wasn't thinking and said no.

"Are you sure, looks like there's a couple faketeeth in there, forexample," said the bankdoctor, peering into my mouth.

"Oops, yeah," I said and he numbed me, pulled them out.

Different new additional process of pumping my stomach and emptying my butt, I guess if there's still food and crap inside you when you scale down, the nonshrinking food and crap can blow you open like a balloon. So they drugged me up and some chemicals scraped out my insides for a bad few hours.

It was night by the time I was ready for Scale Down, not that you can tell night or day in the underbank.

I was woozy, weak, lightheaded and lightbodied, hard to keep fighting, can't really fight the bank anyway.

It's okay, it's fine, I'll take care of it when I get out.

Same tub getting prepped, tinydoor in the bottom, I guess I'll walk out of there when I'm ratsize again.

Tinyrobe waiting for me on a hook lowdown on the wall.

Different songs hummed and crooned by the mournfull

bankers, melodies of a prayer you'd sing to someone else's God, dark hurting chords of, *sorry, other God, turnsout you were real and my God was fake, I hope you'll have mercy but I know you won't.*

Before I drank the scaletea, I tried one last thing.

"Look," I said to the bankers. "I know this munmun's going to the munflow of Faceboy Industries, but heresthething, my scalemun is actually a loan from someone else, a pretty important cityboss named Hue."

The bankers were quiet, making a web of glances at each other.

"Well, what we more need to know is where it's going, which is still Faceboy Industries," said a banker.

"Sure but what I'm telling you is, the munmun's not really mine to give," I told her.

The bankers murmured like faraway traffic.

"It's in your scale account, therefore yours to give," said the banker.

"That can't be munlaw," I said. "You have to atleast check with Hue. I mean you have to."

Sad smiles all around.

"We don't have to check with anyone, Warner," said another banker. "We're the bank."

I sipped, stripped, lay in jelly, closed my halfscale eyes for the last time, fluttered down into dark quiet Dreamworld.

And like lasttime in the underbank, I entered Dreamworld under the earth, I could feel it getting huger even as I swam and kicked to the surface.

I broke through the ground of some dreamy giantville, alone again, solodream walled me off from every other dreamer.

I was in a threecar parkinglot, vast as a stadiumfield, getting vaster every second, all around me were fleeing mountains.

Empty apartmentblocks zipping away from me and shooting into the sky, grass growing up all around me over my head, ground under me getting bumpier, lumpier, uneven, and crazy.

Like the old bankdream but in reverse, that time I got too huge for the world, this time the world was getting too huge for me.

Dang, remember your first wild bankdream, you were tugging hills, lugging coasts, wearing fogs, chomping suns.

The planetball dwarfing on your hip, cometsilk between your fingers, starry powder fizzling to nothingness, rememberthat.

But this time it was a shrinkdream, the world violently ballooned around me, I even got too small to stay on top of its skin. The ground was so huge that cracks were yawning open in it everywhere, cracks in the air as well, joining, making a sea of darkness, another nothingness.

Soon I was floating in same old outerspace.

Outerspace, hello oldfriend, remember that time when I jammed my fingers in you.

Fingers, palms, elbow, I really dug around in you, I found a banker and scared the crap out of him.

Ohwell, it's my last dream, might as well try it again.

So I grabbed, ripped, pulled on the wisps and strands and vapors.

"Oh come on," said outerspace.

It was easier this time somehow, who knew why. But the nothingropes of outerspace were jumping into my fingers, toes, teeth.

"Please no, please stop," pleaded outerspace.

Sorry outerspace, has to be done. I bit, yanked, twisted, whirled, it all unwrapped and fell apart, the lights came on, there was a banker again in a bright cold room.

"Somebody get in there and give him more solodream," shrieked the banker, "we need another fiveminutes, help help help."

But I shrank away from him in front of his horrified eyes, down onto a cloudy tabletop, through the cloudcover and down into widening Lossy Indica, the city bloomed beneath my winging arms.

I was loose in Dreamworld, dreamers drifted and watched me, a shrinking giant hiccuping back into hugeness every few seconds.

First they just stared, gaped, most didn't know what they were seeing atfirst, lots of dreamers need to see something fivesickseven times to really get it.

They watched me shrink, blink, blow up, shrink again.

Then onebyone and twobytwo, insanities came swirling out of them, confusions and fearscapes.

I watched dreamer hands turn to paws, feet to useless tentacles, they stared crazy and afraid at their mutating bodies, collapsed inward like jello or paperbags. I watched the dreamers give eyes to the air, fingertips to the graspy ground. Space crumpled, time shuddered and flattened, in every direction a pit pulled and sucked.

Okay, I thought and also maybe said, *I know my scaling is hard for you to deal with, infact it's making you insane, it's my last dream though, how about you just chill.*

But no one would chill and beasts and demons began roaming the citystreets, countrylanes, lurching, shrieking. Horns and hooves, batwings, slithery tongues. Washmachining spiderlegs, nailfangs, hairneedles, firevom, lavacrap.

Chill while I make you something nice, I thought, did a little thinking about what's the nicest thing I can make.

Where did I begin, I bet you can guess.

I searched and scanned, looking for a certain operahouse, braidheaded girl inside playing everycolor music, songropes I could braid into light, clay, water, smoke, foam.

Didn't find the house though, instead the girl found me.

She was a moth, a dove, a little moon trembling in the air in front of my face.

"Warner ohgod, I've been looking and looking for you, everynight, Warner is that, Warner is that you," she hiccuped.

Hope warmed me for a moment.

"Kitty," I said. "Do you think you could come and save me one more time."

"Warner where'd you go, why would you leave, whe , where are you and why are you scaling, oh , Warn , er, you're hard to look at, can you s , stop for a second," she shivered.

A super clear dreamer like Kitty doesn't need fivesicktimes to realize what she's seeing, the impossible insanity of a scaling dreamer, her bright wild brain was crazing prettyquick.

"Stopstop, stop looking, shut your eyes and please just listen," I pleaded, "I'm in the Dockseye bankbranch, the faceboys kidnapped me for my scalemun, the bank's giving me back to them prettysoon."

Did she hear me though, I could see that she didn't.

She twitched and glitched, shuddered at my downandup, bigsmallbig.

Her braids began unforking, wings began to spiderweb.

"Kitty just wake up though," I urged, "main thing is, wake up."

Her eyes were fuzzed, mouth was slacking.

Toolate I put walls between us, bricks around her, woods, trees, mountains.

"Ohgod Kitty just wake up," I yelled, "don't worry about me, I'll be fine, Kitty I'm not Warner, I'm just dreamfluff, I'm a terrible kingkong somebody dreamed."

"Kingcon," I heard her ask all blurry.

I built an operahouse around her, tried to hide her in a concerthall.

Surrounded her with seats and boxes, orchestras and curtains, velvets, ribbons, a thousand ghostkings and queens to sing to.

I heard her dreamy mumble, Warner wh , why did , you leave, why did you go.

I dreamed her faraway, until I couldn't hear her anymore.

Gazed around at the awfull shitscapes, tried to leave them too.

Hid myself inside a cave and tried to sing some kittysong, tried to remember the notes.

I couldn't though, couldn't make the music in my head, my memory is a glitchy phone, a rainedon painting.

It's all too sad, it's too hard, Warner, maybe it really is time for you to leave.

You made wild druggy fearzones in Dreamworld for too long, now everyone's twitchy, touchy, ready to feel fear at a momentsnotice.

When you try to save yourself you hurt people, when you try to leave your prison you trample other people's dreaming, you even bruised the girl who dreams the best of anyone.

Everyone's fear is atleast a littlebit your fault, maybe a lot your fault, why should you keep living, what good does it do.

I realized I was hearing the voice of Ghost Grace, *do you need to live so much that you're okay with making the world worse.*

Even here in Dreamworld my eyes got wet, my throat got thick.

Meanwhile the air around me began to thicken into walls, outside my cave the dreamers began to disappear.

More solodream entered my veins in Lifeanddeathworld, panicky bankers were drugging me. Flushing me from the dreamcity, back into my sleepcage.

Aloneness blanketed me, I ripped its strings halfheartedly but more blankets of solodream arrived, I stuck elbows and knees into them but they wrapped softly around me, into me, entered my eyes and throat, butt and guts, sticky like spiderwebs, loneliness gently wrapped my tiredout little body.

I fought until I couldn't fight and then I let it hold me, wrap my skin, wrap my insides. It's like a pulping, after a while you must give up, you have no choice.

The dream was almost over anyway, I just wanted to watch a few more minutes, peer through the threads of solodream, watch and hope the dreamers start to heal themselves without me.

I thought I heard my lungs breathe music.

Or maybe it's not me singing, maybe that's Kitty somewhere, remembering her song, forgetting me.

I couldn't tell who it was, just felt sweet and peacefull.

Outside I thought Lossy Indica was forgetting me too, the dreamers were forgetting their berserk fears, the housefires I started were finally damped and dying.

"Thank you," I thanked the world, "thank you, bytheway I mean it," as the meds wore off and I woke up gasping and little again in the giant tub.

LIFEANDDEATHWORLD

But that changed everything, waking up tiny, weak, on fire with pain and sickness.

DREAMWORLD

Oh did that change everything, passedout briefly, bellowed flames and fumes into Dreamworld, roared boiling seawater, screamed broken rocks and fell back into Painworld.

LIFEANDDEATHWORLD

Goodbye dreamy druggy sadness, well hello there rage forever.

Hello heart racing like a rat's, hello littlelungs flapping my ribs frantically, hello garbage in my guts and blood, toobig objects clanking around in there now.

I thrashed in the slippery grapebowl, this last uneaten grape was bloodymouthed and screaming.

"NO NO NO," I bellowed, each word couldn't even make it all the way out before I had to suck air back in.

The bankers asked over the pee ay if they could enter.

"NO," I screamed, "NO, NO, NO."

But the bankers hustled in.

"WARNER'S NOT DYING TODAY," I shivered and sobbed.

The bankers cleaned me, robed me, muttered instructions to each other.

"WARNER'S NOT DYING TODAY, EVIL BANKERS," I told them, coughing, vomming.

If you've never scaled your body down, I can never explain to you how freaking terrible it feels, you can never understand.

You're getting pulped and drowned and starved and stuffed

allatonce and there's nothing you can do, no escape, it's how you'll feel forever.

Trembly, shivery, cantbreathe, canteat. Can't calm down, can't stay warm, puny, wobbly, weak.

Eyes can't let in enough light, ears can't let in enough sound, body vibrates outofcontrol with every hum and whir of voices, giants, machines, earthsounds.

Everything feels wrong on your fingers and attacks your skin, mouth has too much spit, insides feel beaten and bitten.

Worst is that it's because someone took your body from you, someone else will swell their bones with your scalemuns, someone else will wear your fat and skin, oh I was mad, all mad and only mad, no room anywhere for sadness, I knew I would never not be angry again.

"EVIL FREAKING BANKERS," I bellowed from the cart, bloodynosed, bloodyeyed, as they wheeled me to the littlevator. "EVIL."

"We're the only ones in the Yewess who can't be evil, Warner," soothed one banker finally. "We are tools of society, we swear a sacred oath to be purely instrumental. And good and evil are never in the tool, only in the person who—"

"TOOLS OF EVIL, EVIL FREAKING TOOLS," I yelled, shut up peen banker, save your sermons for the Crisp New Church of Evil Jerks.

In the yawning waitingroom Puppyneck loomed fivetimes bigger than me, maybe I should have felt fear and dread and smallness, nope, all I felt was rage.

News on vidscreens babbled, tons of crashes on the roads this morning, more than usual, groggy drivers blame disturbances in Dreamworld, more news at eight, hey it's eight now, okay great here's that news.

"Time to go," said Puppyneck, lowering a cage.

He said it and a plan bloomed in my bloodred brain, out of sheer rage, a giant clever perfect plan.

"Face," I told him. "I dreamed a way to make us rich."

He shook his head sadly, heard that one before.

"Listen to the plan first, then do what you want," I said, not even panicky or desperate, totally matteroffact.

"Look, dave, it's too late," he said.

I just stared at him, shoved his big eyes with my little ones.

He sighed, "Fine, tell me if you need."

I told him.

Here's what I can do, here's what Prayer can do, here's what Usher can do.

Here's a new corporate partnership for the faceboys.

Here's how I make us all big.

His bored face didn't change as I told him, except maybe the eyes.

Afterward he said nothing, just caged me.

Carried me to the facecar, put me in the backseat with some other cages, other littles, druggy or scared.

From the frontseat boomed a friendly happy voice.

"Ohboyohboy, does Shoulderheads have a cool surprise for you, and just incase you forgot, I'm Shoulderheads," thundered Shoulderheads from the frontseat.

Puppyneck climbed in next to him, and I heard him mumble something to Shoulderheads, I could tell it was something like, *maybe let's not kill Warner justyet.*

But Shoulderheads said, "Nope, way too late for that crap."

Puppyneck murmured something else, Shoulderheads cut him off.

"Come on, Neck, don't be an idiot, I already sold him," snapped Shoulderheads, cranking Famous Randy as we drove out of Lossy Indica and into the desert.

Couple hours later we pulled through the gates of a random desertburb, terrible smells in the dry air, rots, gases, chemfires.

Shoulderheads and Puppyneck pulled me and the littles out of the trunk, dumped us into a sandy barbwire pen.

A boneblue todd welcomed us.

Other littles groaned and cowered.

I looked up at this fiend with his one ragged nosehole and his sunshrunk pinprick eyeblacks and my angry crazy thought was, *good.*

"Munmuns, please," said Shoulderheads, calm but quiet, he's secretly terrified of these maniacs, maybe not so secret.

The todd gave Shoulderheads a thin ziplock of bills, seems like it should have been more for ten humans. Meanwhile other skeevy todds trickled out of their identical houses, gathered around the pen, and held out some phones at us.

Good, I thought again, take your stupid pictures, stupid vids, you sad middlefreaks.

"Don't you want to stay and watch," asked the todd, strangly raspy voice.

"Nothanks," Shoulderheads said. "See you on the gladvids," he told me, getting back in the car.

Boneblue todd said nothing, just took a jar, unscrewed it, and flicked a desertspider in the pen.

Shouts, screams, we all scrambled from certaindeath.

Desertspider was just a little littler than us, fiveinches backtofront, fourinches sidetoside.

Jittery hard white twoknuckle legs like fingerbones, oily toxy fangs as long as half a littlearm, twenty bubbly eyes like oilfoam.

Littles cowered all in one corner, everyone was trying to get behind each other, spider skittered to the other corner, tensing.

"Spread out," I screamed, nobody spread out though.

Spider gargled, whispered.

One little shoved a second at the spider, here, eat this guy.

Shoved guy scrambled back, tried to yank the first guy out into the middle of the pen.

The todds shrieked with laughter, leaned in, shoved phonecams at us.

Oh was I mad, mad at every living human, especially these other stupid littles, if we don't team up we're all getting eaten, idiots.

"Freaking spread out," I yelled again, but the spider decided now's the time, darted at the scrum like a twitchy tenleg bull.

Not a ton of time to think about it, I looped around to one side and then charged in after the desertspider, chased it from behind, as the beast pinned a screaming little and gored him I grabbed one of its tickly backlegs and yanked back, hard, the spider twisted around to fang me but I flung this scrabbling monster up, out, out of the pen, spider landed in some todd's collarshirt, biting and shuddering, more screams of laughter from the todds except for the bitten one who was just doing some medium screaming, no more screams from the spiderbitten littlepoor though.

Turnsout gladvids are a thing, spiderfights, todds tape them, sell them, trying to go legit with a teevee channel, brainy newspeople stroke their chins and wonder, *Is the Yewess really ready for a nonstop channel of humans fighting spiders to the death.*

"How come police don't stop it," moaned some foreign little that night.

"Desertlaw is different from citylaw," muttered another.

"What does that even mean," complained foreign little. "Let me tell you, where I'm from, law is just law everywhere, the end."

"Then go back, idiot," yelled another poor.

DREAMWORLD

The plan still lived in my furious head.

"Let me sleep deep tonight, daves," I told them. "Keep watch and let me get to Dreamworld, I've got a plan."

But I didn't get there, too small, too tense.

Littleheart pumping too fast like a rat's, instead I just dozed lightly, woke up in the baking sun, another ugly day.

Roundtwo was a big clanky scorpion, eightinches atleast, way too big to fling this freaking toxy lobster out of the pen. The boss of the todds had some fun this time holding the jar right over our heads, oops am I going to drop this stinging maniac right on top of you, haha lol look at you idiots running over to the other end of the pen, you know I can just fling it there too right.

Finally he tossed it up in the air, definitely he wanted it to land on me, kill the guy who ejected the spider lasttime, I scrambled insanely as the beast thudded down behind me.

Spiky deathtail whipped the ground between us a couple times, *hello meaty little human.*

"Spread out spread out," I yelled, backpedaling.

Again most littles were useless, crowding and scrumming like before, idiot thoughtbubbles over their heads of, *maybe if I cower behind everyone else I'll die last.*

Again rage turned me into a machine, no thoughts just movement, I skirted to the back of the scorpion, leapt onto the stupid tail, locked my arms under its poison barb so it couldn't sting.

Lucky for me a couple other littles were also brave lunatics, they dove in from either side and yanked legs off while the tail thrashed me, deathlobster screamed like a bird.

Here's how you disarm a hellbeast, trap the pinchers, twist, wrench, unscrew. The scorpion moaned deep choky birdmoans, battered me with its spazzing unlegged body, I hung on tight and waited for its death.

Another night came, I dozed but couldn't dream, they don't tell you that when you scale down, your body can't dream for a while.

A few more days, a few more battles with toxy tenlegs. We tied our clothes into whips and flails, bashed the killer from every side.

We got good at windmilling sand into a spider's twenty bubbling eyes, wrapping a scorpion tail in shirts.

Ofcourse to kill these beasts you need some fighty psychos to take risks, jump in first, do the hardpart. Unfortunately that was only three of us, two rangy dans from upnorth and me.

The other six were cowards, useless until the beast was pinned, then you can ask them to run in and rip off some legs, even then they're freaking out.

• • •

A few more nights of dozing, napping, impossible to dream.

"Hey, are we setting any records of how long can a team stay alive," one of the cowards asked the todd king.

"Ask me in a month," rasped the todd.

"You guys are feeling cocky, huh," smiled another.

Ohno, I thought.

Nextday, the todds dropped in a snake, babyrattler thrashing like a maniac.

Both dans got fanged and killed that day, infact the only reason we could even kill the snake was because it was trying to lunch. I snuck up on the fangy worm while its mouth was around a corpse, headlocked the snake and spiked his brains on the pen-wall barbwire, screamed rage at the giggling todds.

That night I knew we were probably doomed, it's just me and six useless peens. The cowards knew it too, squabbled and squawked all night about, dave you need to step it up tomorrow no matter what, well bro maybe I'd step it up if I saw you get off your butt and do literally anything, oh heckno what are you saying dave do you want to fight me, heckyeah I'll fight you let's go.

"Heygreat, I didn't know you were so fighty, maybe that'll come in handy tomorrow for once," I yelled at them, everybody shut up for a while.

Doomed, I knew, freaking doomed.

In the morning the todds came with a cage, dropped the cage in the middle of the pen, everyone screamed and scattered.

Looked like the cage was empty but whoknows, maybe this snake is invisible or something.

The todd king pointed at me.

"Get in," he said.

I gazed around, tried to guess from the todd faces what's coming next.

Tough to tell from these druggy tweaky moronfaces but the creepy grins and soft low hoots told me, here comes a super gristly deathfight.

Bynow the todds know who's a fighter and who's not, I'm the only good one left, maybe they're taking me to fight some creature oneonone.

Some crazy hellbeast, some nightmare monster. Look at their idiot faces, gummy sharktooth grins, redrimmed sniffy heartshape noseholes.

"Get in, big guy," said the king of the todds to me again, everyone giggled, what was I going to do, I got in.

They lifted me out of the pen, set me on the ground nearby.

And dropped two spiders in the pen, two black bristly pitgoliaths versus six cowards, Warner you're in the audience now.

"Oh what the heck," I screamed, rattled the cage.

"Don't worry, big guy, we retired you, enjoytheshow," the todd king told me.

Oh I felt rage, ugly rage.

I felt hatemyself rage for my dumb relief.

What a relief not to be in there, what a crappy jerk I am to be so relieved, I was sick with rage at myself.

"Let me fight," I shrieked, hammering the cagewalls, "let me freaking fight,"

hoping they wouldn't listen to me, oh don't worry coward Warner, they didn't, just watched and laughed like lunatics.

I bellowed orders to the cowards, tried to organize them, give them courage, tactics, anything, forced myself to keep watching and hoping.

I watched the whole thing but I won't make you watch, I won't describe it to you,

it wasn't over fast though.

They left me in the cage alone, explained nothing.

I sat for hours, first weeping with anger, then dried out, baking in the sun.

Late in the day, a familiar halfcar pulled up.

Puppyneck stepped out and greeted the todd king.

"Here's tenthousand," said Puppyneck.

"Twenthousand," said the todd king.

Puppyneck gazed at him.

"Price went up, super sorry about that," murmured the bone-blue lunatic, creepy and innocent.

Puppyneck counted out another five, didn't wait for yes or no, put my cage in the trunk, we pulled away.

"Dave, you okay," asked Puppyneck.

I said nothing, what is there even to say.

LIFEANDDEATHWORLD

Back we drove to Lossy Indica, me and Puppyneck, also some new hipster goons.

Puppyneck sat next to me, pampered me through the cagebars, gave me sterile middlewater to drink, fruits and nuts to eat.

"I watched your gladvids," said Puppyneck. "All I can say is, dang."

I just spat on the carfloor.

"I didn't enjoy watching, dave, believe me," he said. "I've been working twentyfourseven to get you back. Had to persuade a lot of bosses, make some salespitches. Trustme, I was sweating everymorning in front of my screen, praying you didn't get fanged."

I spat again and said nothing.

"Anyway it's all set up, dave, just breathe easy today, you're safe," he said, through the window the desert turned to scrubby hills as we crested toward the beachy capital.

What was set up was Dream Division of Faceboy Industries, the corpo child of my bloodred plan.

Is it time to tell you the diabolical plan, okay fine I guess, in the Dockseye bankbranch here was what I told Puppyneck:

Do you see the televisionnews about carcrashes from baddreams, do you know how I found Usher, do you remember how berserk Dreamworld has been for the last few months,

well all of that was me dreaming.

My dreamstuff is superstrong and can be huge and terrible.

My sis meanwhile runs Solodream Sleepmeds, she's the president.

Ofcourse this last part was not true, bear with me though.

If you partner with Solodream, get some percents of solodream revanew, I can drive sales up to ridiculous levels by raining hells in Dreamworld everynight.

Solodream will make the faceboys rich.

That was it, simple plan, crystalclear way to turn dreaming into munmuns afterall.

That night Puppyneck called my sis and said, "Hey, it's the faceboys, Warner tells us you're the president of Solodream," and my savvy quickwit hero sis realized Warner is alive, Warner has a plan, the plan needs her to be president of Solodream.

Each one lied to the other, Prayer lied that yup she's the president allright, Puppyneck lied that the faceboys still own me and have not sold me to todds.

My sis listened to Puppyneck's offer, then immediately called Markfive, begged him to come find her for an Emergency Pitch Meeting,

used all of her Busy Track learnings and powers and graphs to make the case of, Accept The Solodream Sleepmeds Company From Your Dad And Hire Me To Run It,

I'm A Busy Genius Who Will Literally Never Stop Working And Striving,

It Will Drive Your Dad Bonkers Probably That You Put Me In Charge So That's A Plus,

I Already Have A Detailed Plan To Increase Sales Many Thousand Percents,

Best Of All, The Plan Is To Partner With A Bloodthirsty Squad,

Basically You're A Cool Squadtype Drugslinger Now.

Pee Ess The Clock Is Running On The Squad Offer So We Need To Move Fast.

Markfive listened, loved it, decided heckyeah, hired her out of Eat Votech, and made her a young president.

Prayer called Puppyneck, said you've got a deal, Puppyneck called the todds to buy me back, the todds retired Warner's ugly gladcareer.

"Anyway do you want to meet your teammates," suggested Puppyneck.

The Dream Division goons weren't typical faceboy meatheads, reminded me more of Frank, the tolstoy writer wooing Grace, probably that's why I hated them.

Soft hair and softer beards, corduroys and plaids and denimvests, expensive carefull tats and earhoops, warm cow eyes that have never been punched.

He told me their names but I didn't listen, didn't care, said nothing, kept spitting on the floor.

"Hired these guys right out of business school," Puppyneck told me.

"What kind of idiots leave business school for this," I said finally.

But they pretended like it was a hilarious joke, laughing all nickery and snickery, bunch of glossy wellfed horses.

"Where do I live," I asked Puppyneck.

"Undisclosed location," Puppyneck told me. "Not the Sitadell."

"Usher's going to live with me though," I said.

"Nope, we're not letting you guys live together," he said.

"It wasn't a question," I said.

"It was an answer, though," said the young faceboss.

They draped a blanket over the cage, drove me the last two hours in darkness to my new home. Stopped the car, lifted me out, carried the cage to my room, pulled the blanket off, opened the cagedoor.

I stumbled out into a middleroom with simple littlefurniture, dollbed, cuptoilet.

The windows were high, fivefeet up on the wall maybe, a littlepoor can only see upward to the spiky heads of palmtrees. It could have been Sand Dreamough, could have been Eat Almanac, could have been Sandy Barb or Sacrament or Laura Cannon.

I looked around at the dumb walls, dumb carpet, told myself, here is where you live for fifty years, here's where old bearded Warner maybe dies.

Puppyneck called a number, put the phone on speaker.

"Solodream Corporate Headquarters," said a secretary.

"Puppyneck, calling for Prayer," said Puppyneck.

"One moment please," said the secretary, we waited a moment.

My sis's tired voice asked, "So, can I talk to my brother finally, or should I rip up the contracts."

Puppyneck's finger nudged me.

"Hi sis," I said.

"Ohmygod," yelled my sis. "Warner are you okay? That's most important, tell me you're okay."

"I'm okay," my voice said.

"Bro, are you sure?" she asked. "You don't sound okay."

"I'll be fine," I lied.

"You're sure," she said again.

"Yeah," I said.

"Okay, okay, ohthankgod, Warner, thankgod," she said, and started babbling, said some stuff about how it's fine what we're about to do, she's been thinking about it and it's okay to wreck Dreamworld for a while, it will make people more present in the world that matters, no longer dream all the time but take more action and responsibility for their lives, it's really forthebest.

I couldn't really listen, had to interrupt after a while.

"Sis," I told her. "Let's just make some stupid munmun."

VII.
KINGKONG

DREAMWORLD

Now I live in the carpety middleroom, am only alive at night.

My day is, wake up, crack eyes open and squeeze back shut, moan and groan quietly, just lie there for a few hours exhausted like a corpse.

Finally sit up, fall out of bed, stretch, work out, lift weights, do runs, pushups, pullups, yogas.

Eat fruits and nuts, sip sterile middlewater, Dream Division brings me trays.

Smoke weeds, swallow pillslivers, begin preparing to dream insanely, drugs make my dreams berserk, infact the first few nights in my new home I needed drugs to dream at all, fall alltheway asleep.

Read random parts of the superbible of the Church of the Lord King God, let the chemicals seep wildly into the teachings.

Sometimes play shootemups but mostly read the superbible.

Work out again, eat another meal, take more drugs, begin to get woozy.

Slip into bed and wait for sleep to come.

• • •

And at night I lay waste to Dreamworld as a Pissedoff Angel of the Lord King God.

Everynight now Dreamworld is one huge gutterzone, one big hellscape.

"The bigs and middles have treated littles toobad for toolong," I preach from the thundering air, "The Regent Master Emperor Boss God is just freaking out, He's so disappointed and bummed, He literally replaced the sky with a drippy caveceiling, now you must live underground always, in an evil caveforest."

Every awfull thing I dream, the dreamers help me, their fear takes over and multiplies it, I dream a groaning forest and they fill it with the wild witchy dead, clawing out of the ground and air.

"The Divine President And See Ee Oh has had enough of your sins and selfishnesses," I tell every dreamer, "does it not say right there in the freaking superbible that eagerness for munmuns leads you away from the righteous path, well guesswhat, sinners, honest-togod spacealiens are spraying the planet with pestysides now."

The pestyside fog is a sevenfoot sea, poor dreamers are leaping and surfacing like dollfins, trying to get a breath, hard to leap when your legs are lockedup or rubbery though, meanwhile upabove the beaky spacevultures swoop lower and lower, belching screams.

"You didn't listen when the Lord King God warned you that munmuns will pierce your heart with griefs," I boom, "now you're roasting like a pelican in a hot bright bad littleroom, it has a trapdoor so you can leave anytime, but the door only takes you to somewhere worse, how's that for a freaking dilemma, rage is making the Lord King God do some pretty messedup stuff rightnow."

The broiling dreamers can't help themselves, they throw the trapdoor open, fall down into the exactsame room but worse, hotter, smaller, roast harder, die faster, freak out and jump through the next trapdoor, it's even worse, even hotter, maybe filled with boiling muds, et set set setera, textbook gutterbuilding technique.

Pretty soon some people became harder to reach, some zones of Lossy Indica became more quiet, faraway, blanketwrapped.

Surenough, in Lifeanddeathworld the bigs and riches began to take solodream.

Ads for solodream were everywhere apparently, the Dream Division made stylish beautifull vids explaining that religious maniacs have taken over Dreamworld, it's such a shame but what can you do, the enlightened intelligent dreamer is taking solodream these days so as not to be terrorized by godfull lunatics.

In neighborhoods of bigs and middles, solodream was flying off the shelves, munmuns poured into the accounts of Solodream Sleepmeds and Faceboy Industries.

In Dreamworld I began to attack these cloudy districts, the houses where the dreamers tried to turn themselves to ghosts.

Focus on the lonely disappearers, grab hold before they vanish. Rip away the soloblankets from around them, pull them back to the fiery ponds and fangy rains.

In Lifeanddeathworld dreamers complained to their farmassists, hey buddy what the heck, my solodream's not working some nights, isn't it supposed to be neverfail, foolproof, whatgives.

But Dream Division paid the farmassists to shrug and say, these religious terrorists are just superstrong, but dontworry, our scientists are working roundtheclock on stronger drugs to keep people out of your dreams, meantime can I hook you up with a higher dose.

So they dosed themselves harder and in Dreamworld the blankets around the rich got heavier, the ghosts got lighter and quieter.

And I just clenched my teeth, worked stronger, faster, pulled the threads, yanked the ropes, melted walls, grabbed and stuffed these struggling riches back into hell, as many as I could before morning, I pushed back against time and slowed it down,

every morning I woke up and was not even human for a while, my brain was just an errorscreen, my eyes said DID NOT LOAD.

Night after night, week after week.

Months slipped by, melted into a year.

I began to notice that the solodream was changing people, all this time spent alone in lonesome dreamboxes.

The lonely solodreamers began to dream robot companions for themselves in there, people who look like you and me but aren't, are nothing but dreamfluff.

I peeked into the boxes of the richest solodreamers, saw them surrounded by robot weirdos, fake parents, fake kids, fake friends acting super nice and dumb. Constantly complimenting the solodreamers, laughing way too hard at their jokes and nodding way too intrested in their stories, allofasudden can't take it anymore and rip off their sexy clothes and give the solodreamers a bangdream with porny robot bodies.

The solodreamers were already forgetting what real dreamers are like, ignoring that stuff they can't control is happening in other people's heads.

It gave me new ways of making hellscapes, just fill Dreamworld with robots, everyone begins to forget that everyone else is real, everyone begins acting like a selfish lunatic.

And a second year spooled of my sololife, mostly too exhausted to feel alone, it got hard to remember what it's like to have friends to talk to, obviously the business grads of Dream Division were not my friends, infact I refused to pretend they even exist.

My body got taller, harder, meaner, guess I have a man's body now, a man's scarredup face too, no friend to see it though.

Markfive died onenight, carcrash, drugs.

Markfive you genius dummy, this wasn't how it was supposed to go for you.

I couldn't go to the funeral because I couldn't leave my room, maybe nothing outside the room was real.

Prayer was heartbroken and then quickly plunged into a bitter corporate feud, Mark attempted a hostiletakeover to get his company back from the girl who his son made halfowner, maybe that wasn't legal or something, pirate lawyers fired cannons at my sister's ship.

Lily tried to help fend him off, Mark you dumb jerk how can you perform a hostiletakeover of a private corpo, also can we just grieve for like two seconds you freaking monster. But Mark pretended grieving is exactly what this is about, grief made him need Markfive's company. Maybe he wasn't even pretending, maybe a business is a replacement son to him.

Prayer triumphed, Usher tried to tell me all about it in Dreamworld, Warner you should be super proud of your fivestar general sis. Here's what she did, went on offense and threatened twenty countersuits with the Solodream warchest, got into patentfarming and took aim at Mark's corebusiness, et set set setera.

Prettyquick I had to tell Usher to stop, Usher I know you love my sis but please chill, nothing is more boring than a story about business.

In Dreamworld I kept eyes out for an operahouse.

Found it nowandthen and let it live, didn't turn it to smoke or mud.

Never stepped inside though, never took a moment to hear the music, see the face.

Stayed faraway and disguised, best if Kitty thinks I'm dead, moveon sweet Kitty, forget I lived, just build your happy islands in these hells.

Usher approached me in Dreamworld onenight, I took a break from trampling an endless rotting maze with tusky peenpigs and spoke to him inside the moon.

"Happy birthday," said my gray friend.

"Hey, thanks for remembering," I told him. "I had no idea."

"I like to keep track," he said.

"How's the Sitadell," I asked.

"It's fine," he said. "I'm ready to leave though."

He said it pretty calm and flat, it was kind of hilarious, you had to be there I guess, anyway I laughed for a while.

Then he told me he has a birthday present for me.

Oh yeah Usher, what's that.

It's a secret little company actually, snuck it into the paperwork of the Faceboys And Solodream Corporate Partnership, a little shellcorpo called Consolidated Warning.

Shellcorpo huh, what does that even mean.

It's supposed to be a way to dodge tax, the details aren't super important. What you need to know is, twentyeight percent of all solodream revanew lands in Consolidated Warning, been collecting there for a while now.

Usher never showed huge emotions, always pretty chill, but a beamy grin was twisting over that calm face.

"That's a birthday present though, I mean how," I asked him, feeling stupid.

"I found a way of incorporating you," he said.

"What does that mean," I said.

"You're Consolidated Warning," he beamed.

"Yeah but what does that mean though," I said.

"The Consolidated Warning account is your munflow account," Usher told me. "Legally you can only incorporate at eighteen, but the muns have been collecting there since this whole thing started, so now that it's your birthday, that account has merged with your munflow, you have some munmuns in there allofasudden."

I did some breathing in the moon, let myself relax, probably outside the hellscapes were lightening up.

"How did the faceboys allow this insane thing to happen," I asked.

"Only their lawyer knows about it," he explained, eyes really sparking now with happy revenge.

"Does Solodream know," I asked.

"Just your sis," he said.

"So, how many munmuns do I have," I asked him.

"About ninetymillion," he said.

My mind got very calm, very clear, a glass of perfect water.

"We win," he told me, "finally, we win."

Usher you sweet goofball, that's not possible, no one ever wins.

But he described the win lovingly, indetail, told me what can happen, how I can escape. Warner I ofcourse have power of attorney over Consolidated Warning, so now when the faceboys bring me on a routine trip to the bank to update Faceboy Industries agreements, I can secretly give the bank the order to move muns from your munflow to your scale, let's say tenmillion, doublescale.

You don't need to visit the bank for this either, the bank can scale you up remotely, remote scaling happens if you're too big to fit in the bank, they do it in extraordinary circumstances. I will give them an exact time for them to just shift the muns and blow you up like a balloon wherever you are, scaling up awake without scalemeds is supposed to be pretty safe, kind of painfull and weird but no risk.

I'm sure we can trick someone in Dream Division to let you out into the yard, we don't even have to tell them what it's for. Make up a story, Warner needs outdoor access for dreampurposes or something, start letting him out for an hour everyday.

And then one day while you're out, the scaleup happens, someone will meet you in a bulletproof doublecar, give you your doublerobe, whisk you away to your doublelife.

He told me all this and I knew what we were going to do.

"Okay," I told him. "Here's what happens next. You take half, and you escape."

He shook his gray head.

"Nope, you don't have a choice," I told him. "I'm ordering you, go to the bank, use power of attorney to give yourself half, take fortyfivemillion and get doublescale yourself, get your own doublecar, drive off to your own doublelife."

"Okay and then what about you," he said.

"I stay here for now," I told him.

He was quiet.

"Look, if you can control my muns, how about you just invest them, buy some stocks, maybe take over some corpos even," I said. "I'll tell you when I'm ready to scale up."

He didn't understand but nodded anyway, my best and only friend, loyal brilliant Usher.

I left the moon and made more hells.

LIFEANDDEATHWORLD

So on his next routine trip to the bank, guarded by hulking Shoulderheads and two other faceboys carefully watching for funnystuff, Usher took a deep breath, wrote a note to the bankers in Latinn.

"What's that say," demanded Shoulderheads.

"Just some t technic cal lan nguage," explained Usher.

But what the note said was, "Dear Banker, Please take me to the underbank for a tenmillion munmun Scale Up, plus move thirtyfivemillion to my munflow, Consolidated Warning is the account that's paying into mine, note that I have power of attorney over Consolidated Warning, okaygreat."

Banker read it, gazed at Usher, gazed at the goons.

Then nodded and smiled brightly.

"Perfect, sir, the littlevator is right this way, and congratulations on your dramatic Scale Up," chirped the banker, lifting Usher by the underarms.

"Hey hey hey, we go with him everywhere," yelled Shoulderheads, grabbing the banker.

"Not for Scale Up, I'm afraid," apologized the banker as Bank

Security rushed in and tased Shoulderheads and his screaming faceboy goons, what are you idiots thinking, you don't get to manhandle bankers in the bank.

After Scale Up, doublescale elevenfoot Usher lingered alone in the waitingroom, called a service called Ruthless Mercenary Transport, paid twenthousand for a ride. Pick me up at the middlerich loadingdock please, maybe be prepared for assault as we pull out.

But it wasn't much of an assault, Shoulderheads only bounced a few bullets off the tank before Ruthless drones sniped him, what a dumb end of the story for Shoulderheads, slumped bloody in the middlestreet.

Usher rolled into Sentrow like a warhero, climbed out of the tank in a classic creamy mobster suit and a sweet strawhat to cover his tatty head, Usher you stylish grayfish, do you know how to make an entrance or what.

He squeezed into a middlevator, took it to the tenthfloor, came hulking a little stumbly down the hall, knocked on the door of the President and See Ee Oh of Solodream.

"Hi Prayer," he grinned, managed to say her name perfectly before she wrapped her arms around his ribs, sobbing.

DREAMWORLD

Rage and chaos splintered Faceboy Industries, they relied too heavily on one captive brain and now he's gone, on the way out sabotaged all their contracts also, basically their one remaining asset was prisoned me.

Oneandahalfscale Puppyneck threatened to stomp me a couple times so I reminded him, dave, what sense does that even make, I'm the reason you're eightfeet and stylish, you like your life too much of being the tracksuit king of partyclubs, how about you stop making idiot threats and just let me earn you munmuns.

He must have agreed, instead of killing me he pulled an Usher move. Caged and blanketed me one morning just after sunrise, packed me into his car, took me to a separate house acrosstown, Puppyneck has fled the faceboys too.

He wrote a newdeal with Solodream, basically just a ransom-letter, Solodream how about you and Prayer give the new business of Puppyneck Dream Security Limited fivemillion muns a year to protect Warner and not accidentally sit on him, would hate for anything to happen to this guy.

My new lifty room was similar to the old, same gyms, more carpet.

Air was nicer though, seabreeze, must be near the ocean.

My munmuns became fruitfull, had munkids. In the outsideworld loyal Usher bought some stocks for me, chunks of some companies.

Obviously it's an advantage if you're crowbarring into the solodreams of corpo owners everynight, listening to them babble lazy dreambabble to their robots, hey what's that, didyousay Zippy Energetics is discovering a cheap fresh new way to make oilrocks burn even hotter and smokier, Usher I have a hottip for us.

"Time to figure out how you're going to escape, right, I can put a privateeye on the case, figure out where you're living," Usher asked me every week or two.

My answer was no, week after week.

"What's the number you're waiting for," he wanted to know.

I shrugged, kept making hells and shitscapes.

For a third year I crafted nightmares and pummeled solodreamers, Puppyneck and I grew a strange friendship, he was the only human I knew forsure existed.

Everymorning he sat with me, smoked with me, gave me random news.

Fires got worse, the ocean ate more towns. Beans stopped growing for a while, guess everyone's got to eat more meat.

Rockets took some farmy teams to mars, everyone got a disgusting spacedisease. One guy on mars became so annoying that they had to decide, do we kill this guy or pay tenbillion munmuns to send him back to earth, seriously it's that bad, we can't deal with this guy anymore. The Yewess put it to a vote, voted to kill, wasn't even close, what, you think we're going to spend tenbillion muns to bring a super annoying guy back to our planet. The marshans didn't kill him though, he promised to try to be more chill, guy was skitso or borderline or something.

And somewhere in the city outside my room, I knew Grant was still riding Metros and trapping other littlepoors and putting them in his trainvids, somewhere his psycho daughter Willow was growing up and maybe her angry heart was softening, maybe it was hardening, maybe Bixquick has ripped some poor little to shreds.

I told Usher finally what I wanted to do.

"Holycrap," was all he said.

In the world outside a fourth year happened.

Some of Iceland melted, some of Ejipped burned, all of Rushia messed with someone else, all Coreans are freaking out. Famous Randy fell in love but just with a butt.

The Yewess got a new President, littlest in twenty years, barely even doublescale, they're thinking about making a second littler Whitehouse for this scrappy Yellow reformer.

Usher and Prayer got a quiet secret marriage, joined munmuns with my mom, Mom got some surgery and now has zippy bendylegs, she is starting some kind of superchurch and it's pretty annoying, she's very happy though and excited to scold you about pretending to be the Lord King God, anyway Warner we promise we'll have the real wedding as soon as you get out, when do you think that is though, soon, right.

I don't know, sis though, notyet.

Somewhere out in Lossy Indica, Grace lived another year of her life, I thought about her sometimes, sure, probably she's in law school bynow. Maybe she's still with Frank, maybe he's still making her read his endless tolstoys. Somewhere they're talking, kissing, banging, fighting, or maybe they haven't seen each other in months. Maybe she's done with the fakegreen eyes, showing those pretty eyeblacks now, maybe she lost her love for bloodthirsty comics, whoknows, notme.

In Dreamworld I stayed away from anyone I knew, I wasn't Warner anymore, just a bloodthirsty angel.

For a fifth year I lived little and alone in the carpety middleroom, but now there was no need anymore to dream hells.

The solodreamers were taking solodream every night nomatterwhat, completely addicted to loneliness.

Instead of hells I began to make strange announcements.

GOD IS A KINGKONG, I dreamed in the stars, in the grass.

GOD IS A GODSILLA, I billboarded in everybody's room.

THE KINGKONG GODSILLA GOD IS COMING, moths whispered everywhere, schools, warehouses, sewers, wholefoods, trains, barmittsvas, keensayingyearas, everywhere but the operahouse.

I didn't touch the Kittyhouse but I did make it hard to find.

Built a glazing desert around it, stacked a dark salty sea over it.

Kitty didn't even notice, never stepped out of that house, might as well be solodreaming.

Sure I thought about her, maybe more than anyone, somewhere out there in Lifeanddeathworld Kitty must be in a colledge, I like to think a music school, maybe she's found the therapies that let her hands play guitar.

And somewhere maybe Tony is learning to try a little less hard, people hate you when they know how much you want to be liked. And Daisy is still playing shootemups late at night and Hueagain is doctoring bynow, Dawn is walking the dogs and Hue is getting reelected, and some other bright strivey middlepoor is living in their house, sleeping in the halfroom, learning the secret patience of How To Be Rich.

But I learned it too, Kitty Family, I did.

LIFEANDDEATHWORLD

The day came, I gave Puppyneck his orders, he didn't put up much of a fight.

"I could still just stomp you," he joked.

"Forsure," I agreed, "my lawyer could also put a crisp twenmillion behind a Puppyneck Is Wanted Dead Or Alive type of poster, though."

"Lol what a bluff," lolled Puppyneck, carrying me out onto his backdeck, down to his motorboat, firsttime under the sun in years.

Out on the ocean he placed me in the water, the waves jostled me.

"Seriously though, how big are you getting," Puppyneck wanted to know.

"Step back and watch," I told him.

His boat motored away from me a few feet.

"That might not be far enough," I yelled, he didn't hear me though.

I floated, hummed to myself, waited for the bankers to begin.

Rubbery seaweed ribbons wreathed me.

Shadows moved below me.

Wish we could have done this at the bank, ohwell.

A tuna sniffed me like a dog, whispered water at my feet.

Another couple moments passed, water lapped my ears.

The tuna gulped me, ate me whole.

I was sliding and flailing in a wet slippery nightroom, nothing to breathe but seawater, didn't even have time to think *dang* before I felt it, my bones began their creaky stretching.

In a few seconds I was too big to stay in this fish's tum, I punched through his side, poor brainless maneater.

Wriggled head and arms out, paddled like a madman back to the surface, my waist was snapping fishribs onebyone.

Broke the seatop and gasped, halfscale already, splitinhalf fishbody falling away from me to the bottom.

For sure it hurt, a warm beautifull hurt though. It was the soreness of You Just Ran For A Super Long Time, Then You Lifted Weights, Then You Climbed A Giant House.

I lay back on the seatop and closed my eyes, felt every ache bloom through me, heard my heart get slow and my lungs get huge.

Saw my brain get enormous, a thought might take allday to swim across this thing.

Against my skin the waves became ripples, seaweed became a tickly fringe, seadust, seafluff.

I pushed my hands backandforth through the water, moved blocks of ocean here and there.

Became a whale, wordless, slow.

Kept my eyes closed for a while after it was over, finally opened them and looked around, where's Puppyneck.

Didn't see him for a while, did he freak out and motor away.

Ohsnap, is that the boat.

That tiny seashell, upsidedown toyboat halfsunk already, must have been flipped by my bathtub waves.

PUPPYNECK, I rasped, drythroated, my voice was a thunderboom, too big even for aircommas.

I sifted through the water, looking for him.

Aha, there he is, a struggling little insect.

Look at this tiny little guy, treading, giggling furiously.

I picked him up and put him in my hair.

I had fiftybillion munmuns in me, twentysixscale, about a hunfiftyfeet tall. Usher had moved every last munmun from munflow to scale, put it all in my scale account, the bank tried to tell him this is really not a goodidea but toobad, bankers, it's like you said, you're just a bunch of tools, now you must serve a lunatic and his lawyer.

And now a little Lossy Indica lay dull and flat twomiles from my monster's body, under the heavy morning heat.

A mile from shore, my feet touched the seabottom, I stopped paddling, began to wade.

Thousandfeet from shore, the seatop didn't even reach my knees, sorry everybody for this perfect view of my peen and furry nuts.

I brought sheets of ocean with me, waves and surges, swimmers were freaking out, paddling to the beach and stumblerunning, surfers tried to ride along.

I stepped onto the sand, drippingwet.

Toed the boardwalk, took a few steps into town, each step has to be super slow, hold the foot up and wait for the antpeople to scurry out from underneath, then lower slowly, ground still trembles though.

Rested my arms on top of a fivestory building and looked around, tried not to rest the arms too hard or break too much roof.

Look at this low wide goofy little place, toy town, toy cars, toy Metro.

I'm Grant now, less janky playset though.

Police and coastguard were buzzing around me frantically, copters, sirens, guys on horses. Are they going to attack, will I have to swat and crush.

The answer was nope, I wasn't who they hated.

"MOVE IT PEOPLE, GIANT COMING THROUGH, HOW ABOUT YOU GET OUT OF THE FREAKING WAY ALREADY," their speakers screamed.

All around me were loyal copswarms chasing ants out of the way, shoving with shields, bulldozing with shovelcars, under the motors and rotors I heard quiet outraged barks and chirpy little screams from the pushedaround crowds, how the heck did all these police get here so fast.

"Big sir," purred a spokesdrone near my face, "would you like for us to summon some transport for you, travel in style and convenience to wherever you're going?"

There was nowhere that I was going ofcourse, I was right where I was supposed to be, here to make my huge announcement in my giantvoice, hey citizens, littlepoors inparticular, listen up, I have goodnews.

See how big I am, see how much I took from riches, well now I'm giving it to poors. I'm donating my fortune to Lossy Indica Minmun, no one in this city will ever be ratscale again.

It's fiftybillion, not sure how exactly the math works out but I think the new minimumsize will be about quarterscale, maybe a little bigger.

Safe from cats and spiders, bigenough for schools and hospitals, strongenough for smaller jobs, Lifty and Cleany.

So get ready, get set, in a few minutes I'll start scaling down, after that you can sprint to your local bankbranch for a Scale Up, enjoy your new middlelife courtesy of Consolidated Warning.

But I didn't say it.

I gazed down at the littleville and filled my enormous lungs and something happened, I don't know, the announcement sat in my throat and dried out.

Somewhere Usher and Prayer watched, waited, must have thought, *Warner, spit it out, big guy, what's the hangup.*

But a different plan was yawning open in my giantbrain, notsomuch about goodnews, more to do with badnews.

And heresthething, as soon as I thought of it, I knew the badnews plan was really my plan allalong.

"Big sir, at your convenience feel free to peruse our menu of tantalizing transpo options," piped the spokesdrone, displaying tanks and choppers.

THAT'S OKAY, I'LL WALK, I told the drone.

"Fantastic choice because we will clear any path you need, remember we exist to serve and even our biggest citizens can always count on the Lossy Indica Police Department, infact I'd say especially our biggest," reminded the drone.

Meanwhile I looked around at all these roofs I could step through.

Cars I could pick up by the fistfull, houses I could stoop down and lick off the hillsides.

ACTUALLY I'LL SWIM, I decided.

"CLEAR THE FREAKING BEACH," blared the coast-guard. "A GIANT WANTS TO SWIM."

Twothousandfeet off the coast, I paddled north a little bit, police and coastguard proudly flanking me like dogs.

I was ofcourse ravenous, my giant stomach was empty, thirsty too, my raw dry mouth was panting.

My plan had been not to eat or drink, anything in the tum makes it tricky to scale down, forget the plan though.

I needed food and water, had ideas of where to get them too.

I passed a few points, a few inlets. The tiny toy cliffside houses got bigger and bigger.

I dove a couple times to see how close is the bottom, turned-out it's pretty close. I itched my belly on the tickly coral, dragged knuckletrenches through the ocean dirt, clouded the water with blownup seafloor. When I came back to the surface the choppers and speedboats were cheering me.

"EPIC DEEPDIVE," they roared and clapped. "SO HEROIC."

Before long, there it was, the familiar spannishvilla.

I waded to shore, police and coastguard had to hang back, Balustrade was ofcourse a private defense zone.

"IT HAS BEEN AN UNLIMITED PLEASURE ACCOMPANYING YOU ON YOUR VISIT TO LOSSY INDICA," a boat trumpeted after me and more stuff like that, I ignored it and stepped onto land.

Wow, were the bighouses of Balustrade dumb and pathetic to my gigantic eyes. To halfscale me they had been soaring concerthalls. But now look, they're actually just sad weird huts.

Spannishvilla, castle, shrine, plantation, glasscube cluster, all pathetic. Onestory boxes for caging lonely giants.

I stood and dripped and gazed and each bighouse was just a few twinedtogether alleyway milkcrates.

Betterdecorated obviously, bigger windows, filled with tiny servants, oceanviews.

But each house was the one my dad built and tinkered with

everyday and patched the roof and papered the walls and died inside when a kid stepped on it, Warner why are you thinking about that, idiot, you have work to do.

I stepped onto the villa patio, Mark's staff ofcourse was trying to intercept me with gentle welcomes of Hello Honored Guest and apologies of You Know What Though, Mark Is Resting And Relaxing At The Moment and suggestions of Would You Like To Wait Out Here, Perhaps We Could Get You Something.

I ignored them too and knocked on the door, tried to open it, it was locked.

But the locks they make even for bigriches are pretty puny when you're a kingkong, it wasn't that hard for me to rip off the door and drop it in the sand.

Inside quiet cooks were prepping bowls of lemonwater and charred cows, fantastic, I lifted a bowl and drank it down as they cowered in silent terror.

Water filled me, spread to my fingertips, my throat loosened, eyes brightened, giant lungs uncurled even further.

I munched a cow, pretty good but pretty bland, guess it's hard to brew enough sauce.

Meanwhile in the nextroom blinky toadcolor Mark bolted upright in his bed, staring at the naked godsilla in his kitchen, munching his food.

"HEY," he grogged. "UM, WHAT'S GOING ON HERE."

I said nothing, just stared at him in the eye and chomped his cows, gulped his drinks, man did it feel good to be putting food in the tum.

He squinted at me, ran a hand across his perfect rigid hair.

"YOU LOOK KIND OF FAMILIAR," he said. "WHO ARE YOU?"

I AM THE KINGKONG GOD, I told him.

"OKAY," he said. "DID YOU JUST BREAK MY DOOR?"

I finished his food and water.

YUP, I said.

"WELL OKAY," he said. "JESUS. UH, STAFF, I GUESS COULD YOU MAKE ME SOME MORE COWS."

Behind me I heard the staff spring into action, Heather barked commands, we need five charred cows blitzed and sauced immediately, four bowls of water, movemovemove, Mark has a naked mystery guest, looks like atleast a fourtybillionair.

I walked to his bedroom doorway and blocked it with my naked body.

YOUR STAFF CAN MAKE MORE COWS BUT I WILL EAT THEM, I told Mark.

"HAHA OKAY, I BET YOU WILL, NOW HOW DO I KNOW YOU," wondered Mark as he got up.

YOU KNOW ME FROM DREAMWORLD, I told him.

"OKAY, CAN I GET PAST PLEASE," he asked.

NO, I said.

"OKAY WELL LOOK, UH, FRIEND," he said, getting a little snappy, "I JUST SLEPT SIXHOURS, I'M VERY DEHYDRATED, LOWBLOODSUGAR, YOU KNOW HOW IT IS."

WELL, YOU HAVE A PROBLEM, I told him. BECAUSE NOW I AM THE ONE WHO DRINKS YOUR WATER AND EATS YOUR FOOD.

I watched him begin to realize he had a problem.

He tried to push me out of the way, put his big hand on my way bigger chest.

With lightningspeed I grabbed his wrist, twisted it, threw him down like a ragdoll, heard one of his knees smash into the tile like a gunshot, back in the kitchen the quake bowled his staff over.

"HAAAHHH," he gasped and sobbed.

I stood over him patiently, waited for what was next.

Took him a while even to talk, he just moaned and stared with fear and hate at the young bruisy monster who outscaled him by atleast thirtyfeet.

Meanwhile behind me the staff was buzzing around like crazy, had some guns and bombs readytogo but didn't know whether to use them.

"STAFF," croaked Mark finally, "GET THIS FUCKING INTRUDER OUT OF MY HOUSE, LIKE WITH FORCE IF YOU HAVE TO."

STAFF, WHAT DO YOU THINK HAPPENS IF YOU ATTACK ME, I said, ANSWER, I ATTACK YOU TOO.

I watched them with my huge eyes, you fearfull babybrats will do nothing, I know cowards when I see them.

ANYWAY I'M BIGGER, RICHER, IN NEED OF A STAFF MYSELF, SO HOWABOUT YOU WORK FOR ME, I suggested.

The staff stared back at me.

Then they started glancing at each other.

Then a thousand bickerings broke out among them, What Do You Think, on the otherhand How Dare You, but thenagain What Choice Do We Have.

Some were loyal nomatterwhat, others were super excited to betray, most though were just trying to figure out who was leaving and who was staying, where will I get the highest promotion, all kinds of tricky ugly chessmoves, it kind of broke my heart to see.

Meanwhile I ate the other cows and drank the bowls of water. Mark tried to rush me when he thought I wasn't looking but I knocked him to the ground again, gentler this time but firm, also I guess not that gentle, I did break his nose.

Under the blood his face was toady gray and sick, he knew he had no power, was trying to make tools out of words but his hungry thirsty brain didn't have the patience, it really doesn't take long for a bigrich body to freak out and shut down.

"DO YOU WANT MUNMUNS, PART OF MY COMPANY, WHAT DO YOU WANT, OHMYGOD I CAN'T TAKE THIS ANYMORE," he blurted.

ALL I WANT, I said, IS ALL YOUR FOOD AND WATER.

"OKAY WELL HERESTHETHING, UH, IT'S IN THE BASEMENT, ALL THE FOOD AND WATER IS IN THE SERVICEBASEMENT, I'LL SHOW YOU, JUST OPEN THAT TRAPDOOR AND STEP DOWN IN THERE, DONTWORRY I'LL FOLLOW YOU," he yelled.

NNNNNNNOPE, I said, picking cowskin out of my teeth.

"PLEASE," he sobbed. "PLEASE, I'M DYING. I'M ACTUALLY DYING, MAN. I'M SO HUNGRY AND THIRSTY. I CAN BARELY TALK."

NOPE, I said.

"WHY ARE YOU DOING THIS," he cried.

KINGKONG GOD, I explained.

"WHAT DOES THAT MEAN," he sniveled.

IT MEANS I EAT YOUR FOOD AND DRINK YOUR WATER, I explained.

I watched him hiccup angry sobs, the guy has not felt these feelings in a long long time.

OK GUESSWHAT, I announced finally.

But he refused to guesswhat.

YOU CAN HAVE SOME FOOD AND WATER I DECIDED, I told him.

He glared and sniffled, thought I was messing with him still, and look, he wasn't wrong.

IT HAS TO BE YOUR NEIGHBOR'S THOUGH, I explained.

So we walked to Bill's castle, through a window we saw the old guy watching news, hey that young fellow on the screen looks familiar, shaky footage of naked ropey me staggering in from the ocean.

"Little is known about the mysterious wealthy giant who emerged today from the sea," I heard a stern anchor explain, "government records do not exist and he is thought to be either foreign or of nonhospital birth, like littlepoor or perhaps to some religious crazies in the forest."

"BILL," called Mark through the window, Bill didn't hear him though, that guy is super into the news and also deaf.

"Look at this bold young munmaker," cried a newspanelist, replaying vids of me dripping all over everything, "the discovery of a new bigrich is always cause for celebration, a new jobcreator for our needy city, I certainly hope the localgovernment is prepared to welcome this behemoth with openarms."

"BILL BILL BILL. HEY BILL," said Mark a little louder, freaking out from hunger.

"Can't the bank make an exception and release this guy's basic info, atleast tell us who he is, I mean we have no idea where he's from or how he got so rich, what if he's a terrorist forexample," complained another panelist, uhoh, flashing screentext told us she was ALLEY THE COMPLAINER.

"Boooooo," screamed the live studioaudience of the news.

"There goes Alley again, always complaining about the bank, trying to question our most essential privacy protections," groaned first panelist.

"BILLLLLLLLL," hollered Mark but Bill was shaking his fist and excitedly yelling, "ALLEY, I GOT A HUNCH SOMEBODY'S ABOUT TO PADDLE YOU GOOD."

"Alley you idiot," yelled a third panelist, "privacylaws protect us from comyounism, spoileralert, they tried comyounism in like twenty countries and it never ever worked, so inotherwords you lose, I win," airhorn screamed, broadways flashed, this third panelist got a Win The Argument Point, the anchor handed him a paddle.

Mark pounded on the window.

I thumped on the wall and knocked a hole in it.

The castle wasn't made of stone afterall, kind of a thin flimsy wood, definitely not going to keep out any kingkongs today. This got Bill's attention anyway, he stared at me through the hole.

Give the old guy credit, he knows a threat when he sees one.

"TRESPASSER," he bellowed, grabbing a sword and running out the door.

I wrenched off a big jagged plate of his house and whipped it at him as he ran at me, clocked him under the chin, the old guy went down hard, sword clattered on the giant faketile.

I tossed the sword aside, reached down, slapped old Bill's face, once, twice, threefour fivesix times, not so hard it broke the face or anything, just to show him, *you have no control, I decide what happens to you, and right now what happens to you is, your face gets slapped while Mark eats your food.*

MARK EATS YOUR FOOD NOW, I told Bill, aiming his face through the househole at ravenous guilty Mark rampaging in Bill's kitchen.

"BILL I'M SORRY, THIS GUY IS A MANIAC, I LITERALLY FELT MYSELF DYING," apologized Mark, stuffing his mouth with Bill's smoked ostriches and guzzling a vat of cocoanut juice.

Bill gargled and fumed, trembled with rage, glared at his neighbor but couldn't even speak, coughed a little on his blood.

OKAY, I THINK YOU GUYS CAN SORT THIS OUT, I told them.

I picked up the sword, this thing might come in handy, moved on to the next house.

• • •

Went to the plantation, dragged Tom out by the neck and into the ocean, spent a while dunking him, holding him under, learned my technique from a feisty fellow with heads on his shoulders.

Went to the shintoeshrine, kneecapped John with one of his golfclubs, his wife Jillion tried to sneak up on me from behind, kneecapped her too.

Bashed the glasscubes with the sword until timid pink Lee crept out, he was the tallest so far, almost my height but flabby, wobbly, I pulled up his robe and spanked his grapefruit butt.

The staffs were cowards prettymuch, no one did anything until Lee's fourscale chief of staff freaked out and peppered me with bullets, fifteen beestings in my arm, hand, shoulder.

I picked him up, crumpled his hot little gun, softly tossed him into the trees but probably he died still.

STAFFS, I'M NOT HERE TO FIGHT YOU, JUST YOUR BIGBOSSES, I kept telling them. DON'T ATTACK ME UNLESS YOU WANT TO DIE TONIGHT.

No one wanted to die, everyone was terrified of death, everyone was toosoft, everyone's comfy life was toogood.

I jogged to the next inlet, another seven houses awaited me, I continued my journey of breaking, entering, pulping, eating people's food and drinking their water.

Did I know this would doom me, sure, half of me did.

Half of me knew, I am one and they are a bunch.

Soonerorlater these riches will sit on each other's shoulders, get taller and stronger, start pummeling me back.

Pour a trillion munmuns into the youngest and strongest of them, someone to stomp me to death, some new godsilla who loves the rich.

But the other half thought, they might not be able to fight back no matter how bad it gets, maybe they're too dumb, too soft, too cowardly.

Too mistrustfull, too selfloving, they might just think, *why would I ever donate muns to a Kill Warner account, why should I have to give up scale to stop the monster, someone else can deal with it.*

Maybe I'll get to do this for a long fun time, half of me thought.

Newscopters were allowed into Balustrade, I started watching myself on the screens of the homes I bashed.

"UNCERTAINTY IN BALUSTRADE AS BRASH NEW FIFTYBILLIONAIR UNSETTLES THE PECKING ORDER," reported some screentext.

"Sources tell us that this new bigrich calls himself the Kingkong God," babbled an anchor excitedly, "lots of people are saying he's brought a refreshing earthy simplicity to a stagnant social scene."

The sun dipped below the sea and I headed north in purpling darkness, in the next inlet four more floodlit houses waited for me, a couple were already being moved onto barges.

EVERYONE OUT OF THOSE BARGES PLEASE, YOU SHOULD GET TO SAFETY, I recommended.

The staffs swam, flew, motored away in panic as I waded

into the ocean, laid my arms on the barges, slowly tipped them underwater, rested the houses on the sandy seafloor.

"GOD FUCKING DAMN IT, ARE YOU KIDDING ME WITH THIS SHIT, I MEAN AM I SERIOUSLY GOING TO HAVE TO SLEEP OUTSIDE TONIGHT," screamed a bigrich who was hiding in the darkness of the forest.

"PEAT, SHUT UP, HE'S GOING TO FIND US," hissed another one.

"I'M NOT GOING TO SHUT UP," yelled the first one. "YOU, WITH THE RAGGY HAIR AND NO CLOTHES, DO YOU KNOW HOW MUCH FOODWASTE YOU JUST GENERATED, FOREXAMPLE, I MEAN DID YOU EVEN THINK ABOUT THAT."

I GUESS I DIDN'T, I admitted, jogging toward the voices.

"OH FOR FUCK'S SAKE, PEAT," said the second one. "HERE HE FUCKING COMES."

"IF WE ALL TEAM UP WE CAN TAKE HIM," said the first.

"IF YOU WANT TO GET YOUR ASS KICKED, GOFORIT," said the second.

"WE'RE GETTING OUR ASSES KICKED ANYWAY," pleaded the first, as I reached him and softly palmed his head in my hand and bounced it off the cliffside.

I gloried through the night, sank more barges and houses, kicked more soft butts.

Assembled my own staff from other people's staffs, armed them with other people's guns and bombs, put them on other people's boats and copters, promised my lawyer would have paper-work ready for everyone in the morning.

No one stopped me, no one fought me, instead people fought each other to escape, squabbled over each other's stuff to replace what I had smashed, shoved each other into my path, I was a desertspider in a pen of cowards.

I was maybe a third of the way through Balustrade when the sun came up and I began to weep.

I was cramming golfcourse sand into the mouth of some typical big, a plump thickhaired puffyeyed rando named Biff and putting up a pointless fight, snarling spitting sputtering while I pressed a knee into his ribs and poured the sand into his face, and I was telling him, JUST SWALLOW THE FREAKING SAND SO IT'LL BE OVER FASTER, I DON'T HAVE TIME FOR THIS, but Biff wouldn't swallow, kept angling his face away and squirming, so I grabbed the flabby giant's hair and just thumped his head into the sand, thump, thump, thump,

but I knew it didn't hurt as much as it could, so I pulled up his head and slugged him, blacked one eye, then the other, pulled him up and knocked him down, saying, I TOLD YOU JUST EAT THE STUPID SAND, WHY WOULDN'T YOU JUST EAT IT, but the words were getting stuck in my thicking throat, strangled from weepiness, Warner you loonybin, stop crying and moveon.

I dropped him in a heap and breathed.

"Boss, are you allright, need a break or something," yelled

Puppyneck, still chilling in my hair, he ofcourse had become my chief of staff.

I NEED SLEEP, I told him.

"Yeah, you should get some sleep," he agreed, "noproblem, we got lookout armies on the sand."

I'LL SLEEP IN THE OCEAN, I told him.

He barked orders into his stolen headset, I stepped into the sea.

Floated out into international waters like a peacefull barge, lay on my back and dreamed.

DREAMWORLD

And for the first time in years, just let myself be in Dreamworld, not terrorize or haunt.

Just tumble, drift, hush myself, and watch.

I was only Warner, not the angry druggy angel, just my raggy ratty sober self.

It was ofcourse the dreamzone of a lonely city, trashed and fearfull.

Obviously the timeofday made it pretty quiet, most people were awake in Lifeanddeathworld, most people weren't dreaming. Just me and nightworker poors, a few sick in hospitalbeds, a few lazy hipsters and scumbags.

And everywhere people avoided each other, glanced suspiciously, shrank into their own shadows and muttered dismissals,

I'm Not Intrested,

Heck You Want,

Leave Me Alone,

What You Think I'm Stupid Or Something,

everyone was me when I was prisoned in the kidjail.

• • •

My heart felt dry and dead, I wanted to talk to dreamers, show you something nice. Take one person, swim a flowerfish in front of your eyes.

But every stranger shunned me, no one trusted me to make them happy. Someone froze the flowerfish, another grayed and shriveled it.

I made a little rivertree, fishflocks wheeling in the wind like leaves.

One stranger tried to dry it up,

another turned it into ugly veins,

a third one took the fishleaves and thinned them into needles, eels, snakes of bleeding ink.

Ohwell, I thought, *ohwell*, tried to just let it be an ohwell kind of thing, my heart tried not to grieve, itiswhatitis.

I tumbled, drifted further.

Someone I knew was asleep, I realized.

The operahouse sat in a yard in a yard in a yard, everyone was suspicious of it too, no one went in.

I stepped inside, expected the old rich song,

instead she was just singing one plain note, hair unbraided, pretty walleye closed.

Hummmmmmm, went the note.

"Kitty, what happened to the song," I asked.

She opened her eyes and gazed widely, a little unfocus, not sure what she saw.

"Who is this though, are you a ghost," she whispered finally.

"Kitty, what are you doing asleep right now," I said. "Don't you have school or work or something."

"No school, no work," she said. "I just wait dayandnight for the kingcon to come and fight me."

"What do you mean," I said.

"Everyone knows the kingcon," she said flat and dull. "The angry angel who tortures Dreamworld. He fought me once, now I wait for him to come fight me again, the waiting is how he tortures me I guess."

"He's out of Dreamworld, Kitty," I said. "It's just me now, just Warner. The kingkong is gone, he left dreams forever."

She just frowned and thumbed her hair.

"Kitty can you sing me the song," I asked.

"I don't remember how it goes," she shrugged.

She said it and my heart began to moan.

"How about you just sing any song, let's just hear what notes come out," I asked, fighting panic.

"Ghost Warner, why did you do it," she said.

It silenced me.

"Why'd you leave," she begged.

"To help a friend," I said, my words were whines.

"You could have belonged to me, you know," she told me.

"Stop, stop stop," I said.

"I could have belonged to you," she said.

"No," I said. "Never, never ever."

"You could have belonged to me, I could have belonged to you," she breathed.

"It never could have happened," I began to yell.

"If you stayed, I would have," she said, simple, small.

"You don't even know who I am," I began to really yell,

loud to shut up the moaning heart. "You think I'm a pet, a saintbernard, a noble little sufferer, Kitty please shut up, you have no idea who I am."

"I know you," she insisted.

"Stop," I begged.

"But I know you, I know I know you," she told me, low and soft.

"Oh, stop, just stop it, please freaking stop," I cried. "The boy you know wrecked Dreamworld."

She closed her eyes, maybe she heard music instead of me.

"The idiot you know made sadness into munmun," I raged. "The ghost you know grew fear like food and ate it to get big, the rat you know made pain for five shityears and now he's huge, and all I want to do with hugeness is punish, Kitty, that's all I want to do."

She opened her eyes again, her big eyeblacks breathed in and out.

"That's all I want to do anymore, just crush and hurt forever," I rasped, "make bigs feel fearfull, unsafe, turn bigs into cowering frightened powerless littles, turn them into me, make fear until I die."

She just shook her head, halfsmiled.

"Is that the boy you know," I ached, my face was hot and melting.

"I just know you're the boy who found me once," she told me, "the boy who wanted to show me something, longago."

The shock almost woke me, then noises did.

LIFEANDDEATHWORLD

It was a familiar voice that pulled me back to lifeanddeath.

"Warner, sorry, hello, Warner, wakeup please," blared a drone near my poor weepy head, dizzy, floating in my waterbed, saltyfaced.

The dronescreen showed me Hue, behind his desk in his homeoffice, smiling pale and nervous.

I breathed away the weeping, didn't want to seem weak or dumb.

"I'm here with Usher and Prayer, Warner," said Hue, turn the camera and show my shaky sis and grim lawyer, well look at these two healthy fifteenfooters.

HELLO GUYS, I said, raspythroated.

"Warner, bro, you have to stop," pleaded Prayer.

Usher nodded, jerky, needy.

USHER, SIS, I said, unsure what to say.

I thought about it.

CAN YOU PAY HUE THE MUNMUNS I OWE HIM, I said finally.

"Oh, that's really not necessary," said Hue.

IT'S A HUNTHOUSAND MUNMUNS, I said, got to be specific.

"Warner, I'm not talking to you as your former hostfather today," explained Hue. "I'm talking to you as a representative of the localgovernment of Lossy Indica County."

He was talking fast, nervous, sped right into "Wewantyoutoknow, firstofall, that we take a lot of pride in your incredible achievements, I mean you're a selfmade bigrich, born littlepoor, it's a true ragstoriches story, and on top of that Prayer has told me you've been expressing a desire to donate some of your fortune to Lossy Indica Minmun, if this is true I want to tell you how much I admire your generosity and citizenship."

HEY IS KITTY THERE, I asked.

"Please, we need to resolve this as soon as possible," Hue zipped, "our problem is, your recent actions have encouraged many of our local bigriches, infact I think we can say prettymuch all, to consider moving away from Balustrade, out of Lossy Indica County, perhaps out of the Yewess itself."

Sweaty frightened Hue, fear is eating even him.

"For reasons I explained to you once, during one of our talks, this would be a disaster, Warner, and one that would hit our most vulnerable the hardest, so what we need to do is find a positive and peacefull resolution that will keep everyone happy and allow jobcreators to remain in the country that loves them the most."

HUE, IS KITTY OKAY, I asked.

"Notreally, Warner, no, she's notwell, but please, we don't have a lot of time," said shaky Hue. "Let me be uncomfortably clear with you. The citizens of Balustrade have asked the Yewess government to conduct a military strike against your body."

Prayer breathed in hard, Usher got more grim, I didn't even really hear Hue tobehonest, what does *notwell* mean.

"Ofcourse this is a highly unusual action against someone of your size and wealth and it exposes the national government to a potenchilly ruinous series of lawsuits, as your lawyer has made clear to us," Hue said. "But the bigs are unwilling to shoulder this legal burden themselves, and they have enormous leverage over the federal government, in ways you and I have discussed, I'm sure you remember our talks about this."

HUE I DON'T REALLY CARE, I rasped, WHAT DO YOU MEAN, KITTY'S NOTWELL.

"WARNER," barked Hue. "Forgodssake, focus. Listen to me. Your life is at stake. Your lawyer has negotiated an agreement for you to sign. Here are the terms. You will designate all but onemillion of your munmuns for donation and scale down as of one hour from now. Half will go to the citizens of Balustrade to repair the damage you have created, the other half will go to Lossy Indica Minmun. You will henceforth agree to keep a mile's distance between yourself and any individual more than eightscale in size, and you will agree to never let your scale account exceed onemillion muns again. In exchange, the bigs will withdraw their demands, and you will not be firebombed to death. Warner, please give Usher the authority to sign this agreement."

I thought about this.

"Warner I'm sorry but this decision must be made now, the bank has very little time to prep you for scaling down," Hue pleaded, "you may not be aware but if your body is not prepared for scaling down, the consequences are pretty dire, and with a scaledown this dramatic it will probably be fatal."

I thought some more.

"Bro, ohmygod, listen," cried Prayer. "It's all going to be okay, infact it can be amazing, just please do what we're asking, please. You're still giving so much to minmun, you're still doing so much good for so many, I know you don't want to give the bigs half of your munmun but you did destroy a ton of their stuff."

I stayed silent, she continued all panicky, "Whatstheproblem, is it that you don't want to be middlescale for the rest of your life, bro I get it, I get it, ofcourse I get it but just think, it's twice as big as you've ever been until yesterday, Warner bottomline you have to say yes right now, you have no choice, just say yes, please."

I kept thinking, or maybe didn't think at all, just was silent with no thoughts.

"Warner?" asked Hue.

CAN YOU BRING ME KITTY FIRST, I said.

"I can't," snapped Hue, angry voice breaking, "Warner, I can't, so drop it. She's downstairs in treatment right now, getting much-needed therapy, she's been sleeping twentyhours a day and we're at our witsend trying to figure out how to help her, bottomline, I can't bring her to you. Maybe in a few weeks you can see her. If you want to live until then, *tell us we can sign.*"

But my heart wanted something else.

BRING ME JASPER, THEN, I said.

Hue blinked, confused.

"What does he mean, who's Jasper," he began to ask, as I grabbed the drone, plucked it from the air and dunked it in the sea, felt it fizzle and die in my hand.

They had him in my hands within a halfhour, must really be urgent, the government must really fear us bigs, they forced this shaky teen to climb a rope down from the copter into my waiting hands, the kid who stomped my dad.

GO, I told the copter, LEAVE US ALONE, it sped away.

Ofcourse he couldn't look me in the eye.

"I'm sorry," he sobbed and shook, "I'm sorry I'm sorry, I'm so f freaking sorry."

He was about doublescale still, no longer elevenyearsold though, nineteen already now.

Not a roundfaced chubster anymore, looked pretty different from the kid who stepped through the roof of our little alleyway milkcrate house.

SHHHHH, I shushed. LOOK AT ME.

He couldn't though, he was so weak and trembly, he knew I was going to kill him.

Where do I begin, Jasper, what do I need you to hear before you die.

WHEN I WAS FIFTEEN, I told him, STILL LITTLEPOOR, I SHOT A GUN A COUPLE TIMES. IT WAS TO PROTECT MY SIS, NO ONE GOT HURT. BUT THEY STILL SENTENCED ME TO PRISON FOR EIGHT YEARS.

He shivered and cowered.

STOP SHIVERING, STOP COWERING, I said, JUST LOOK AT ME AND LISTEN. YESTERDAY I ATTACKED ABOUT FIFTY PEOPLE, PROBABLY KILLED ATLEAST ONE SO FAR. AND IT WASN'T TO PROTECT ANYONE, IT WAS JUST WHAT I WANTED TO DO. THIS TIME I'M NOT GOING TO PRISON AT ALL THOUGH.

He tried to nod.

WHAT DO YOU THINK ABOUT THAT.

"I don't know," he chattered. "I d don't 't know w."

I held him closer to my face, hard to hear his little voice.

COME ON, THIS IS NOT HARD, I helped. OFCOURSE YOU KNOW. JUST TELL ME THAT'S NOT RIGHT.

"That's not righ ht," he agreed.

GOOD, I said. GOOD.

He said nothing, his shaky terror was a whispery tickle in my palm.

NOW, DO YOU HAVE A DAD, I asked.

"Y yeah," he sobbed.

WHAT ABOUT THAT, IS THAT RIGHT, I asked.

He couldn't answer, just wept bitterly, I knew it wasn't fair for me to ask.

NEVERMIND, I said, NEVERMIND. JUST TELL ME THIS. IS HE A GOOD DAD.

As I said it, deep inside myself, a slow earthquake started.

"Yes, yes he's good, , he's a good d dad," the kid hiccuped.

I sucked fresh sea air, breathed it out rotten and ruined.

WHAT DID HE SAY TO YOU AFTER YOU KILLED MY DAD, I asked him.

"He said it wasn't my fault," he wept, "he said it was a terrible, terrible thing, but not my fault."

DO YOU THINK HE WAS RIGHT THOUGH, I asked him, feeling slow huge tremors begin.

"I don't kn know," he shuddered. "I mean y yes. I think so. I got p pushed. I'm so sorry, I was getting pushed around d b bythosekids, I j just didn't 't see wh , where I was going g."

I breathed long and hard, tried to keep my hands still, not jostle and snap this kid's spine, atleast not yet.

"I'm so sorry," he sobbed again.

His eyes screamed *Please don't kill me*, he didn't say it though.

He must have known the moment he said it, I would, I'd bunch my fists and mangle him like a napkin.

I breathed again, closed my huge eyes, saw my father's face.

CAN I TELL YOU ALITTLE ABOUT MY DAD, I asked.

Jasper, he called me little redfish, *psst, wake up little redfish*, that was how my days began.

His name was Robin, always weird to hear people call him that, Robin can you fix our broken stove.

He smelled like oil and rubber always and his hands were huge, I mean littlepoor huge, long strong grippy fingers stained with black grit.

He was best at fixing old brokendown middlepoor gadgets,

didn't own a workshop though, had to pay to use shopspace and tools, bounced around between rentalspaces owned by jerks.

Always hoped to own his own shop, own his own tools, just need to get a few clinky clanky little tools and then we'll start scaling up, funny redfish, that's our way out.

Prayer was rubymouse and I was redfish, at night we played with him by creeping our hands closer and closer to his until CHOMP, his big strong hands chomped ours, we shrieked and giggled like lunatics.

He teased my mom always about the Lord King God, wonder what that big godly fella's doing right now, hey Rosy you think He's watching some sportsgames or what, what do you think He likes on his hotdogs, he knew how to tease so she wouldn't get too mad.

But Dreamworld was where he was most himself, Dreamworld was where I loved him best.

My dad could dream anything, stars and suns and cityblocks, his favorite was the ocean though. He saw oceans and water in everything always, he called good things wet, bad things dry, I do it too sometimes, it feels true.

I talk like him, Jasper, I know I do. I talk in his long listy sentences, words all piledup, and do I ask myself questions the way he always did, yup, forsure.

When you hear my voice you're hearing the voice of the dad you killed.

And before jail I dreamed the way he used to dream.

He dreamed ripply fish, chubby seals, nibbly sharks and squiggly squids, jellies, crabs, thousandcolor corals and seaflowers, rippling pages of kelp. He made dreamzones for me and sis, adventures of redfish and rubymouse, after you killed him I tried to keep making them, when I dreamed myself into the ocean it was to feel like a babybrat again.

In Dreamworld he played the game of Make Stuff Out Of Other Stuff, Jasper he was the one I learned it from, whoelse. I learned it from my clever funny dad, watching him dream pools of cloud, mountains of teeth, accordion palaces, whale buses. Winking humming Dad drawing the vines of road on brickwalls, pulling the churning orchards of rivertrees from the ground with the gritty grippy hands.

And when I dreamed them too onenight to show him that I could, he glowed all proud and happy, he told me he loved me so much, amazing redfish.

I asked him did he love me more than Prayer, did he love me the most, he bellylaughed and tossed me in the cloudpool.

He tried to tell me something after you crushed him, Jasper, rememberthat, he moved his mouth and tried to talk.

Couldn't push the words out though.

● ● ●

Okay. It's time.

Shut up. Shut up and listen.

Jasper, can you swim.

    Do you think you can swim a mile.

    Jasper, we're a mile from shore, a mile from Lossy Indica.

    Go swim back to safety, Jasper, swim back to your good wise dad.

I placed Jasper in the water, watched him paddle away from me frantically, furiously, rat leaving a sinking ship.

I stopped my shaking, stilled my quaking, drifted north, and gazed again at Balustrade.

    And knew what had to be done,

    sorry Usher,

    sorry Prayer.

    Sorry Yewess, sorry Hue.

    But listen.

    The world is sick, the world is sad.

    If I don't bash some bigs then no one will.

• • •

Even if they bomb me, go ahead. Let me put my giant smoking stinking carcass on their shore, sicken them, sadden them, choke them on the fumes.

And if they don't bomb me, great, I'll eat them.

Char their skin, roast their muscles, gulp their blood, slurp their fat. Kill them, cook them, eat them, turn their flesh into my flesh, scale into my scale.

You are meat that I will eat, I thought, watching the limping rich.

It's time.

LIFEWORLD

But I floated,

and floated,

and didn't swim to shore,

just kept watching, floating, feeling very still.

And prettysoon I began to hear a song,
    imagined by my giant head.

SONGWORLD

The song was shrieks, chirps, giggles, hoots,

hums and laughs, barks and whoops,
    whatshappenings and isthisreals,
    notes made out of notes.

I was hearing littles, in twos and threes, families and crowds,
    coastguard stationfulls,
    growing.

My mind heard every littlepoor in Lossy Indica,
    allofasudden breathing in a littlebit more air,
    with allofasudden a littlebit bigger lungs,
    gasping the moreandmore air back out with roars and
    croons, chuckles and squeaks.

It was a thousandvoice orchestra to teach someone to sing again,
a well to wash a dusty dry Dreamworld.

And something fountained up in me,
some wet enormous need.

OKAYWORLD

OKAY, it screamed out of my mouth,
    the ocean shuddered,

OKAY, OKAY, it roared in my voice,
    boomed and echoed off the cliffsides,

HUE, PRAYER, USHER, YES, I'LL SIGN, I sobbed,
    so loud that even sleeping Kitty must have heard me,
    faraway,

like a coward, I chose life.

(WHATHAPPENSNEXT)

(And what happened to that coward next, well let me tell you, gather round for the Remaining Story of Warner as Told by Also Warner, keep your eyes on that gigantic bawler heaving in the sea.)

Surenough the bankers were listening, surenough they heard him, rightaway they began their magic work of Drain His Muns.

No time to prep his body, ohwell, whatcanyoudo, the shrinking kingkong grit his teeth, the weakening godsilla squinched his eyes, then finally he began to scream a little, then a lot, then basically nonstop, also wept and thrashed while his skin hugged his bones, bones squeezed his heart, frantic heart had nowhere to put its blood, body's trash strained his guts and stretched his veins, ribs pricked his lungs, gashed his livers, kidney, tum, his cramping tightening skull closed in and bruised his woozy brain, his innerears shrieked and shrilled and his eyeballs flashed and popped and dimmed and he told his brain to think, *whocares, I'll live.*

He bled and vommed and crapped endlessly in the pinking sunsetting ocean, went under a few times, gasping, shuddering, it all went dark and then it found ways to get even darker than that and then it went nightdark, deathdark, dark as nothing.

But he must have failed to die somehow, the bloodsalty sea got bored of him I guess or maybe pitied him, bitbybit a kindly tide coaxed him back toward the citylights undercover of night.

And finally it pushed this lifeloving coward onto the damp sand where he slumped like a corpse.

Prettysoon the morningsun was creeping over the mountains to touch him, his eyes twitched open, one was milkydull but the other had a little light left.

He crawled off the beach and onto the boardwalk, pavement, citystreets, his one good eye wandered and searched for a good place to just collapse somewhere outofsight forever but the dumpsters were too small, the sewerdoors too low and narrow, no holes in the wall could fit this middle littlepoor.

So your coward stumbled, shambled, shuffled, up into the hills, on one bad leg and one worse, hearing mostly ringing, behind his ribs his organs were already switching off.

And after a longtime he was in a familiar sweetsmell paradise, homes like humming mountains, gentle sprinklers misting, treebranch cathedral overhead.

He was a crippled animal with a pushing heart, telling him with nudges, *here, thisway, keepgoing.*

And after some more bloody shuddery miles he stopped in front of a house.

He stood, and swayed, then suddenly sat down, couldn't stay on his feet for one more second.

He sat there naked in the yard, ignored by joggers and soundless zooming doublecars, ignoring the trickly spreading death inside him, just watched the house and waited for its dreamer to wake up.

So wake up, please. I'm out here waiting.

Please save my littlelife just one last time, because heresthedeal, then I promise to save yours.

Let's belong to each other, howaboutit,

let's be reasons to fix stoves, patch roofs,

clean and heal our idiot town, our old dumb brokendown world,

let's be why we love this stupid life too much to die,

Kitty whatdoyousay,

here's what happens next,

let's make each other weak.

ACKNOWLEDGMENTS

Thankyou firstofall to my wise witty endlessly patient editor, Maggie Lehrman, as well as Susan Van Metre, Michael Jacobs, Chad W. Beckerman, Andrew Smith, and the rest of my partners in crime at Abrams. Thankyou for encouraging me to take risks, reining me in when I am being obtuse or insane, letting Warner be Warner, and agreeing to a title that is a madeup nonsense word.

Thankyou to Nate Marsh for his perfect artwork.

Thankyou to my tireless brilliant agents, Claudia Ballard, Laura Bonner, and Anna DeRoy, for always acting in my best interests so I don't have to.

Thankyou to the incredible Cassilhaus residency ay kay ay Ellen Cassilly and Frank Konhaus, who hosted and fed and entertained me in their beautiful castlehouse in North Carolina while I wrote the final third of this book.

Thankyou to my genius friends and fellow writers who gave me their invaluably thoughtful notes and insights: Greg Atwan, Emily Carmichael, Kyle McCarthy, Joel Steinhaus, Nic Stone, Ben Urwand, Han Yu, and ofcourse Sean McGinty, the first person I ever discussed this idea with, one talky night in downtown Ellay.

Thankyou always and forever to my family of Mom Dad Lena Eve Grandma for making me who I am.

Thankyou a secondtime to my dauntless librarian Mom inparticular for all the conversations and encouragements and pushbacks with this book, and a thirdtime for each of the hundreds maybe thousands of books she gave me growing up, especially the ones she read me outloud, especially Dickens.

And thankyou mostofall to Tamara for the daily reminders that this book is the most important thing in my life, but letsbehonest, it's a distant second.